THE
KEYS
TO THE
REALMS

Also by Roberta Trahan:

Aftershock

The Dream Stewards series:

The Well of Tears

The Keys to the Realms

THE KEYS TO THE REALMS

BOOK TWO OF

THE DREAM STEWARDS

ROBERTA TRAHAN

47NORTH

Text copyright © 2014 by Roberta Trahan

Published by 47North, Seattle
www.apub.com

ISBN-13: 9781477849958
ISBN-10: 1477849955
Library of Congress Catalog Number: 2013946477

Cover Designed by Mark Winters

For AJ and Morgan

THE PROPHECY

E ven before the seeds of the first civilizations were scattered, sorcerers walked this world. For a time they trod in the formidable footfall of the Gods, serving the fledgling societies as the arbiters of faith and fate. With their guidance, humankind flourished. But with prosperity came avarice, and with avarice came ambition. Before long, the world knew unrest.

Dark and terrible times followed. Chaos descended upon the land, and for a thousand years her peoples suffered at the hands of tyrants and marauders. Yet, somehow, the seeds of salvation survived.

In the province Ystrad Tywi of the Kingdom of Seisyllwg, a handful of those devoted to the old ways found refuge in the abandoned sanctuaries of their ancestors. Hidden deep within the mystical woods of Coedwig Gwyn, nestled near the tiny village of Pwll, stood one such ancient and sacred place—the all but forgotten temple called Fane Gramarye.

Cloistered within an enchantment that hid the temple from the eyes of the world, the last remaining mages to serve the Order of the Stewardry at Fane Gramarye endured to fulfill a single sacred vow— to protect the king who would one day unite the peoples of Cymru in a long and lasting peace. An age-old prophecy foretold that a son descended from a line of noble rulers would rise to rule a new era, and that by his hand the ancient beliefs would be resurrected and the sorcerers returned to reverence. And so it was that for nine generations the Stewards served in silence, awaiting an omen in the birth of a boy.

In the year 880 AD, it came to pass that the first begotten son of Cadell, King of Seisyllwg, was delivered unto the world and anointed by the Gods. Soon after reaching manhood, the child called Hywel would begin the journey to his destiny, and the ancient prophecy would finally be fulfilled. The Stewards of Fane Gramarye would be called to raise the first sorcerers' council to serve a high king in more than a millennium.

But it was also foreseen that there were those among men and mage who would stop at nothing to usurp such a powerful alliance. As the age of peace approached, the Sovereign of the Ninth Order moved to protect the prophecy, secretly naming four sorceresses of uncommon power to the sacred council. He then sent the sorceresses into hiding, scattering them to the four corners of the known world so that even if one were discovered, the others might survive.

For more than twenty years they lived in waiting, until the summons to return finally came. But their homecoming was overshadowed by sorrow. The ravages of time and unrelenting conflict had decimated the lands and disheartened the people. The Stewardry at Fane Gramarye had faded even further into obscurity, and insurrection had weakened the Order. And when the first of the sorceresses arrived, the enemy was waiting.

While dark forces besieged the Stewardry, dark times befell the rising king. The unexpected death of his father reawakened a generations-old dispute over land and title, forcing Hywel to defend his claims against family, friend, and foe alike. Determined to seize the destiny he had been promised and unite the disparate kingdoms as one nation under his rule, Hywel declared a bloody and ruthless campaign against all those who dared stand in his way. But his rivals were just as determined to resist him, and the battles raged, unrelenting, until Hywel's only hope of victory lay in the fulfillment of the prophecy. While he fought to hold his ground, his last refuge was Fane Gramarye, and his only allies the mages of the Stewardry.

ONE

Wintertide in the White Woods, 906 AD

Evil slithered through the low-lying mist along a dark and rarely traveled route. With cunning intent and deadly speed, it approached its unsuspecting prey unhindered. The victim, wounded and weary, paused to rest before reaching refuge. In the distance, a solitary sentry recognized the danger and cried out, but the warning came too late.

Glain clawed at the edges of the vision, frantic to escape the malevolence in her subconscious and return to the safety of wakefulness. But the dream would not let her go. The layered haze that shrouded her senses was dense and cloying, like cloth soaked through with tar.

Still, the deep sleep had not overtaken the whole of her mind. Over time, Glain had learned how to hold a piece of her consciousness apart from the sensations created by her visions. In this way she could maintain a thread of awareness—a necessary defense against the vulnerability of the dream state. She felt the warning now. A separate danger threatened, nearer and more urgent. Glain struggled harder.

At last she broke through the trance, startling herself awake with a gasp and a prayer. "Gods help me!"

The young Steward was almost surprised to find herself alone in her chamber. The nearness of something *other* had made such a strong impression that she half expected to find it standing next to her bed. But nothing was there.

Glain focused on the late-night stillness, straining to hear or feel unrest in Fane Gramarye. Her rampant heartbeat and shallow breathing were like a deafening roar in the dead hush, but no other sound pierced the quiet. When a few moments of wary anticipation still failed to reveal a threat, Glain cursed her over-anxious nature and snapped her fingers at the bedside candle stand.

"Alight."

At her command, the tallow wick-end on the pricket sputtered to life. Its pale glow beat back the shadows in her room but did not hold the power to banish the dark images that dwelled in her mind. Nor did the silence quell her misgivings. Evil was lurking, here in the waking world. She was sure of it.

If only to appease the relentless niggling of her intuition, Glain tied back her ginger-brown locks, retrieved her house shoes, and pulled the white robe of the acolyte over her nightdress. Leaving nothing to chance, she snatched the indigo velvet sheath that protected her wand from the wall hook and fastened it securely at her waist. And for good measure, she took the bone-handled dagger from the ritual altar next to her hearth.

Practiced stealth and well-oiled hinges allowed Glain to leave her chamber without alerting the other acolytes housed on the hall, but as soon as she stepped outside her room, she reconsidered the wisdom of venturing on alone. Her intuition flared and foreboding rippled along her spine.

Thank the Ancients for the apprentice who had remembered his duty and lit the lamps in the halls. Still, the smoldering flicker of liquid tallow cast more shadow than light. And the dark silence beyond her door was not empty. Before she'd taken half a dozen steps down the hall toward the entrance to the Sovereign's quarters and the third-floor landing that separated the east annex from the west, Glain sensed an unearthly presence. A sickly sweet odor lingered on the air, as though something rancid had passed only moments before.

Ahead, a door latch slid from its brace, and Ynyr stepped cautiously into the corridor. Glain nearly collapsed with relief. Ynyr, the eldest and the leader of the acolytes, seemed only mildly surprised to see Glain already on the prowl, and he motioned for her to join him. She had to run to catch up—he was already striding down the passageway as though he knew where to go.

"Did you see anything?" he whispered.

"No. What woke you?" Glain asked. Ynyr was not a seer.

Ynyr's nose wrinkled as he caught a whiff of the rank air. "I heard a rustle, but it passed so quickly I almost dismissed it. I heard voices earlier in the king's chamber and assumed it was just another of his late-night distractions making her way back to her own room."

If Hywel had indeed returned to the temple, this was a more than likely explanation. Much as it galled Glain to know it, the king was rarely without "distractions" in his quarters. "But now you think it was something else?"

He paused to squint at her as if the question were rhetorical, reaching reflexively for something at his waist. It was only then that she realized Ynyr was armed with more than his wand. "Don't you?"

"Yes," she confessed. "I am sure of it."

"Stay close, then." Ynyr tipped his chin ahead, toward the shadows. "Aside from mine, his are the only rooms occupied in the west annex. Assuming, of course, that he is here at all."

"I thought you said you heard voices in his rooms."

"Yes, but that was hours ago. For all I know, Hywel has already gone."

"How is it possible that you would not know whether he is on the grounds?" Glain was perplexed, and a little annoyed. "You are his personal attendant."

Ynyr cast a quick, sidelong scowl in her direction, keeping his focus in front of him. "I know what Hywel decides I should know, and that tends to be very little."

A muffled thump silenced them both. Glain heard what she believed to be a stifled shout, and then Ynyr bolted for the king's chambers with her on his heels. Together they threw open the door and charged into the dimly lit rooms.

Hywel had engaged the first of two shadowy figures near the hearth in hand-battle, a fierce grappling struggle against a disembodied force. The second infiltrator had overtaken a naked form, a woman Glain could not recognize through the shadows. She appeared to be completely overcome and unable to resist.

"Ynyr!" Glain shouted, suddenly recognizing the danger for what it was. She had never seen such demons, but they were such a deadly threat that all Stewards were taught how to fend them off. "*Cythraul!*"

Ynyr lunged over the bed to aid Hywel's companion. He would realize, as she had, that his physical strength would be used against him. The only defense against such a demon was to dispel its form.

Hywel, however, did not understand this. He fought hard against his attacker and was quickly faltering under the smothering of the Cythraul's darkling shroud. Death would come swiftly.

"Cease your struggle, Sire." Glain unsheathed her wand and positioned herself as near to the wraith as she dared. "You only make it stronger."

Hywel growled with fury and frustration, but he did as she bade him. He let his arms fall to his sides and dropped to his knees. Submission would slow the effects, but not stave off the end for long. Glain hoped there was time.

Grasping her wand at mid-staff, Glain held it at arm's length, leveled on the horizontal plane. She focused her every thought on the Cythraul before her and called the command to disperse. "*Ymadael!*"

The shadowy wraith shimmered and thinned slightly before regaining its mass. It was more resistant than she'd expected. The sorcerer that had brought this spirit from the netherworld into this one was accomplished and wickedly powerful. The wraith had been shielded against ordinary magic, and she knew of nothing else to do.

"Stand fast, Glain." Ynyr was managing to hold the second wraith at bay using the same wand spell. He was no more successful that she at destroying it, but Ynyr had weakened the demon enough to allow its captive an opportunity to escape. "Ariane! Don't just stand there, you vapid girl. Give aid or go for help!"

Ariane did neither, apparently frozen in place by her own fear. The only effort she made was a lame attempt to cover her nakedness with her robe, but even the white wool of the acolyte's mantle could not hide her shame. How had Ariane come to be here like this? There was only one reasonable answer, and Glain's dismay nearly shattered her concentration. But she dared not falter.

Prevented from reclaiming Ariane by Ynyr's strength and unrelenting resistance, the wraith turned its menace on the king as well. Ynyr immediately brought his spell to Glain's aid, but it still was not enough. Hywel was fading, and it felt to Glain as if the Cythraul were trying to pull her power away from her through the wand—but that was impossible. A Steward's wand was cured in her own blood. None but she could wield it. But then, she had never confronted dark magic before.

For the first time since the Hellion had stormed the Fane, Glain was afraid. Perhaps she had been wrong to think she was mage enough to overcome this threat. Even with Ynyr's help.

She dropped the dagger she carried to clutch her wand with both hands, and felt the hornbeam bark warm from the force of her magic. "*Ymadael nawr!*"

One of the Cythraul shuddered, as if it were wounded. Glain sensed weakness. She took two steps toward the demons, focusing her thoughts on the entity she had affected.

"What are you doing?" Ynyr shouted. "You're too close."

Glain had no idea what she was doing or why she was defying her own terror. A sorceress with good sense would have backed away, but Glain let her instincts guide her. She could not destroy the Cythraul, but she could draw it away from Hywel.

"Glain!" Ynyr realized what she had in mind. "If you get any closer you'll be caught in the shroud."

She knew he was right, but her idea was working. Glain had engaged the wraith. It was turning away from Hywel and toward her. If she could keep it distracted and drain enough of its strength, Hywel might break free. Glain backed away slowly, suddenly realizing that she could only lead it away for so long before being swallowed up herself.

All at once, another presence joined theirs, tripling the strength of her spell. Nerys, the last of the four acolytes, appeared beside her, lending her magic to theirs. The wraiths were not shielded enough to withstand sorcery thrice made. At last they retreated, disappearing in a cloud of black mist. Hywel was released from the darkling at last, shaken and winded, but apparently unharmed.

The king recovered so quickly one might think he faced demon assassins every night. His chest heaved from the effort of his deadly struggle but he stood tall and true, leveling upon Glain a gaze iced with dark rage.

"Tell Alwen I wish to see her. *Now.*"

* * *

Glain left Ynyr to see to the king and ushered Nerys and Ariane out of the bedchamber. "Take Ariane back to her room and see that she stays there."

Nerys gave Glain a glare of resentment, but she did not protest. Nerys was particularly critical of the awkward and less accomplished Ariane, and Glain had always been quick to reproach Nerys for her unkindness. This time, however, Glain felt as Nerys did. Ariane had embarrassed them all.

"Before you go," Glain asked in afterthought. "How did you know?"

Nerys frowned at Ariane, who appeared to be far more troubled with tying the sash of her robe than she was by her own humiliation. "I heard voices in the hall and came to see what was wrong."

"Well," Glain said awkwardly. There had never been warmth between them and it was uncomfortable to find herself obliged to express it now. "I am glad you did."

Glain turned and raced back along the length of the corridor as if there were white-hot coals beneath her feet. Hywel would not be far behind, and Alwen deserved fair warning. It had taken less than the turn of three moons for tales of his rages to reach legendary proportion, outstripped in infamy only by the rumors of his womanizing.

Glain reached the door to the Sovereign's chambers at a dead run and threw it open, only to find Alwen already dressed and seated on the small dais in the receptory that centered her chambers.

"Breathe easy, dear girl." Alwen waved her into the room. "When you've recovered, find fresh cups and pour."

"*Cythraul*—in the Fane." Glain forced the words out between panting gasps. "Hywel is coming."

"Yes, I know." Alwen, serene and gracious, gestured toward the hearth. "The aleberry, Glain."

Glain obliged, wondering whether the mulled spirits were meant to calm Hywel or to fortify Alwen, and how it was that Alwen was not at all surprised. Glain poured first for her mistress. "It was over nearly as quickly as it began, and I came to you straight away."

"Just now I awoke knowing that a threat had been thwarted." Alwen accepted the cup with a nod of thanks and a pensive frown. "Tell me what happened."

"Hywel was quick to react, but we were nearly too late." Glain began to recount the incident, but the pounding echo of determined boot heels in the hall stopped her short. "He is angry."

Alwen almost smiled. "And wouldn't you be, if a soul-sucking wraith had come for you in the dead of night?"

Hywel burst through the door with unspent rage, Ynyr close on his heels. "*That* one."

Hywel pointed directly at Glain, staring at her beneath a glowering brow and shaggy dark curls. He carried himself with a stag-like grace and the physical confidence of a man who knew how to handle himself. Even half-dressed he was a commanding presence. If Hywel knew fear, he would never admit it. "Fortunately for me, she is fierce, and quick-witted."

He snatched the cup from Glain and gulped the contents, wiped his mouth with the back of his hand and held the cup out for more. "What manner of creatures were they?"

"Very old and very obscure black magic," Alwen said. "The Cythraul demon is a taker of souls, brought from the netherworld and given new form in this one. They are mindless creatures that serve this one purpose, and they answer only to the mage who summons them. You were very lucky. They rarely fail to accomplish their task."

Alwen gestured to Glain. "Bring another chair."

"I will stand." Hywel swallowed his second cupful and seemed to find some comfort in the spirits, if not in the Fane's defenses. "You claimed I would be safe in this place. I trusted in that."

"Indeed, you *are* safe, Hywel. Are you not standing before me now, in full form? And was it not my second you only moments ago credited with your rescue? Had the Cythraul come for you anywhere but here, you would not have survived."

Hywel snorted and glared even harder at Alwen. "Had I been anywhere but here, I wonder, would the Cythraul have come for me at all?"

Alwen offered a half-shrug, as if to concede the point, and handed Glain her cup, still half full, and folded her hands in her lap. "How is it you are in residence tonight, Hywel? We've heard nothing of you these last few weeks."

"I came seeking respite from a bitter campaign." Hywel's scowl turned somber. "My father passed on to the next life some weeks ago, and ever since I have been forced to defend his borders—*my* borders—from that thieving marauder Anarawd of Gwynedd."

Alwen raised one eyebrow in a show of reproach. "I believe that 'thieving marauder' is the rightful king of Gwynedd. And your uncle, if memory serves me."

"There has never been love between the House of Aberffraw and the House of Dinefwyr," Hywel explained. Aberffraw was the castle court of Gwynedd, and Dinefwyr the ruling seat of Seisyllwg. "When my grandfather divided his lands, he also divided his sons. My father's death has given my uncle cause to rejoice and an excuse to extend his reach. I have had no peace at all this past fortnight."

Emrys, interim captain of the castle guard, bulled into the room flanked by the headman of Hywel's personal guard. "My apologies, Your Grace. I've only just heard that you had arrived and about the threat on your life."

Hywel barely acknowledged Emrys. "And just how long do you suppose I would live if I announced my every step?"

"If I had been alerted once you were on the grounds,"— Emrys struggled to maintain the proper deference—"we might have taken other precautions."

Glain felt a twinge of empathy for Emrys. He was the most capable ranking officer in the Cad Nawdd, aside from Aslak, and the appropriate man to serve as captain in Aslak's absence. However, Emrys lacked the confidence that might have come with winning the post on his own merits, and it showed.

Hywel spoke without taking his eyes from Alwen. "A soldier of merit is always properly prepared, most certainly in times of war. Surely the security of this compound is not dependent upon whether or not I am expected—or any other guest of your palace for that matter."

He turned to glare now at Emrys. "As it stands, Captain, your defenses have been breached. How do you account for *that*?"

"If evil crossed our walls we will know soon enough. I've sent Rhys to scout the grounds." Emrys had recovered his command, personally and professionally. The Cad Nawdd was an unequalled regiment and worthy of his pride, though the castle guard had suffered great losses in the battle for the Fane. "He will report to us here."

"So we wait." Alwen had a look of deep thought. "In the meantime, let me hear from each of you your own account. Perhaps we may glean something useful from the details. Were you awakened in your rooms, Hywel, or did the wraiths assault you in the hall?"

Hywel crossed the room to the hearth and back again. He paced as if he didn't know what else to do with himself, as if the frustration he must be feeling would explode inside him. It made Glain nervous and she braced herself against the shame he was surely about to place at Ariane's feet. There was no saving her friend now.

"It came upon me in my rooms, as if it passed through the closed door, and without a sound. By the time I sensed any presence at all, I was already in its grasp. I've never faced a thing that holds form but has no substance. How does a man fight a foe he cannot strike?"

Glain felt gratitude for Hywel's discretion, though she could not imagine what advantage keeping Ariane a secret would give him. Hywel was not known for his selflessness.

"There were two," Ynyr spoke up. "Glain went to the king's defense while I tried to free Ariane."

Glain glared at her brother acolyte. If Hywel could be discreet, why couldn't Ynyr?

"It was Nerys who saved us all, really. Had she not come when she did—well, I'd rather not imagine." Ynyr made no attempt to hide his disdain. "Ariane was apparently overcome by the shock of the attack, though I am at a loss to explain how she came to be there in the first place."

Glain half expected the king to say that Ariane had been there at his invitation, but it seemed Hywel's gallantry did not extend that far. Not that Ariane's was a singular indiscretion; it could have been one of a dozen other women of the Stewardry in Hywel's bed on any given night.

"The three of you are accountable to Glain. It falls to her to address an acolyte's conduct when need be." Alwen frowned, but offered no further comment on Ynyr's concerns. "Something alerted you two to the threat?"

"I dreamt of danger," Glain recalled. "But there was something else, something that caused me to wake. Ynyr, did you not say you heard a noise?"

"I cannot honestly say whether I heard anything, but I did sense that there was something amiss. And there was that awful smell."

Alwen nodded. "The Cythraul leave a scent in their wake. They can be tracked once they have entered the earthly realm, but it is impossible to anticipate their coming. How were the wraiths destroyed?"

"Dispelled by word and wand," Glain explained. "But it took the three of us combined."

Rhys arrived and Glain's heart leapt, though he cast only a passing glance in her direction before addressing Emrys and his mother. Their friendship was a poorly kept secret, but out of respect for Alwen their relationship was private. Not that there was much to hide aside from a few stolen kisses, but there was the promise of more. At least Glain thought there was, one day when they weren't all caught in the throes of chaos. But for now, Rhys maintained a serious devotion to his service in the Cad Nawdd, and Glain was committed first to her duty as proctor.

"I have news," he said. The look Rhys exchanged with his mother was furtive and begged for privacy.

Alwen nodded and turned back to Ynyr. Her voice had taken on a somber tone. "Thank you, Ynyr. You've done well tonight. I will trust it to you to see that the Fane itself is secured. No need to disturb any more sleepy Stewards, but I am sure Emrys can spare the guardsmen to help you make sure there is no evil still lurking about the halls."

"Take my men with you," Hywel ordered. "They've been of little use to me tonight. Perhaps they will be of better service to you."

Ynyr was clearly unhappy to be dismissed, but nonetheless gave his bow and left to attend to his duty with Hywel's guardsmen in tow. Glain felt regret, but she understood Alwen's caution. Those closest to Alwen had known since before Madoc's death that there were traitors among them. And although Ynyr had shown nothing but loyalty and devotion in the weeks since Machreth's Hellion horde had decimated the Stewardry, the circle of trust remained tightly drawn.

"Not helpful news, however." Rhys closed the door behind the men and faced his mother and the king. "The grounds and the surround appear undisturbed. If anything or anyone has transgressed upon us, there is no evidence I could see."

Hywel began to pace. "The lack of evidence is hardly proof that there has been no transgression."

"Nothing?" Emrys queried further. "No tracks or a trail?"

Rhys looked perplexed. "Nothing I would not expect to find, save a foul odor near the rear gate that raised my hackles a bit. The remains of a wolf kill, a stag or a wild boar maybe."

Glain's heart skipped, and all eyes turned on Rhys.

"What?" Rhys stepped back a pace. "What have I said?"

"It seems there is evidence, after all." Alwen sighed. "The odor you noticed was the scent of the Cythraul, Rhys. If the magic that wrought those wraiths was strong enough to pierce the veil that hides us from the world, we are in far worse straits than I feared."

Rhys was puzzled. "How do you mean?"

"To think the Cythraul were conjured by a traitor within our walls is disheartening enough," Alwen explained. "But only a master magician, one well versed in the dark arts, could summon them from the netherworld and march them right through our defenses."

"Machreth?" Glain nearly choked on the name. The former proctor of the Stewardry was the only black mage she knew, and the only enemy with the motive and the means to threaten them. Despite Alwen's many and varied attempts to discover his whereabouts during the twelve weeks since his failed attempt to take control of Fane Gramarye, he remained at large.

"Or Cerrigwen." Rhys raised another gruesome possibility. "They are allies, after all."

This was still an unpleasant thought. Cerrigwen's disappearance just before the last attack had suggested she was complicit in Machreth's first campaign to overthrow the Fane. It was difficult to believe the guardian of the Natural Realm had forsaken her destiny and the prophecy she had sworn to uphold, but whatever the reason, her defection was indefensible. Even if it could be proved that Cerrigwen had not collaborated with Machreth the usurper, it was painfully evident she had done nothing to stop him.

Alwen's brow furrowed as her thoughts deepened. "Whether Cerrigwen is truly Machreth's ally or was merely a means to an end is still unclear. I have long suspected she is driven by her own motives. We should assume they are separate threats."

"Your mages are but two more enemies among many." Hywel allowed a wry smile to soften his scowl. "Apparently it isn't enough I must fight my uncle and my brother."

"Your brother?" Alwen's faint frown belied her surprise.

Hywel's eyes narrowed. "Word reached me not three days ago that Clydog is gathering support in hopes of taking Seisyllwg by force."

"By law he is entitled to half your father's holdings." Alwen eyed Hywel with suspicion. "What reason would he have to take anything by force?"

"Clydog may have been fostered in my uncle's house, but his first loyalty should still be to our father. So long as he supports Anarawd, he is entitled to nothing," Hywel roared. "Instead of returning to Seisyllwg to renew his fealty to the House of Dinefwyr, he rides upon it with his sword raised and the cry of victory for Aberffraw on his lips."

"This is unfortunate news," said Alwen.

"Clydog may be foolish, though I can hardly fault him for his nature," Hywel admitted, his rage softening as suddenly as it erupted. "I might even admire him for it. We are both sons of Cadell, after all, and the thirst for power is bred in our bones.

However, if Clydog thinks to set his ambitions against me, well,"—Hywel paused to drink—"*that* is another matter."

"So it begins." Alwen spoke as though sorrow were swallowing her. "We are now at war on every front."

The stark pronouncement silenced the room and set everyone in it to thinking on the consequences. Images from her dream resurfaced, and Glain's stomach churned with dread. Perhaps the visions had been an omen of something worse yet to come.

Alwen sighed. "We have squandered the weeks since the siege, withdrawing like the defeated to nurse our wounds and our worries, while our enemies have spent the winter fattening their ranks and sharpening their teeth.

"The scrying stone has shown me Thorvald on his way home from the North with Cerrigwen's daughter and the third guardian, Branwen. Bledig may well have found Tanwen by now, or he may still be searching. This I have not yet seen. But sooner or later Cerrigwen will be caught and the others will return. Once we have reclaimed all four keys to the realms, it will fall to me to unite the Circle of Sages and provide Hywel his Stewards' Council. Until then, if it can even be done, there is little hope of securing Hywel's reign. But I will not waste another minute waiting."

Suddenly, Alwen's expression ignited as if her resolve had rekindled. Her fingers gripped the scrollwork arms of the chair as if at any moment she might spring from the seat.

"Hywel." Alwen stood abruptly. "Despite the events tonight, you are safest here, in this castle. I suggest you bring your armies to you here. Mount your campaigns from our gates as you must, but make Fane Gramarye your stronghold for a time."

Hywel's glower darkened further as he inclined his head in an unmistakable display of resentment. "A wise precaution, for now. But if Clydog marches for Dinefwyr, I will be there to defend it."

Alwen took this as agreement and continued to list commands. "Emrys, send scouts east and north. If Thorvald or

Bledig can be found on any of the roads home, let us hasten their return. The sooner the remaining Guardians of the Realms are safe within these walls, the better we will all rest. Glain, gather those among the Order you would trust with your life, and bring them to me at dawn."

Alwen returned to her seat. "You may take your leave now, all of you, save my son. Rhys, I fear there will be no rest for you tonight."

Glain wished for an excuse to stay behind, hoping to hear what errand Alwen had in mind for Rhys. Maybe he would find her later. For now she had her own tasks, and Ariane still owed her an explanation.

TWO

Glain wandered the hallways for what seemed like hours, thinking on Alwen's order to choose her most trusted. By the time she returned to her chambers, her decision was made. To her surprise, Ynyr was waiting outside her door—with a summons from Hywel.

"He can be very intimidating, but he loathes a bootlicker," Ynyr advised as he escorted her to the king's quarters. "Which I find interesting, because he has a way of making a person desperate for his favor. Which, of course, he never grants. You'll see what I mean."

Glain wiped her dewy palms on her robe and hoped that she'd managed to tame the flyaway locks around her face. "Why would he want to see *me*?"

"I imagine he means to offer you his thanks. You did save him from the Cythraul, you know." Ynyr paused with his hand on the door clasp. "Glain. I trust you to have more sense than Ariane."

"Really, Ynyr." Glain was appalled, and then a little worried. "You don't think *that* is why he has summoned me?"

Ynyr gave an apologetic shrug as he sprang the latch, as if to say he wished he knew, but did not. "Ariane is hardly the only girl he has charmed, though she is the most smitten. Nerys says she can't stop nattering on about him."

He pushed open the door to the master's chamber that Hywel occupied and waved her in, whispering as she passed, "I will be right here, in the hall."

Glain was too nervous to respond. All of the third-floor suites were spacious and finely appointed, especially when compared to the small plain rooms she and the other acolytes occupied. The proctor's official suite was second in finery only to the Sovereign's, and as such had been offered to Hywel. By right, and under less chaotic circumstances, the chamber would have been Glain's. She was proud to hold the title but had no desire to ever claim the suite. These rooms had last belonged to Machreth, which forever soiled their appeal for her.

Hywel's was the only presence evident now. He could not have appeared to be more at home, sprawled sideways across a tufted armchair and reading a book by firelight.

She made a slight bow in his direction. "Sire."

"That's twice you've used that particular address." Hywel glanced at her over the top of the book. "My countrymen call me 'brenin'; others say 'king' or 'lord.'"

"And Alwen calls you Hywel," Glain responded without thinking, then realized that she ought not to have spoken so plainly. "Which do you prefer?"

"I have little regard for titles, though I will answer to any I've earned, by birthright or battle." Hywel folded the book closed and studied her instead. "But it is my opinion that the man who claims the laurels a title demands must be deserving of them, or else the title is meaningless."

"Madoc had a saying," Glain recalled. Though she knew she shouldn't, Glain felt quite at ease with him. "Something about a pig dressed in fine fur and silver still being a pig."

A smile widened the long lines of Hywel's narrow and angular face, softening the edges of his naturally stern expression. "I have heard him say it."

"How shall I address you then?" Glain asked. "What does Ynyr call you?"

"To my face—or behind my back?" Hywel chuckled. "If 'sire' comes naturally to you, so be it."

Glain tried hard not to smile, but she liked his humor. "Sire, then."

Hywel folded himself into a proper sitting position and beckoned her closer. "I have questions, Glain. Will you answer them for me?"

Glain took several small paces nearer to the hearth, less sure of herself now. "If I am able, Sire."

"Good." Hywel nodded at the small divan adjacent to his chair, indicating she should be seated. "It's already late, and we may be a while."

Glain felt obliged to accept his hospitality, though she wasn't quite sure it was proper. Suddenly, she wasn't quite sure *any* of this was proper, but Ynyr was just outside. "I can't imagine there is anything I know that Alwen does not."

"Is that so?" Hywel's brow furrowed, and one eyebrow slid into an arch. "Does she know you better than you know yourself?"

"I suppose not." Glain was puzzled. What could Hywel possibly want to know about her?

"Nor did she know Madoc well," Hywel asserted. "It seems to me she hardly knew him at all."

"Alwen had only a short time with him before he passed, and those were frantic days." Glain felt compelled to explain. "She was twenty years absent, after all."

"But you...," Hywel said, leaning forward in a way that seemed to suggest affinity between them. He looked at her with a directness that should have unsettled her, but it did not. "You were close to him."

"I was his last apprentice. I spent most of my life attending him, learning from him." Glain noticed that he still gripped the book, an old historical text. Hywel was clearly learned, but his hands were broad and coarse, more like those of a tradesman than a man of letters. "Everything I am, I owe to him."

Hywel nodded as though this information reassured him, and Glain found herself noticing other details like the small jagged scar crossing the ridge of his nose, and the particularly warm brown hue of his eyes, which were a lighter brown than his long curls. There was nothing overtly threatening about him, though she had seen his rage and heard him lauding his own ruthlessness.

"You mentioned before that a warning came to you in a dream." Hywel was engaging, and yet an air of self-possession ensured that anyone in his presence knew he held command. In this way, Hywel was intimidating. But he also appeared to her to be a much less obvious man than she had presumed. He was gentlemanly, even charming. "Do you have these dreams often?"

Glain was unprepared for this question. She had never openly discussed her dreams with anyone but Madoc, though she brought her visions to Alwen when she thought they might help. She was reluctant to answer but had no legitimate reason to avoid it. The safest response was the simplest one.

"Not so often that I dread sleep," she offered. "But the visions are more common these past several months."

Again he nodded, as if she had given the answer he expected to hear. "These visions, do they always come to pass?"

"Yes." Glain was surprised how quickly this answer found its way out. The intense focus of his gaze had a way of making a person want to oblige him, if for no other reason than to escape it. "In some form or another."

Hywel wetted his lips with the tip of his tongue and then pressed them tightly together, contemplating his next approach. This made Glain exceedingly uncomfortable, but also curious and a little flattered.

Finally he drew breath to speak. "If ever your dreams involve me, I wish to know."

Glain could see no reason that this should be at issue. "Alwen will keep you informed, of course."

"I am sure she will, when it suits her," Hywel said. "But you misunderstand, Glain. I wish to be the *first* to know."

Glain did not know how to respond. She could not possibly agree, nor could she refuse. Hywel was the very embodiment of the prophecy the Stewardry existed to serve, but she answered to Alwen. No matter whose interests she chose to serve, one or the other of them might feel betrayed. Before Glain could decide what to say, Hywel stood and walked the book he was holding back to its place in the shelf on the wall behind the chair.

"You are in possession of something very rare, you know," he said. "Very few people can say they are owed my favor."

Glain, who was still struggling to find a way to respectfully decline his request, found herself at even further loss. "You owe me no favor, Sire."

"But I do." Hywel returned to stand directly before her and held out his hand. "You saved my life tonight with your quick thinking and remarkable skill."

Not knowing what else to do, Glain put her hand in his and allowed Hywel to help her to her feet. When he did not immediately release the hold, her stomach fluttered, but she did not resist. His touch was warm, and her cheeks burned. Not from embarrassment, as they should, but from a more base response to the subtle sensuality of the gesture.

"One day you will have need of something I can provide." Hywel led her to the door, and then took both her hands as he captured her again with his gaze. "And when you do, you must not hesitate to ask."

Before she knew what was happening, Glain found herself taking her leave of the king in a silly, schoolgirl stupor and feeling all a-flush. It wasn't until she was out in the hall and Ynyr had closed the door behind her that she realized how much Hywel had affected her. And only then did she realize that she had never actually refused his request.

* * *

Morning dawned too bright on an angst-filled and sleepless night. Glain had spent the remains of it in tortured thought, assessing each of her colleagues. In the end, the decision was not so difficult to make. Of the three score and four Stewards who remained at Fane Gramarye, Glain trusted only four enough to count them among her chosen.

The acolytes Ynyr and Ariane were her closest friends, and the apprentices Verica and Euday had supported her in the early days following Machreth's insurrection, when Alwen had first appointed her proctor. All had served the Stewardry with distinction, though to varying degrees and ability. For these comrades Glain would sacrifice her own life, and they would vow the same for her. What else Alwen would ask of them, Glain could only guess.

"So few?" Alwen seemed surprised, taking in the small group from the Sovereign's chair atop the small dais in her private receiving room. "I see you continue to exclude Nerys from your confidence, Glain. She is an acolyte as well. Her experience and leadership might be useful."

"Yes, Sovereign." Glain choked the urge to bristle with indignation. "But you charged me to bring only those I would trust with my life."

Alwen's brow creased. "And still you do not count Nerys among them, even after her actions last night?"

"I have no evidence yet, but there are reports of subversion, clandestine meetings with her own inner circle." Glain's frustration refused to be contained. "And I have not forgotten her allegiance to Cerrigwen."

"We have no proof of any allegiance to Cerrigwen beyond what duty demanded of her. Nerys was in service to Cerrigwen, just as you are in service to me," Alwen reminded her. "But you are correct, Glain. The choice was yours to make. So be it."

Alwen surveyed the Stewards before her, her gaze lingering long enough to make them all even more anxious than they were already. Glain worried when Alwen's eyes turned toward Ariane. What must Alwen think of her? And what would Alwen think of Glain, once she knew of her own private encounter with the king—*if* she were to know. It was only a passing thought. It would be wrong to withhold this truth.

With her elbows cradled in the ornately carved armrests, Alwen rested her chin atop clasped hands and continued her contemplation. The silence stretched on, straining Glain's nerves until she was sure they would snap.

At last, Alwen looked directly at Ynyr. "Madoc held the opinion that the Order never healed from the fracture that took place before you all were born. Nearly half the membership defected from the Stewardry then. Madoc thought this was how Machreth was able to encourage sedition among those who remained. Glain agrees. She thinks the discord still survives. What have you to say? Have recent events unified our Order, or does the Stewardry remain divided?"

"The Stewards have always been of two minds, Sovereign, have we not?" Ynyr was scholarly and given to practical, well-considered opinion—qualities that provided a welcome counterbalance to Glain's instinctive responses, even when she disagreed with him.

"Some of us are purists, true believers one might say, those who take the prophecy of the Ancients in its most literal sense."

"As did Madoc," Alwen affirmed.

"Yes," said Ynyr. "And then there are others who see the prophecy as an allegory which was meant to be interpreted in keeping with the ever-changing tides of time. These are the members to whom Machreth appealed, and some of them supported his course of action. However, the fact that any of us question or even argue either belief does not necessarily mean our loyalties are at odds."

Alwen acknowledged his point with a sideways tilt of her head. "And yet, there *was* a defection, and Machreth's recent insurrection had support. Clearly there are ardent believers who have been willing to take the issue beyond argument. How many of them remain within our walls?"

"That there is no answer to this question is a worry that plagues us all day and night, Sovereign," Ynyr agreed. "Save your interrogating every one of the sixty-odd Stewards who remain, we may never know."

Glain was surprised by Ynyr's not-so-subtle reference to Alwen's power over the psyche, which he knew as well as anyone she would never employ in such a way.

He raised his hands in petition. "If any one of us here were called to account for the contents of our thoughts, how might we be judged? In the end, it is our actions that define our loyalties."

Alwen nodded. "Every Steward here has sworn an oath to the Ancients and to the protection of the prophecy. Until I have evidence of wrongdoing, I take them all at their word. As Madoc would say, trust is the very essence of faith."

"When Machreth attacked Madoc and the Fane, he attacked us all," Verica offered, "including his collaborators."

"Even so," Glain said, urging caution, "we should assume there are some who would still join him if they could."

Alwen sighed. "I'm afraid this is a risk with which we must live. Even if I were to offer his supporters amnesty and let them go, I doubt any of them would reveal themselves. Nor would they leave the safety of the Fane." Alwen straightened in her chair as though to signal her authority and then stood. "We have more urgent concerns. Come."

Glain and the others followed Alwen to the adjacent chamber—once Madoc's personal scriptorium—to the massive hornbeam and hazelwood desk that now anchored its northeast corner. Alwen had ordered it moved out of the receptory in order to work in private.

"I have been studying the ancestry of the Stewardry." Alwen settled herself in the seat behind the desk and gestured to the giant leather-bound tome that lay open before her. "This ledger is the official chronology of the founding bloodlines. Naturally, there are five separate delineations, each beginning with the Ancient of origin and continuing with the direct descendants of every generation that follows. The last permanent entries are the known births from each clan that mark the beginning of Madoc's era, as recorded by his predecessor."

Alwen reached for a small stack of parchment rolls and gathered them into her hands. "Each of *these* is a record of the current generation, the offspring of the last hundred or so years. Those among us who are descendants of the Ancients, like myself, are named here. Most of our membership, however, are wildlings and halflings. The founding bloodlines have grown so thin they are nearly extinct."

"Wildlings?" Verica's lack of training showed itself in the worst possible moments, but Glain had only herself to blame for that.

"Mages born at random to plain folk." Ynyr tried to satisfy her with the shortest possible answer and minimize the embarrassment of her ignorance. "A halfling is bred when a mage mates with plain folk, but a wildling is a true mage that just naturally springs up. It happens from time to time."

"Many people in these parts have sorcerer's blood in their family lines and either do not know it or do not admit so." Alwen was ever kind and always welcoming of an opportunity to teach. "Long ago, when the Stewardry was still known to the world, it was common for children who showed an inclination toward magic to be brought to us. But eventually, a mage birth became a dangerous thing, and to keep themselves from being found out, the families began to abandon the babes."

"Or kill them," Euday added.

"Yes, Euday, a sad truth," Alwen acknowledged with obvious regret. "And the favored practice these days, I'm afraid. It used to be that Madoc would make regular travels outside the Fane in search of the wildlings and bring them back here. He called them his foundlings. But I understand it has been many years since any abandoned witches or wizard babes have been found."

Alwen loosed a short sigh and redirected the discussion. "As for the scrolls, as you can see, I have only four." She let the rolls drop, one by one, naming each as they fell upon the desktop. "Caelestis, Eniad, Uir, and Morthwyl. The fifth scroll, the continuation of the Primideach line, Madoc's heritage, is missing. As is his last testament, which was left for me but never recovered after his death."

Frustration sharpened the tone of her words. "This, of course, presents a dilemma on the issue of Madoc's successor. I am his proxy, not his heir. My birthright is to lead the Circle of Sages. It was also Madoc's express desire."

Glain was riddled with prickles of guilt. She shared Alwen's distress for all the same reasons, but she had one that was all her own. Long had she been Madoc's confidante, but in the frenzied hours of his last days, Madoc had gone to great lengths to safeguard his legacy. He had handed her his absolute trust and in return demanded a vow of silence. This quickly became a difficult pledge to keep, and Glain had struggled with it every day since. Madoc was a masterful keeper of secrets, but she had never quite acquired the stomach for it. At the moment, Glain felt as though she had swallowed far too many—and the morning meal was curdling in her gullet.

Alwen leaned forward, elbows propped upon the open pages of the ancient book and hands clasped, contemplating them all again. "It has been suggested to me that Cerrigwen somehow found Madoc's hiding place and stole away his testament when she escaped. I do not believe this to be the case. His testament remains in this castle, as does the record of his lineage. We must find them both."

"Might they not just as easily have been destroyed as concealed?" Verica wondered.

Glain went cold all over. This was an impossible thought. What if the scrolls were never found? The knowledge they contained had such great value that Madoc had protected them like precious treasure. What was to be done if they were lost?

"I have considered this," Alwen said. "But the information in those documents is too precious. The only person who might gain anything by destroying them is Machreth, but even he would be more likely to leverage the knowledge. I am also convinced that neither he nor Cerrigwen had access to these chambers. They couldn't have taken the scrolls."

Glain could not help but wonder if Madoc had somehow not foreseen the potential for theft or destruction of the scrolls by some other traitor. And then again, perhaps he had, and this was all a test of her faith in him. Madoc had held a hard line when it came to revelations. What knowing came to a Steward by way of visions and signs was meant to be used to guide others toward a wiser choice. But when a person would not be persuaded, the fates were meant to unfold of their own accord—no matter how tempting it might be to force a different outcome. Whether or not a supernatural power should intervene was for the Ancients to say, and this had been where Madoc and Machreth had become so fatally divided. Madoc believed guidance still came from the Ancients, through signs and visions, whereas Machreth believed they had long abandoned their followers to their own designs. Glain had always sided with Madoc's beliefs and would never have questioned his wisdom when he was alive. But in this moment, she was discovering an understanding for the alternative view. It was misery.

"No," Alwen proffered. "I believe the scrolls remain intact and within the Fane. Whoever has them effectively holds the Stewardry and the prophecy hostage. An intolerable situation. I have decided to charge Glain with retrieving them, and thereby the rest of you."

It took all the strength Glain had to keep from sighing aloud with relief. Salvation had arrived. She could think of no happier task than to find the scrolls, which would put at least part of her conscience at rest. Still, carrying the authority of search and seizure was not altogether appealing. The role of the inquisitor was somber, even harsh. It was not a responsibility to accept lightly.

Alwen held up one of the parchments. "Both scrolls are likely to be similar to this in size. The vellum Madoc favored is quite distinctive, as is his handwriting. If the original seal is intact, you will recognize his signet. You shall investigate relentlessly and under the full authority of my name. Look everywhere, question everyone, and let no one refuse you. Discretion is a waste of valuable time and serves no one's interest save the person who took the scrolls in the first place."

"Why *would* someone take them?" Euday voiced what they all wondered. "What reason could there possibly be to keep them from you?"

"I do not know, Euday, though I do have my suspicions." Alwen pressed her lips together in a grim line, as though those suspicions were painful to entertain. "Whatever the reason, my first concern is the scrolls themselves. We will have our answers later."

Alwen abruptly swept the scatter of scrolls aside and closed the huge book with a bang. "If there is nothing else?"

Glain gave her friends a dismissive glance and waited for them to leave. "Perhaps I should see to your comforts before I go."

Alwen had already turned her attention back to the stacks of journals and parchments amassed on her desk. "Your time is best spent searching. If there is anything I need, I can see to it myself."

Glain stalled, still struggling with her conscience, hoping to receive some sign to guide her. Over and over she heard the echo of Madoc's words: *Let the fates unfold on their own.* Perhaps the assignment Alwen had given her was just that—the will of the Ancients at work through her. But what if she were wrong?

Before long, Alwen noticed the lingering and looked up. "Tell me what troubles you, child."

The words wanted to come; they clambered over each other in her mind, clawing at her throat. Glain's misery was threatening to exceed her ability to withstand it. Part of her was desperate to be relieved of the burden, and part of her considered that to tell what she knew might be the right thing. But something rooted within her far more deeply than her conscience made her hold her tongue.

Alwen waited, attentive but not prodding, offering Glain every opportunity to speak her mind. For a moment, Glain worried that Alwen might decide to look into her thoughts. Panic burbled in her chest, but still she said nothing.

"Well, then." Alwen broke the gaze and reached for another of the books piled upon her desk. "When the time is right."

Glain's heart sank. Would the time ever be right? And how was she to know when it was? The uncertainty was awful enough, but the thought of failing Madoc in any way was worse. Her duties were at cross-paths and where one wanted her to go, the other could not follow. The conflict was soul rending.

She owed oaths to Madoc and to Alwen, and now, by default, to Hywel as well. It was all too possible that her loyalties might never be aligned toward the same end and that one day she might find herself forced to choose between them. But not today—today the best and safest solution was to choose not to choose.

THREE

Thorne Edwall pushed back the hood of his cloak, removed his gloves, and shook the rainwater from the leather as he surveyed the motley lot that one could expect to find in any alehouse just shy of the closing hour. A pair of well-dressed and well-soused traveling merchants; a handful of local tradesman pissing away their wages; two serving maids who were likely willing to warm any man's bed for the right price; and at the bar, a young swordsman who knew how to carry himself. He was making conversation with Aldyn, the innkeeper.

Though he behaved as if he weren't, Aldyn was aware of Thorne's arrival. Thorne had come at the innkeeper's request. It was a tidy arrangement, though not without risk to them both. Thorne made regular visits to the alehouse, and Aldyn passed on information. The collaboration had worked well over the years and Aldyn was one of the few men Thorne trusted. If Aldyn thought a meeting with the young swordsman would interest him, Thorne was willing to come.

He seated himself at the corner table nearest the door, his back to the wall, and waited. It wasn't long before the two merchants noticed the raven signet ring on the forefinger of his right hand, though they were quick to pretend they hadn't. Thorne found it perversely satisfying that his presence made others so uneasy.

He nodded to a serving girl offering him a cup, though he rarely took ale or wine. When he did, it was only to give the illusion of being at ease. A mage hunter never dulled his senses with spirits—sharp wits were often all that stood between him and his end. But Thorne was not on the hunt tonight, not as yet, and there was neither mage blood nor charmed thing in this place. If there were, the skin at the scruff of his neck would be tingling with the heat of a thousand pinpricks.

The girl returned with a platter, which Thorne accepted for two reasons—to make his presence less conspicuous and because he could not resist the savory smell of rosemary-encrusted mutton slow roasted in its own juices. He often spent weeks in the wilds, and a proper meal was a treat he never denied himself. By the time Thorne had picked the plate half clean and finished the ale, the merchants had gone, and the small group of locals had dwindled to two sorry souls who looked to be too drunk to leave on their own.

"Thorne Edwall?"

Thorne stopped chewing long enough to spare half a glance. "And who are you?"

"Aldyn sends his regards." The swordsman started to take the seat across from Thorne and then decided to ask, "May I?"

Thorne tossed a terse nod in the direction of the chair. "You have until I finish my food to convince me that whatever job you're offering is worth risking my life."

"And then what?" The swordsman straddled the seat and leaned in, his arms folded on the tabletop.

Thorne cocked an eyebrow at the man's bravado. "And then I leave. Whether I take your silver with me depends upon whether I like how you answer my questions."

"Ask, then."

"I believe I have already asked who you were." Thorne directed his gaze across the table and waited to see how the brazen lad handled himself.

"A messenger, come on behalf of the Stewardry." The swordsman leaned in farther still. "*Who* I am is not nearly as important as *why* I am here."

"So Fane Gramarye still stands?" Thorne felt the other eyebrow arch in surprise. He'd heard rumors, tales of the guild disbanded and the temple in ruins. "On whose authority do you speak?"

"The Sovereign herself."

"*Herself?*" This was unexpected. Thorne wondered what had become of the old wizard—but not enough to chance revealing his own knowledge. Then he remembered his food and resumed gnawing on the meat. "Go on."

"The Sovereign requires a seeker of particular skill and discretion. She asks for you by name and will accept no other."

"How does she know me?"

"She has Madoc's writings, access to his records. She is under the impression that mage hunters are useful for retrieving magical things and that you are the best."

Thorne's interest was roused. "What does she seek?"

The younger man frowned, drew a deep breath and then let it out slowly, as though what he were about to say was so dire the words themselves were dangerous. "There are Cythraul on the prowl."

"Small work—nothing any mage hunter hasn't managed a dozen times over." Thorne grew wary. "Cythraul are easy prey."

"Yes, well," the man hedged, "there is more."

"Ah." Thorne was beginning to think he might have been wiser not to come. "So now we get to the heart of things."

"The wraiths will return to the sorcerer who summoned them." The younger man shifted in his chair. "That is your prey."

Despite his skepticism, Thorne was curious. "Such a mage must be powerful, nearly invincible, or else you would not have come to me."

"Yes."

Thorne smiled in spite of himself. He found it difficult not to like this young man. There was something in his ways that Thorne admired, including the flagrant appeal to his vanity. "You have a suspect?"

"Yes," he offered, a bit too tentatively. "There are two."

"Two?"

"One or the other, most likely," the swordsman explained. "Though it could be both. They are known collaborators."

"Either your Sovereign has been misinformed, or accounts of my exploits have been stretched beyond exaggeration." Thorne reassessed the younger man while he finished chewing a bit of bread. The reticence he sensed was beginning to irritate him, and Thorne leveled a scowl across the table. "Out with it all, or we are done here."

His guest swallowed hard and then cleared the reluctance from his throat. "The first is a high sorcerer, some say the most masterful ever, and the heir to the Stewardry. Until Madoc renounced him."

Thorne's mouth went dry, and he seriously considered calling for more ale. "Machreth."

The younger man looked surprised. "You know of him?"

"I am Ruagaire." Thorne was a bit piqued by the lad's ignorance. "Of course I know of him."

The younger men bowed his head briefly in what Thorne supposed to be deference. "Then you know he is now marked a traitor and a murderer. It was at his hands that Madoc met his end."

The food was turning to stone in his gullet, but he took another bite of the meat to keep his surprise from showing. Apparently the Brotherhood's spies were not as well informed as they should have been. This was nearly as serious a concern as the information itself, but the lad was still speaking.

"Machreth now draws on the dark magics and seeks to destroy the Order," he explained. "The second renegade was his consort and turned traitor as well, but for reasons of her own. She is a potent threat herself."

Thorne was piecing together a bigger picture, and he did not like the looks of it. "By what name is she known?"

"Cerrigwen," the younger man nearly whispered. "She abandoned the Stewardry in the midst of a siege as Machreth led his Hellion Army against the Cad Nawdd."

Thorne's jaw clenched involuntarily. These events were beyond dire, and signs of a rift that was far beyond his ability to rectify. How was it that this news had not reached him by way of the Brotherhood? It was troubling to think that he might be the first to hear of it. "Cerrigwen is a Guardian of the Realms."

The swordsman paled. "How could you know that?"

"I am Ruagaire." Thorne no longer tried to hide his irritation. Surely this messenger could not be as oblivious as he appeared. "Do you really not understand what that means?"

"Apparently not as well as I should." The younger man shrugged, undaunted by Thorne's exasperation. "But well enough to know you are not to be crossed."

Thorne stared hard at his guest, masking his bemusement with intimidation. "The Brotherhood exists to protect the balance of power in the magical realms. It is our duty to know who and what might affect that balance. *How* we know is none of your business."

The younger man nodded, apparently sobered by Thorne's terse tone. Not sobered enough, in Thorne's opinion. He wanted to be sure his point was made. "The Guardians of the Realms hold the power to unmake this world. They control the very elements through which it exists. I think you already know this, and if what you say is true, this is far more serious business than you would have me believe."

Thorne felt the younger man studying him, likely wondering just who and what else Thorne knew. The lad's questions would go unanswered if he were brash enough to ask, for his own good. Thorne had silenced men for less.

"You have brought me a fool's errand." Thorne narrowed his eyes at the younger man, intending that his displeasure should show. "And I am not a fool. No mage hunter has ever faced a guardian before, nor challenged a sorcerer of Machreth's ilk and survived. What you ask is impossible."

The messenger pulled a leather coin sack from his vest. He placed it on the table and slid it forward. "Not for you."

Thorne folded his arms across his chest and sagged against the chair back, not in resistance so much as contemplation. The young swordsman was wrong. It was impossible, even for him, but he had no choice. He had to try.

"Not here." Thorne indicated the coin with a jut of his chin. "There is a ramshackle old hut, or rather the remains of one, not far from the small gate on the northeast wall of the Fane. Do you know it?"

The other man's brow arched slightly, but his reply was even. "The shack or the gate?"

"I wager you know them both." Thorne nearly smiled. It was just the sort of quip he might have offered up himself. But when he saw the probing question forming on the other man's lips, Thorne cut him off. "Deliver your silver to the ruins at first light on the third day after tomorrow. Bring a talisman as well, from each of your fugitives. A lock of hair will do or a piece of clothing—something with a scent."

The younger man nodded despite his obvious confusion, but Thorne was done with his meal. He pushed away from the table and stood. "When I see you next, messenger boy, by what name shall I greet you?"

The younger man rose to meet Thorne eye to eye. "I am Rhys, son of Bledig."

"Come well armed and ready for the hunt, Rhys, son of Bledig," Thorne spoke over his shoulder as he took his leave of the alehouse. "Or do not bother to come at all."

* * *

Finn MacDonagh was weary from the unending dread. It had wormed its spiny tail into his gut as soon as he'd followed Cerrigwen out of Fane Gramarye and had been settled there ever since. But follow her he had, even as she'd led them in circles for nearly three days after they left the Fane, along deer trails and faerie tracks. They'd mucked through the dense stands of alder, oak, and rowan that made up the White Woods until finally she'd brought them here, to bide her time.

The old crone's cottage had been Cerrigwen's first home, one of several such places Madoc had fostered his foundlings and the mageborn babes until they were old enough to be brought into the Stewardry. It was long abandoned when Cerrigwen, Finn, and Pedr had arrived, but the roof was whole, and with a little work it had become a tolerable refuge. Still, this time of year the fog never lifted, and it was nearly as cold and damp during daylight as it was at night. At least there was no rain today.

"Cerrigwen," he barked at the back of her head as she stood at the edge of the clearing, staring into the eerie depths of the White Woods. "Won't you at least give me some idea where we are headed?"

"You don't really expect an answer," Pedr said, leading their mounts and Cerrigwen's silver mare from the woodshed they had fashioned into a makeshift stable.

"No," Finn confessed, taking a moment to assess his son's raggedy looks. Pedr's blue eyes had sunk into the hollows on either side of his nose. Several days' worth of reddish-brown stubble bearded his cheeks and jaw and his roan-colored curls had grown long. It had been a hard twelve weeks in the wilds, and

Pedr's spine was bowed by the weight of his duty. He seemed far older than his twenty-seven years, and it troubled Finn that his eldest boy seemed so much worse for wear. "But it would be nice to know."

"Unless she has decided to return to the Fane, I care not one whit where we go." Pedr set to saddling the horses, making a less than half-hearted effort to hide his surly mood. "I lie awake at night, wondering what has become of the castle—and Odwain."

Finn had suffered some long nights as well and worked hard at ignoring the niggling of his conscience. It only gained him heartache to dwell on thoughts of the Stewardry, of the men and the honor he had abandoned in the midst of a siege, including his brother and his youngest son. He could do nothing to right that wrong just yet, but he had to hope he would, one day.

Pedr let the conversation lag, which suited Finn fine enough. More talk would only make matters worse. Finn preferred to pass the time in quiet observation of their circumstances. It was in dark times like these that a man most needed to concentrate on the world in which he walked.

Cerrigwen was his single focus, from the moment she rose until she finally fell into fitful dreams each night. It was his sworn duty as a member of the Crwn Cawr Protectorate. And after twenty odd years in her constant company, he could not help but be concerned. Finn knew better than any person alive how strong she was and all that she had endured in order to receive the glory that was her birthright. Somehow it had all gone terribly wrong, and he blamed himself. He had not noticed her slipping, though he realized now that there must have been some sign, a moment when her soul had splintered.

Truth be told, she *was* mad. There was no doubting it. He had seen it in her eyes when he had found her working the mysterious dark ritual outside the temple walls. He knew her power and respected it. But what if she never returned to take her place in the Circle of Sages? The prophecy depended upon the joined power of the Guardians of the Realms. Even worse, he now realized, what if she did return? Cerrigwen frightened him now more than ever.

"You should have killed her when you had the chance," Pedr muttered.

"Hold your tongue." Finn's bristle was for duty's sake alone. His gut agreed with Pedr, but he'd made his choice. "She is still Guardian of the Realms, Pedr, no matter what she's done. Before all else, we are men of the Crwn Cawr. The blood oath binds us."

"Then let's hope she leads us to better shelter." Pedr tugged at the cowl of his tunic as if he hoped there was some stretch left in it. "If we'd known what to expect, we could have come on the road better prepared. A hooded cloak might have helped."

"Aye." The list of Finn's regrets grew longer each day. They'd slipped out of the Fane still dressed in battle gear and carrying only the piddling provisions Cerrigwen had brought.

"Always take time by the forelock, Finn MacDonagh." Suddenly, Cerrigwen whirled around and swooped toward her mare. In a blink, she was astride and turned toward the rough path they had made on their ingress. "Will you never learn?"

He never had understood that adage, but he knew she meant for him to follow. The narrow trail forced the horses to travel single file, putting Finn and Pedr in a poor position to intercede should they encounter a threat. The best Finn could do was stay close. All the while, he watched the gait of her mare and listened for the whisper of his woodsman's instinct.

After plodding for hours on a nor'easterly vector, Finn noticed a point ahead where the trees were thinner. A furlong farther, the stands were sparse enough that he could make out the changing landscape and, finally, the position of the sun through the clouds. Midday, and at last they had reached the edge of the forest.

Beyond the trees they found easier terrain for the horses—the pebbled dales and rolling, grass- and snow-covered foothills of the Cambrian Mountains. Less than a league after they entered the lowlands, they intersected a proper road. A vaguely familiar road, in fact, and Finn was not at all surprised when Cerrigwen led them northwest along one of the narrow vales that cut between the hillocks. Before long he found himself anticipating what lay on the other side of the next rise, and suddenly he knew exactly where they were.

"Cwm Brith," Finn spat.

"What?"

Finn ignored Pedr, intent on what was ahead. Sure enough the hillocks gave way to the bowl-shaped expanse that formed the valley head, where the road reached its end. Less than half a league ahead they would reach the gates of a secluded and well-fortified keep.

"Curse that woman, and curse my soul to the darkest depths of Balor's realm," Finn muttered. "I'd hoped to never see this place again."

FOUR

"His Eminence will see you." Elder Algernon waved the smoldering rush stalk in the direction of the inner courtyard, indicating the rectory on the other side with dripping wax and spitting embers, and then proceeded to lead the way at a maddeningly deliberate pace.

"I have come on a matter of some urgency," Thorne said. It required fair effort to restrain his pace enough to keep from trampling the frail, elderly man—and a good deal more to find the patience to be polite. "I remember the way."

"You've been too long in the wilds again, Brother Edwall." Algernon paused, obliging Thorne to do the same. "You forget your manners."

Thorne gritted his teeth, offered a bow of respect, and then followed Algernon plod for plod across the stone pavers that floored the central round of the keep. Courtesy was a small price, given how rarely he returned to Castell Banraven to pay tribute. "Thank you, Elder, for granting me entry at such a late hour."

"Is it late?" Algernon gave a chortle that was more a short-winded cough than a laugh. "I hadn't noticed. The business of the Ruagaire is almost always conducted in the dead of night."

One side of the double entry to the rectory stood open, and Algernon waved him in before shuffling away. Thorne quelled a sudden flare of warning and announced himself as he entered the antechamber. "Your Eminence."

Master Eldrith nodded to him from behind his desk. "Close the door."

Thorne obliged and then returned to the customary position of address at the center of the room. "I have unexpected news."

"I assume it must be grave, given how rarely you trouble yourself to return." Master Eldrith's stern gaze had a sobering effect. "How many weeks' service do you owe, Brother Edwall?"

Thorne struggled with humility. "A matter of months now, I believe. I'm afraid I have lost count."

"Hmm." Eldrith folded his hands and rested them on the desktop. "We shall discuss your tithe later. What is your news?"

Thorne had not realized how tightly he had been clenching his gloves in his right fist, and tucked them into his scabbard belt in an effort to relax. These visits were always uncomfortable—this one more than most. Master Eldrith was not a particularly warm man, but tonight he seemed unusually aloof.

"An emissary from the Stewardry has approached me with an unusual request, but perhaps even more unusual than the request are the circumstances that prompted it."

Now Thorne realized he had taken to fidgeting with his ring, twisting the signet back and forth on the forefinger of his right hand. "More troubling even than *that* is the fact that I did not already know.

"Master Eldrith," Thorne queried pointedly, watching his superior's face for signs of surprise, "are you aware of recent events at Fane Gramarye?"

Eldrith's expression was essentially unchanged. "Go on."

Thorne had a vague sensation of foreboding. "Madoc is dead. Machreth has turned rogue and taken the guardian Cerrigwen with him. I have been engaged for the hunt."

Eldrith released a heavy sigh and glanced down at his hands before returning a now saddened gaze to Thorne. "Have you anything else to report?"

"No." Thorne was suspicious, though he wasn't sure why. "The last information I heard came to me by way of Trevanion, months ago. I would guess he reported to you as well."

Eldrith nodded. "Tell me, have you had any word from the Brothers Steptoe?"

"I have not." Thorne had the distinct impression of doom gathering like storm clouds in the near sky. Eckhardt and Gavin Steptoe were among the few men he counted as blood kin, though they were his brethren only by way of the Ruagaire oath. "Not since the cold weather settled in, but I imagine they would winter at Elder Keep unless you have ordered them elsewhere."

"Elder Trevanion is dead."

"What?" Thorne's entire inner being ignited from the shock. He had been Martin Trevanion's last apprentice and his closest confidant for many years. Suddenly, the lack of communication made sense. But Eldrith's vague and cryptic questioning did not. "How? When?"

"Some weeks ago, I'm afraid. I am truly sorry, Thorne. I wish it were not so." Eldrith appeared genuinely mournful, but he did not disclose the details of Trevanion's death. "I wish many things were not so."

"Master Eldrith," Thorne began to question further, trying to wrest understanding from what he realized was an intentionally evasive conversation. He then noticed that Eldrith's eyes were focused somewhere beyond him. "Are you expecting someone?"

"Forgive me, Thorne." Master Eldrith rose to a stand, his hushed voice far more pained than his expression. "There are powers at work here that are no longer in my control."

As Eldrith spoke, Thorne's instincts were already goading him. The need to escape was unmistakable. Thorne sidled back two steps and positioned himself perpendicular to the master's desk, his back to the exterior wall and his fingers coiled around the hilt of his sword. He heard the echo of footsteps crossing the cobbled courtyard. Thorne calculated four men or more, still half a minute away, maybe a few seconds less.

On his right, Thorne heard the metal tongue of a latch clasp slide back, and a hidden door behind the banner on the wall swung in. Elder Algernon beckoned from the threshold. "This way, Edwall. Quickly, now."

Thorne glanced at Eldrith as he started for the door, gauging whether or not his superior intended to hinder or help. Not that it mattered—Thorne had already assessed the odds of success and had made his choice. He would leave or die trying.

Eldrith stood at his desk, for all appearances impassive—even removed. Thorne suppressed a flare of anger. Such emotions were no aid under threat. It was harder, however, to ignore the betrayal—it tempted him to stay and fight if he must, if only to find out what had gone wrong. Fortunately, he was trained to respond to his reflexes, and Algernon was providing a way out.

"We will distract them as long as we can," the Elder whispered as Thorne passed, offering his sputtering rush dip for light. "Take the tunnel, and avoid the gaolers."

Thorne accepted the advice and the light with a nod of thanks, as he broke into a dead run down the stairwell a few feet beyond the rectory. If there were gaolers, there were prisoners. As far as he knew, the hold had not been in use for years. There was no time now to wonder further about Algernon's cryptic remark, though Thorne understood the message. He also understood that somehow he now had more enemies than friends in Banraven.

The short passage at the base of the keep ran in a straight line directly to the dungeon, with but one slightly curving turn. Once past the curve, anyone traveling the passage would be visible to the sentry standing watch at the hold, and likely to some of the occupants of the pens. At the end of the tunnel was an exit used to put prisoners to work in the fields. Thorne stopped just short of the turn. He knew another way out.

Angry voices echoed from above, with the strike of boot heels on stone steps soon following. With only a minute or two to spare, he waved the rush dip over the right-hand wall of the passage until he found the hatch to the wastewater sluice. It took a good tug to wrench open the metal cover, but good fortune was with him—at least this far; the hinge was well-oiled and moved silently. Thorne tossed the burning rush stalk into the culvert, to douse the light and free his hands.

Gripping the top of the hatch for leverage, he swung his legs through the opening and perched on the narrow shelf just above the drop, so he could pull the hatch shut behind him. The effort unbalanced him, sending him plummeting down the narrow chute in a feet-first gut slide. Less controlled and less prepared than he had intended, but at least the hatch had closed.

The culvert was set at a straight, steep incline that ran a good forty feet before letting out in the cesspool. Thorne wondered briefly which was more nauseating—the stench rising from the rancid pool as he barreled toward it, or the thought of landing in the wastewater itself. The landing was worse by far.

He was out of the cistern nearly as quickly as he had entered it. From the pool edge he only had to kick the cantilevered vent out of its housing to get free of the keep. Then it was a short scramble down the steeply pitched earthen mound that formed the defensive foundation of the castle, and a short wade across a ditch that once had passed for a moat.

It wouldn't be long before his pursuers discovered his route, but by that time he would be nearly a league ahead of them. He'd left his horse tethered in a small copse of ash trees a dozen yards from the moat. Fresh clothing was still some miles off. However, far more discomfiting than the fetid, wet cloak and shit-soaked leather leggings, was the fiery tingle he'd felt at the nape of his neck, just before he'd slid down the shaft.

* * *

Glain positioned the hornbeam wand-rough she had brought from her room in the center of the spell room floor. Any rigid thing of similar size and weight would do—a rush stalk or even a candle. But Glain believed that something of meaning and value to her, something inherently magical like the length of consecrated wood she had chosen to become her next wand, would bring her luck. She had been trying all morning with a raven's quill with no result.

The finding was a complex invocation. The act of envisioning an object and calling it forth seemed simple enough on the face of it, but to coax the thing to reveal itself actually required remarkable control and concentration. The wand-rough was merely a conduit, a medium of sorts that connected her to the object of her desire. It would respond by pointing out the object—a bit like a divination stick or a south-pointing needle.

Handling it lightly, Glain held forth her wand and called to mind an image of parchment rolls fixed with the wax impression of Madoc's signet—a bearded wizard encircled with a wreath of laurel leaves. This had long been the sigil of the Stewardry. Once she had the vision of the scrolls firmly fixed, Glain then imagined them in as much detail as she could summon from memory—the faint mottled texture of the fine vellum that Madoc favored, the scent of tallow and pipe smoke, and his sprawling letters penned in the signature blue-black ink. For years she had prepared the unique mixture for him—from albumen, soot, and honey—and just a drop of indigo dye.

Anguish unsteadied her, like a chill rippling along her spine. The memories were reawakening her sorrow and making it hard to think. Madoc's loss was still fresh. The chaos of the last weeks had prevented a proper mourning, and any plans for a public tribute had been put off for a better time. A practical decision under the circumstances, but there were days when Glain resented being forced to hold onto her suffering. The strain would weaken her if she let it.

Two deep, slow breaths helped to quiet the pain. She wanted to find those blasted scrolls, more now than ever, if only to bring some small part of this nightmare to an end. Again she focused her mind on the scrolls. If she tried very hard, perhaps she might even envision the words on the pages.

"Think on the vellum," Glain murmured to herself. "Think hard on the seal and the script."

"Alwen had you teach me the finding spell in this very room."

"Good Gods, Ariane!" Glain had been working with her back to the door and was caught unaware. Ariane had startled her silly, completely fracturing her concentration.

"Do you remember?" Ariane continued, oblivious to the disruption she had caused. "The magic went wild."

Ariane's oblivious rambling annoyed Glain nearly as much as the reminder. "Yes, I remember, and no, it did not go wild."

Ariane laughed. "What would you call it, then?"

Glain bristled at her friend's insensitivity. Had Ariane forgotten that it was in her defense that Glain had overreacted in the first place? Besides, Glain had not actually lost control of that spell; it had been accidentally fueled by her anger. Perhaps her pride as well—but Glain was wiser now. She turned her back on Ariane and tried to pick up where she had left off. "Hush now, or leave me in peace so I can work."

"Cupboard doors banged and books went flying across the room," Ariane continued, as if she were regaling an audience with a dramatic reading. "If I recall, even the floor stones shifted."

"There are half a dozen spell rooms on this floor," Glain said through clenched teeth. "There must be at least one left for you to search."

"Perhaps I should stay"—Ariane continued to poke at her—"in case you need my help."

Exasperated with the taunting and still piqued by Ariane's indiscretion with Hywel the day before, Glain lost her composure. She spun around, almost eager for confrontation. "The sun will set in the south before I need *your* help, Ariane. And who are you to mock me? How many times have I rescued you from your mistakes? I may count you as my friend, but when it comes to duty and skill, we are not equals. You would do well to remember that."

Glain might have regretted her harsh words, were it not for the unexpected flash of defiance that illuminated Ariane's usually dull chestnut eyes. What had come over her these last several days? Ariane was a shy, slightly awkward girl who rarely spoke, and certainly never in disrespect or contempt.

"Ariane," Ynyr's firm baritone interrupted from the doorway, "Euday needs your help in the scriptorium."

There was a fleeting and indecisive moment before Ariane decided to leave, in which Glain was sure she sensed a challenge brewing. At the very least, she had seen the looming shadow of something intentionally left unsaid. It was unsettling.

Ariane had barely passed into the hallway before Ynyr rolled his eyes and let out an exaggerated sigh. "I will never understand why you take up for that halfling." He propped his shoulder against the doorjamb, with one leg crossed over the other and his arms over his chest. "She is not as deserving as you like to think."

"Everyone deserves a chance to become their best." Glain turned back to the wand-rough, more disgruntled than ever and equally as determined. "A halfling witch is still a witch."

"If she chooses to be," Ynyr argued. "She could also choose to suppress her magical side, to live among plain folk and never be noticed as anything other than ordinary."

"Doesn't that make her choice to embrace her magic all the more admirable?" Glain countered. "It is certainly the more difficult path."

Ynyr shrugged. "One could say it takes courage to choose to be extraordinary rather than ordinary, but I think you miss my point. A halfling will only ever be half a mage, no matter how hard they may wish to be more. Some will be content with their limitations, and some may actually grow beyond them, though that is exceedingly rare. And then there are those who will only ever make the smallest effort and then feel sorry for themselves when they fail, all the while secretly resenting everyone else."

"You are such a cynic, Ynyr," Glain said. "And a snob."

"If by 'snob' you imply that I am proud to be mageborn, so be it," he admitted. "I am proud, and so are you, if you are honest. But that does not mean I think any less of the wildlings or the halflings. I am merely pointing out there are differences."

"Hah!" Glain huffed. "You are pointing out Ariane's differences—and not the flattering ones."

Ynyr smiled at her. "Food for thought, little one, that's all."

She glared at him. "If you insist upon staying, please be quiet."

Thoroughly flustered, Glain tried to ignore Ynyr and focused even harder on the wand-rough. He meant well, but she thought he was overly critical of Ariane. Unfortunately, his was the prevailing opinion, and for the moment, Glain was finding it hard to oppose.

A heavy sigh and a good shake of her shoulders brought her close to calm, and Glain started afresh. She held forth her wand

and made a concerted effort to cast off any lingering misgivings. Alwen had told her the spell worked itself to the expectations of the mage who conjured it, so Glain was careful to invoke only the specific objects she wanted to find. As the detailed vision of the scrolls began to form again, the wand-rough waggled. And then a stray thought threaded through the images she held in her mind. *What other secrets might be hidden here?*

The wand-rough spun sunwise twice and then back full around once, stopping abruptly, with the narrower end pointed at the west wall. Glain was perplexed, but relieved that she hadn't lost control. At least this time the drawers hadn't flung themselves out of the desk.

"Odd," she wondered. There were no furnishings on this wall, nothing at all of interest but for an iron torch sconce and a tapestry depicting a celestial view of a full moon in a night sky. "Could there be a keepsafe within the wall?"

"Or behind it." Ynyr was already examining the wall face, testing the mortared seams between the stones with his fingertips. "From where you're standing, do you see anything amiss? It would be subtle."

Glain stepped back to take in the expanse as a whole. "Near your right knee, Ynyr. There is a brick that seems off."

Ynyr knelt and felt around the edges of the slightly raised stone, and then pressed his palm against it. The brick depressed slightly, and when Ynyr removed his hand, it sprang back, extending an inch or so from the wall. Glain crowded closer as Ynyr gingerly pulled out the brick to reveal a hollow behind it.

"There's something inside." Ynyr reached tentatively into the small opening, which was barely wide enough for his hand.

"Be careful." Anticipation drove her heart faster. "What is it?"

"It's not deep enough," Ynyr said, meaning the hole could not hold a length of parchment. "But there is something here."

Ynyr slowly withdrew his hand, and in his careful grip was a black, velvety-looking bundle covered in dust and cobwebs. "It feels like a bag of rocks."

He held it out to Glain and waited for her to take it from him. Her curiosity quickly bested her disappointment, but Ynyr had discovered the treasure. "Go ahead, Ynyr. You open it."

"No," Ynyr resisted. "This is your honor, Glain. You are Alwen's proctor. Don't be so quick to give up your privilege."

"Give it here then." Glain winced a little, as the reproach was all too familiar. Rhys often chided her for the same fault. She was too slow in taking ownership of her new role, and she knew it.

"Heavy," she said as she brushed the pouch clean. "But not rocks exactly. I think this is a woman's jewel pouch."

Ynyr followed her to a small desk and watched while she worked at the drawn and knotted silk cord. "It's cinched tight. You might have to tear the pouch apart."

"I think I can get it." Glain was excited to see what might be inside, but she didn't want to destroy the bag. "The threads are rotted. They'll give way."

It took a few strategic picks and pulls, but in a few quick moments the knot came apart as the individual threads of the braid gave way. Glain tugged the cord free of the cinch hem and set the bag on the desk. She spread the mouth of the bag as wide as it would open and laid the folds back.

"Great Gods!" Ynyr stepped back half a pace in shock.

Glain would have gasped, if her heart hadn't already leapt to her throat. Before her, encased in glistening silver scrollwork and hung on a glistening silver chain, was the bloodstone amulet that was the key to the physical realm. Or at least she thought it was. It perfectly resembled the one Alwen wore, except that Alwen's pendant was lapis.

"This cannot be real." Glain looked at Ynyr for reassurance. "It must be a forgery."

"It must be." Ynyr did not sound wholly convinced, but he knew as well as she that the real bloodstone amulet had gone into hiding with the Guardians of the Realms twenty years before. "But Alwen will know."

"Yes." Glain hurriedly gathered the amulet and chain in the velvet fabric, suddenly uncomfortable to have it in her possession, forgery or not. "Alwen will know."

FIVE

"**I** know this house." Pedr's memories of his youth had rekindled. For a good while, in the early days of hiding, King Cadell's stronghold had been their refuge.

"Aye," Finn muttered, eyeing Cerrigwen as she approached and hailed the watchmen tending the entry. "As well ye should. Stay close to her, and keep yer wits about. We'll not be welcome here."

The gates of Cwm Brith were heavily guarded. Finn counted four dozen armed men in the yard and figured at least three dozen more might be in the outbuildings or elsewhere on the grounds. Enough sheep and cattle were penned nearby to feed a healthy army.

To his surprise, the gates were opened to them, and Cerrigwen rode onto the grounds as though she were still favored royalty. Finn and Pedr were relegated to escort. Like it or not, the only thing in their control was how well they were prepared to respond to whatever they were about to face. While keeping a wary eye trained on their surroundings, Finn wondered if Pedr recalled their unceremonious booting out of these same gates all those years ago.

The caretaker met them outside the manor house, and Cerrigwen had dismounted before Finn could bring his own horse to a full halt. She handed over her reins and smoothed her skirts, as though she were arriving for an audience. It struck him then that her arrival could be expected. The thought soured his stomach all the more. Perhaps Pedr had been right. Perhaps Finn should have ended her life weeks ago, when she had ordered them out of the Fane and he had first realized she had lost her mind.

"Wait for me here." Cerrigwen, crazed and bedraggled, looked up at him through amber-colored eyes that rested too deep in their sockets. Forest dew had pasted her honey-brown tresses flat round her face, which was too gaunt, and she looked aged by the newly grayed locks at her temples.

"Oh, no." Finn jumped from the saddle and waved at his son. "Pedr will mind our mounts and stand watch on our backsides from here. Ye'll not be going in there alone."

She hesitated, as though she was prepared to protest, but it was fear he saw in her face. "Just tie your tongue, then, Finn MacDonagh. Bear witness, and take arms to hold our ground if you must, but don't you dare speak on my account. Not one word."

"Cerrigwen," Finn whispered, truly worried for her. "Do you know what you're doing?"

Tears welled in her eyes. *Tears.* Finn was flabbergasted. In the more than twenty years he had served her, he'd never once seen her weep. He honestly thought her incapable of it, not to mention bereft of the feelings that might cause a woman to cry. Could one go *beyond* madness?

"Cadell's already denied you once and banished you from his holdings," Finn reminded her, making a genuine effort to be kind. "He also made it quite clear what he'd do if you ever dared make claim against him or so much as showed your face again in his presence. Those were no idle threats, Cerrigwen. Long ago as they might have been, he will not have changed his mind. You *know* this."

She swallowed her breath and closed her eyes, and when she opened them again, they were clear and fierce with intent. "I may have cursed what is left of my own life, but there is still a chance for Ffion."

Finn sorrowed for her. It was true—she had no honor left, no place else to go. Whatever betrayal she had committed against the Stewardry—and Finn did not dare imagine what that might have been—there could be no doubt she was an outcast, a fugitive. But it was not only madness that had driven Cerrigwen here. It was desperation and remorse. And—he could see it now for the first time—her love for her daughter.

"Cerrigwen, I must ask you this, and you *must* answer me this one time." Finn dreaded to ask, but if he were to follow her in and still hold on to his own honor, he had to know. "What vile curse did you unleash in that clearing the day we left the Fane?"

"It was a dark spell, but not a curse." She was humbled by failure. "I thought I could undo what I had done. But it was too late. The veil had already been breached."

"What are you saying?" Finn kept his voice calm, though calm was far from what he felt.

"I weakened the veil so that Machreth's forces could invade the Fane," she confessed. "But it was all for nothing."

Finn watched her eyes while she spoke, the only sure way he knew to tell if there was truth in her words.

"One betrayal begets another." Cerrigwen gave a shaky sigh. "He has forsaken me anyway, despite all I did for him. I waited, and he never came for me."

"I see." Finn felt pity for her. It made sense now, all those weeks hiding at the old crone's cottage. Whatever she had done, it was not his place to judge her, nor was it for him to decide whether she might be worthy of forgiveness. But he was grateful for her account—and a little less hateful of her. Her explanation put him enough at ease to see his duty through without piling any more guilt on his shoulders.

"So be it." Finn straightened his mail and leather armor and adjusted his scabbard, knowing he was nowhere near prepared for what was to come. "Whatever it is you've a mind to do, go on then. I'll be there to see you survive it."

For a moment he thought she might actually smile. What a sight that would have been. Instead she returned to her more familiar airs—squared shoulders, chin held high, and the gait of a queen. Finn admired her courage. Whatever else she was, she was an unstoppable force.

The residence was still as he remembered. Cadell had it built half as a fortress and half as a private retreat, a place where he might escape the demands of his rule and his wife. More hunting lodge than manor house, it was too small to be called a proper castell and too utilitarian to host a court. No, this place was a man's solace. Most of the space on the ground level was given to the butchery and the kitchen. The only other room, aside from a good-sized vestibule, was the dining hall where they now waited, unattended.

"Too quiet here," Finn mumbled.

"Cadell never did keep many servants," Cerrigwen said.

So that he mightn't worry about wagging tongues, Finn thought. As he recalled, though, Cadell's personal guard numbered a dozen at least, and there was the caretaker who'd met them in the yard. There was better than a full garrison manning the grounds, but there was nary a soul inside. Still, the well-nursed fire in the massive hearth at the far end of the room signed that someone was in residence here—as were the creaking floorboards overhead.

A moment later the footfalls of several heavily booted men echoed in the stairwell. As five men came into view, Finn was surprised to see that Cadell was not among them. Cerrigwen was caught off guard and instantly offended. Her shoulders went rigid, and her jaw clenched hard. Finn wondered if she had noticed how much the copper-headed youth in the center of the group bore Cadell's resemblance.

"You've come seeking my father." The youth stopped at the head of the long, narrow table that centered the room. "Cadell is dead. This is my hall now."

Finn was careful not to show any reaction, but this was startling news. Not so much that Cadell had died—given the never-ending border skirmishes between Cadell and his kin, it was not unthinkable that he might meet an untimely end—but what his death signified was momentous.

Cadell's son, Hywel, Hywel had begun his ascent to power, just as the prophecy had foretold. Very likely the new king of Seisyllwg had already begun to assert his dominion over the headmen of the smaller kingdoms, even campaigning against their challenges. And it seemed Hywel would now need to count his own brother among the contenders. He would be in sore need of the Stewards' Council that had been pledged to his aid.

"Hywel is firstborn, not Clydog," Cerrigwen retorted. If the news of Cadell's passing disturbed her, it didn't show. "That you claim his hall only makes it yours as long as you can hold it. And I wager that won't be long."

The youth bristled, puffing out his chest like a peafowl, but Cerrigwen paid no mind to his posturing. "How long since Cadell's death?" she demanded. "What took him? Not *your* sword, that's certain. You're just a boy."

Finn remembered his promise and held his tongue, though he wished Cerrigwen would tread lightly. The youth—barely of age maybe, but a man nonetheless—was the son of a king. She'd be wise to show him a little respect.

Clydog showed restraint, though not well. "Three weeks now, nearly four. I hear infection took root in a battle wound that should have cost him no more than a day's bed rest. Whatever business you might have had with my father, you now have with me."

"My business will be settled with the son who has the authority to speak for your house. Would that be you, Clydog? Do you speak for Seisyllwg?"

A flash of rage lit his glare, but Clydog was quick to quell the spark. He knew enough not to show her a weakness she could exploit. "I know who you are, Cerrigwen of Pwll. Have you come hoping my father might yet recognize your daughter, that he might bring you both under his protection again?"

Finn noticed Cerrigwen tense again. She had not expected Cadell's pup to confront her with her past, and Clydog had clearly been lying in wait for this moment. Finn's hackles stirred as he caught the scent of threat.

"Take care you hear the meaning of my words, Lady. Let there be no mistake." Clydog exaggerated his point. "Cadell has no bastards."

Finn felt his gullet close in. Cadell had been careful to let none of his illegitimate heirs live—save Cerrigwen's child. He had spared Ffion at birth, but only because he understood her worth should Hywel's destiny be cut short. Through this daughter, Cadell then had a second tie to Madoc and the prophecy. All the same, no one had ever doubted how quickly and brutally his favor would have been rescinded had Cerrigwen ever given him reason, especially after the birth of another son. And so it was a queer surprise a few years later when Cadell had spared Ffion a second time. When Cerrigwen unwisely attempted to gain title and lands for her daughter, Cadell had declared them exiled, with the warning that death awaited them both should they ever return.

"How would you know this?" Cerrigwen queried, more suspicious than shocked. "Cadell would never have told you, nor would Hywel, if he knew."

Finn's gullet cinched tighter as the only other possibility came to mind. Machreth had a hand in this. His next thought was to affect a quick escape, but Cerrigwen had moved closer to

Clydog—and further from the vestibule. What could Cerrigwen possibly hope to gain here now?

Clydog continued as though he had not heard her question. "But if there were, somehow, a child whose lineage was tied to both the reign of Seisyllwg and the legacy of the Stewardry, I might be persuaded to acknowledge this sibling and offer my protection against any threat my brother might pose."

"No." Had she been near enough, Cerrigwen might well have spat in his face. "You will not use my daughter to further your gains, Clydog, nor Machreth's. I will not aid usurpers, not anymore."

Clydog smiled at her. "Upon further reflection, I've decided you will accept my hospitality and remain here until Machreth can join us. Then, together, we will claim your daughter and the prophecy, in *my* name."

Cerrigwen backed away as she realized the danger, and reached under her cloak to pull the little bone-handled dagger tucked into her belt at the small of her back. Finn readied himself to intercede and hoped Pedr was close and alert.

"My men search for her as we speak, and when she is found, she will be brought here, to me. So you see, Cerrigwen, there is really but one choice to be made." Clydog moved the four soldiers at his sides into motion with a tip of his head. "And I am prepared to help you make it if you fail to see the way on your own."

Before Finn could put himself between her and Clydog's guards, Cerrigwen made her move. In a swift, fluid twist she had unsheathed the dagger and slashed open the half-healed gash across her left palm. The cut was deep. Clydog's men froze in horror and fear as the sorceress held forth her hand and allowed the blood to pool in her cupped palm.

"Behold *my* power, Clydog." Cerrigwen swept her arm left to right, in as wide an arc as her reach would allow, blooding a thin trail across the stone floor between her and the guards. She stared piercingly at Clydog, muttering spellwork in an old tongue. "*Dial ar sawl croesi fy rhybudd.*"

Though Finn did not understand the words she spoke, it was easy enough to recognize that they were a threat. The four soldiers stood their ground and drew arms, but remained well out of striking distance. Finn pulled his own blade and prepared to defend the line that Cerrigwen had drawn.

"You will carry this blood curse the rest of your days, Clydog, son of Cadell." Cerrigwen rubbed both palms together and held her reddened hands outstretched, confronting her enemy with her magic. The room fell into shadow, as if her words had conjured a sinister cloud above the lodge.

"Take care you never cross my path again," she commanded. "Neither you nor any man or beast or vile creature sent on your bidding—lest you be visited with suffering so horrible, even death will bring you no relief."

The fire in the hearth behind Clydog sputtered and flashed, giving the young prince and his men a good start. Cerrigwen turned and brushed past Finn, eyes wide and wild. She had the look of the banshee again. Finn lagged long enough to stare down Clydog's captain, hoping to make him think twice about following. With a little luck, by the time the guardsmen shook free of their daze and found a way around Cerrigwen's hex, Finn would have her well away from here.

"What happened?" Pedr waited astride, holding rein on the other horses.

With a swift step and a spry leap, Cerrigwen was seated in her saddle before Finn had found his stirrup. She yanked the leathers from Pedr's grip and spurred the silver mare toward the forest at a full gallop.

"Gods' piss and shit," Finn cursed as he hauled himself up. "Get after her, Pedr. The sooner we're in the trees, the better. But don't you lose sight of her."

Pedr gave chase, and by the time Finn reached the edge of the thicket, he had lost sight of his son. He'd follow the hoof trail, but Finn knew Cerrigwen would head for the heart of this smaller copse before turning toward the vast expanse of the White Woods. Even she would not enter the enchanted forest alone.

Finn came upon them where he expected, in a clearing that was really no more than a widening of the trail in a dense grove of bare-limbed alder and birch trees. Cerrigwen had dismounted and stood with her face turned toward the heavens and her arms stiff at her sides. He was beguiled for a moment by the sight of her in her indigo Steward's cloak, a shock of color against the pale wintering landscape. And then he realized she was spell casting yet again.

Pedr waited nearby with her mare in tow, eyes downcast to avoid bearing witness to whatever wickedness she might wreak. Finn cursed under his breath and edged his horse near enough to hear her mumblings. As he drew closer, he could see the tears as they dripped unhindered from beneath her lashes—her eyes were closed, her arms now reaching skyward, beseeching. It was not a spell she muttered; it was a prayer.

Cerrigwen's eyes snapped open, and her anguished gaze fell upon him. "Take me home."

Finn stalled, but only because he couldn't trust his voice not to break. He would take her wherever she asked to go—the oath-bound warrior in him could do no less. And to be fair, the father and brother in him understood why she would resign herself at last to such a fate. Whatever she had done, the Stewardry was the only family she had ever known. In the end, she could have no peace until she had done whatever she could for her child and faced her judgment. He felt compassion for her again, which was a welcome respite from the soul-burning hatred he had been working so hard to squelch these last weeks.

"Return to the Fane?" Pedr was as incredulous as he was relieved, and quick to finally give voice to his worries. "For all we know, it no longer stands. And if it does, who knows who rules it."

Finn nodded at Cerrigwen. "All the more reason to hurry."

A look of profound gratitude washed over her face before her intractable haughtiness returned. Cerrigwen resumed her saddle and led them once again into the enchanted groves of the mysterious White Woods.

SIX

Glain held out the velvet bundle, eager to be relieved of it. Forgery or not, having the amulet in her possession was making her uncomfortable. Her palms were dewy, and her fingers tingled. "It was discovered in a keepsafe behind a wall stone in the large spell room."

"Place it on the altar." Alwen approached with caution and obvious anxiety, toying with the lapis amulet that hung from her neck. The casing and chain were identical to the one Glain had found, except that Alwen's was the key to the spiritual realm.

Glain did as she was asked and stepped away to watch Alwen examine the necklace. "It looks remarkably like the real one."

"Yes." Alwen reached out with tentative fingers, as if she were unsure whether it was safe to pick it up. Glain remembered the scorch mark at the base of Alwen's throat, left by the lapis amulet when she had called upon its power to defeat Machreth's Hellion Army.

With slow and careful movements, Alwen lifted the necklace by the chain with one hand and cradled the pendant in the palm of the other. The bloodstone luminesced, as though it were drawing heat from her skin. She flipped the pendant over and held it close for a better view, searching the backside for something. "That is because it *is* the real one."

"How is that possible?" Glain was stunned, but not nearly as deeply as Alwen appeared to be.

"It isn't." Alwen was quick to return the necklace to its velvet wrap and then took a step back, as if she were protecting herself. "And yet, here it is."

Almost reflexively, Glain crossed the room to retrieve the pot of aleberry always left warming in the coals. "Shall I pour for you?"

"Pour for us both, my dear." Alwen had begun a slow, arcing pace from one end of her ritual altar to the other, pausing now and then to rest against the back of the Sovereign's throne and gaze quizzically at the amulet, while absently fingering the nearly identical pendant hanging at the base of her throat.

"Does it burn?" Glain asked.

Alwen was so deep in thought, it took a moment for the question to resonate. "What did you say?"

"Your amulet," Glain said, "does it burn?"

"Oh." Alwen realized she had been fidgeting with the pendant and let it go. "Yes, it does, a little. The power of the stones is amplified when two or more come together. Even more so when two or more guardians bearing keystones come together."

"I don't understand." Glain returned with two pewter cups full to the brim with the mulled spirits that Alwen brewed from a recipe she refused to share. It was a bit too sweet for Glain's taste, but she was so rarely invited to partake that she would force herself to sip at it in order to accept the intimacy it fostered. "How can the key be here when the sorceress is not?"

Alwen shook her head in bewilderment. "Obviously, Tanwen left it behind, but did she do so intentionally?"

Glain wasn't sure whether she was expected to answer. Alwen began pacing again, sipping absently from her cup and never taking her eyes from the bundle on her altar.

"But how could she have hidden it?" Alwen might well have been speaking to herself. "Madoc placed the amulets round our necks only moments before the four of us left the Fane. There was neither time nor opportunity."

"The necklace had been in that keepsafe a good long while. Years and years." Glain had a heretical thought. "Could she have returned?"

Alwen shrugged, admitting the possibility. "For all I know, she might never have left."

"That is impossible," Glain said. "Madoc sent you each in the custody of an escort. You left through the labyrinth. None of you could have found your way back without help. And even if she did return, where could she have hidden all this time?"

Alwen stiffened and then slowly turned toward Glain. A glimmer of suspicion tinged her quizzical gaze, but her expression was placid. "I would ask how you know all this, but I expect you would rather not answer. Isn't that so?"

Glain thought she might choke on her tongue. Any truth she gave would be revealing that there was something to disclose, and a violation of her oath to Madoc. A lie was unthinkable, not only on principle but also because Alwen would never be fooled. Silence was the only possible response.

"Just as I thought." Alwen's smile was a relief. "You needn't worry. I would never ask you to betray Madoc's trust. Though I cannot help but wonder what else you know."

Glain's misery nearly breached her capacity to contain it. Even the aleberry had little effect on her guilty conscience, though she sucked her cup dry in an effort to find some comfort for her nerves. There was no escaping Alwen's all-knowing ways.

"You are a mystery, Glain." Alwen had resumed her pacing back and forth in front of her altar, one hand grasping her cup and the other toying with her amulet. "Most people, be they plainfolk or mageborn or something in between, reveal themselves to me without my having to search very deeply. More often than not, I find that I must make an effort to avoid learning things I'd prefer not to know."

Glain pretended to drink from her empty cup, suddenly desperate for an excuse to appear distracted. Alwen had the power to see into a person's psyche if she wished, and even to alter their intentions. The conversation was taking a dangerous turn.

"But your thoughts…" Alwen altered her pacing and looped around the Sovereign's throne to meet Glain face to face. "They hide themselves from me."

Glain's mouth fell open, but thankfully none of the garbled thoughts in her head escaped before she could pinch her lips shut. Glain was desperately confused and a little afraid. It was uncomfortable to look Alwen in the eye, but she could do nothing else.

"I confess," Alwen spoke in an even tone that was far more unsettling than any of the alternatives Glain could imagine. "I have tried to look into your mind more than once. Every instance was an invasion of your privacy, and I am not proud to admit my transgression. I must also admit that I failed at every attempt. I was more than a little surprised to discover that the best I could glean were particularly strong feelings. Your grief for Madoc, for instance."

Alwen let these words linger a few moments, so their underlying intent could surface. A tightening resonance took hold in Glain's chest, and her heart trembled as if exposure were imminent and escapable. Glain knew Alwen's power, and it was unthinkable that she was somehow invulnerable to it. It could not be true.

"A very rare ability," Alwen continued, and though there should have been, there was no accusation at all in her words or her voice. "Cerrigwen could evade my intrusions, but not completely repel them. The only person I have ever met whom I could not read at all, not even a little, was Madoc."

Glain felt as though she were utterly transparent and completely lost. "I don't understand."

"Nor should you, I suppose." Alwen's head tilted slightly to one side, and a faintly bemused look crossed her indecipherable face. "Odder still is your origin. Try as I might, I cannot seem to find any written record of you. If you were a wildling, your arrival would be noted in the membership ledger along with the other foundlings and the halfling births here in the Fane. That was not so surprising because I assumed you were mageborn and expected to find your birth inscribed in the record of one of the original bloodlines. But I did not."

Again Alwen paused as if she were baiting Glain to explain or own up. The answer was obvious, and the missing scroll would destroy any doubt of her identity. By remaining silent, she risked Alwen's trust, but if she spoke she would betray Madoc's. Glain felt as though she were daring fate by dancing on a thread that was stretched too thin, with no safe place to fall.

"Curious," Alwen commented, and before Glain could decide whether to respond, the conversation changed course yet again. "I understand you have been to see Hywel."

"Yes." Glain was still dancing on a thin thread, but this one seemed a little less tenuous. At least she could give an honest answer. "He wanted to know about my dreams."

Alwen nodded, as though this did not surprise her. "A born seer is rare, Glain. Divination may be a common magical art, and most any mage can acquire some mastery through the runes or a scrying stone, but unbidden foresight like yours is a gift. Even with the bequest of the dream-speak, I struggle to find guidance from beyond. The language of the Ancients does not come naturally to me, and their messages are so obscure. I had hoped to find Madoc's voice among them, but I have yet to hear him. However, the dream-speak was never intended to be mine."

"Whatever foretelling comes to me I give to you." Glain meant to offer reassurance of her loyalty, but to her own ear she sounded defensive. The dream omens had been visited upon her all of her life, and she had always accepted the responsibility to act on their warnings. "I withhold nothing from you."

"Of course you don't. It would never occur to me to think otherwise." Alwen returned to the altar, hovering just out of reach of the amulet. "This is the mystery that most needs solving just now. Though we may not yet know how and why it came to be here, it is a good omen that the key is now in our possession. One less challenge to overcome."

Alwen turned to Glain again, taking her thoughts in yet another direction. "I expect you will want to know that Rhys has also been charged with a finding task, though his will take him away from us for a while. He leaves at first light."

This time the clench in her chest was so tight if felt as if her heart might be crushed. Glain did her best not to show her distress, but Alwen would know. Glain's fondness for Alwen's son was a secret none of them tried very hard to keep.

"Go." Alwen smiled slightly. "He's been waiting outside my chamber doors for some time now, but not to see me."

* * *

It was harder than he'd thought to contain his excitement. He would miss her; at least he expected as much, but the opportunity had awakened a longing for purpose and adventure that Rhys had stifled for too long. He had hoped she would understand, but Glain was having none of it.

"Your mother has commanded that you go?" She made an effort to edge indifference into her tone and turned toward the window, just to keep from accidentally catching his eye. "I am surprised she would knowingly put you in reach of danger, with your sister lost to the faerie realms and your father still away."

"I did not say she commanded it." Rhys tried a smile, hoping somehow to lessen the tension. Glain would not look at him. "Only that she has agreed to it."

He saw her delicate frame square and her neck stiffen, a subtle yet telling reaction. She might be angry, she might be frightened, or she might be both. He had seen the same posture on more occasions than he cared to recall, but he'd never before been the cause of it. Rhys steadied himself.

"Then you have *asked* to go?"

"The mage hunter requires it," Rhys explained. Thorne Edwall would not have taken the assignment otherwise, and his mother had made it clear he was to do whatever it took to engage this particular Ruagaire monk. To be invited along on the adventure could be considered an honor, though Rhys doubted Glain could appreciate that just this moment.

"But you would go anyway, if you could." Glain finally turned to face him, the full measure of her disappointment revealed on her face.

Rhys knew better than to admit it, but she was right. He would go, even if it pained her, which it obviously did. The Cad Nawdd was a duty of necessity, and he had been sincere when he'd taken the oath, but it was not a calling he would have sought for himself. Glain had heard him complain often enough of his need for purpose of his own choosing. He could not refuse this adventure and still feel true to himself. Surely she must know that, and yet she argued. "We must have Cerrigwen's amulet."

"But at what cost?" Glain's voice trembled.

"A very fat bag of silver, to start."

Rhys regretted the quip as soon as he'd said it, but he really couldn't help himself. A bit of a jest was the best way he knew to deal with difficult situations, though it wasn't always as helpful as he meant it to be. He felt compelled to make some offering of amends and moved closer to take her hands. She stiffened even more, twisting her fingers together in a tightly clenched ball. He reached for them anyway, but she would not allow it.

"And what next?" she challenged him. Her eyes lit her entire being with their fire. "Your life?"

It was then that he realized he was abandoning her, as she saw it. During the fight for the Fane a bond had taken root in the midst of the maelstrom and bloodshed. They had survived dark times together and shared an understanding that few could. But there was also desire between them that defied denial. Intimacy, at any level, was complicated by their respective duties to his mother and the continuing uncertainties within the Fane. The times were still dark, and the new order demanded a great deal more of Glain than she felt qualified to give. She had not yet found her stride. Nor had he.

Rhys tried again to cajole her into a lighter mood. He flashed her a rakish grin and took her hands in his, whether she liked it or not. "I believe you may miss me, just a little."

Her bottom lip trembled. "Make fun if you like, but there is cause for worry."

Realizing his attempt to alleviate the tension was not having the effect he intended, Rhys decided to stand on principle and duty. "Of course there is cause for worry, but not on my account. No one of us is safe while Machreth lives."

If it were possible, Glain looked even more aghast. "So you intend to hunt him down and kill him?"

The idea sounded far more chilling coming from her, or perhaps it was the rising hysteria that tinged her words. "I imagine the seeker will do most of the hunting and likely all of the killing."

And then Glain's wide-eyed stare widened further, as though she'd been struck by an unexpected and horrifying revelation. "And Cerrigwen too?"

Rhys felt his shoulders sag along with his bravado. It was an unthinkable thing, to send an assassin after a Guardian of the

Realms, and a decision that his mother regretted. Rhys was none too proud to be the one to carry it out, but he agreed that it was necessary. "She will be given every chance to return or to surrender the amulet. But yes, if there is no other way."

Glain stared at him, almost blankly, and then pulled back her hands to wrap her arms around herself. "This grows more unbearable by the minute."

She laid the words out so plainly that Rhys couldn't tell what to make of them. He understood she was distraught; only now, he suspected that there was more to it than his leaving or even his part in a despicable plan. He searched her eyes for some clue to her distress and was caught unprepared when their dappled-gray depths clouded with tears. *Blazes*, he cursed himself. *What to do now?*

"Glain." He was halfway to pleading with her, partly because he truly wanted to know what the trouble was, but mostly because he couldn't bear for her to cry. "Tell me."

She teetered on the edge of indecision, and Rhys was miserable for her. Whatever the worry was, the struggle was bitter, and he found himself wishing she would just let it all out, for her own sake. Her lips parted slightly, as though she were prepared to spill all her fears. And then, the clouds passed.

"We all have our duty." Glain blinked twice and almost managed a smile, though she couldn't quite keep the quiver from her voice. "But I do wish yours would keep you here. I am stronger when you are near."

Her admission had an unexpected effect on him, evoking anguish and pride and a sort of protective desire that was both fierce and tender at the same time. Rhys was confounded, but his instincts urged him toward action. He took hold of her shoulders and pulled her close. This time Glain allowed his embrace to swallow her up. She buried her face against his chest, and he was content to let her stay just as she was for as long as she wanted.

It gave him relief to hold her and seemed to quiet the strange emotional storm she had unleashed in him.

But misgivings lingered, and he was no longer so eager to leave. He could be gone for weeks—even longer. What if she needed him while he was away? And then another possibility crept into his head.

"Ynyr tells me you were summoned," Rhys ventured. "To Hywel's quarters."

Glain pulled back enough to peer at him. "Ynyr talks too much. But yes, Hywel asked to see me."

A frown formed without his willing it, though the news warranted more than a little displeasure. "What business would Hywel have with you, in his chambers?"

"As it so happens, he wanted to know about my dreams." Glain pushed against his hold, trying to wedge more distance between them. "Not that I am required to justify any of my business to you."

She was defensive, which only irked him more, and now he had the distinct impression that she was hiding a guilty secret. Rhys was not at all comfortable with the conversation, but he would not let it go. Hywel had power and wealth and the romantic appeal only a legendary warrior-savior-king could have. He was also the sort of man other men would follow to their deaths, and women would do anything to please.

"Hywel has a... reputation."

"So what if he does?" She wriggled until he released her, and then stepped away to glare defiance at him. "Must I then be guilty by association, Rhys, or is it that you think me so naïve that I would not recognize his advances for what they were, if in fact there were any such advances, which there were not." She crossed her arms across her chest and narrowed her eyes at him. "Or maybe you are afraid I might encourage him."

Rhys withered a little, but only a little. She could claim insult all she wanted, but the pink stain on her cheeks gave her away.

She was flattered by Hywel's attention, maybe even welcoming of it. Rhys had no reason to think there was any more to it than that, but that was enough. He didn't like it.

"I only mean to point out that Hywel is more complicated than people tend to think. He holds his own interests first at heart."

"The same could be said of you. Or any other man I've ever met." Glain smiled when her retort caused his eyes to snap wide and his jaw to drop. "And all things being equal, I fail to see why Hywel should be any less appealing for it."

She was toying with him, and Rhys deserved it, but he was still going to make the most of the opportunity to point out Hywel's less attractive qualities.

"He stalks the grounds like a caged beast barking orders at everyone, and then he helps himself to every comfort the Fane has to offer, if you take my meaning, *and* he is pigheaded. He will hear no counsel but his own. Poor Emrys is tasked beyond his limits."

"Hywel is restless," Glain countered. "He worries his people will lose confidence with their king so long away from his court. He does have a home, you know. Perhaps he misses it."

"He has a wife as well, though that seems easy enough for him to forget. No, it's the battlefield he misses," Rhys argued. "His soldiers have begun to arrive, which only agitates him more. I doubt that his promise will hold him at the temple much longer, but my mother won't hear a word against him."

"She sees him as he is, the best and the worst of him," Glain assured him. "To serve the prophecy, we must also serve the man, Rhys. You must make your peace with him."

He squinted at her, as afraid to question her meaning as he was angered by the implications. "Have you?"

"I think I shall devote myself to the effort in your absence," she sassed. "Perhaps then I won't notice it."

Rhys had taken all the banter he could stomach and reached round her waist with both hands. He pulled her hips to his and held Glain hard against his groin, making it impossible for her to ignore the bulge she had caused. The sighing gasp she let out was satisfying, at least for his ego, and when she tilted her head back, she was rose-lipped and flush-faced again. But this time because of him.

"Oh, you'll notice," Rhys said. And then he kissed her long enough and deep enough to be sure she would.

SEVEN

The old cob and thatch dwelling was nearly indistinguishable from its surroundings. One had to look hard to see the shape of the structure beneath the wild growth that was slowly composting its remains. Only two of the four walls were still standing, more or less, joined at one corner and tilting at a precarious angle under the weight of age and disrepair. A pallet-sized patch of matted roofing sagged between two nearly collapsed framing poles, providing a flimsy barrier between Thorne Edwall and the wintry drizzle.

After retrieving a change of clothing from the stores Aldyn the tavern keeper held for him, Thorne had spent the day before making sure he hadn't been followed. He'd taken up position in this corner of the ruins a good two hours before sunrise—not for shelter, but for cover.

From here he could watch the Sovereign's messenger boy as he arrived—if he arrived—and see how he carried himself when he thought he was alone. This was a simple but telling test of veracity—the first of the four virtues of the Ruagaire Brotherhood.

He had passed the first hour in silence and soggy darkness, crouched in a frosty, ankle-deep drift pile of dead leaves, twigs, and mud. His heavy leather boots, leggings and gloves, and the hooded cloak that was the signature uniform of the Ruagaire hunter were all made to stave off the cold. But the infernal sputtering mist was aggravating. Thorne resented the rain. It made it more difficult for him to maintain his patience. Forbearance was the fourth virtue, and the one that Thorne had struggled most to master.

At the turn of the second hour, anticipation began to make him restless. To relieve the increasing urge to move, he slowly raised himself to a stand by gradually increasing tension in his haunch muscles. Done properly, the movement was so controlled that the motion barely unsettled the air around him. A stealthy effect that was yet a further challenge to the fourth virtue, but if Thorne's hunch proved true, the wait would not last much longer.

As a general rule, he was reluctant to hope, but it would be nice to be right about this. What had happened to him at Banraven was clear evidence that something sinister had taken root within the Brotherhood, and Thorne could not rest until he made sense of it. If the young swordsman bore up to Thorne's assessment, he could be of use, and Thorne was considering an arrangement that would benefit them both.

Not a quarter of an hour later, a soft and far-off rustle caught Thorne's attention. Well-trained hearing detected both the distance and direction of the movement. His quick reckoning put the advance from the southwest, about at a furlong away and closing. Thorne was impressed. Rhys, son of Bledig, was early.

From where he stood, Thorne had a fairly unobstructed view of the surrounds on the north, east, and west sides of the cottage, but no sightline at all on the south. He would not be able to see Rhys unless and until he rounded the structure. But what he could hear told him almost everything he needed to know.

Drawing nearer at a wary pace was a single man, leading a shoed and fully dressed horse that was trained to travel as quietly as its rider. Thorne detected the slight scraping sound made by a leather sword scabbard rubbing against doeskin leggings that had been worn smooth by use. The man wore heavier-soled boots than Thorne's—suited for the weather, but not for stealth. His approach slowed, and as he drew within ten yards of the cottage ruins, he hesitated—likely taking time to listen to his own senses and assess what risk he faced.

Thorne was confident that this young man was smart and seasoned enough to be of more help than harm. So far, the lad had acted in accordance with good training, just as Thorne had expected. Next, the swordsman would decide he was alone and come forward to investigate the cottage and the surrounds.

"Your horse and your dog are clever," the swordsman called from where he stood. "Neither so much as twitched a tail, and I passed close enough that I could have reached out and scratched the mutt's ears."

Thorne grinned to himself despite being caught unaware. "You were wise not to try. Maelgwn is half warg, half hellhound. He'd have taken off your hand."

Rhys stopped a few feet short of entering Thorne's view. "Well then, I suppose I'll just wait here for you to show yourself."

"I'm beginning to like you, Rhys, son of Bledig." Thorne stepped out of the shadows and pushed back his hood to greet his guest. "I hope you won't disappoint me."

Rhys offered a wary half-smile. "I'm hoping the same of you."

This sobered Thorne and reminded him of his duty. He circled Rhys and his horse, giving them both a critical review. The swordsman was adequately outfitted for the wilds in woolen and leather, and armed with a good skinning knife and a boot dagger. He also carried a pair of finely crafted throwing blades on his belt. His horse was battle dressed but not overladen, and the saddle sacks were fat enough to be holding a properly measured store of provisions, but not overstuffed—a sign of experience.

"Your Frisian is too big to be fast, but he is made for the cold and the long hunt. A good choice. But your boots, they give you away."

"I prefer these for riding." Rhys tipped his head toward his saddle sacks. "If I'd meant to go unnoticed, I'd have worn the others."

"I see." Thorne squelched another satisfied smile. "Did you bring what I asked for?"

Rhys reached beneath his cloak and brought out a wad of green silk. "A handkerchief of Cerrigwen's, one she was seen carrying. It has her scent, I'm certain of that."

"This will do." Thorne took the silk because his glove afforded him a bit of shielding. He had felt the warning trill at the base of his neck the moment Rhys had brought the fabric out into the air. To touch it barehanded would have been very unpleasant. "What else?"

"Hairs retrieved from Machreth's grooming tools." This time Rhys went to his saddle bags to retrieve a small roll of plain linen, knotted at both ends. "I couldn't stand to have anything of his on my person."

Thorne looked sidelong at Rhys, curious. "But the handkerchief didn't trouble you?"

"No more than I'm used to. Magical things have always stirred my hackles. I even know a witch or a wizard on sight. But this"—he held out the second bundle—"makes the skin on the back of my neck burn."

Thorne had hoped for this. It was a telling trait that all of the Ruagaire shared, but it was too soon to be sure. Perhaps this young man had been born to the calling, and perhaps he was merely sensitive to mage sign. Either way, Rhys was a natural tracker. Thorne would have to add a tithe of gratitude for this good fortune the next time he gave thanks. His list of tithes was growing too long to remember. It had been too many months since he'd last knelt before an altar.

"How will we track the Cythraul?" Rhys asked.

"I've already found the trail. It leads south, to Castell Banraven." Thorne dropped to one knee and let out a long, one-noted whistle. A half-minute later Maelgwn crept out of the woods with the stallion in tow. He let loose the reins and sauntered up to Thorne, who rewarded the warghound with a well-deserved scratch behind his ears. "Hand over that bundle with the hair."

Rhys did as he was asked and then retreated a few paces. "Now what?"

"Now Maelgwn will tell us what he knows." Thorne put the linen on the ground and pried it open a bit so that Maelgwn could nose at the small clump of black, coarse strands tied together at one end with a bit of string. Maelgwn took a sniff and then turned aside. "This bit doesn't interest him. Let's try the other."

Before Thorne had even opened his hand, Maelgwn voiced a deep-throated purring growl. When Thorne placed the cloth on the wet, leafy mulch in front of the dog, Maelgwn backed away and prowled in a circle, making short snarling yips.

"The way he's pacing about means he recognizes the scent. If we follow him, he'll take us to where he first caught it." Thorne stood and handed both the bundle of hair and the green silk back to Rhys. "As good a place to start as any."

Rhys stored both talismans in his saddle sacks and then turned to Thorne. "Shouldn't we first follow the Cythraul trail?"

Thorne swung himself astride his stallion. "My guess is one trail will lead to the other, eventually. Come on."

* * *

Thorne's strange beast was fast. Maelgwn's silver-black fur melded into the shadowy silhouette of the White Woods, masking his movements as he darted through the trees. Only the soft, fleeting rustle of his monstrous paws skimming the forest floor gave his presence away, but by the time the sound traveled, he was already long gone. Maelgwn gave no howl or bay to signal the hunt, and he never slowed or doubled back for his master. It was up to Thorne and Rhys to follow or be left behind.

Maelgwn led them into the dark heart of the woods, through oak and alder stands so dense it felt as if the trees were closing in around them. Rhys had never liked this forest. Legend claimed the oak trees rearranged themselves, trapping unsuspecting travelers in an endless labyrinth from which they never emerged. And although Rhys hadn't seen any moving trees for himself, he'd seen enough these last weeks to believe the White Woods were deadly to anyone who did not know his way around them.

His instincts were afire with dread, and Rhys began to second-guess his decision. The Frisian stallion eased off in keeping with his rider's hesitant thoughts, letting the distance grow between them and the hunt. Rhys had never been so deep in these woods and wondered how wise it was to go any deeper. Already he was uncertain of his bearings—and it was far too late to question whether Thorne knew his. Perhaps Rhys should turn back while he still could. He held the Frisian at a brisk but cautious gait, watching the lag stretch to precarious lengths.

Blazes, he thought, cursing his qualms. What was he thinking? Rhys dug his heels in hard and spurred his mount on, determined to leave all his doubts in the duff. He was committed to the chase and whatever came after, even if it took him to his death.

At the edge of what looked to be a small but intentional clearing, Maelgwn's steady lope abruptly slowed. The horses pulled up without prompting, a sign to Rhys that the animals were working in consort. This was reassuring. His father had taught him the value of the bond between man and beast. The wolf, as the warg was also known, was the sigil of their tribe, and Rhys was naturally inclined toward kinship with Thorne's strange beast.

Thorne signaled caution and Rhys followed his lead, holding the Frisian at a safe distance while Maelgwn prowled along the tree line. Rhys marveled at the mysterious creature. Its features were wolf-like, as was its shape and stance, but the beast was far larger than any lupine Rhys had ever seen. And thus far, Maelgwn had shown a man-friendly nature, which was a decidedly canine behavior. Rhys admired its graceful stalk and obvious intelligence.

Suddenly, the beast stopped. He circled once and sat facing the clearing. Then Maelgwn lifted his nose skyward and let out a long, haunting howl that sent a chill trilling along Rhys's spine. And then the warghound disappeared.

"That takes some getting used to." Thorne urged his massive black stallion toward the clearing. "Let's take a look around."

"What takes getting used to?" Rhys prodded his Frisian into motion, keeping pace with Thorne. "Where did he go?"

"Maelgwn is as much a creature of the netherlands as he is a beast of this world. He comes and he goes."

"Then he is magical." Rhys had thought as much, but he was still a bit stunned. "He is trained to your command?"

Thorne laughed. "Some days I think it's more that I am trained to his. I suppose you could say we have an understanding. Look." He nodded toward the far side of the small clearing. "He's found the witch's lair."

"You mean that cottage?" Rhys wasn't exactly sure what Thorne meant. "There's no one here now."

Thorne twisted in his saddle to look quizzically at Rhys. "Is it your eyes that tell you that, or your instincts?"

"Both." He took a moment to sort through his senses. "Stale manure, three, maybe four days old, and the newest tracks are leading east, into the trees. Three horses, all mounted. They were here a good stay, or at least planned to be. The roof's been patched recently, and there's a fair-sized pile of freshly split logs."

"But the door is standing wide open." Thorne pointed to the small stone chimney on the roof of the old house. "And that fire has been cold almost as long as the horse shit."

Rhys paused to examine another niggling tingle. "The magic lingers."

"Good." Thorne grinned. "That's the remnants of spellwork you're feeling. Take a look inside. See if they've really gone for good."

Rhys dismounted and peered through the doorway into the one-room dwelling. "There's nothing here but a wooden cot and a table. No provisions, no bedding, no belongings of any kind."

"Three horses." Thorne spoke as though the thought had just occurred. And then his expression soured. "Who is she travelling with?"

Rhys hesitated, suddenly realizing he'd never mentioned the escort. "A Guardian of the Realms is always accompanied by at least one member of the Crwn Cawr Protectorate."

"I should have remembered that." Thorne was obviously annoyed. "But *you* should have told me."

"You're right. I'm sorry." Rhys was concerned. He did not want to test the newly forged trust between them. "Finn MacDonagh and his son, Pedr."

"The damned blood oath." Thorne blew a huff of frustration. "They will die defending her."

Rhys felt sick. He had not done as good a job assessing the risks and consequences as he'd thought. "I hope it won't come to that."

Thorne shook his head at Rhys, as disappointed as he was distressed. "And I hope there isn't anything else you've failed to mention."

A shard of white lightning fractured the clouded sky. No more than a breath later, thunder exploded, shaking the ground beneath them. Rhys was half afraid he'd evoked a dark omen with his overconfidence, and swore to himself he'd not make the same mistake twice.

Thorne stared at him, hard, and Rhys held the gaze despite the urge to turn away. He intended that Thorne should see his regret, if not some better evidence of his merit. Words, at this moment, were meaningless.

Again lightning cut across the heavens, and Thorne broke the stalemate with a blink and a duck of his head. "Rain," he muttered.

"We might as well make use of the shelter." Thorne swung out of his saddle and handed his reins to Rhys, leveling another pointed but less glaring look as he planted himself on the ground and stood eye to eye. "Perhaps the storm will give us time to become more accustomed to one another."

EIGHT

Glain paced at the open end of the west annex corridor. It was too early to call upon anyone, especially the king, but the dream that had invaded her sleep the night before had forced her awake. Its meaning was unmistakable, and the urgency embedded within the imagery would not be suppressed. She had to tell Hywel.

Or so her first impulse had said. It wasn't that the king had requested it so much as it was that she was certain the message was intended for him. Alwen would not agree. She would want the opportunity to judge the dream for herself and then decide what to tell Hywel, if anything. Glain had seen it before. It was how Alwen leveraged what little influence she had been able to exert over him thus far. If Madoc were here, Glain would never have hesitated. She would have gone to him first, and Madoc would have delivered the message to Hywel exactly as Glain had perceived it. He had always trusted her to know her own dreams. But Alwen was not Madoc, and Glain was conflicted.

And so she paced, waiting for the sun to breach the horizon and for her conscience to decide what she should do. That she was undecided at all was as troubling as the conundrum itself. She owed Alwen the first debt, as both a Steward and as her second, and because Alwen was deserving of the title Madoc had given her. Glain had no doubt as to whom she was duty bound. So why was she even entertaining Hywel's request?

Because she did doubt. Not whether Alwen should rule the Stewardry, but whether she should rule Hywel. Glain was startled by the thought, but she could not deny it was the truth. At first she had seen Hywel as Alwen had—impulsive and headstrong and in need of guidance. But the man who had presented himself to her these last days was tempered, worldly and wise in ways, she thought, perhaps Alwen was not. He was the king of the prophecy—the king the Ancients had foretold would one day rule them all.

And so it was that Glain found herself at Hywel's door, well before cock's crow, realizing that the decision was already made. She would tell Hywel first, and then Alwen, honoring her duty to them both as best she could and with as little transgression as possible.

She presented herself to the guard. "I have business with the king."

The sentry knocked on the door without questioning her, which made Glain feel both entitled and abashed. There was more than one type of business a young woman might have with the king at such an hour.

The click of the door latch startled her, and Glain retreated a step as one half of the double door was pulled in. Hywel greeted her with a sleepy scowl, wearing only a silk undershirt and breeches. This was a second startle, on another account altogether.

His scowl quickly relaxed into bright-eyed curiosity. "And what brings you here so early?"

"I've had a vision." Glain sounded more eager than she intended, but the dream was so vivid, she could not contain it.

Hywel stepped back and waved her in. "And so you've brought it to me?"

Glain ignored a pang of regret. "Yes, Sire. Just as you asked. Besides, I believe the message was meant for you."

Hywel eased the door closed, manipulating the latch so that it re-engaged silently. He then took a touchwood to poke life back into the fire and light an oil lamp, which he placed on a candle stand between the divan and the armchair.

"Alright then." Hywel seated himself on the divan, folded forward with elbows propped on his splayed thighs and his chin resting on the thumbs of his clasped hands, staring expectantly at her. "Tell me."

His words were more command than inquiry, and Glain was reminded that favor or not, she was not his equal. Even in his undergarments Hywel could never be mistaken for anything but the powerful ruler that he was. Glain was suddenly as terrified as she was thrilled, and tried not to look at Hywel directly for fear her courage would falter.

"A regal stag preens atop a hill, master and defender of all he surveys. Hidden by the mist below, a pack of black wolves is creeping toward him, encircling his stand. They move silently until they are close enough to strike, and then the wolves let loose a mighty howl. The stag is surprised by the attack, and yet he fights valiantly until his strength begins to fail. The pack is too much for him alone. The wolves tear at his flesh with fang and claw until he is dragged down, to kneel upon his forelegs. The end has come, and just as the stag accepts his fate, another buck appears at his side. The wolves retreat, and the first stag is heartened by the unexpected alliance."

Hywel's haunted stare never moved from her face, and he never once interrupted. Glain wondered if he even breathed. She had his full attention as she spoke, which was almost as intimidating as the loose drawstring that allowed the fabric folds at his groin to gap. Given his posture, it was difficult to keep her eyes from focusing where they should not.

"But then the second stag turns on the first, and the battle begins anew, antlers clashing and hooves flailing. Were he not so weakened by the wolves, the first stag would have easily bested the second, but weary and wounded, the best he can do is to hold his ground. The wounds the bucks inflict upon each other are deep, and the blood runs, thick and red, until it becomes a great flood drowning the land. And still they fight."

Glain took a steadying breath and engaged Hywel's gaze. "That's where the dream ends."

Hywel was silent a long while, holding her captive in that searching gaze that should have completely unraveled her nerves. A proper girl would have made an effort to withdraw from it, but for some reason Glain felt emboldened. His searing scrutiny, however, made her uncomfortably warm and caused her heart to run rampant. Anticipation dampened her palms and the back of her neck, and mortifyingly, the private places beneath her skirts. Why did he stare so? How she wished he would speak. How she wished he were properly dressed.

"And what does this dream mean to you?" Hywel sat back and folded his arms across his chest without breaking his stare, or shifting the position of his legs. "What does it have to do with me?"

That he did not immediately understand the symbolism so surprised her that she forgot everything except the message she had come to deliver. Glain plopped herself on the armchair adjacent to the divan. "Don't you see? You are the stag, the first stag. The wolves are Machreth, or perhaps your enemies joining forces against you, and the second stag—well, of course, *that* is Clydog."

Hywel's frown signaled sobered thoughts. "So this is a foreshadowing of betrayal."

"Yes, but only in part." Glain was impatient to help him see, and her earnestness brought her to the very edge of her seat. "It is also a warning about the consequences of vengeance and the cost of rivalry."

He abruptly pulled himself back to his previous perch, knee to knee with Glain and tensed by sudden realization. "The blood flooding the land."

"Yes!" Glain was pleased that he had gleaned the most valuable part on his own. "As long as it lasts, your feud with Clydog will cost you everything you gain, maybe even more."

Hywel's eyes glinted and narrowed. "Then the sooner I end him, the better for us all."

"No, Sire." Glain was taken aback. She had misjudged his thoughts and now attempted to counsel him toward a more benevolent solution. "There will be bloodshed and loss and betrayal. This will all come to pass. I would venture a guess that some of it has already. And there will be more. It cannot be avoided. But *I* believe the true meaning of the dream is that in the end, the lasting peace and unified nation you envision is only possible once you've made peace with Clydog."

Hywel's frown soured, as though he had been force-fed a bucket of maggots. For a moment Glain worried she had overstepped her privilege, and wondered what might be the price of his displeasure. Outside the dream, Hywel was far more bear than stag.

Finally, his expression softened to a look that bespoke a more measured line of thought. "You are suggesting an alliance."

He said it as though the idea were worthy, albeit distasteful, but Glain was gratified that he had heard her.

"It is only one of many destinies, of course," she admitted, "but yes. United, the sons of Cadell would create a dynasty so strong, few would dare to challenge you, and certainly none would succeed. It may well be that Clydog cannot be redeemed, and perhaps he is meant to come to a bitter end after all. But if such an alliance were possible, would it not be worth considering?"

Again, his gaze was searching, as if he believed she had the answers he needed. As if he trusted her wisdom. Not until that thought did Glain realize how near she was to violating Madoc's prohibition against intervening in the fates, nor did she realize she had hold of Hywel's knee until he covered her hand with his.

Glain was reminded of how harshly she had judged Ariane. Now she understood how easy it was to fall prey to his magnetism, how intoxicating his attentions were. Already she had risked too much to please him, and to her disgrace, she thought herself quite likely to risk far more.

"Thank you, Glain." With her hand still in his, Hywel stood and bade her rise as well. He was so close to her that her nose nearly touched the hollow at the base of his throat. "I am grateful for your confidence. You've given me a great deal to contemplate."

And then Hywel was at the door, dismissing her with just a hint of a smile. "I remain in your debt."

Finally, humility and modesty and some small measure of good sense returned to her. Glain gave a polite nod and escaped before another embarrassing thought could arise. But no sooner had she left his room than she wished herself back. It was like stepping out of the heat of the sun into cold shadow.

"Oh great Gods." Ynyr confronted her in the hall just outside Hywel's door. "What were you *doing* in there?"

"Hush, Ynyr." She was mortified, and yet strangely thrilled. "Keep your voice low. I had honest business with the king."

Glain turned to make a quick escape, but Ynyr blocked her path. "What business could you possibly have with Hywel, honest or otherwise? Did he summon you? Did Alwen send you?"

And then, because she felt guilty and trapped, without an answer that she could possibly justify to him, Glain employed the only defense she had left. "I am Proctor of the Stewardry, Ynyr. Bear that in mind before you question me."

"I meant no offense, Glain." Ynyr looked like he'd been slapped. "It's only that I...it's just that you..."

"I'm sorry, Ynyr. There are some things I cannot explain, not even to you." Glain tried to make light of it, but she was not proud of her behavior. "Bring the others and meet me in the scriptorium after the morning meal. We'll start a fresh search for the scrolls."

* * *

Glain lingered while Ariane finished primping in front of the mirror on her dressing table, tempted to unburden herself. Her meeting with Alwen had been awkward and tense. Glain felt out of sorts and a little adrift, and without Rhys she felt profoundly alone. Ariane was a good friend, but there were only so many troubles Glain could confess without disclosing more than she should. Besides, Ariane was a little too simple and unsophisticated to offer any true wisdom. Ynyr was the better choice, but his counsel would come wrapped in reproach. Just now Glain wanted a more sympathetic ear.

"You're up very early," Ariane noticed. An innocent observation that Glain knew was actually an invitation to gossip—one of Ariane's favorite pastimes, much to Glain's dismay. "What duty was so important that it got you out of bed before dawn? No more demons, I hope."

"I had business with the king." She could admit this much. "And then with Alwen."

"What business could you have with Hywel?" Ariane's first reaction was defensive, and then concern that bordered on distress overtook her. "Not *personal* business."

"Of course not." Glain knew right away what Ariane was suggesting, and was almost annoyed enough to call her out. "I was honoring a request, one I ought to have refused."

"That doesn't sound like you—not at all." Ariane stopped fussing with her hair and turned to face Glain, fully rapt and trying a bit too hard to mask her curiosity with concerned interest. "What did he ask?"

As soon as she said it, Glain realized she had fed Ariane's slightly perverse fascination with other people's missteps. "It doesn't matter, really, except that I went first to Hywel with something and then to Alwen."

Ariane's frown unfolded into wide-eyed surprise. "What did Alwen say?"

"Very little," Glain explained. "But it was clear she was not particularly pleased."

"You mustn't be so hard on yourself. Hywel is a man who gets what he wants. It does not surprise me that you could not resist, whatever it is he has asked of you." Ariane's earnest expression shifted to a look of knowing and an illicit sort of smile that made Glain uncomfortable. "I certainly can't."

"Ariane." This was not the conversation Glain had wanted to have, but there was no avoiding it now. "Are you really that foolish?"

A look of wounded denial washed over Ariane's face. "If love is foolish, then yes. Yes, I am."

"Oh, good grace." Glain dropped to a perch on the edge of the bed to bring herself to even terms with her friend. She was crestfallen. "It can't be love. Or at least it shouldn't be. You are a Steward, Ariane. Your duty is to fulfill Hywel's destiny, not his desires. Besides, he has a wife."

"He married for title and land, not for love." Ariane's chin jutted. "Don't be such a priss, Glain. There are many ways a sorceress might serve a king. I consider it an honor that he seeks his comfort from me. He *needs* me."

"That is the most ridiculous thing I have ever heard." Glain was so stunned that she forgot to be kind. "Even you could not be this naïve."

Ariane took offense, and the backlash was immediate. "Your lusting after Alwen's son is every bit as foolish.

Just because he hasn't bedded you doesn't make you any less his whore."

Ariane's biting anger was unexpected and unsettling. For a moment she was another person than the girl Glain knew. Even her generally plain appearance seemed altered, strangely beautified by the gleam and flare of her passion. This was not Ariane's character, or so Glain would have said before these last few days. Within the simple, unassuming and obliging girl that Glain had taken into her trust coiled a stirring viper. Glain, who had always taken pride in seeing potential in Ariane that others did not, had somehow failed to see this.

Glain stood up and straightened her robe to keep from appearing uncomfortable, and took a few steps toward the door, to keep space between them. "I count Rhys among my friends, just as I do you."

"You count me as your friend because it makes you feel superior to do so. But I know better." Ariane's usual vacant calm resurfaced as she returned to the mirror on her dressing table. "You have just as many failings as the rest of us. You're just better at hiding them than most."

Glain was hurt, and a little disturbed. "The others are waiting for us in the scriptorium."

"Good." Ariane pulled herself away from the mirror, wrapped her white robe around her, and proceeded to the doorway, putting herself in the lead. "It's time we quit avoiding the obvious."

Glain followed Ariane into the hall, scurrying to match her pace. "What is that supposed to mean, Ariane?"

As if she'd just remembered her place, Ariane slowed as she reached the third-floor landing and waited for Glain to overtake her. "I simply mean to point out that some might think you are too quick to favor your friends, myself included."

Glain reached the second-floor landing a few steps ahead of Ariane and waited. "I don't understand."

Ariane ignored her and gestured toward the scriptorium doors. "They are waiting for you."

NINE

Ynyr had brought Verica and Euday, and was waiting for her inside the scriptorium, just as she had instructed. He was faithful and reliable no matter what she asked of him, which only made Ariane's comments about appearances all the more annoying.

Glain looked to Ynyr, hoping to redeem her earlier bad temper by deferring to his leadership in front of the others. "Will you give us an account of our progress?"

He avoided her eyes as he responded, making her even more miserable. "We have searched all the outbuildings, including the barracks and the officers' quarters, the stable and forge, and the old residence halls. The acolytes' dormitory was too badly damaged during Machreth's incursion to enter safely. Emrys has assigned men to shore up the walls enough to allow us in, but that will take another two days. Inside the Fane, we have finished with all of the common areas, including the spell rooms."

Ynyr was careful not to mention finding the bloodstone necklace, just as Alwen had asked. "That leaves us with the scriptorium, the kitchens, and the apprentices' residence hall."

"There is also the dungeon beneath the kitchens, and the tunnels and chambers beneath the west annex," Euday added. "But much of that is even more impassable than the dormitory."

"What about the grounds themselves?" Verica wondered. "Isn't it just as possible that the scrolls could be hidden in a well or a hollow tree? Or even in a hole in one of the exterior walls?"

"Alwen is convinced they are somewhere within the Fane itself," Glain explained. "How she can be so certain I have no way to know, but I trust her judgment. I think we can forego the grounds for now, but I will speak to Alwen about the dungeons and the catacombs."

"You are all so ridiculous." Ariane, who had been so reserved that she'd nearly been forgotten, suddenly chirped in agitation, "You actually believe you will somehow discover the scrolls without casting aspersions on anyone."

"I hardly think it ridiculous to exhaust the less unpleasant possibilities first." Glain was beginning to regret having ever brought Ariane into her circle. "None of us is eager to implicate our friends."

"And yet it must be done." Ariane was exasperated. "Even if we were to find the scrolls in some impersonal place, the investigation will not end there. *Someone* is guilty of taking them to begin with. Do you really think Alwen will be satisfied to leave a traitor running loose in the Fane? Will any of you?"

Ariane's argument was well made, and they all knew it, though no one was ready to agree with her. They had spent valuable time eliminating the least likely prospects, and Glain had to admit to herself that she had happily followed the path of no resistance. Perhaps Ariane was right. Perhaps the time had come to confront their worst suspicions.

Ariane let out a huff of frustration. "How is it that you all do not burn with righteousness? How are you not so offended, so angry that you would tear the stones from the walls to find Madoc's scrolls? There is a *traitor* among us!"

Ynyr looked exhausted, almost defeated. "Then what would you have us do, Ariane?"

"It is not for me to say." Ariane hesitated in an attempt to show deference, but she made no effort at all to hide her self-satisfaction. "But I would suggest we go straight to the most obvious culprits, to those among us who have motive and the opportunity."

"You mean the acolytes," Ynyr sighed. "You mean Nerys."

"I mean us all, Ynyr," Ariane sniped. "But search my room first, if it makes you feel better."

Ynyr's bright blue eyes grew dark and narrow with anger. "If you insist."

Verica did her best to defuse the sudden tension. "Perhaps we could start with the apprentices' sleeping porches. Neither Euday or I would mind, would we, Euday?"

"It is all equally ugly to me." Euday shrugged. "Though I must say that any of the apprentices, myself included, would gladly do the bidding of a superior and without question. I would suggest that some delicacy might be in order if one of them turns out to be complicit, some allowance made for an underling acting out of deference."

He cleared his throat. "I'm afraid I must also point out that you have failed to mention the third-floor residences—the docents' quarters and the private suites, not that I am suggesting we barge in on the king—or Alwen, for that matter."

"And yet it must be done." Ynyr appeared to have resigned himself to some inner misery, but his puffed-up chest and crossed arms did little to mask his resentment. "But we will start with Nerys."

"Then let's get to work." Ariane glared at Ynyr, gathered the folds of her robe in clenched fingers, and marched toward the staircase.

"Wait," Glain declared, more forcefully than she intended. "*I* will lead."

At last Ynyr smiled as he drew close to be sure she could hear his whisper. "Perhaps there is hope for you yet."

* * *

Nerys obliged the demand to search her quarters without a word, not a single huff of objection or even a resentful scowl. Glain was surprised, given her naturally fiery personality. Nerys was even willing to wait in the hall, under guard.

Ariane insisted on searching the room with Glain. Verica and Euday bore reluctant witness from the doorway, while Ynyr waited in the hall with Nerys. He tried to be officious, but his sorrow seeped out of him with every breath he expelled. He and Nerys had been close all their lives, like siblings. They had both been born to the Fane the same year, and Ynyr had always been protective of her. Whether it was for his pain or Nerys's discomfort, Glain felt regret. No matter how much she distrusted Nerys, she could not take pleasure in the humiliation of her peers, deserved or not.

Ariane, however, would not be hindered by compassion, especially not when it came to her rival. Nerys was everything Ariane was not—gifted, accomplished, and confident in her power. Nerys was also a graceful beauty, whereas Ariane was awkward and plain. And wherever it was that nature did not pit them against each other, Ariane was sure to try. And so far, had failed to succeed.

Before Glain could stop her, Ariane took it upon herself to begin the finding spell. She placed a raven's quill on the hearthrug and withdrew her wand, positioning herself between the quill and the door. For several moments she stood stone still, every wisp of her being focused into a single thought. The feather quivered.

As Glain and the others watched in anxious silence, the mystic forces tugging at the feather grew stronger, and the quill twitched back and forth, as though it wished to turn both ways at once. It seemed to fight against itself at first, and then the feather began to spin ever so slowly clockwise. It turned a full circle and a half and then stopped.

"Which end is the indicator," Glain asked. "The plume, or the nib?"

Ariane looked bewildered. The feather tip pointed toward the hearth, and the stem pointed at the bed. "I don't know."

Ynyr snorted. "She didn't bother to decide before she started the spell."

"Then it could be either," Glain said reluctantly, "or both."

"The plume," Ariane announced, starting toward the hearth. "It is the plume."

"No," Glain ordered, beckoning the two sentry men in from the hall. "Stand outside with the others. The guards will search."

Ariane obliged, but not without pouting. "As you wish, Proctor."

Glain ignored her and instructed the guards, "Search the bed and then the hearth."

It was a painful wait. Under Glain's close watch, the mattress was turned over, and the boards and posts disassembled. The coverlet and pillows were patted down and shaken out. And last, the floor beneath and the wall behind the bed were examined for loose stones. Nothing.

Then the sentries turned their efforts to the hearth, one on either side of the chimney. Glain stood before the fireplace, looking for any obvious irregularity in the facing. There were no breaks in the mortar, nor unusual discolorations or obviously displaced bricks. The hearth base itself was worn and crumbling, and deep enough to hold treasures much larger than the scrolls. But the guardsmen, searching on hand and knee, failed to find any hollows or recesses.

It was by happenstance that one of the men discovered the false mantle, when he took hold of the one end to help pull himself up. The scrollwork support mounted on the right side of the fireplace came free of the sill and clattered to the floor, revealing a carefully made and very small, perfectly round tunnel bored into the mortar between the brick framing and the oak mantle.

"Oh, great Gods." Glain was exhilarated. The scrolls were found, and she was saved. "Stand aside."

The guardsmen stepped back to make room as she approached. Glain knelt on the hearthstones to peer inside the small opening and caught sight of the end of a small roll. Taking care not to damage it, she tweezed the edge between the first two fingers of her right hand and pulled with gentle, even tension until the roll was freed.

"Well?" Ariane, hovering just inside the door, could not restrain her curiosity any longer. "Have we found them?"

Glain examined the parchment with a delicate touch, afraid she might tear it. The seal on the scroll was broken, but it was unmistakably Madoc's. As gently as she could, Glain unfurled the exposed edge far enough to see the first few lines of script.

"One." Glain let the parchment curl back into place and cradled the roll in the palms of both hands. "We have found one of the scrolls."

Ynyr pushed past Ariane into the room. "Are you certain?"

"Yes." Glain heard agony in Ynyr's voice. "I know this must be difficult for you, but this is clearly one of Madoc's private writings. I believe it is part of the registry, the record of the Primideach line."

"Glain." Ynyr looked at her with pleading eyes. "I know you have never cared for her, but if you have ever had any faith at all in me, you must believe me now. I do not know how it came to be in her room, but Nerys is not to blame for this."

Her heart bled for him. She had never understood his blind devotion to Nerys, no more than he had understood her unyielding support of Ariane. Misplaced or not, she and Ynyr shared a commitment to the same values, friendship and loyalty. And so she extended him hope she herself did not have. "It is not my place to judge, only to report what we have found. Nerys will be allowed to plead her case. Perhaps there is an innocent explanation. But that is for Alwen to decide."

* * *

Glain went straight to Alwen with her evidence. She found the Sovereign already dressed in the gold-trimmed indigo velvet mantle that denoted her rank, as if she had been expecting to give an audience. The formality made Glain feel a little intimidated, but she was pleased to present what she'd found.

"This is how you found it?" Alwen held the scroll delicately with the fingertips of her right hand.

"Yes." Glain could not keep herself from staring at Alwen's frostbitten fingers. The stain of Alwen's ill-fated attempt to save Madoc from drowning in the Well of Tears affected all four fingers from the first knuckle to the tip. It was all the more noticeable because of Madoc's signet, which she wore on the middle finger of the afflicted hand—as much a macabre reminder of Madoc's absence as it was a bizarre but convenient alternative to Alwen's gaze. "The seal was already broken."

Alwen carefully unrolled the vellum to read its contents. "It is, in fact, just as you had guessed. This is the continuation of the Primideach line, from the beginning of Madoc's generation forward. It seems Madoc had no progeny of his own, but he did have three siblings. Among them, only one child was born to the Primideach line—a son, brought forth by his sister, Saoirse." Alwen's expression soured, and she paused to clear her throat. "This son, Alric, was fathered by one of Madoc's brothers, the eldest of the Primideach clan."

Alwen looked at Glain. "You don't seem particularly shocked, or even surprised."

"Madoc told me the story once, as a cautionary tale. In a cloistered society, certain risks are inherent." Glain quoted his words almost verbatim. "'Inbreeding,' he said, 'is inevitable.'"

"Hmm." Alwen resumed her study of the document. "It seems Madoc's nephew begat three children by a sorceress of the Eniad clan named Brigid, but it appears the eldest two, both boys, did not survive infancy."

Her expression skewed to puzzlement. "The birth of this third child is recorded by date," she sighed, "but not by gender or by name."

"And even stranger," Alwen glanced at Glain again, "two days later both Alric and his father died. At each other's hands, it says here. Another family scandal?"

Glain knew only what Madoc had told her. "A duel to the death between father and son over a debt of honor so immense it cost both their lives. Madoc did not say what the debt was, but it saddened him deeply to speak of it. I always thought it must have had something to do with Saoirse."

"These writings show that Saoirse abandoned the Stewardry later that same year, along with a handful of devotees, but there is no mention of why. She was a respected elder. I recall Saoirse's name spoken with great reverence by the docents during my early years here. Losing her must have been difficult for Madoc." Alwen frowned. "But I never knew any Brigid, and I don't believe she was ever in residence here. Her name appears in the Eniad family lineage, but not in the Stewardry membership rolls."

Alwen looked at her pointedly. "Did Madoc never say what became of her, or of Alric's child?"

Glain had expected this question, but that did not make it easier to answer. "No, Sovereign. He did not."

"He never mentioned a name?"

"Never." In the strictest sense, Glain was telling the truth. Madoc had never mentioned the name given to his nephew's child at birth. Glain did know where it could be found, but so did Alwen.

Alwen rolled the vellum sheet into a tight curl, appearing to struggle a little with the practiced serenity that was her signature trait. This constant calm was the temperament with which she greeted everything, but for the first time Glain saw ripples of disquiet beneath the carefully composed façade.

"This is disappointing." Alwen tapped the scroll with her fingertips, her eyes focused on some invisible point, speaking to no one in particular. "We need Madoc's last testament. Apparently it is the only hope of ever finding his heir."

Unsure whether a response was expected or even wanted, Glain remained silent. Alwen appeared to be searching, somewhere within or beyond herself, for an answer that refused to be found. Glain was hopeful now that the first scroll had been found, and the traitor.

"Now." Suddenly, Alwen returned to the moment at hand. "You are wondering what I will do with Nerys."

"She is waiting in the hall, under guard." Glain was puzzled by Alwen's comment, which was more an observation than a query. "I assumed you would question her. If she has the one scroll, it stands to reason she has the other."

"So it would appear," Alwen said, straightening even more in her seat. "But I have my doubts. Don't you?"

"I don't understand." Glain was now befuddled. "The scroll was found in her possession."

"In her room," Alwen corrected, "not on her person. The two are not the same."

"Are you suggesting that Nerys is *not* the traitor?" Glain did not accept this theory. "That she is but a dupe for the one who is?"

Alwen's widened eyes and the tilt to her chin seemed to say exactly that. "I suggest the possibility, yes. Nerys has the support of many of her peers, including Ynyr. And I have neither seen nor heard anything to give me cause for concern, aside from your suspicions."

Glain bristled. "Is that not enough?"

Surprise widened Alwen's eyes further still. "It would be, if those suspicions were founded on something other than rumor and her petty rivalry with a sister acolyte who has your favor. I trust you take my point."

"I do." Glain could not deny the favoritism, but she could still protest. "But it is more than that. My own intuition tells me Nerys has been hiding something all along."

"Hmm," Alwen smiled. "We all have secrets, Glain. They are not in and of themselves a sinister thing. Nor is the keeping of them grounds to charge treason, at least not without a better understanding of what has been concealed, and why."

Glain felt as though she had been caught in a lie. Was Alwen still speaking of Nerys or of her?

"I will speak to Nerys alone. I believe she will open her mind to me freely, but one way or another I will have the truth as she knows it," Alwen said. "And then I will decide what is to be done. I will expect your support, Glain, even if you do not agree."

"Of course," Glain promised, though she had no doubt that her suspicions would be proved. "I have nothing but respect for your wisdom, Sovereign."

Alwen looked at her for a long time through narrowed, discerning eyes. For a moment, Glain wished she were not immune to Alwen's probing. Perhaps the best thing for them all would be for Alwen to see Glain's truth.

Alwen closed her eyes and released a long, slow breath, as though she had resigned herself to an unavoidable conclusion. "Send me Nerys."

TEN

The entire hearing, in Glain's opinion, had been a travesty. The interrogation had amounted to little more than a few pointed questions, for which Nerys had no defense but denial. Finally real evidence of betrayal had been found, and Alwen had all but forgiven it. She had taken the accused's claims of innocence seriously and taken the entire matter under advisement. Alwen had then deferred formal judgment and confined Nerys to her quarters until further notice.

Glain had wanted to argue for a proper inquiry, but she had promised Alwen her support. Which she would give, at least publicly, but it had been difficult to contain how appalled she felt. And so, Glain had silently steeped in her resentment until the hearing was over, and she was finally free to seek refuge in solitude.

The scriptorium was a common gathering place for study and quiet conversation, especially after the evening meal. At this late hour, however, Glain could generally expect to study or contemplate alone. She waited for the apprentice to tend to the room, lighting the lamps and stoking a last blaze in the hearth, before settling herself in one of the overstuffed chairs in the sitting area to stare at the fire, and sulk. She had called for ginger and spice tea, but what she really wanted was a strong, properly aged claret.

"Is it really so awful?"

Glain winced at the sound of Ynyr's voice and purposely kept her eyes trained on the hearth. "I was expecting the attendant with my tea."

"I intercepted him in the hall." He set the small pewter serving tray on the candle stand nearest her chair and handed her the steaming cup. "It gave me an excuse to intrude on your gloom."

She accepted the cup but refused to acknowledge him, hoping Ynyr would reconsider and leave. He did not. Glain fought the urge to order him out of the room. Ynyr deserved better from her, and she sensed his concern. But if he forced her to speak on the issue of Nerys at this very moment, she was not at all sure she could be kind. "At your own risk then, Ynyr. Consider yourself warned."

Ynyr hovered behind her in the half-shadow cast by the firelight against the book stacks and shelving on the near wall. "You think Alwen's judgment was too lenient."

Glain sighed aloud, exaggerating the huff to declare her aggravation. "What does it matter what I think? Alwen has said that Nerys deserves the benefit of the doubt, and so it shall be."

"Yes." Ynyr took to nervous pacing. "But what do *you* say?"

"It is not my place to *have* a say." Glain's indignation underscored her tone, despite her intention to temper it. "Alwen is Sovereign, not I."

"And not Madoc." There was compassion in his voice that Glain felt she did not deserve. "What would he have done?"

"He would not have shown Nerys every little kindness and treated her as though *she* were wronged, I tell you that. Not with only her word against the evidence," Glain blustered. "Treason is a high crime. The punishment is death."

"I admit the evidence is damning, but even you must see that there are more questions than answers. Nerys has not been convicted, but neither has she been acquitted. Isn't it enough that she is confined and under guard?"

"Confined," Glain scoffed, "in the comfort of her own rooms."

Now Ynyr sighed, but his exaggerated huff was one of exasperation. "Where would you have her, in the dungeon? I wonder if Madoc would have been so harsh."

"He might well have set down the same sentence, at least until the whole truth is found out. But he would have respected the concerns of his advisors rather than dismissing them out of hand." Glain realized she had found the true root of her discontent. "And he would have called for a formal inquiry before witnesses and a jury of her peers, as the canons dictate."

"You are right." Ynyr finally emerged from the shadows and plopped himself into an adjacent chair. "Madoc certainly had a more democratic bent."

Glain took his subtle reference as she knew it was intended. It was difficult to accept Alwen's more solitary and interpretive approach to authority. Madoc had made it a practice to invite the counsel of others, Glain's in particular, but in general he took the opinions of others into consideration on matters that affected the entire Order. And he strictly adhered to the rules of order that governed the Stewardry.

"We all miss him, Glain," he said. "But I know it is hardest for you."

"She has never asked me what you just did." Glain was too close to tears and swallowed a gulp of the tea, hoping the ginger vapors would help. "Not once has she ever asked me what Madoc would do."

Ynyr attempted to placate her. "It may be that Alwen believes she already knows."

"How could she know?" Glain argued. "She lived half her life outside the Fane, away from his company. She tells me every day that she still cannot find his voice in her dreams. Her only connection to him is through me."

Ynyr's smile was born of empathy. "No one knew him better than you, and Alwen would do well to seek your insight. Not to speak ill of her, as I confess I am glad for the mercy she has shown Nerys, but Alwen does seem reluctant to take a hard line."

"I often wonder if she ever will," Glain said. "Perhaps when there is no other choice. I tend to think that times of unrest require a stronger hand, not a softer one. But as I said,"—she forced a smile over the rim of her cup—"*Alwen* is Sovereign."

* * *

The rain had let up by morning, but the clouds clung to the sky, gray and bloated and soon to start seeping again. Thorne had slept well for the first time in weeks, partly because of the shelter of the old hut and partly because of the company. He had forgotten what a relief it was to share the watch.

Rhys was eager to please after his carelessness the day before and had offered to find food. As it happened, he was particularly skilled with an unusual looking shepherd's sling, fashioned from exotic leather. There had been rabbit meat on the spit for supper and entrails soup for breakfast—a veritable feast that had gone a long way toward easing Thorne's misgivings. Today was a new day.

Maelgwn had reappeared during the night and was waiting with the horses in the small lean-to that the last residents had erected as a makeshift stable. Rhys had already loaded the saddle sacks and was now contemplating the warghound. Thorne watched with amusement as Rhys screwed up the courage to approach the animal. It seemed important to him to have Maelgwn's respect.

"Do not bend to him as you would a dog," Thorne advised. "You put yourself at risk of losing your nose or an eye. And for Gods' sake, do not just stretch out your hand. Stand close, but stay still and let him decide."

Rhys did as he was told, waiting for Maelgwn to respond. Thorne wasn't sure what to expect. Aside from him, the only person in this world Maelgwn had truly taken to was Martin Trevanion. It was Martin who had found the warghound pup in the first place and offered him to Thorne to raise. The memory pained him. Everything Thorne valued Martin had given him.

Maelgwn appeared disinterested at first, but Rhys was patient. After a minute or two of completely ignoring the man, Maelgwn began a lazy circle around Rhys while pretending not to notice him. The only sign of the warghound's interest was the slight flare and flutter of his nostrils. The second pass was closer than the first, and Thorne found himself feeling a little anxious. Even he could not always predict Maelgwn's decisions, and he wasn't absolutely certain the move was not predatory.

Rhys never so much as flinched. He remained calm as Maelgwn prowled around him, which Thorne thought incredibly brave. Maelgwn's size alone was intimidating—his head was nearly level with the messenger boy's chest. If the warghound should strike, Rhys would be dead before he realized he'd been attacked.

Maelgwn finished his second circle and came to a standing stop facing Rhys. Thorne's throat tightened, trapping his breath in his lungs. He wasn't sure that Rhys knew better than to stare the warghound down, but he didn't dare speak up for fear of startling either of them into motion.

Then Rhys made an unexpected gesture that gave Thorne a good fright. He knelt on one knee, as he had seen Thorne do the day before, and extended his hand. Rhys placed something wrapped in cloth on the ground and then laid back the folds to reveal its contents. He'd brought an offering—a second rabbit carcass, salvaged from his kill.

It was a good gambit, though Thorne thought Rhys lucky Maelgwn hadn't decided to take it from him rather than wait for it to be given. The warghound would have smelled the meat on Rhys long before the approach had begun. It was a good sign, though, and Thorne began to breathe again.

Maelgwn barely hesitated before snatching up the rabbit. He swallowed it whole, but without taking his eyes from Rhys, which gave Thorne pause. To his credit, Rhys had not assumed that he'd passed muster and held his position. Then, at last, Maelgwn sat.

Thorne let out a sigh of relief. "You can pet him now, if you like."

Rhys was tentative, but he took the opportunity to touch the beast. Maelgwn's fur was softer than it looked, and the warghound loved a good scratch. When Rhys went to rub between his ears, Maelgwn tilted his head so that his jowl was exposed and Rhys obliged. "The gray wolf is the sigil of my father's tribe and an honored spirit among his people."

"Maelgwn is part warg, a Norse wolf," Thorne said. "Perhaps he senses a kinship."

"Perhaps," Rhys grinned. "But I think it was the meat."

Thorne laughed. "Well, whatever it was, you should know he doesn't generally take to people." A change in the air tamped his humor. The hairs on his arm stood on end, and the back of his neck burned. Mage sign. "Someone approaches."

"From the east," Rhys said as Maelgwn's ears flattened. "He hears it too."

"They are close." Thorne lunged for his saddle sack to retrieve his septacle and a length of mage tether, thoroughly annoyed that he had not sensed the danger sooner. "There isn't much time."

"What do you want me to do?" Rhys stood with his hand poised above the hilt of this sword.

"Tell me again who we're facing." Thorne held the coil of mage tether in his teeth while he looped the chain anchored to the seven-chambered silver septacle around his right wrist so that he could cradle it in his palm.

"If it is Cerrigwen, we'll have her to deal with and then the two soldiers of the Crwn Cawr, the father and son who are her protectorate." Rhys was staring at the septacle. "What *is* that?"

Thorne tucked the coiled tether into the top of his belt, where it could be easily reached when he needed it. "A tool of the trade."

"Yes, but what does it do?"

Thorne watched Maelgwn as he edged around the clearing, looking for a place in the trees to hide himself. "The septacle is a spell catcher. It captures the burst of magical energy that drives a hex or an incantation."

"A protective device?"

"When it works." Thorne made his stand in the open. "Prepare yourself."

"I am known to them. Perhaps I can encourage a surrender."

"Not likely, once they see me, though you're welcome to try." Thorne had come to a resolution he hoped he wouldn't regret. "I aim to take Cerrigwen alive, Rhys, but if it comes to a fight, I will strike to kill. And so should you."

Both men fell silent, waiting for first sight of the riders closing in on the clearing. Odds were best that it was Cerrigwen and her escort returning to their shelter, but Thorne was prepared for anything. The White Woods were the first and last stronghold of the magical realms, the birthplace of the Ancients, and the final refuge of the mystics and the mageborn. All manner of enchanted beings still made these woods their home, some more deadly than others.

Like all the Ruagaire, Thorne knew this forest well. During the dark era, when the Brotherhood had unwisely turned from their once noble path, they were charged by the Christian bishops with ridding the White Woods of the witches and wizards who defended the old religions and sought sanctuary here. To this day every Ruagaire apprentice was required to survive the rite of Twelve Nights and find his way out of the forest alive before receiving his ring.

Thorne alerted to the scuff of hooves thrashing through the duff. The riders made no attempt to conceal their approach. Either they were unaware of the danger, or they had no fear of it. Thorne expected the latter. The back of his neck burned, and a road-ragged sorceress astride a silver mare emerged from the trees.

Despite the dust streaking her face and the nettles matting her long, unraveled locks, she would never be mistaken for ordinary. Her mage sign was stronger than any Thorne had previously encountered. This was not just any sorceress of the Stewardry. She wore the indigo robe, marking her rank at docent or better, and at the base of her throat hung the moss agate—the legendary keystone to the natural realm. This could only be Cerrigwen.

The sorceress acknowledged Rhys with a slight nod and then turned to Thorne. "You wear the ring of the Brotherhood. What is your name, mage hunter?"

"Dismount, sorceress." Thorne ignored her question. It was an obvious distraction. She was too calm, and her escort had yet to show themselves. "Where are your men?"

"Close enough." Cerrigwen slid from the back of the mare with easy grace and stepped forward as if to submit. Thorne quickly pocketed the septacle and pulled the mage tether from his belt to bind her hands. No matter how compliant she appeared, he knew better than to leave her any advantage she could exploit.

In the few instants it took Thorne to close the dozen paces between him and the sorceress, fate turned against them all. The moment the first horse soldier broke through the tree line and entered his visual periphery, Thorne's subconscious imprinted two instinctive conclusions on his stream of thought: the soldier would immediately interpret Thorne's approach as a deadly threat to his mistress and act without questioning, and then Thorne would be forced to kill him.

The dread that had settled upon him the day before descended into soul sickness as his training took over. Before the tip of his sword cleared the scabbard, Thorne already knew how the last moments of this soldier's life would unfold. The horse would charge full on and break slightly left so that the rider could engage from his strong side, leaving him open to Thorne's left-handed strike.

His timing was so practiced and the movements so fluid that not even Rhys, who was remarkably quick to understand what was happening, could intervene in time to prevent the inevitable. But Rhys tried anyway, adding another stone to the sack of regrets Thorne carried.

Just as the horse banked, the soldier raised his sword, giving Thorne aim at the underarm seam where the chain mail shirt-front was connected to the sleeve, and the protection was weakest. As he threw into the upthrust, Thorne called to mind a prayer for forgiveness, but the one that actually left his lips was a plea for deliverance.

Salvation—of a sort—came in a flurry of fur and teeth. For all his arrogant reckoning, Thorne had failed to take Maelgwn into account. The warghound, sensing the threat to his master, did exactly as his nature would call him to do. Maelgwn sprang from the shadows in a single swift and sure bound and tore the soldier from his saddle before Thorne's sword could reach its mark.

"Leave him, Maelgwn!" Thorne dropped his sword and fell to his knees beside the wounded man. Maelgwn backed away, teeth bared and hackles raised in protest. Rhys edged around the warghound and knelt to help, easing the soldier's head into the crook of one bent knee.

"The other one," Thorne demanded as he tried to assess the damage. "Where is he?"

The wounded man's color was poor, but his breathing was good. Maelgwn had snatched him from the horse by his shoulder, gnashing through chain mail and leather and shirt cloth and flesh. The skin and sinew were torn from the clavicle, and the blood gushed. But at least Maelgwn had not ripped out the man's throat.

"He won't be far." Rhys tore cloth from his undershirt to use as a compress. "Cerrigwen, where is Finn?"

"A furlong behind, maybe less." Cerrigwen hovered closer but stopped short of imposing. "Let me see to him."

"She is a gifted healer," Rhys offered. He masked his concern better than most men would manage under similar circumstances, but he was worried. "And Pedr means something to her."

Pedr. It always made things worse to know their names. Now this soldier was also a son, a husband, a father, a brother, a friend. The last thing Thorne wanted was an undeserved death on his conscience.

"Do what you can for him, sorceress." Thorne heard the muffled thunder of hooves drawing nearer. He snatched up his sword as he rose and stepped back to make room, edging slightly to his right to keep the tree line behind her in his line of view. "But know I am watching."

With her hands still bound, Cerrigwen knelt beside the wounded man and placed her right palm over his heart and her left on his brow. She muttered an incantation in the old tongue. It had been so long since Thorne had heard the language of the Ancients that he could recall only a handful of her words, just enough to recognize a sleeping spell. He was surprised that her healing magic worked so well through the binding power of the mage tether. As impressed as was, he was reminded to be wary. Cerrigwen was powerful.

Pedr's eyes closed, and his body ceased its violent trembling. Cerrigwen next removed a drawstring pouch from her belt, a healer's bag, and handed it to Rhys to hold for her. She then pulled a dagger from its sheathing somewhere beneath her cloak and cut away as much of the clothing the armored mesh would allow.

Thorne resolved to remember she was armed, and then looked for Maelgwn. The warghound had disappeared, either into the woods or the netherworld, but he was no longer a threat. Thorne was relieved and turned to face the second horse soldier as he barreled into the clearing.

"What's happened?" the second soldier shouted. He leapt from his mount, quickly taking account of the situation and coming up nearly as bewildered as he was horrified. "Rhys?"

This second soldier was older than Thorne by at least a dozen years and closely resembled the wounded one. *Father and son.* Thorne's remorse turned to self-loathing. How had he made such a foolish mistake? How could he have allowed this to go so terribly awry?

"Keep your wits, Finn MacDonagh. Your boy is alive," Cerrigwen answered before Thorne could swallow his sorrow and speak. She selected two glass vials from the bag as Rhys held it open. One held a clear liquid; the other, a yellowish powder. "Pedr intervened to protect me, but things were not as they appeared. He had no way to know I was under no threat. The mage hunter was only defending himself."

"Mage hunter?" Finn turned his furious and stunned glare on Thorne. "This is your doing?"

"His hound, saving his master as any dog would," Cerrigwen said. She unstopped the vial and drizzled the liquid over Pedr's wound. "Moonwort oil will stave off an infection from the beast's drool and ease the pain some. I can make a paste from the turmeric to slow the bleeding, but I need fresh water and clean cloth to dress this wound."

Thorne took on the tasks to cure his feelings of helplessness and guilt. He had a new linen undershirt in his saddle sack, and good water could be got from a spring a few yards behind the old cottage. By the time he returned to the clearing with the supplies, the others had moved Pedr inside.

Rhys met Thorne at the door. "Cerrigwen says she'll have him strong enough to travel by morning. She's asked to be returned to the Stewardry, in shackles if you insist, but she says she will come willingly."

"From what you know of her, would you take this as a sincere show of contrition?" Thorne wasn't convinced, but neither did he feel particularly suspicious. "It could just as easily be a ruse of some kind."

"I wondered that as well." Rhys shrugged. "But I figure her reasons don't much matter, so long as she and that amulet are brought back to the Fane."

Thorne nodded his agreement. "I am sorry about your friend."

"We're all alive, and Cerrigwen's been found." Rhys smiled in such a way that Thorne felt understood and forgiven. "It could have gone worse."

That thought brought Thorne an unexpected bit of comfort. It was a simple but profound truth that reminded him to be mindful of even the smallest of blessings. Rhys was right—it could have gone worse, far worse. But instead, the renegade sorceress had been brought to heel, and Thorne had been spared the gruesome task of taking yet another life. The elders at Castell Banraven would claim that these were signs that the Ancients were once again listening to the pleas of their believers and that they still visited their grace upon the world of man. Thorne would not go so far as to say he had actually felt the hands of the Gods intervening, but he had gotten what he asked for.

ELEVEN

The sentry rapped twice on Alwen's chamber door to signal his arrival, and Hywel was obliged to wait for permission to enter. Since the attack of the Cythraul, he could hardly piss without one of the Cad Nawdd soldiers watching over his shoulder. And now it seemed Madoc's successor intended to remind him yet again who was keeper of this castle.

The seeress Glain, a wistful beauty with full lips and shining ginger-brown hair, opened the door and ushered him into the suite. Hywel found the girl interesting. He valued her magical talents, but she was also pleasing on other accounts. She had noble features, a proud nose and aristocratic brow, and intelligent eyes that shifted from one shade of gray to another, depending upon the intensity of her mood. Glain averted her gaze to avoid his, but he smiled at her anyway. Although she presented herself as docile and dutiful, he knew there was fire in her soul.

What he hadn't been able to determine to his full satisfaction was her station. The governance of the Stewardry was as complex as that of any monarchy or religion, but the distinctions between the leadership and the membership were less strictly drawn and apparently adaptable to circumstances and familiarity. Glain answered to Alwen where before she had answered to Madoc, but the relationship between the two was not the same.

Glain set two silver cups on the hearth to warm and then made a discreet exit, leaving Hywel to await Alwen's audience.

There was no one in this world unto whom he would willingly submit himself, but he had always understood that his destiny was tied to the Stewardry. With Madoc gone and its leadership in question, it was only prudent to cultivate alliances with whoever held the power or might one day come into it.

Waiting, however, was intolerable to Hywel, unless there was a strategic advantage to be gained or it was passed in some purposeful way. Elsewise, it was a waste of valuable time. While he paced the receptory to keep from losing his patience, he examined the room.

Alwen's receptory was, as far as Hywel could discern, still Madoc's. Her presence had not supplanted his, which surprised him. In fact, Hywel could find nothing in the appointments that appeared to belong to Alwen except for the implements on the ritual altar against the wall behind the throne—a small, hammered silver plate and bowl, a handworked silver chalice, a long-bladed dagger with an exquisitely carved bone handle, three beeswax candles, and an assortment of jars and vials filled with oils and herbs. Hywel particularly admired the wooded landscape and the celestial imagery in the tapestry hanging on the wall above the altar.

Hywel decided to wait near the hearth in the adjacent alcove, tempted to help himself to the brew Alwen habitually kept heating in the coals. It was a sweeter drink than he usually liked, but the recipe had a unique spice to it that had a calming effect. It was so appealing that he had wondered once if the brew were a magical potion that Alwen used as a method of control.

She entered from the bedchamber, dressed in a simple gown made from exotic cloth. This was appropriately regal attire, but not the formal dress of the Sovereign. He had been prepared for the robe. Perhaps this was not the official audience he had presumed.

She joined him at the hearth and gestured toward the divan facing the fire and two upholstered chairs positioned on either side. She seated herself in the chair facing him. "Sit, so we may speak plainly."

Hywel obliged, taking the other armchair and eyeing the pot in the coals. "Shall I pour?"

"If you please." Alwen watched him closely, ever assessing him. "Then we'll get straight to the matters at hand."

Hywel filled the silver cups and handed one to her before folding his tall frame into his seat. "I was surprised to receive your summons. The hour is very late for an audience."

Alwen smiled. She knew full well it wasn't the hour that annoyed him. "Like you, I favor discretion in my dealings. I find the later the hour, the more assured I am of true privacy. I trust I have not intruded on anything more important than your rest."

Hywel's smile was sly, almost lecherous. "Nothing that can't wait until my return."

"Good."

Hywel imagined her squelching her scorn, wondering whether she was more offended by his philandering or the willing women of her Order who obliged him.

She sipped at her cup, pacing the conversation. "The captain of my guard has advised me that you have requested workers be assigned to clear the catacombs. You are aware that it is by my direct command that those tunnels remain undisturbed?"

"I was granted free access to those tunnels by Madoc himself." Hywel drank deep from his cup before continuing. "I have relied on the labyrinth for years. The obstruction inconveniences me."

"Fane Gramarye is always open to you, but those catacombs were blocked when Madoc met his end. They are known to our enemy," Alwen argued. "Clearing them makes us vulnerable to ingress."

Hywel shrugged. "Then guard the junction where the maze breaches the understructure of the Fane, if it concerns you so much. I doubt our enemies know as much about those passages as you fear. There are many routes, stretching for leagues in every direction. To my knowledge, none but my men and I have traveled them in decades, if not generations."

"I see." Alwen could not hide her surprise. She had not known the extent to which the labyrinth reached. "Then you know the tunnels well."

"Every twist and turn. They are an advantage that I am unwilling to abandon. With all due respect, Sovereign," Hywel set his cup on the floor in front of him and folded his hands as he leaned forward to make his point. "Do not expect me to respond politely should you decide to rescind any favor Madoc has granted me."

"You speak of Madoc in such familiar terms," Alwen said. "You and he were very close?"

"Close enough that I am as wounded by his loss as I am my own father's." Hywel's brow furrowed reflexively and he wished for more of Alwen's strange brew. It pained him more than he expected to speak of either man. "Madoc is missed."

"Yes, he is." Finally Alwen sipped from her own cup. "It would seem we share his loss. We have something in common, Hywel, something other than your destiny."

"Perhaps we do." Hywel reached for the ale pot and poured more into his cup. "And perhaps we might yet forge a true alliance. But I do not know you, Alwen of Pwll."

"Is this why you flatter my second?" Alwen smiled, but the smile was arrogant. "To learn from her what you think I might withhold?"

Hywel recognized the territorial tone in her comment. He also understood now why she had summoned him. Alwen understood the value of alliances. "She is useful to me."

"Because she was close to Madoc," Alwen challenged, "or because she is close to me?"

"Both." Hywel could be diplomatic when it was prudent, but Alwen was drawing boundaries and close to daring him to cross them. "But more so because of her dreams and the keen way she interprets the foresight."

"I see." Alwen clenched her fingers more tightly around the cup in her hands.

"The girl has a remarkable talent," Hywel continued, aware that his comments had evoked a twinge of envy. "She will be an asset to me when I am high king of all Cymru."

"You claim the throne to a kingdom that does not yet exist," said Alwen, "a throne that can never exist without my help. I stand in Madoc's stead today, but when his heir is found, it is I who will lead the Circle of Sages. It is the power of the Guardians of the Realms that will protect you."

"I know the prophecy." Hywel was careful to keep his tone level, controlled. "Perhaps even better than you. It is my sacrifice, my leadership that guides it to being."

"And my hand that stays its course," Alwen bristled, and the thunderstone flooring beneath them trembled. "Do not challenge me, Hywel. Sorcery can either bring your greatness to light or eclipse it altogether."

A steely smile ever so slightly widened Hywel's lips. She had reached the limits of his tolerance. "And so might sorcery be eclipsed, Sovereign, by my hand. This is the world of man. Were it not, your prophecy would not call forth a mortal king. Nor would you be hiding here."

"Come now, Hywel." Alwen's lips pursed and her eyes narrowed. "Enough parry and chase. I do hope we will not need to battle wits at every turn. We need each other to survive."

"Agreed." Hywel had grown weary of her attempts to cow him. "But it was you who called this fight, Sovereign. I may not be mageborn, but I have felt you skirting the edges of my mind since the moment I entered this room."

Her eyes widened slightly. She had not expected this.

"Oh, yes." Hywel could not help but gloat. "I know of your power. You could easily pluck any thought from my head at whim, and yet you goad me. What exactly do you hope I will reveal? Some uncontrollable deviance or sinister motive?"

Alwen maintained her impenetrable calm. "How and what a person chooses to share—or hide—reveals things about their nature that are far more useful to me than what they readily admit."

"Then I shall be direct." Hywel leveled a pointed gaze at her. "Madoc disclosed only what he believed I needed to know, when he believed I needed to know it. This I accepted, because I knew and trusted him. Never once did he misguide me or fail me when I was in need of his aid. You I neither know nor trust. Perhaps you and I will eventually come to better terms, but for now I extend you very little credit. I will value your wisdom as it proves its worth, from one minute to the next."

"A prudent practice, and one that I am also inclined to follow, given the luxury of time." Alwen regarded him carefully, considering her response. "But time is a luxury we do not have. I suggest we each make a leap of faith."

"What makes you think I haven't already?" Hywel piercing stare grew even sharper. "I remain in your audience by choice, Sovereign. If time is turning against us, if Machreth's power grows as he seduces my allies, what is gained by waiting?"

"Perhaps nothing," Alwen said, "perhaps everything. But none of the greatness you desire will come to you unless the fates unfold as the prophecy foretells. Until the last two Guardians of the Realms return, your destiny is at risk. For now, you must fight to hold your ground, and we must fight to hold ours."

"Then support me in my campaigns," he insisted. "With your sorcery alone I can bring the rogue lords to heel and crush

Clydog's threat. Then none will dare lay their loyalty at Machreth's feet, and your rule will be secured as well as mine. When the rest of your sorceresses return, I will acknowledge the Council and pay the debt I owe to the prophecy."

"How like Machreth you sound," she accused. "The prophecy is not an entitlement that can be bartered or bought, not even with the wealth of reason and good intentions you possess. It is a divine decree that must be obeyed. I am bound to the rites as set forth by the Ancients on the day they foresaw and decreed your rise."

An impasse had been reached, but Hywel was not ready to acknowledge it. He would not leave without securing some kind of victory. His pride would allow no less. "Then, in the meantime, allow me to reopen the labyrinth. Rotate my men into your ranks if you cannot spare enough of your own soldiers to guard the tunnels against ingress."

"Agreed." Alwen accepted the compromise more readily than he had expected. "Provided your men will also work to excavate the cavern that holds Madoc's remains."

"Of course." Hywel felt more placated than satisfied, but that was enough.

"I require one more thing, however." Alwen rose and crossed the room to the altar on the wall behind her throne.

Hywel followed, wary but curious. With a snap of her fingers the candles on the altar alighted. From its rest on an embroidered silk cloth beside the silver bowl, Alwen retrieved the long-bladed knife and turned to Hywel.

"There shall be a vow between us, Hywel, sworn here and now."

"A blood oath?" Hywel was surprised. "To what end?"

"If we are to succeed, I must have your trust, and you must have mine."

Alwen pulled back the right sleeve of her robe, exposing the hand that had been blackened in her battle with Machreth and Madoc's signet ring. With the tip of the blade, she slit a small vein at the base of her wrist and allowed the blood to dribble into the chalice. When enough had pooled in the bottom of the vessel, she stopped the bleed with a puff of her breath. The incision vanished.

"A blood oath is ever binding. No pledge is more sacred." She turned to face Hywel and offered him the knife. "Are you willing?"

Hywel was moved by her gesture and stepped forward to take the blade. He slashed through the thin flesh on the underside of his forearm, cutting a lengthwise gash that was deep enough for the blood to course freely, but carefully placed to avoid tendon and artery. There was no vow worth risking full use of his sword hand. Hywel held his arm over the chalice and waited for enough of his life force to join with hers, before pulling back.

"Here." Alwen held out her hand. "Let me."

Hywel offered his arm for her healing. To his amazement, a gentle exhale across the bloody gape instantly sealed the gash. He swiped the residual mess on his trouser leg and watched as Alwen lifted the chalice with both hands and swirled the contents to mix their separate lettings together into a single elixir. Then she raised the vessel skyward to invite the Ancients to bear witness and proclaimed the oath.

"On the blood of our now inseparable essence, we pledge to one another our unrenounceable loyalty, unrelenting faith, and unquestioning devotion. Ever shall we be joined by this oath and bound to its demands so long as we each shall serve the prophecy to which we owe our lives or until death shall release us from this debt."

"I so vow." She lifted the chalice to her lips, sipped the blood of their bond, and then offered the vessel to Hywel.

He accepted the cup without question, but not without hesitation. The only faith Hywel knew was his sure belief in his destiny. The prophecy was the purpose to which he had been born, and the only thing more valuable to Hywel than the promise of this destiny was his word. He did not give it lightly. In fact, he rarely gave it at all.

He raised the cup to drink. "I so vow."

TWELVE

Glain arose far before dawn, anxious and ambivalent. Nothing good had come from several hours of fitful meditation once the dreams had departed. Certainly not sleep, which lately was almost as dreaded as it was necessary.

Since the premonitions had begun nearly two years before, very few nights had passed undisturbed, and the dreams that came were always ghastly. She had long ago given up hoping for visions of glad tidings. That was not her gift. However, a forewarning of an ugly fate was preferable to no warning at all. And sometimes Glain was able to effect a change for the better.

Such was the obscene nature of these precognitions. The visions revealed, often in incongruent scenes of metaphoric horror, a destiny that was already unfolding and all but inevitable should events progress unchallenged. The revelations did not, however, offer any indication of *how* one might intervene. That was a matter of interpretation and, very often, accidental discovery. And this was the dilemma that truly kept her up nights and the one that troubled her so deeply now.

Glain dressed in the dark, too distracted to bother with the candle ends or the hearth. Twice more the grisly vision of the clashing stags had come to her, each reiteration more urgent and bloody than the last. She had believed her conversations with Hywel would alter the outcome, but the dream remained the same. Apparently an improvement in Hywel's perspective was not enough, and Glain had the distinct impression that the time for change was waning.

She took to wandering the second-floor corridors so as not to disturb the slumbering souls in the third-floor residences with her restlessness. Not that the answers were any more likely to find her as she prowled the Fane than they had while lying awake in her bed, but somehow Glain felt less useless.

The rhythmic whisper of her soft-soled house shoes scuffing the stone floor created an illusion of companionship at first, filling the quiet with something more than the sound of her breathing. But soon, given the dark images and brooding thoughts occupying her mind and the shifting shadows cast upon the corridor walls by the guttering torches, she began to feel vulnerable.

It was still an hour at least until the novices assigned the house duties would be up and about, and Glain decided to wait out the time until she could call for tea by pondering her worries in the scriptorium. She eased open one of the heavy double doors partway and slid inside, feeling a little sneaky, but she did not want her solitude interrupted by someone investigating a suspicious noise.

The ember glow from the remains of yesterday's fire was welcoming, but the huge room with its alcoves and shelved recesses and towering book stacks was a less reassuring refuge than she had hoped. Glain snapped her fingers and incited the charred, half-spent logs in the hearth into a short-lived flare, then sat in the nearest armchair, facing the dying heat.

The room was still too cold and too dark to be comfortable. Alone with the memories of her night terrors, Glain's attention began to wander from the soft crackle of barely burning wood toward the random creak and clunk of settling foundation stones and the hushed moans of the walls breathing. A breeze, sneaking through a gap in the framing of one of the oversized arched-transom windows that punctuated the exterior wall, rustled the coverings. The drapes were drawn over the leaded panes to keep out the cold, but they also shut out any celestial light. Glain went to the window and pulled back the heavy curtain on one side, hoping for moon sign.

The clouds were too thick to see stars but thin enough that the sky was a paler shade of black than the silhouetted trees of the forest beyond the walls. The enchanted mist that veiled the Fane kept to the trees, forming a ring of wispy white fog around the castle that she could see even from two furlongs away. But inside the walls, the grounds proper were shrouded in black and even blacker shadows that created a monochromatic landscape where only motion distinguished one thing from another.

Though it was too dark to see detail, Glain could orient her view from memory. This window was north facing and overlooked the rear of the keep—the herb and vegetable patches directly below and the sheepfold and old orchard beyond. The apple grove was ancient and stretched all the way to the outer wall. To the east, in daylight Glain would have a glimpse of the ruined dormitory that had once housed the apprentices; and to the west, a portion of the faerie meadow.

The apple trees swaying with the breeze caught her eye, and Glain wondered if the waning winter was whipping up a last bluster. For a while she watched their spindly, naked boughs bend and wave against the misty white background of the enchanted veil, and then she noticed something else in motion on the ground.

It was coming closer toward the Fane. Glain stared hard into the shadows, waiting for the dark and indistinct mass to take recognizable form. The shape moved with the cadence and intent of a living thing like a stag or a horse. As it drew nearer, she realized it was more than one, a pack or a herd. And once they were very near, Glain knew it was neither.

Approaching the Fane from the apple grove was a cluster of hooded and cloaked persons. Three, or maybe four—she couldn't be sure, and they were completely indistinct in the dark and from this distance. Presumably Stewards, but who, and up to what? This was odd and unexpected, but not unheard of, and probably nothing more sinister than a few of the novices daring themselves to brave the grove at night. But given the frightful happenings taking place in the Fane, it was more than a little possible that something far more dangerous and even illicit was afoot.

Glain watched until the group disappeared beneath the eaves, assuming they would enter the castle through the kitchens. If she hurried, she could be in the corridor on the main floor by the time they made their way back to the sleeping porches in the east annex. And if any of them happened to be one of the new prefects she had assigned or any of her fellow acolytes, they would have no choice but to face her.

She took the stairs as quickly as she could, growing more suspicious and angry as she ran. Just as she reached the grand vestibule, she paused, thinking she heard voices down the west annex hallway, just ahead of her. Instead, she realized the murmurs, now accompanied by footsteps, were overhead. They had taken the service stairs.

Cursing herself for not having thought of it first, Glain ran back up the stairs, as far as the second-floor landing, and paused again to listen. She waited and waited, but heard nothing more. Somehow she had missed them.

Suddenly, a rustle from below reached her ears. She leapt down the steps to the vestibule and turned down the west annex hallway toward the kitchens and the sound of approaching footfalls.

"Will you be taking your morning tea in the scriptorium, Proctor?" The attendant was startled and clearly embarrassed to see her so early, thinking he was late to his duties.

Glain struggled to give a polite nod and turned straight around, winded and aggravated beyond words. She made her way back up the stairs to await her tea and mull over what might well have been the longest night of her life.

* * *

Master Eldrith could not stop wringing his hands. Whenever his fingers were not purposefully occupied with a quill or a cup or a task, they took to nervous fidgeting as though they were under the direction of a mind other than his. And so Eldrith had unconsciously adopted the annoying habit as a way to keep himself under control.

It did not seem to be helping much, the wringing of hands. If anything, it keyed his nerves to an even more frantic pitch. Eldrith tried clasping them on his desktop while he waited, and then in his lap. Lastly he held them clenched at the red and gold tasseled sash that belted his vestments as he took to pacing back and forth behind his desk, beneath the leaded glass window depicting the sigil of Castell Banraven—a white raven rising on a red shield.

Drinking did some good, but he found it difficult to partake of wine without sodding himself into a stupor. He glanced at the cabinet on the opposite wall, reassuring his conscience that just one cup couldn't hurt, and then remembered he had thrown out the last of the port in an effort to keep himself from succumbing in moments like these.

The door latch clicked and nearly sent him to his death by way of terror. But it was only Algernon, thank the Ancients, come to report. Eldrith was almost too afraid to ask.

"Well?"

Elder Algernon scuttled into the rectory and closed the door behind him. "The Hellion scouts have returned. They have abandoned the chase for now."

Eldrith sighed aloud with relief. "Then Thorne got away."

"If he did, it's no thanks to you," Algernon snipped. Gnarled and shriveled as he was, the old man had plenty of snarl left. "If I hadn't stepped in when I did, you'd have gone through with it. You'd have given him over."

Eldrith hoped not, though he wouldn't dare swear it. "But you did step in, Algernon, just as I knew you would."

"No more men of the Ruagaire Brotherhood will come to harm so long as I can do something about it." Silver cups clattered as they rocked back and forth on their stems. Algernon had gone to the cabinet and was rooting through it. "Where the bloody hell is the port?"

Eldrith winced a little and reluctantly reached behind the draperies for the silver flacon he had hidden on the windowsill, setting it down on the desk a little too hard. "Here. It's claret, though, not port. Might as well bring two cups."

Algernon gave him a reproachful scowl but brought two cups anyway. "What excuse did you give?"

"That Thorne sensed mage sign more quickly than I expected and ran before he could be stopped." Eldrith eyed the wine sloshing into the cup far too eagerly. "Not so hard to believe really, given Thorne's reputation. But our new prelate was not pleased."

"Hah," Algernon scoffed. "Where is he now?"

"Retired to his chambers, finally." Eldrith was sickened to think of it. He missed the featherbed in his former room and the other creature comforts the dark mage had commandeered.

"I have no idea what goes on all night in those dungeons, and I hope to never know."

"Thorne will be back. He will want answers."

Eldrith knew this was true, and in fact he was counting on it. "If anyone can save us, it is Thorne."

Algernon coughed out a wry chuckle. "If he tries, he'll end up no better off than Trevanion for his trouble. Even the great Thorne Edwall is a small challenge to this black sorcerer. He'll need an army of mage hunters, all of them at least as good as he is, if not better."

A shiver rippled along Eldrith's spine. The blackened, malformed remains of Martin Trevanion had burned visions of unimaginable horrors into his mind. At night, he could still hear Martin's screams. And yet, despite several days of soul-gutting torture, Trevanion had died without uttering a single word, not even a hint at the whereabouts of the oldest mageborn stronghold in the White Woods.

Eldrith swallowed the wine in one gulp and pounded the empty stem on the desk. "Keep pouring, Algernon. And keep praying that you're not the next 'inquiry' on his list."

"I doubt the black mage worries much about me." Algernon narrowed his eyes and unfurled a thin, mocking smile. "I am a very old man with a very poor memory, Eldrith. And you forget. I've spent all my days in Banraven. I believe I just may be the only one of us left who has never been to Elder Keep."

Eldrith tasted the salt of his own sweat as tiny, cold droplets erupted on his upper lip. He snatched the cup up nearly before Algernon had finished filling it and sucked the wine down. "By the time this is finished, you may well be the only one of us left at all."

Algernon no longer bothered to hide his disgust or dress it up with sarcasm. "How could you have been such a fool?"

"How was I to know what he had done?" Eldrith snapped back, trying to sound less defensive than he felt.

"You knew enough," Algernon accused. "For years we've heard rumors he was inciting sedition. Drydwen herself warned you against him, and then there were Trevanion's reports of odd happenings near Fane Gramarye."

"I never imagined what he had become." Eldrith's knees would no longer hold him upright. He wobbled to his desk chair and slumped into its overstuffed arms. The empty cup still clutched in his hand mocked his defeat. "What he was capable of."

"You underestimated him. Or worse, you overestimated yourself." Now Algernon mocked him. "To my knowledge, your grace, arrogance is not one of the four virtues."

Eldrith was mortified. When the dark mage and his legion had arrived at Banraven, demanding the Brotherhood surrender their sanctuary, Eldrith feigned submission and opened the doors to evil. He had believed he could contain it, even conquer it. He had been wrong.

At least he now understood Machreth's intentions, though the knowledge kept him up nights. Having been thwarted in his attempt to overtake Fane Gramarye and the well of knowledge it guarded, the dark mage had set his ambitions on Elder Keep and its secrets. Eldrith now had no choice but to accept that Machreth would spare none of the Order in the end. The power of the Ruagaire, should they ever regain their strength in numbers, was the only force Machreth still had any reason to fear.

"I have to hope you are right about Thorne," Eldrith said. He had taken to wringing the stem of his cup. "If somehow we could get word to him, he would find a way to warn Drydwen. At least then the prioress could prepare a defense."

Algernon showed a faint glimmer of interest. "If Eckhardt and Gavin Steptoe are still alive and Thorne can find them before the dark mage does, Drydwen might stand half a chance."

Eldrith nodded, though he didn't really believe there was even half a chance. Thorne was uncommonly skilled, but even with Eckhardt and Gavin to help him the odds were insurmountable. The best mage hunter who had ever lived had already fallen. But if the Ancients were still listening, perhaps Eldrith's prayers would count for something. Drydwen was a powerful guardian, and the last three mage hunters of the Ruagaire Brotherhood were the strongest of their generation. With the blessing of the Ancients, anything was possible.

Failing that, however, Eldrith's last recourse was the hemlock he'd saved for himself. All he would need was the courage to take his own life before the black mage decided he had no more use for him.

THIRTEEN

Glain stood as regally as she could at Alwen's right side. The Sovereign had taken her seat to await the presentation, and Glain was nervous. She was also exhausted and still concerned about the mysterious band of cloaked figures she had witnessed in the orchard that morning. Even worse, the black camlet robe itched, and she fought the urge to dig her nails into her arms. It did not suit her, the proctor's mantle, no matter how hard she tried to make herself comfortable in it. There had been thankfully few occasions that had called for it, but this was a day of days. Cerrigwen had surrendered.

The hurried, late-day inquiry was closed to all but those Alwen herself had summoned. Ynyr and Ariane had been invited to hear the testimony, as had Hywel. The king and his two most trusted men had taken a distant position to Alwen's left, against the wall that separated the receptory from the scriptorium. Glain presumed he meant to observe inconspicuously, but Hywel was the sort of man who drew attention whether he intended to or not. Ynyr and Ariane lingered just inside the main door, clearly as uncomfortable to be called to the proceedings as they were to be in each other's company. Emrys and three lieutenants of the Cad Nawdd, including Odwain, who was the youngest of the MacDonagh clan, guarded the entrance.

Glain had never seen a mage hunter, but every Steward knew of the Ruagaire Brotherhood. Indeed, all the magical beings and plainfolk in the neighboring provinces both admired and feared them and their mysterious ways. The Ruagaire were a centuries-old sect of enforcers that had been commissioned by the first Sovereign's council, in the long-ago days when there had been many guilds. Their order, though now little more than a band of magical bounty hunters, had once been given the sacred charge of upholding the laws and edicts set forth by the leadership council that governed the practices of all of the mageborn societies. But like the Stewards, they were a dying breed. An encounter with one of their kind was extraordinarily rare.

The hunter called Thorne Edwall led his party into the Sovereign's receptory. He walked with an athletic grace that was uncharacteristic of a warrior, but he carried himself with the confidence of one. Everything about this man was dark and intimidating—his mood, his manner, and his dress. Even his hair and beard were black. All was dark but his eyes, which were the most luminescent blue Glain had ever seen.

Flanking Thorne was Rhys, which pleased Glain so much she had to remind herself not to let it show for fear of embarrassing them both. She had missed him more than she'd expected. Last came Finn MacDonagh, who escorted Cerrigwen as if he were a lord accompanying a noblewoman to a royal court. Except that Cerrigwen was bedraggled and covered in muck and blood, and her hands were bound. It was a somber sight to see a Steward shackled, even when it was deserved.

Thorne addressed a proper bow to Alwen. "Your wayward sorceress is returned to you, Sovereign. Not without incident, I'm afraid, but that was no fault of hers."

Alwen nodded in somber acknowledgment. "You've earned your silver, then."

"No," Thorne said, more assertively than most would dare speak to Alwen. "Not yet. There is still the matter of the Cythraul and their master. I shall return to the hunt just as soon as you've finished with me here."

"You are more than welcome to rest and reprovision yourself from our larder," Alwen offered. "Whatever you may need is yours for the asking."

"You are more than gracious, Sovereign, but the sooner I am on the trail the better, and I have everything I need." Thorne paused. "I do have one request."

"Yes?" Alwen was still listening to Thorne, but her gaze had travelled past him and was now trained intently on Cerrigwen.

"If you'll allow it, I should like to keep your young soldier in my company for the remainder of this commission. He has proved himself a valuable partner."

Alwen's attention returned fully to Thorne, and her expression softened, almost enough to allow motherly pride to show through. "It is his choice to make, but I grant my leave if he decides to go with you. Aiding your efforts also serves our interests."

She looked past Thorne, at Rhys. "Well?"

Glain's breath caught in her throat. It hadn't occurred to her that he could leave again so soon. She remained silent and stoic at her post, ignoring the crushing ache in her breast. It would be beyond improper to speak out, unless she was asked. And even if she were, Glain would never admit her objections. Her personal concerns had no place here.

Rhys answered without hesitation. "If you can make do without me, I would very much like to see this business through to the end."

Glain's hands clenched so hard the nails dug into her palms. He had yet to look at her, and she was forced to consider that he might be intentionally avoiding her eyes. If Rhys were struggling with the conflicting desires that were plaguing her, it did not show. If anything, he seemed eager to leave again. The realization gnawed at her heart.

"I can think of no better use of your talents,"—Alwen's expression hardened again, and her tone turned cold—"considering only half the threat to the Stewardry has been found and contained. Finn MacDonagh," she commanded. "Step forward, and account for yourself and your charge."

Rhys and Thorne stepped aside to make room for Finn, who led Cerrigwen toward the small dais with an air of nobility that Glain could not help but admire. The Crwn Cawr were the most honorable of all the guardsmen ever to pledge their lives to the Stewardry, and oddly, Finn's unwavering devotion to Cerrigwen inspired hope. However it was he had been carried astray, he had held to his pledge.

"I would not presume to speak for Cerrigwen even if I knew what to say," Finn said, his voice soft and plain, but still dignified. "But I will account for myself and my son. Pedr and I have done as the blood oath demands. There is but one duty of the Crwn Cawr Protectorate: to do whatever must be done to keep the guardians safe, no matter what the cost."

"That may be the literal word of the oath," Alwen said. Her eyes widened with restrained although obvious anger. "But wouldn't even the most blindly devoted member of the Protectorate recognize the wrong path and at least question the wisdom in following it?"

Glain was surprised by Alwen's disdain and irked by what she believed was an unfairly delivered reproach. Alwen had shown Nerys considerably more compassion for a far worse betrayal. Finn could not be faulted for following his orders.

If he was disturbed, Finn did not let it show. "Oh, I questioned plenty, Sovereign. But in the end I made my choice. I make no excuses for it—or apologies, for that matter."

Alwen scowled as she regarded Finn, as if she were pondering the merit of his existence. He bore up well under her scrutiny, better than Glain thought she would do were she in his shoes. He never pulled his gaze, never lost his air of resolve. After a few moments, Alwen took in a deep breath and let it out in a huff.

"I'm told Pedr will recover," she said. "And no doubt Odwain is glad to know that his elder brother and father are alive after all."

Finn nodded, buying a moment to tamp the emotion that surfaced at her words. "As I am glad that he is well. My boy was at the heart of my worries all the while we were gone."

"Odwain was wounded defending the Fane against Machreth's beasts," Alwen continued as though she had not heard him. Her voice held no warmth or concern for the humbled warrior. "He was fortunate to have survived. Madoc, however, was lost in the attack on the Stewardry, after you fled. As was Fergus."

Finn had earned Alwen's wrath, but it was a cruelty to deliver the news of his brother's death to him this way. Glain glanced at the elder MacDonagh, trying not to stare directly at him for fear of adding to his discomfort. Poor Finn's face took on the look of weathered stone, bleak and fissured with grief. His despair was palpable, though he stood silent and accepting in the face of Alwen's judgment.

The sound of chain mail shifting called attention to Odwain, who had come dangerously close to breaking with the protocol of his post. Were it not for the stern look Emrys fixed upon him, Odwain might have made a foolish move. Worse, Rhys was so startled by his mother's behavior that he stepped forward half a pace, as if he too were thinking to intervene. Glain hoped that Rhys would not risk it; her instincts hinted that to speak out on Finn's behalf would only make matters worse.

"Enough." Cerrigwen's voice startled them all, even Alwen, who glared at her enemy with contempt. "If it is suffering you need, Alwen, carve your due from my heart and soul. Finn does not deserve this misery."

"He abandoned his Sovereign, his family, and his way of life," Alwen snapped.

"At my command," Cerrigwen said flatly. "Which is exactly what the blood oath requires him to do. Had Finn defied me, he would have disgraced himself and the entire MacDonagh clan for generations to come. His devotion to me is no less than was Fergus's to you. Only you know what unthinkable sacrifices his devotion cost him. Think on that before you judge Finn."

Alwen's struggle with Cerrigwen's point caused ripples in the practiced serenity that she presented to the world. Unresolved grief and bitterness tightened her lips and creased her brow. Her eyes narrowed, but she did not lose hold on her temper.

"All right, then," Alwen said. "Whatever blame there is shall be yours to bear. If you have anything to say for yourself, say it now."

Cerrigwen stepped in front of Finn and lowered herself to her knees before Alwen. Even disheveled and disgraced, Cerrigwen still held herself with all the regality she had always possessed. She had abandoned her arrogance and her pride, but not her dignity.

At the same moment Glain noticed the amulet hanging at the base of Cerrigwen's throat, so did Alwen. The bloodstone pendant glimmered as though it were warmed from within. Though she could not see it from where she stood, Glain knew the lapis amulet that Alwen wore would be responding in kind.

Alwen beckoned to Rhys. "Take the talisman from her."

Rhys hesitated for a moment and then retrieved his riding gloves from his belt. He put them on before removing the necklace from Cerrigwen's neck and carrying it to his mother. Alwen was unwilling to take it into her hands.

"Put it on the altar," she instructed Rhys and then focused again on Cerrigwen. "Speak now or never."

Cerrigwen met Alwen's glare as her equal, though she did not protest her defeat. Her hands were still bound, and her eyes had the hollow look of a lost and haunted soul. A muddle of emotions shifted across her face, but fear was not among them.

"It was I who weakened the veil," Cerrigwen said plainly. "I brought down the Fane's defenses so that the Hellion legion could invade, and I conjured the wall of thorns."

Alwen waited, perched on the edge of her seat as if she expected more. "Out with it now, Cerrigwen. Confess it all."

"I will not confess a crime that is not mine, Alwen," said Cerrigwen. "I cast the incantation that wrought the vines, but it was Machreth who turned the spell dark. I am guilty of betraying my oath to the guild and to Madoc, and of laying the Stewardry open to attack, but no matter how much you may wish to believe it, I did not curse your daughter."

Alwen stiffened, but she did not speak. This was not what she expected to hear, but even Glain could feel the sincerity in Cerrigwen's words. Despite their suspicions, there was no denying that in the hours after the poison had first taken root, Cerrigwen had made every effort to help.

Cerrigwen steadied herself, gathering the last few remnants of her poise. "Every choice I have made since I first felt the quickening in my womb has been for my child. I did not understand it then, but the day Ffion came into this world I was no longer fit to be called Guardian of the Realms. Nothing could ever come before her in my heart—not the Stewardry, not Madoc, not even the prophecy. For her I have harmed and been harmed. For her I have sacrificed my conscience and my destiny and broken every covenant I have ever made. For her, I have traded on the lives of those who trusted in me, and I would do it all again. But I would no more harm your child than I would my own."

She pressed her lips together to keep them from trembling, but it was clear she was dangerously close to unraveling. "This is my defense: that I am devoted to my daughter above all else. It has been my failing all along, though I worked hard to hide it. And so it is that I come before you as I am, for my daughter's sake and none other."

"Your daughter's sake?" Alwen appeared unmoved, but her angry tone made a subtle shift toward sorrow. "How does your shame do anything but destroy her?"

Earnestness overtook Cerrigwen. "Ffion is innocent in all of this. There has never been an indignity I would not endure or any loyalty I would not betray for her best interest, but she knows nothing of my deceptions. I have hidden it all from her, even her father's name. I've kept that secret since the day he cast us out, at first to save her from his blade and later, from his connivances. But Ffion is in danger still, even now that he is dead. I can no longer keep her safe."

Cerrigwen appealed to Alwen as one mother to another, attempting to reveal something of her character beyond the self-furthering opportunist she had thus far shown herself to be. Glain could never absolve Cerrigwen for the loss and devastation her alliance with Machreth had wrought, but she might understand that something other than ambition could have driven Cerrigwen to treachery.

So could Alwen, a woman whose destiny had called upon her to sacrifice her own child. Glain could already see the weight of empathy straining Alwen's rigid stance, and she began to worry that Cerrigwen might have discovered the one plea that the new Sovereign would hear.

"I fail to understand how you could think that betraying the Stewardry could possibly protect your daughter?" Alwen was unconvinced. "If anything, it has brought her to greater peril."

Cerrigwen's jaw clenched, as though the answer on her lips was sour. "Exile made me bitter, and Madoc's favoring you when we returned only angered me more. Machreth told me what I wanted to hear. He offered me the power I had always desired and promised my daughter would have everything she deserved.

Alwen shook her head. "And you believed him."

"I am not so foolish as to ask forgiveness for myself. I am beyond mercy." Cerrigwen swallowed hard. "But I *will* beg you to pity Ffion, if for no other reason than her having had the double misfortune to have been sired by a tyrant and born to a traitor. I will submit to whatever judgment you impose upon me if you will bring my child under your protection, just as you would your own."

Alwen managed to appear indifferent. "If I were inclined to agree, what would you have me do? Ffion is still on the travels that you insisted she take. She is outside my influence."

"But it has been months. How can she not be here by now?" Cerrigwen struggled to her feet, clearly panicked. "Clydog's men will find her on the road, or Machreth will."

"What has Clydog to do with this?" Hywel forced his way to the dais. "What is he to you?"

"He is less than nothing to me," Cerrigwen spat. Her face twisted ugly and dark with hatred and then settled again into the flat, resolved expression of a woman facing her end. "But he is of Cadell's seed, the same as she, the same as you. My daughter is your sister, Hywel ap Cadell. She shares your blood. She is also mageborn, like me, and heir to my legacy as Guardian of the Realms."

Hywel's shock, if he harbored any, was stifled so deep within him that not a single sign surfaced. He stared at Cerrigwen as though he were examining an intricately detailed map.

"My father made a careful practice of eradicating the product of his affairs," he said, nodding. "But I remember you at Cwm Brith for many a hunting season. I was just a boy, though, and took you for one of the servants at my father's lodge."

Cerrigwen nodded. "Think of it. A sorceress with blood ties to the two most powerful legacies in the land, and no more willing to submit to your brother than you are. The only person Clydog could ever want dead more than you, is her."

Hywel circled Cerrigwen slowly, considering the possibilities, and then faced Alwen. "Cadell would have let such a child live, if for no other reason than to give him a legitimate claim to the Stewardry, another stake in the prophecy should I not succeed."

"Yes." Alwen looked at Cerrigwen again, as though she had suddenly made sense of it all. "That's why you forced Aslak to send Ffion on the expedition to retrieve Branwen. To keep her away from Machreth."

"We were friends once, Machreth and I. When the time came to return to the Fane, I hoped we might renew our acquaintance, that I might still have an ally in him, but I knew better than to trust him blindly," Cerrigwen explained. "I was not about to put Ffion within Machreth's reach before I was sure of him."

Alwen stiffened, digging her fingers into the chair arms as if she were holding herself back. "You were allied with him from the beginning."

"Yes," Cerrigwen confessed. "In the year before Madoc sent us away, Machreth had begun to talk of reform. There were factions within the guild who supported his more progressive views, and I admit I found his ideas appealing. I never advocated defection, and certainly not revolt, but I did share Machreth's interpretation of the tenets and the prophecy. I was nearly condemned for it, but I supported his views, and in return he supported me."

"You also shared his bed," Alwen sniped.

"So I did." Cerrigwen affected a dismissive shrug. "He was revered then and very powerful. Nearly every sorceress in the Stewardry coveted his attention. I enjoyed his favor, as he did mine. I counted on Machreth remembering me fondly enough that he would agree to take Ffion's cause as his own."

Cerrigwen turned to Hywel. "Ffion is as entitled to your father's name and his lands as you and Clydog. But Madoc would never have agreed to approach Cadell on her behalf."

"Not Cadell," Hywel said. "But he would have come to me. Had he known, Madoc might well have petitioned me to acknowledge her."

Cerrigwen's chin lifted, but her lips trembled. "And would he have succeeded?"

"Not while my father still lived," Hywel admitted. "But Madoc would have protected her, knowing that I would eventually see how a blood bond between the Stewardry and Seisyllwg strengthened my claim. Instead, she is outside my protection as well as yours."

Tears glistened in Cerrigwen's eyes, but not a single drop spilled. "And as vulnerable to Machreth as she is to Clydog."

Hywel frowned. "Then they both know."

"I took Machreth into my confidence when I first returned here," Cerrigwen explained, "and he disclosed the truth to Clydog."

Glain could see the new King of Seisyllwg already plotting and planning, and she was uneasy. She envisioned the two stags on the hill and the river of blood from her dream, and she knew destiny was about to take a dangerous turn. Though she had envisioned a path to peace that circumvented the carnage, Glain now realized that no matter what path Hywel chose, his destiny would ultimately lead him into it.

Alwen obviously saw the same. She stood abruptly. "Hywel."

"We must intercede," Hywel announced, "and quickly."

"Hywel," Alwen said again, more forcefully. "I caution you to remember who rules here."

"On what heading will Aslak's expedition travel?" Hywel all but ignored Alwen's warning. "From what direction?"

"From the east," Cerrigwen offered.

"How do you know that?" Alwen was aghast and quickly losing control of her own audience. "Hywel, be silent!"

"So, I will take my men east, through the woods." He addressed Alwen directly. "We will intercept the expedition, warn your guard of the threat, and send them on their way here. And then I will press on to Cwm Brith and deal with Clydog."

"Enough!" Alwen ordered. "That is *quite* enough from the two of *you*! Be still, or I will have you both removed."

Emrys and his lieutenants snapped to attention, prepared to assert their authority should Alwen command it. Cerrigwen looked a little chagrined, whereas Hywel seemed smug and even a little amused. The rest of the room hung on the tension and worried they were about to witness a battle of wills between the Sovereign of the Stewardry and the king of the prophecy.

Alwen lowered herself back into her chair, sighing as though the happenings had pushed her past exasperation. "Have we any idea where Machreth is now?"

Cerrigwen responded cautiously. "Three days ago, Clydog claimed to be expecting him at Cwm Brith, but Machreth had yet to arrive."

"The Cythraul trail leads southwest toward Castell Banraven," said Thorne Edwall. He stepped into the conversation with such command that even Hywel deferred to him. "It is possible that Machreth is there."

"It is more likely he is already at Cwm Brith," Hywel countered, "or at least well on his way."

"All the same," Alwen said, wearily, "with the mage hunter in pursuit of the Cythraul, and you on your way to meet the escort, one of you is bound to come face to face with him. Thorne Edwall is well prepared to confront magic, Hywel. Are you?"

A fair point, but Glain was surprised by Alwen's lack of diplomacy. Surely it would be better to support the king than to try to subdue him. Hywel had no reply, at least not one that he was willing to voice, but his expression said more than enough.

"Perhaps you should not presume to commit horses and men to a campaign that is not yours to issue and that you are woefully unprepared to undertake." Alwen's sarcasm was slightly undercut by exhaustion. She seemed taxed beyond her willingness and unable to see a clear path ahead of her. "I will decide what is to be done about Ffion, and your brother, but before I can even begin to consider *that*, I must first decide what to do with the traitor before me now."

Whether she meant to or not, Alwen had completely undermined Hywel's authority, and in front of a room full of his subjects, no less. Such a misstep, were it an unmindful one, was an insult that might yet be redressed. But if Alwen's intent was to force Hywel to accept her rule in place of his, she foolishly risked the freshly forged relationship between the two of them. Hywel's reign might well come to pass without their alliance, but the Stewardry would never survive without it. Glain could not begin to fathom how Alwen had managed to lose her equability and her wisdom all at once. The Sovereign seemed in need of counsel but showed no sign that she intended to seek it.

Hywel's posture squared, and his jaw clenched tight. Glain dared not wait for Alwen to find her way. In another moment, Hywel's self-preserving nature would drive him to confrontation. The result would be ugly.

"Sovereign, if I may." Glain stepped into Alwen's line of view. "It seems clear to me the king's plan has the potential to solve our problems as well as his. If the most urgent task is to reunite the Guardians of the Realms, sending aid to the envoy can only help to ensure their safe return. Branwen travels with them, as well as Ffion. And if I may be blunt—"

"As if you weren't already," Alwen said, more bitter than sarcastic. "But go on."

Glain continued with the confidence that came from deep conviction. "You will need Ffion to complete the circle. Someone must take Cerrigwen's place, and her daughter is the only possible choice. And if the king is to ride into battle with Machreth, as you have pointed out, he will need the means to fight magic or, at the very least, defend against it. Aside from you, there is only one Steward among us who is powerful enough to confront Machreth."

Alwen's eyebrows had arched so high her eyes looked like they might pop out of their sockets. "Just what are you suggesting?"

Glain expected full well that Alwen and Hywel and likely everyone else in the room knew exactly what she was suggesting. It was a heretical idea, but it was the right one. All the same, it was not an easy thing to say. She took a slow breath to steady her nerves.

"Send Cerrigwen with him." Glain swallowed. "No matter what crimes she has committed, none of us doubts her dedication to her daughter. For this single purpose, I believe she might be trusted. She and Hywel have a common interest in defeating Clydog, and as it stands, she is the only Steward you can spare."

Alwen stared at her, her eyes stark and almost vacant, as though she were shocked out of her wits. Glain felt her hands shaking. She could hardly believe she had spoken the words aloud, but Glain knew she was right.

"Get out." Alwen spoke so calmly at first that no one reacted. "Every last one of you, get out of my receptory."

"It may be a questionable solution, but it is the best one." Glain stood her ground, although she expected she might very well suffer for it. "It is what Madoc would do."

Alwen's eyes narrowed, and then the room darkened. Glain felt a sudden foreboding just before the thunderstone floor shuddered. There could be no mistaking the warning. Glain had breached the bounds of Alwen's benevolence.

The Sovereign pulled to her feet. "I will not say it again."

Thorne Edwall was the first to break ranks and Rhys was close on his heels. The soldiers of the Cad Nawdd took Cerrigwen and Finn into their custody, and Ynyr escorted Ariane out of the room. Hywel's lieutenants waited for him at the door.

Glain lingered long enough to be the last to leave. She barely had the nerve to meet Alwen's angry glare straight on. Glain forced herself to stand strong just long enough to convey her resolve, but just shy of showing defiance.

Alwen was unmoved, and Glain was forced to break the gaze. She offered Alwen a slight bow and then turned away to take her leave. To her surprise, Hywel was still standing between the dais and the entry. He fell in step just behind her as she passed, and followed her out. Glain felt reassured and a little flattered by the king's show of support, but she was more than a little afraid.

FOURTEEN

Glain nearly stumbled down the stairs in her hurry to catch Rhys, but Ynyr stopped her on the second-floor landing. Concern had carved deep lines into his brow that made him seem decades older than he was. It frustrated her to be detained, but she knew why he was worried, and she could not ignore him.

"Perhaps if you had spoken to her in private," Ynyr said, working hard to keep his voice hushed.

"And what good would that have done?" Glain glanced through the open doors of the scriptorium to be certain they would have privacy and then gestured for him to follow. "It had to be said right then and there."

She led Ynyr closer to the stone hearth. The fire had been left a good while, and it wouldn't be long before someone came along to tend it. The gloomy chill in the room only made her more impatient, and her skin begged for relief from the itch raised by the black camlet robe. It required more and more of her focus to resist the urge to rake her fingernails along her arms and over her neck.

Ynyr gripped her shoulders to force her to face him. His pale eyes had turned a brooding shade of blue. "You do realize that you have put yourself in a dangerous position. You came uncomfortably close to siding with Hywel against her, and worse, if Alwen were so inclined, it would not be a far stretch to accuse you of defending a traitor."

"Don't be ridiculous. I suppose I am guilty of insubordination, strictly speaking, but no one in their right mind could think I was defending Cerrigwen." Glain pulled free, dismissing the entire idea out of hand, and then thought again. She stared hard into the ashes. "But then Alwen was not herself."

"My point, precisely." Ynyr hovered behind her, so agitated that he had difficulty keeping his voice low. "The whole thing was odd, the entire proceeding. It was as if Alwen were a completely different person. I have never seen her truly angry, and in there she was almost vengeful."

Glain sat on the edge of one of the armchairs adjacent to the hearth, absentmindedly scratching her right forearm and contemplating the possible explanations. "It's not her anger itself that was so bizarre. We are all angry. And given all that Alwen has suffered personally at Cerrigwen's hands, I imagine she was fighting a powerful rage. But that's just it. As you said, we have never *seen* Alwen angry. She is always, *always* serene. It's a matter of pride for her, you know, to keep her emotions from clouding her judgment."

"Not today," Ynyr said. He shifted from one uncomfortable stance to another—first next to the hearth and now across from her. "Today, I'd say her emotions were actually undermining her judgment."

In hindsight, Glain could see a subtle but discernible pattern of alterations in Alwen's usual behavior ever since the night the Cythraul appeared. Of course, there were reasonable explanations. Not the least of them, the stress of governing under constant chaos, but now Glain was beginning to wonder about the not so reasonable explanations. Something was amiss.

"I will speak to her again," Glain decided, thinking she might still find Rhys before some other crisis got in her away. "After the evening meal."

"You might only make matters worse," Ynyr cautioned, and then cleared his throat. "We have company."

"What?" Glain focused fully on Ynyr again, who was looking over her head at something or someone behind her. One of the novices must have come to rekindle the fire. Hoping Ynyr felt she had given him a good hearing, Glain stood and turned to acknowledge the attendant and take the opportunity to leave. Instead she found Rhys, uncharacteristically sober.

"If you will both excuse me, I've a thing or two to see to before the day is over." Ynyr was a true gentleman and a good friend. "The small storeroom down the hall is on my mind. I started in there earlier, before all the excitement, but got interrupted before I could give it a good search. Something about the room seemed off."

"Thank you, Ynyr." Glain was so grateful she would have kissed him on that aquiline nose of his if Rhys hadn't been in the room. It was a convenient excuse, but also a critical mission. The search for the second scroll had all but been forgotten in the uproar of the last two days. "Do let me know what you find."

She could have sworn Ynyr winked at her as he left. He had earned himself a favor or two for this. Perhaps there was some kindness she could offer Nerys.

"I was just coming to find you," she said to Rhys, whose grim expression remained unchanged. "Is there something wrong?"

"The mage hunter wants to know when we can expect my mother to resume the proceedings," Rhys said. "His intention is to leave as soon as they are concluded."

Glain sighed, suddenly realizing that the business left unfinished was as problematic as the business itself. "Hywel will want to know as well. No doubt he is just as eager to go."

"I tried to speak to her myself just now, but she made it clear this particular business was none of my concern." Rhys offered half a smile. "I hate to ask you."

"It's alright. I had already made up my mind to speak to her later," Glain said, reluctantly, "but it seems sooner would be better."

"Yes, I'm afraid it would." Rhys fidgeted with the decorative tassel tied round the throat of his scabbard, looking everywhere but directly at Glain. "I've never seen my mother so unsettled, at least not in public, and even then it was for far better cause than what happened today."

"It hasn't been her best day." Glain shared his distress and his dilemma. They were both of them answerable to others now, and not as free to address their personal concerns as directly. "I never meant to disrespect her, only to help her see all of the possibilities."

"I'm sure she knows that." Rhys still would not look directly at her, but at least he didn't think she had overstepped herself. "She'll come around."

"I hope so." As perplexed as she had been with Alwen's decisions these last days, Glain made an effort to see her as Rhys did—with compassion. "She seems to be tasked beyond her means, but then she resists looking beyond herself for help."

"That's just her way. She would rather suffer alone than trouble others with burdens she believes are hers to bear," Rhys said. "She takes her obligations to heart; that's all."

"That she does, though I do worry her commitment to her duty might make her a bit, well, shortsighted." Glain felt quite certain there was more to it than that, but she had come as close as she dared to criticizing Alwen. The last thing she wanted to do was make the son feel the need to defend his mother.

Rhys nodded, accepting of the realities and seemingly consumed by thoughts that obviously had nothing whatsoever to do with her. Glain had been hoping the avoidance she had sensed earlier was for the sake of decorum. She was still feeling the kiss he gave her the last time they parted, and once they were alone, she had intended to show it. Instead, Rhys appeared even more uncomfortable.

"I am happy to see you, though, in spite of all this," Glain invited, "even if it is only in passing."

"Not much of a visit," Rhys said, attempting an apologetic smile that wasn't very convincing. "But as I said, Thorne is eager to resume the hunt."

Whatever response she had hoped for, it was not this half-hearted apology. He was trying to lay blame on the demands of his new taskmaster, but it was obvious to her that Rhys was intentionally keeping distance between them. The unbearable itch on her arms and neck was insignificant compared to the hollowing ache this new sadness dug into her heart.

"We've been lucky so far, aside from Pedr's unfortunate encounter with the warghound." His eyes brightened as he spoke, and some of his natural exuberance surfaced. Rhys was taking pains to contain it, likely for her sake, and failing miserably. "Machreth won't be so easy to find as Cerrigwen. But at least we have a trail to follow."

"This work seems to suit you." As much as Glain wanted his enthusiasm to be on her account, she knew what the adventure meant to Rhys. "Perhaps you've discovered your calling."

"I've waited all my life to know what I want." His expression turned earnest, almost pleading. "I think, at last I may have found it."

She had heard this sentiment from him before, in the difficult first weeks after Madoc had fallen and his sister was lost to the faerie realm. Rhys had joined the ranks of the Cad Nawdd partly because he had needed purpose, but also for his mother's sake, and in some measure because it was the only honorable choice to be made at the time. But he had always known it was not his true destiny. And Glain understood, better now than she ever had.

"Well," she said, resigning herself to the inevitable, "if Alwen will not reconvene the hearing, perhaps she will render an edict through me. I will find a way to suggest it, but it doesn't seem likely we will have any kind of a decision before nightfall. Perhaps you can persuade the mage hunter to wait until morning."

The instantaneous relief that appeared on his face nearly crushed her. "The promise of a hot meal and a dry bed ought to do it."

"Good." Glain forced a smile, hoping to keep her sadness from showing. "I will see what I can do."

This time Rhys was not so quick to turn away. He met her gaze straight on and gave a slow nod to signal his appreciation, all the while acknowledging her with a look that held something more meaningful in its expression. Glain took it for respect, maybe even admiration, and just possibly genuine regret. Perhaps Rhys wasn't as oblivious to her as she had thought.

And then, before Glain could think what to say or do next, he was gone. A withering shudder overtook her as another sorrowful place opened up deep inside. Some of her wondered how much more loneliness she would have to endure in the name of the prophecy. Still more of her feared she might survive it all just to discover that the bright days it promised held no particular reward for her. But none of that mattered to the fates. Unless she could find a way to help Alwen succeed, such worries would be the least of her troubles.

* * *

Odwain had taken the stairs as far as the second-floor landing twice now and still couldn't decide whether to walk down the west annex hall to Pedr's room. Alwen's bizarre audience had been difficult to bear, and Odwain had been torn between his loyalty to her and his need to defend his father and brother, no matter what they had done. The only emotion he had acknowledged for months was anger, in all its many shades, and the concern Odwain was experiencing now came as a peculiar relief. He still wanted answers, though, and he also wanted to see for himself that Pedr was not on his deathbed.

The membership was gathering in the great hall on the main floor for the evening meal, and the corridors were nearly deserted. Odwain loitered on the landing, trying to be inconspicuous and failing miserably, until deciding at last that his only choice was to confront the situation.

The long hallways that extended east and west from the central tower-like core of the Fane were essentially rows of individual chambers adjacent to a central great room. The third-floor chambers were reserved for the ruling ranks of the Stewardry, anchored to the Sovereign's grand suite. On the second floor, instead of a grand suite, the corridors were annexed to a large scriptorium that also served as a parlor. And instead of bedchambers, there were spell rooms. At the ends of each hallway, some of these spell rooms had been converted to accommodate guests. Pedr had been given hospice in one of them.

Odwain went at first to the wrong room. To his right, he saw a door ajar but found the chamber dark and smelly. He closed the door tight and tried the room across the hall. This door was closed, but light slipped out beneath it.

A sober young man dressed in the gray robe of an apprentice answered his knock with a book in his hand. He looked to have been sitting vigil in a chair next to the bed, reading by firelight. He acknowledged Odwain with a polite nod and closed the door behind him as he quietly excused himself.

"You scared off my nurse." Pedr's voice was faint, though not strained. He seemed to be resting easy and was trying to be jovial, but he looked awful. "You can have his seat, if you want."

Odwain felt obliged to sit, although he wasn't particularly comfortable. He and his brother were barely more than acquaintances. When Finn and Fergus MacDonagh had been called to serve the Crwn Cawr and gone into hiding more than twenty years before, each had taken one of Finn's young boys to apprentice. Odwain had lived nearly all his life with his uncle, in service to Alwen. He had not seen his father or elder brother again until they had all returned to the Fane just twelve weeks before.

It had been a glad reunion of kin long parted, despite the dire occasion, and an opportunity to celebrate Odwain's betrothal. And then Alwen's daughter, his beloved Eirlys was cursed and Fergus killed, and the rest of his family had disappeared without a word. It had been the worst two days of Odwain's life.

"They assured me you'd be good as new soon enough." He required himself to express his good wishes. "I wanted to see for myself."

Pedr tried to pull himself up to sit but quickly abandoned the effort. "Where did they take him, our Da?"

Odwain knew, but he wasn't happy to say. "He's being held in the old guardhouse next to the barracks, for now."

"And Cerrigwen?" Pedr asked, struggling a bit between distress and disgust. "Not that I much care, but the damned oath demands that I ask."

"She is confined to her chamber until Alwen can find the sense in it all. Pedr," Odwain continued pointedly. He was through with niceties. "I am about to ask you why you left, and you had better tell me there was nothing you could do."

"Of course there was nothing we could do. You know that better than anyone. You've lived the code all your life, same as me." Pedr's face looked pained, but from a far deeper wound than the one to his shoulder. "The Crwn Cawr indentures us to whichever guardian we are pledged. She is our first duty, before everything and everyone else. Just as Alwen was yours, all those years in Norvik."

"So Cerrigwen ordered you to follow her out of the Fane in the midst of a siege?" Odwain asked. It had to be true, but he needed to hear it said before he could put his worries to rest.

"Whatever befell the Fane, we were gone long before any of it started. That night, Cerrigwen assigned us the late watch at the rear gate, but we were to stand guard from the forest side, from outside the wall," Pedr explained. "It was a strange request, but no stranger than anything else going on in this place. So we stood in that enchanted mist, staring at those damned woods and waiting for whatever was lurking in the trees to swallow us up. An hour later, maybe two, Cerrigwen appeared at the gate astride that silver mare of hers and demanded we let her out. She conjured something at the edge of the forest and then just walked straight into the trees. It's not what either of us wanted, Odwain, but there was no choice but to go with her."

Odwain was accepting, if not forgiving. "You did what you had to do. What I would have done had I been in your place."

Pedr seemed relieved to have Odwain's understanding. "We will accept the consequences, whatever they are. The MacDonagh men are men of honor."

"Did they tell you that Madoc fell to Machreth's dark magic?" said Odwain.

"No," Pedr sighed, "but I figured as much when I heard they had taken Da and Cerrigwen to atone to Alwen."

"And Fergus." Odwain had to steady himself to get it out. He'd managed to avoid speaking of any of it until now, and it was difficult to allow the words to leave his lips. But he intended to be kinder than Alwen had. "He is gone too."

The pained look returned to Pedr's face, an offering of empathy from one brother to another. "I guess this must have been hardest on you."

"All of us are suffering on some account." Odwain would never have guessed how much it helped to hear his personal sorrow acknowledged. Not that he claimed himself to be more bereaved than anyone else, but he had felt profoundly alone—until now. "I am glad to have you both back at the Fane, even with things as they are. I should speak to Alwen to be sure she understands why you did what you did. She is new to the responsibilities of the Sovereign."

"No." Pedr took hold of Odwain's arm. "You'll only put your own standing at risk. Alwen knows the oath as well as any of us. Let her come to reason on her own."

"And what if she doesn't?" Odwain did not want to admit he had any doubt, but he wasn't as confident as he should have been. Alwen was different, more easily unsettled since the onslaught on the Fane, since Eirlys. So was he. But the woman he had seen holding audience earlier was not the woman he had known nearly all of his life.

"She will." Pedr managed half a smile. "Have faith, little brother."

FIFTEEN

"**S**overeign?"

Glain let herself in, carrying the meal tray she had taken from the attendant who was waiting outside the suite when she arrived, having received no answer to his knock. The receptory was empty, but the torches still burned, and the adjacent sitting room was bright and warm with the heat of the fire. Glain set the tray on a table near the divan.

The doors to Alwen's bedchamber were closed, but the private scriptorium was open, and Glain could just make out a robed silhouette at the window. "Sovereign."

Alwen remained unresponsive. Glain paused in the doorway that separated the scriptorium from the receptory, and then realized that Alwen was spirit-faring. Glain had found the Sovereign entranced like this many times before and had been transfixed to witness the psychic sharing of minds. It was inspiring to behold. Such elegant magic required a rare blend of innate talent and acquired skill. Alwen had both in abundance, whereas Glain had discovered she had little of either—at least when it came to this particular discipline. Alwen, however, was a natural master of the spirit-faring. It was an extension of her telepathic gifts, and Glain believed that Alwen could send her consciousness to cohabit nearly any sentient being she chose.

Glain waited quietly so as not to disrupt the sojourn or inadvertently cause Alwen an unexpected shock. A mage was vulnerable in any altered state, but especially so when her psyche was separated from her physical form. It was best to wait until Alwen returned, and then gently intrude.

Half an hour passed in silence. Glain wondered with what creature Alwen was riding. Generally, she preferred the birds, as they had the advantage of lofty vision and swiftly traveled distances, and tended to be most welcoming of her companionship. It could be most any being, though—a wolf or a rabbit, or even a merchant on the road to market.

Another quarter-hour passed, and then Glain noticed Alwen's steady, even breaths grow increasingly shallow and rapid. A few moments later her body shuddered slightly, and with a sharp gasp, the stasis was broken. Alwen had returned.

"Sovereign?" Glain whispered just loud enough to be heard and waited for Alwen to react.

Alwen turned from the window and placed a hand on the nearby desk edge to steady herself. "Bledig and Aslak will soon join Thorvald. Both caravans are closer than I expected, but still several days' ride north of here." She took a single step forward and hesitated, as if she hadn't the strength to go any farther. "Thorvald escorts two cloaked women and a new soldier—Ffion and Branwen, I presume, with her Cad Nawdd guardsman. But Bledig's party contains only men." She sighed, and even her dejection sounded exhausted. "Apparently Tanwen was not to be found."

"How long have you been at this?" Glain was concerned. Alwen was obviously drained by the spirit-faring, but Glain wasn't sure whether to offer her assistance.

"Longer than I intended," Alwen admitted. "The nighthawk led to the owl, and the owl to the ferret, and then another nighthawk, and so on. But I needed to know."

"I think you should sit." Glain decided help was needed and bolstered Alwen with a gentle hand beneath her right elbow, guiding her to the divan in front of the hearth. "Here, by the fire."

"Thank you." Alwen lowered herself onto the divan with much more difficulty than it should have taken. "Some aleberry perhaps."

Glain was already pouring. As she handed the cup over, she noticed that Alwen's fingers trembled. "Your evening meal is on the little table next to you. It would help to eat something."

"Later." Alwen held the cup to her nose. She appeared to be comforted by the vapors.

"Sovereign." Glain perched on the edge of the hearth, directly facing Alwen so that she would not have to move to meet Glain's gaze, but neither could she easily avoid it. "What is happening?"

Alwen's weak smile barely penetrated the layers of pain and exhaustion that seemed to have appeared overnight. Glain had not noticed any of this before, and at first she thought it might just be a trick of the light. However, the longer she looked, the more she realized that weeks of unending struggle had gradually etched the first furrows into the youthful, silky skin of Alwen's face. And now she seemed to have aged years in a matter of a few days.

"I am being overcome." Alwen seemed to shrivel into the stuffed and tufted back cushion. "For a while, I thought it was only the natural aftereffects—the fits of unrest and bad temper that anyone might experience having endured our recent, well, *difficulties*. But eventually, I began to wonder."

Glain waited, out of respect, until the lull between the last statement and the next lasted a little too long, and Alwen's presence seemed to fade. "Wondered what, Sovereign?"

Alwen's eyes centered on Glain's, and all trace of the weak smile slid away. "After Madoc was entombed in the Well of Tears, and the dream-speak would not come to me, my first thought was that somehow I had not swallowed enough of the waters for the enchantment to take hold. But clearly that could not be possible, considering I nearly drowned."

Alwen held out her empty cup and continued while Glain poured again. "Then I thought I was missing something, that there was some secret bit of knowledge Madoc had forgotten to share. So, I studied his writings and searched the scriptorium for clues. I learned a great deal about a great many things, but the one answer I wanted could not be found. Finally, I was left with only one explanation. It could only be that something in me was lacking."

"Sovereign," Glain objected. "I hardly think that could be true—"

Alwen held up a hand to stop Glain from arguing. "It was easy for me to think it, though I do know better. Even then I was beginning to sense what was happening, though it was weeks before I could see the proof."

"What?" Glain was on tenterhooks. "Proof of what?"

Alwen sat forward and pulled back the cuff of her right robe sleeve as she held out her arm. "See for yourself. It's been worse since the Cythraul violated the Fane."

The blackening that had taken over Alwen's fingers when she had tried to save Madoc from the freezing well waters had spread to the outer edge of her palm and was creeping up her arm. Glain was horrified. "Why didn't you say something before this?"

"I cannot afford to show even the slightest weakness." Alwen withdrew her hand and returned to cradling her cup in both palms, as though nothing at all were the matter. "No one else is to hear of this, Glain. The only reason I am telling you now is that I am no longer able to keep the effects from showing. As I'm sure you have already seen."

Glain tried to return Alwen's attempt at levity with a smile, but the effort yielded little better than a nervous twitch at the corner of her mouth. Glain was worried. "Are you sure I shouldn't call for a physician?"

"I am sure," Alwen insisted, but the effort seemed to pain her.

Glain stifled her concern and focused on what she could do to help. "What do we do now?"

"Well…" Alwen let herself collapse back into the cushion. "We will proceed as you proposed. I am in no condition now to hold another audience, so you will assist me by drafting a decree, which you will then enforce on my behalf. The mage hunter will continue his pursuit, with Rhys to help him. Hywel will carry a warning to the Protectorate escort, secure the safety of Cerrigwen's daughter and whichever of the remaining guardians have been found, and then he will engage Clydog, as he must. Cerrigwen will go with him, but send Odwain as her personal guard. He is all that is left of the Crwn Cawr here, at least alive and able and fit for such a duty."

"What will become of Odwain's father and his brother?" Glain went to the desk in the scriptorium and returned with quill and parchment. "What judgment will you pronounce on them?"

"Pedr, I believe, has suffered quite enough. Neither he nor Finn has committed any crime against the Order. If anything, I would have to say they have more than fulfilled the intent of the oath." Alwen was apologetic. "And I suppose it could be said that Finn paid any due he might have owed by enduring that audience the way he did. If there was an offense, it was a violation of military regulation. For all intents, he abandoned his post. Leave it to Emrys to impose whatever penalty is required by the law of the Cad Nawdd—or not, as he sees fit."

Glain nodded, furiously jotting notes and prioritizing her missives. She was profoundly relieved to finally have some understanding and a course of action to follow. And though she was prepared to defend her own behavior, Glain was grateful that Alwen seemed to have decided not to address it.

"That should take care of the matters brought before me today and by all means set it all in motion as quickly as possible," Alwen said. "But see that Hywel leaves enough of his men behind that the work clearing the path to the well continues."

"So that is why you agreed to the excavation." A sudden realization brought Glain to a pause. "You think curing the curse on the Well of Tears will cure the curse on you."

"And free Madoc's knowledge," Alwen said. "In the three months that I have been his proxy, many nights I have dreamt, and many times those dreams have brought me omens, but never once have I heard the dream-speak. There are times when I sense Madoc and the other spirits attempting to speak to me in my sleep, but it's as if they are speaking a language I do not know. Not so surprising, I suppose. The gift of the dream-speak was never meant to be mine. Perhaps I will never be able to master it."

Glain knew how much Alwen had hoped the wisdom Madoc had promised would come to her, and that she considered it her failing that it had not. "The murky well water might be to blame for this as well, you know."

"You may be right," Alwen said. "Even if you are not, it might not matter. We have three of the four keys, and soon we will have Branwen with us, and her amulet. Perhaps, as you suggested, Ffion can be persuaded to take her mother's place in the circle. Then we need only fill Tanwen's seat somehow. But you," Alwen pointed a shaky index finger in her direction, "*you* must find that missing scroll."

Glain nodded, masking a momentary twinge of old guilt. "We must also keep you strong, Sovereign. What more can be done?"

Alwen sighed as though she had tasted something unpleasant. "When you have finished the decree, and before Hywel can take her, figure a way to bring Cerrigwen to me here. Tonight. Quietly, though. No one can know."

* * *

Glain waited outside the doors to Alwen's chambers as though she were one of the Cad Nawdd sentries standing guard. In effect, she *was* standing guard, though she was desperately hoping no one would come along. If Alwen meant to keep her private meeting with Cerrigwen a secret, she would have to hurry. Already nearly half an hour had passed, and Glain was beginning to worry she'd never have Cerrigwen back in her room before the guard she had relieved returned. Or worse, before Ynyr or Ariane or one of the prefects decided to retire for the night.

She dared not interrupt, though impatience tempted her to knock. Her nerves were only slightly less jangled than her thoughts. Once she had finished with Cerrigwen, her next task would be to deliver Alwen's directive to Emrys. She had wanted to take the news straight to Rhys, but it was proper that the captain of the Cad Nawdd issue orders to his soldiers and grant custody of Cerrigwen to Hywel. But once she had informed Emrys, she would give Thorne Edwall his leave to depart, and this would be the last chance she would have to see Rhys again.

Finally, she heard movement near the doors and the latch clack as it opened. Cerrigwen stepped into the hallway and acquiesced to Glain with a slight bow of her head.

Glain pulled the door closed and gestured down the west annex hallway. "Were you able to help her?"

Though she was no longer bound by the mage tether, Cerrigwen walked with her hands clasped in front of her and kept her face fixed straight ahead. She did not respond, and Glain wasn't sure whether she'd been heard or if Cerrigwen simply did not want to answer. Either way, the next two dozen paces were spent in uncomfortable silence.

Just before they reached the entry to Cerrigwen's quarters, she came to an abrupt stop and turned to confront Glain. "You are a very foolish girl."

Glain was stunned, and a little piqued. "I—I beg your pardon?"

"You fail to see the most obvious signs." Cerrigwen cocked her head and peered at her more closely, as though she couldn't believe what she saw. "Remarkable, really, considering how much time and effort you spend trying to make sense of them."

"I'm afraid I don't understand," Glain said, trying to be polite.

Cerrigwen's eyes narrowed. "Of course you don't."

The cryptic retort was unnerving. Perhaps the woman really had lost her mind. Glain started to move past her and open the door, hoping to put an end to the exchange, but Cerrigwen stopped her with a hand on her arm.

"Take care, young lady, when it comes to the men of Cadell's house. They seduce with their sincerity, you see, not with flattery, which is what makes them so much more dangerous than they seem."

"I'm sure I don't know what you mean," Glain bristled, taking the warning as an insult or an accusation of something sordid. Cerrigwen was obviously referring to Hywel, which made Glain feel as though her privacy had been invaded.

"If that is true, you are even more foolish than I thought." Cerrigwen frowned at her and let go of her arm. "There are pretenders among your trusted, you do know *that* much, don't you?"

Glain nodded, though she wasn't entirely sure why. She scoffed at the very idea that she had been misguided in her alliances. Every one of them had earned her trust. And yet, she thought of Nerys, and the cloaked Stewards she'd seen sneaking out of the apple grove, and even Ariane. But why was she entertaining this conversation in the first place?

"Good." Cerrigwen seemed relieved. "You may be foolish, but at least you're not stupid."

Glain took offense. "Take care how you address me, Cerrigwen."

"Well," Cerrigwen said, almost smiling, "at last a little spark, a little glimmer of spirit. I was beginning to worry you had no sense at all of who you are."

Glain was now wary and a little irritated, but she had to ask. "Just what is that supposed to mean?"

Cerrigwen's expression sobered, and then turned quizzical, as though she were listening to voices in her head and trying to make sense of what she heard. This made Glain so nervous, she wished she had never said anything at all to Cerrigwen. Then the sorceress began wringing her hands. Her gaze dulled and her lips moved as though she were speaking, but there was no voice to her words.

"Stop this," Glain demanded, a bit panicked. She couldn't be sure whether Cerrigwen had slipped into some addled state or had entranced herself in a spell casting. Whichever it was, either Cerrigwen could not, or would not, cease.

Glain grabbed Cerrigwen by the shoulders and shook her, hard. "Stop!"

Cerrigwen's gaze refocused on Glain. At first she appeared lost and uncertain, but she was no longer wringing her hands or talking to herself. Recognition registered in her eyes, and then profound sorrow. "It was never me who harmed her child. She knows that now."

It was a random thing to say, but not meaningless. Glain did not know how to respond or if she even should. "Oh. I—I see."

Then the moment of vulnerability passed, and Cerrigwen's gaze hardened. She clasped her hands together again and turned toward the door to her room, waiting for Glain to open it.

"I have lent Alwen endurance, nothing more," Cerrigwen said as she entered the chamber. "What afflicts her will worsen, but more slowly now. You should watch her carefully, but she will sleep well tonight."

Glain whispered her gratitude to the Gods, for never had she been so relieved to leave anyone's company. And blessing upon blessing, she turned toward the welcome sound of the new sentry reporting for his turn just as she pulled the door shut behind Cerrigwen.

The guardsman presented himself with a half-bow and took his position. It was only then, as the full length of the hallway came into view, that Glain saw Ariane standing near the door to her own chamber—between Glain and the stairs.

"Oh, great Gods," Glain muttered to herself. "How long has she been there?"

"She was already standing in the hall when I passed."

The unexpected reply startled her, but the information was helpful. "So you didn't see her on the stairs?"

"No, there was no one else."

"Thank you," Glain said, absently, calculating the potential risk. Ariane had to already have been in her room when Glain escorted Cerrigwen back down the hall, else Glain would have seen her come up the staircase while she was waiting outside Alwen's suite. This was disastrous. What explanation could she give without revealing what must remain hidden?

And then Glain realized that she need not give any explanation at all. She did not answer to Ariane on any matter, and so what if an acolyte was left wondering about things that were none of her affair? Glain squared her shoulders, lifted her chin, and proceeded back toward Ariane with purpose and aplomb, as if there were nothing at all out of the ordinary.

She tipped her chin in greeting as she passed. "Good evening, Ariane."

Ariane's mouth opened as if to speak, but Glain never so much as slowed her pace enough to allow for a polite reply. There would be recriminations aplenty later on, if Ariane were able to find a way to speak to her alone. Glain resolved to make that as difficult as she could, which brought a sly smile to her lips. *How Ynyr would appreciate this development*, she thought, making note to mention her new attitude when next she saw him. She wondered briefly what Ynyr had discovered. It was hours since he'd gone to search the second-floor storeroom, and he'd promised to report. She considered seeking him out, but it was late, and she had yet to speak to Emrys.

SIXTEEN

Despite the anger that dug deeper into his gut every time he thought of Clydog's revolt, Hywel was pleased. All of his senses came alive in the White Woods. The dark mystery of this forest intrigued him. Not that he was ignorant or careless of the danger—he had faced and defeated unthinkable horrors on his many travels through the enchanted woods. But that was exactly why he appreciated this place—its hidden dangers challenged him in unusual ways.

This was but the first of a three-day ride through the forest from Fane Gramarye to the old trade road where, according to Alwen's information, they should intersect the caravan escorting Ffion and the sorceress called Branwen. So far the journey had been quiet. They had encountered nothing more than a few distant sightings of the gwyllgi—spectral hellhounds who preyed on lone travelers—but Hywel knew from experience to expect more from the White Woods.

Hywel always took point, partly because he believed a real leader led and partly because he couldn't stand to follow, not ever. His captains had long ago given up arguing and dedicated their efforts to better watching his back. Twelve men from his personal guard accompanied him on this mission, each of them chosen for a particular expertise, all of them seasoned and loyal, and none of them strangers to this forest. Some had fought for his father and taught Hywel the ways of a true warrior. And some were comrades who had earned his trust in other ways.

Of the fifteen riders that made up the party, only one had not been Hywel's choice. Though he liked the Cad Nawdd swordsman Alwen had assigned to watch over Cerrigwen, Odwain was a brooding sort, and Hywel thought him too serious for his own good.

Hywel pulled back on the reins until his mount fell in step alongside the soldier, who rode behind the sorceress. Thinking Odwain might make a better companion if he relaxed a bit, Hywel struck up a casual conversation. "When I was a boy, my father would take me deep into this forest and leave me to find my way back on my own."

Odwain slipped an incredulous squint sideways, unwilling to take his gaze too long from the woman, or the road ahead of him. "To what end?"

"He meant for me to learn self-reliance—and fearlessness, I suppose. The first time I was lost a full night and day before he came looking for me." Hywel grinned. "I was soaked in my own shit and too scared to sleep in the dark for weeks, but I had come face to face with the púca and lived to brag of it."

Odwain tried hard not to appear amused. "My uncle used to tell stories about the shapeshifters, but I always took them for tall tales meant to keep children from wandering too far from home."

"The púca are real enough," Hywel said. "So are the fearsome creatures they fashion themselves into, though their true nature is not particularly threatening. They mean to intimidate more than anything else, but to a young lad alone in the woods they might as well have been wolves come to feed on me."

"I'm sure you made your father proud."

Hywel snorted at the thought. Cadell had been a hard man. "If he was, I never knew it. As I recall, he made me walk all the way back to Cwm Brith. Never said a word one way or the other, but he sent me back out there again a month later."

"At least he didn't call you out for shitting yourself."

Hywel strangled a smile. "Few men have the stones to speak to me that way, MacDonagh."

"I've a bad habit of speaking the truth as I think it," Odwain replied, more by way of explanation than apology. "I meant you no insult, Brenin."

"None was taken." Hywel appreciated the use of his native Brython title. It was a show of respect that spoke well for this new conscript, but he had learned it was unwise to encourage familiarity too soon. "I don't know you well enough yet to call you friend."

"Nor I you," Odwain said, as straight-faced and bold as before.

Hywel let the grin loose this time, but he also let the conversation come to a close. This plainspoken quality of Odwain's was reassuring to a king who had more enemies than allies. Whatever it was that had so sobered such a young man had likely made him wise beyond his years as well. These were traits Hywel might value, if and when they proved out.

Besides, Hywel knew a thing about being made a man young. He wouldn't tell this story today, but the third time Cadell had forced him to brave the forest alone, Hywel had startled an eight-foot-long, three-headed serpent feeding on a fallow deer. Though he'd been only twelve, he managed to hack off all three heads with his boot dagger, but not before the creature struck. The venom had left him delirious and near death for days. Hywel could not remember how he got out of the woods, but he still had the fang his father's physician had dug out of his hip—and the scar.

A rustling sound caught his attention. Hywel stilled his thoughts, so he could listen harder. He had noticed it earlier, and it had seemed to be following them. Now he was sure it was dead ahead.

Odwain was quick to notice Hywel's distraction. "What is it?"

"The forest is working its magic," Cerrigwen said, pointing ahead. She had been quiet the entire journey until now.

"But is it working its magic for us, or against us. That is the question." Hywel pulled rein on his mount and waited for Odwain to sidle up. He knew what was happening, but he had never gotten used to it. "Watch, up ahead. See there? The road was bearing northeast, now it turns northwest."

"If I didn't know better, I wouldn't believe my own eyes." Odwain was incredulous. "What now?"

"The trick to travelling in these woods is to know your bearings and keep true to them no matter how your surroundings seem to change." Hywel signaled to his regiment to follow and guided his horse off the cart path onto a narrower trail. "This way."

He led the others northeast, through a thick stand of ash and birch trees. On the other side of the stand, they met the proper road again, headed in its original direction. Hywel wondered if he had wisely avoided a lure or had just been duped into a detour. All the same, he was still sure of his course, though he would mind the way with greater care until they were clear of the White Woods.

* * *

Thorne gave Rhys the lead for the first day, making no attempt to guide him, so as to get a full sense of the lad's true talents. It had taken the young tracker only a few minutes to detect the now thin and stale scent of the Cythraul. By midday, Rhys had tracked the wraith trail as far as the narrow river that ran through the White Woods. There his senses had become confused by another scent that was stronger and fresher—and far more pleasant. So had Thorne's senses responded, but he knew how to keep from losing his head.

"River fey," Thorne explained. "There is a Naiad bevy near."

Rhys struggled to concentrate. "The aroma is very strong."

"Naiad magic has a feminine scent. It can be a bit, well, distracting." Thorne decided not to say just how distracting. "The longer we stay, the worse it will be."

"Can't decide if I want to get closer or farther away," Rhys complained, rubbing hard at the back of his neck.

Thorne turned his horse downriver. "That's the point, I'm afraid. Come on. There's a shallows a few yards from here. We'll cross the river and see what we find on the other side."

"You said before that you had already found the Cythraul trail," Rhys reminded him. "Are we close?"

For a moment, Thorne dithered over whether to leave his young friend to fend for himself a while longer, and then he decided it was too much to expect. "No doubt it will be very faint after so long, but my guess is you'll pick up the scent yourself once we've put enough distance between us and the river fey."

"And if I don't, I suppose you will just point us toward Banraven," said Rhys. There was knowingness in his tone, but no accusation. "As I recall, you also said the trail led in that direction."

"So you've just been humoring me all this time?" Thorne cocked an eyebrow and tried to look disapproving.

Rhys grinned. "I figured you needed me to prove something. I didn't mind. I like a good challenge."

"Took you long enough to call me on it." Thorne was finding it harder and harder to conceal his favorable impression of this young man. He goaded his mount into motion and headed downstream. "Let's get clear of this blasted fey magic and stop for the night."

Sure enough, Rhys was quick to scent the Cythraul again, and on the same vector Thorne had tracked them—which did indeed lead toward Banraven. The wraiths would return to their master, and *he* was the real danger. If this renegade mage were powerful enough to conjure and control Cythraul from leagues away, no telling what else he could do.

They made another good mile's travel before the afternoon began to fade. Fortunately they'd come upon a fairly protected spot to rest while there was still light enough to hunt, beneath a cluster of evergreen boughs thick enough to give at least a little shield should it rain. Thorne offered to build a fire and find water so that Rhys might try his luck with that sling of his. He was fond of rabbit stew, and Rhys had very good aim.

But Thorne was also wanting a bit of solitude. He sensed unrest in this part of the forest, and he needed quiet to get to the root of it. Once he had a good blaze stoked in the little pit he had dug, Thorne settled back on his heels and closed his eyes, so he could concentrate on the unseen things in his surroundings—the auras and spectral essences of the woods.

"What are you doing?" Rhys approached quietly, but not so quietly he hadn't been heard.

Thorne held up a hand to stop the interruption, continuing to squat with his eyes closed, searching the in-between places for signs of whatever might be amiss. Suddenly, a thought came to him, and he quickly calculated the days since the last full moon. *Ah, so that's it.*

Thorne relaxed and looked up. "Have you brought supper?"

Rhys held up two fat red squirrels. "Best I could do."

"Hand them over." Thorne reached for the carcasses with one hand and pulled his boot knife. "I'll do the skinning. You do the cooking."

"What were you doing just now?" Rhys kicked at a pile of nearby mulch and fallen branches, looking for sticks thick enough to spit the squirrels in the fire.

"We're passing very close to the next world," Thorne explained, making quick work of the skinning and gutting. He was hungry.

"The moon is full, and a full moon works a powerful enchantment over thin places."

"Alright," Rhys acknowledged. "But what were you *doing*?"

Thorne wasn't entirely sure how to answer in a way anyone other than the brethren would understand. "Listening."

Rhys scraped the bark off the two sticks he'd selected with his own boot knife and handed them to Thorne. "I've got salt in my sack, and some rosemary, I think."

"That's it?" Thorne was surprised. He skewered the squirrel carcasses and staked them in the dirt, waiting for Rhys to return with the seasonings. "You've no more curiosity than that?"

"It's not so odd, you listening to the otherworld. My sister could speak to the faerie folk. She was different that way. She had our father's fey blood."

Using his boot toe, Rhys scraped away damp leaves and duff until he exposed a relatively dry patch and then sat cross-legged on the ground near the fire. "I know more than I care to about thin places and what the light of a full moon can do."

Rhys rubbed salt and herbs on the meat and then anchored the spitted carcasses in the coals. His mood had sobered, giving the impression that the conversation had taken him somewhere he didn't want to go. Thorne thought it best not to tread any closer to the heart of things just yet, but he was curious.

"Then I won't need to warn you to be cautious. No telling what we might encounter. If we're lucky, we might just have Maelgwn with us tonight. You should save the entrails for him."

Thorne suddenly recalled an earlier annoyance. "That reminds me, Rhys, son of Bledig. When were you going to tell me you were also Rhys, son of Alwen?"

Rhys flashed a sheepish grin. "You heard that, did you?"

"Hmm," Thorne said. "I thought we had an understanding about half-truths."

"We do. That bit was a precaution, for my mother's sake. I was going to tell you, but you asked before I got around to it."

"There are four virtues of the Ruagaire Brotherhood," Thorne said, deciding to venture down a slightly different path. "Veracity is the first and most sacred."

"Virtues?" Rhys asked.

"Qualities of character," said Thorne. "Before a man can be considered for induction to the Brotherhood, he must first have been observed conducting himself in accordance with certain merits—veracity, loyalty, righteousness, and forbearance."

Rhys nodded in acknowledgment as he poked at the embers with a twig to keep the heat high and even. "And just who does this observing?"

"Each of us is charged with taking on an apprentice, but finding a suitable candidate is difficult," Thorne said, measuring Rhys for signs of interest or awareness of Thorne's intent. "It is an important decision, choosing someone to inherit his knowledge and his duties. It is also necessary to the survival of the Order, but very few men are born to the calling."

"How would one know if he were born to the calling?" Rhys asked, trying to appear less interested than he clearly was.

"The most obvious indication is sensitivity to mage sign. That burning at the back of your neck, for example." Thorne was trying to be subtle, but it wasn't one of his stronger skills. "That comes from having some measure of mage blood in your lineage."

"So, you are descendants of sorcerers, but not actually sorcerers yourselves."

"Yes." Thorne was beginning to feel expectant, which made him uneasy. He would not allow himself to want this too much. "We are born with a connection to the magical realms, but we have no real power over them. What we do have is a natural resistance to the influence of magic, which is what makes it possible for us to defend against or even capture a mage."

Thorne couldn't tell if Rhys was simply interested in the information or if he had made the connection to his own potential, so he decided to push just a little. "Often the gifts go unrecognized for what they are and more often than not are mistaken for something more ordinary, like a knack for tracking or a strong intuition. But it is much more than that."

"I suppose a person would have no way of telling unless he were to come to know someone like you," Rhys said.

"And it might well not ever happen, such a meeting. The Ruagaire is a breed so rare that one might live his entire life without ever encountering another, aside from the rest of the brethren," said Thorne. "But it is not enough to be born to the calling. There are the virtues, as I mentioned before, and then there is the training. The Brotherhood is a lifelong dedication, to faith and to sacrifice. It is a pledge to be taken by only the most worthy of this world, and I would be lucky to come across just one such man in my entire lifetime."

"Have you?" Rhys asked, screwing up the confidence to meet Thorne's gaze directly. "Ever found such a man, I mean?"

"It is too soon to be sure," Thorne said quietly, struggling to contain the swell of gratitude he felt. He was not yet ready to reveal it to Rhys, but Thorne was about as sure as he could be. "But I think so."

SEVENTEEN

Glain's eyes opened to a warm room and light peeking between the drapery panels drawn over her window casing. She sat up with a start, panicked by the sense of disorientation that came with awaking from a very deep sleep. Was the day waxing or waning? The last thing she recalled was watching Rhys ride away just after dawn. Glain had been up the entire night before, dispatching Alwen's directives and seeing to the Sovereign's comfort.

Good Gods, she thought, throwing off the coverlet to discover she was still fully clothed, except for her shoes. How long had she slept? She had left precise instructions with one of the prefects to rouse her before midday, but it felt as though a good deal more than two or three hours had passed. Glain slid from the bed and threw open the draperies, making a best guess at the time through the cloud cover. It was a good while before noon, maybe just mid-morning, if she were lucky.

Hopping on one foot to shoe the other, Glain thought a moment on whether she should wear the proctor's mantle. She hated that robe, but circumstances did seem to warrant the protocol. Like it or not, the gold-trimmed black camlet called attention to her authority, and Glain had to admit that was an advantage she needed just now.

It wasn't until she was leaving her room that Glain realized that she had slept without dreaming, for the first time in so many days that she had lost count. If only she knew whether that was a good sign, or bad.

As she approached the Sovereign's suite, Glain noticed one of the outer doors stood half open. She rapped twice and then entered the receptory, expecting to find one of the prefects tending to Alwen's comforts. The throne room was empty, but the lamps were lit, and the hearth in the adjacent sitting room well stoked. Perhaps the attendant had been careless upon leaving.

"Sovereign?" Glain crossed the receptory, peering through the doorway into the shadowy scriptorium, thinking she might find Alwen at the window again. But the window was shuttered and the room empty, which left only the bedchamber.

The door to Alwen's most private space was closed, but Glain was worried now. As far as she could tell, the Sovereign had yet to rise this morning. Glain knocked hard as she turned the handle and pushed the door in. "Sovereign?"

"I've been hoping you'd be along soon." Alwen sat on the edge of her bed, dressed but not robed. "Help me with the mantle, would you?"

Glain obliged, reluctantly, easing Alwen's arms into the heavy velvet vestment. The dark blight on her hand did not seem to have worsened overnight, but Alwen did not seem rested. "You needn't rise at all, you know. What would it matter? No one would dare disturb you, not even the prefects if I so instructed. I can well enough manage the day to day matters on your behalf, and by and by, I can come myself to see to your needs."

"And just who will tend to your duties while you tend to mine, hmm?" Alwen's smile was strained, but she pulled herself up to a fairly solid stand. "I am not as frail as I might appear."

Glain resisted the urge to assist Alwen as she walked from her bedchamber toward the scriptorium. "Do you have pain?"

"Yes," Alwen said honestly, stopping midway as though she were reconsidering her destination. "Only needles and pins though, thanks to Cerrigwen, and only in my hand, but I must say the hand doesn't trouble me nearly as much as the fumble-mindedness. It tends to settle over me later in the day, when I begin to tire, and always when I most want a clear head."

"She is a bit off, don't you think?" Glain thought she might be speaking out of place, but she was curious. "Different than she was before, to be sure."

"Cerrigwen?" Alwen turned toward the sitting room and walked with careful steps to the divan. "She has been altered by her ordeals, that much is plain. And she seems genuinely plagued by regret. Certainly she is afraid for her daughter. Whether any or all of that is change enough to warrant my trust, well, that I am still deciding."

Alwen settled herself on the divan with obvious effort. "You, on the other hand, seem to need less convincing."

"What I said yesterday was that I believe she can be trusted within limits." Glain was surprised to hear herself sound so assertive, but it felt unexpectedly natural. "Do you want me to pour the aleberry, or would you rather I called for tea?"

"The aleberry, please," said Alwen. "You think Cerrigwen can be controlled through her concern for her daughter."

"Not necessarily controlled." Glain handed Alwen a cup full to the brim. "But I am absolutely certain she will do anything to protect Ffion, and nothing whatsoever to endanger her. As long as Hywel and Odwain keep this in mind, they will know what to expect from her."

"And how to use her, I suppose." Alwen gestured toward the seat next to her. "Sit. Tell me the state of things. Did Hywel agree to leave enough men to continue the excavation?"

Glain gathered her robe and skirts and sat next to Alwen. "He has taken only a handful of his soldiers, a dozen I think. The rest were conscripted to Emrys, with instructions that the work in the tunnel should not be interrupted. I understand they have made remarkable progress."

"Let me know when they reach the cave," Alwen requested. "Rhys and the mage hunter are well on their way, I presume?"

"Yes." Glain did not want to speak of Rhys. It had been an awkward farewell, and she'd felt a sense of finality that she preferred to ignore. "Do you think when they find where the Cythraul have gone, they will also find Machreth?"

"I would be surprised if they didn't. He is at the root of every treachery that befalls us, I am certain of that, just as I am certain he has help." If Alwen noticed Glain's discomfort with the subject, she gave no indication. "I presume the search for the scroll continues."

Glain was suddenly reminded of Ynyr. "Yes, though I haven't had time yet this morning to speak with Ynyr or the others. I shall make a point of doing just that, as soon as I am sure you have everything you need. Shall I have a morning tray brought?"

Alwen waved the idea away. "Just bring the scrying stone, will you? I heard whispers in my dreams last night."

"The dream-speak?" Glain went into the receptory to retrieve it from the obelisk next to Alwen's ritual altar.

"The stirrings of it, I believe. I have been visited by these whispers before, but I could make next to no sense of them. This time, I have an inkling of something, a message, maybe. I am hoping the scrying stone will help me see it more clearly."

Glain brought the crystal orb from its resting place, wrapped in its protective velvet cloth, and placed it in Alwen's lap. She could not imagine how the scrying stone could be used to amplify the voices from the beyond. The orb neither possessed nor controlled the power of the dream-speak, and it seemed to Glain that Alwen was clutching at straws. But then again, there were many things Alwen knew that she did not, and this was not the time to question such things. "If there is nothing else, I'll go and find Ynyr."

"Yes, do." Alwen, already distracted by the orb, was slipping into her thoughts. "Come to me again later, when you have news."

* * *

Glain left Alwen to her scrying, pledging to return soon, news or not. She had her doubts that Alwen was faring as well as she wanted Glain to think. Still, it was eating at her that she had neither seen nor heard from Ynyr since the day before. Nor had anyone else, she soon discovered. One of the prefects found Ynyr's room cold and quiet, as if he had not even slept there. The last place he was known to have been was with Glain, after Alwen's infamous audience. When he'd left Glain, his plan had been to investigate a second-floor storeroom.

Verica and Euday were inquiring discreetly throughout the temple and the grounds as they went about their daily business, while Glain retraced Ynyr's steps. Ariane had not been included— not just yet—mostly because Glain wanted to avoid her questions. Besides, Ariane had no love for Ynyr.

A large storage closet was located at the end of the west annex hallway on each of the second and third floors, across from the service stairs leading to the kitchens. They were catchalls for things that had fallen out of use and big enough for at least two persons to move about and rummage through. Her first stop would be the second-floor room to see if Ynyr had actually gone there in the first place.

As small as the membership had become, it was unusual for anyone to go missing for more than a few hours. One could make themselves scarce in a castle so sprawling and so replete with secret spaces, but Ynyr normally went out of his way to let his presence be known. He was a watchdog by nature, and a leader through his own example. Glain's most urgent concern was that he had next gone searching somewhere even more obscure than the storeroom and become trapped or injured.

Two of the four spell rooms on this hall were in use by small groups of apprentices testing their skills. The others were open, but empty. Beyond the spell rooms was a matching pair of simple guest quarters just big enough to hold a cot, a chair, and a washbasin and stand, one directly across the hall from the other.

Odwain's brother was convalescing in the south-facing room, attended by a young male apprentice named Ilan, who nodded as she paused at the entrance. Pedr was resting well under the care of the young apprentice, who already had the skills of an accomplished physician and was uncommonly dedicated to the healing arts. Such a pity that Cerrigwen had lost her way; she would have found an eager student in Ilan.

Glain glanced down the hall. On the north side, beyond the unoccupied guest room was the storage closet. The door to the closet was ajar. A sudden wash of relief eased her anxiety. Ynyr had been here.

"Were you sitting with your patient last evening, Ilan?" Glain asked. "Did you happen to see Ynyr pass this way?"

"Not that I noticed," Ilan said. "But I excused myself while Odwain was here visiting for an hour or so. Ynyr might have come then."

Glain crossed the hall and pulled the storeroom door open wide to investigate. "Good Gods. What happened in here?"

Ilan was quick to her aid, oil lamp in hand. "Stay where you are. Don't go in just yet. Let's have a good look first."

He stood on the threshold and extended the lamp into the shadowy space. The closet was in a shambles. What should have been an orderly arrangement of unneeded implements and household goods was a mess of upended crates and broken pottery. The top of an old trunk was caved in where something heavy had landed upon it, hard. And the thick layer of grime that had once covered it all had yet to settle again. It coated the air with its tacky silt and the stale, fusty odor of disuse. Glain was aghast at Ynyr's carelessness.

"Well," she huffed. "I hope he found what he came for."

"Come now." Ilan scowled, disbelieving. "You don't really think Ynyr would do this, do you?"

"No." Glain realized right away how unlikely it sounded and regretted that her first thought had been accusing. "He wouldn't."

"Looks to me as though there was a struggle," Ilan speculated. "Though I don't know how that makes any more sense."

He stepped back into the hall and glanced around, searching. "What is that *smell*?"

At first Glain thought he meant the cloud of dust that had escaped the closet, but then she caught the waft of a second, even less pleasant scent. Faint, but distinctly familiar. Her heart seized. Glain recognized this sickly sweet stench.

"Ilan," she said evenly, drawing her wand from its sling at her waist. "Can you tell the source of the smell?"

Ilan squatted to set the oil lamp on the stone floor and, now steely-eyed and tensed, drew his own wand. He stood again and turned full circle, slowly, tracing the source of the scent. "I can't be certain, but it seems to be strongest right here. What is it, Glain?"

Glain could barely utter the word. "Cythraul."

She admired the look of indignation that settled over Ilan's face, even took courage from it, though she knew he did not understand the horror they might be facing. Still, she was grateful she was not alone.

"Stand ready," Glain said, indicating the vacant chamber across from the sickroom with a jut of her chin. It was the only other place to hide. "Do what you must to keep Pedr safe."

Without questioning, Ilan positioned himself behind her in the middle of the hall, which emboldened Glain just enough to confront the closed door. Logic informed her skittered mind that the scent they were encountering was only a remnant of danger already passed. She could not be certain, though, until they had seen for themselves.

Glain reached for the handle. She could see her hand shaking but could not make it stop. The last time she had fought the soul-stealers, she had not been strong enough on her own to overcome them. She had needed Ynyr and Nerys. Brave as Ilan showed himself to be, he would be of little help were they facing even one wraith now.

Pulling a steadying breath deep into her lungs, Glain gripped the door handle and turned until the latch slid back. She paused for an instant, listening for any sign of being from within. Satisfied there was none, she flung the door in and struck a defensive pose at the threshold. Nothing would pass her unchallenged.

It took a dozen heartbeats for her eyes to adjust to the unlit space. At first she saw only shapeless shadow, like a curtain of black wool draping the entry. Slowly her vision sharpened and the blackness refined itself, until the realization of what awaited in the darkness struck her so hard that she staggered.

Glain stumbled forward and fell to her knees at the feet of the twisted, stiffened figure that lay on the floor between the door and the cot. The room was so rife with the stench of the Cythraul, she gagged, choking on the acrid mixture of bile and stifled sobs roiling in her chest.

Ilan retrieved the lantern and rushed to her side. His light fully exposed the grotesquery and shocked him to a dead stop. Ilan let out a low groan and muttered an angry epithet in the old tongue, followed by a gentle blessing meant for the protection and safe passage of a departed spirit.

"Great Gods, Glain," he said. "He looks unnatural. What happened to him?"

Glain was so devastated she could hardly speak. She forced herself to stand, to tear her eyes from Ynyr's hideously contorted face and to detach from her horror in order to function with at least a little clarity and dignity. If she did not lead, who would?

"His soul has been torn from his body. The darkling shroud sucks out the very essence of a person. It is a slow and agonizing process, even when the victim surrenders to it. Ynyr did not surrender."

Ilan crouched beside the remains to examine them more closely. Glain cringed as he poked and prodded and then pulled at Ynyr's crooked limbs. They were rigid.

"His body is cold," Ilan deduced. "Death came to him some hours ago." Ilan turned to look up at her, alarmed. "Would the wraith still be loose somewhere in the Fane?"

Glain had no idea, but then she could hardly think straight. Still, the last thing she wanted was to admit uncertainty to Ilan. "Once they have overtaken their intended victim, the Cythraul return to whomever it was that summoned them in the first place."

"You assume, then, that Ynyr was the intended victim?"

Was he? Or had he surprised the soul-stealer on its way to attack someone else? Glain envisioned Ynyr trapped in the darkling shroud, helpless and alone. Sorrow nearly cracked the thin and fragile mask of control she had fashioned, and she swallowed the wail that kept rising in her throat. Mustering every ounce of determination, she focused on following the most rational trail of thought. "You said yourself he was overcome hours ago. He was last seen yesterday eve, on his way to the storeroom. I would have to think that was when he was attacked. If the Cythraul were still in the vicinity, someone else would have encountered it by now."

Ilan nodded, reassured. "Outside this room, the scent trail is weak."

"Raise the alarm anyway." Pedr had managed to make his way to the doorway, sword at the ready. "Whether the threat has passed or not, the Fane has still been invaded. And unless you have some idea how and by whom, we are still vulnerable. The grounds must be searched and any breach reinforced. And I'm afraid until you have accounted for the rest of your membership, you cannot possibly know if this one Steward is the only casualty."

"Yes. Of course, you're right." Glain felt foolish for not thinking the situation through. "Ilan, gather help from the apprentices in the spell rooms down the hall. Send someone capable to stay with our wounded warrior here, and then summon Emrys to Alwen's quarters. Order the membership to gather in the main hall and wait for me there."

Ilan scrambled madly down the hall, leaving Glain alone with the corpse. It frightened her, the malformed shell that had once held the essence that was her truest friend. She couldn't stand to think what he must have suffered in those final moments, and yet the thoughts filled her mind anyway. The putrid, inescapable smothering of the darkling, tearing and shredding at his consciousness until he could no longer resist; it was beyond hideous. Agony sent a violent shudder through her.

"Pull the door closed now," said Pedr. "You only torment yourself, standing there staring at him, and nothing good can come of that."

It was kind advice, and wise, though Glain was inexplicably reluctant to take it. It seemed too final an act to shut the door on what was left of him. She could not shake the childish feeling that until he left her sight, Ynyr was not truly gone.

"Come," Pedr said, gently insistent. "Help me back to my bed before you go."

Glain complied, grateful for direction when she felt so profoundly lost. Ynyr had been her guide at times like these, but she could not bear that thought now. She offered Pedr her hand for balance, though he seemed perfectly able to walk all on his own. He sheathed his sword with relative ease, even with only one good shoulder, and stood the scabbard against the wall next to the head of his bead.

"You seem to be doing remarkably well on your own," she observed.

"You needed the distraction." Pedr sat on the edge of his bed and eased himself onto the cot. His attempt at a wry smile was only half successful, and he was perspiring more than he should. "And I'm afraid things aren't always what they seem."

Glain began to wish she hadn't sent Ilan away. "Are you in pain?"

"No more than I was before. Just not as steady on my feet as I'd like to think," he confessed. Once he was still, the color returned to his face. "I'll be fine."

"Are you sure?" Glain pulled the blanket up to his chest and then noticed Pedr was watching her.

"Yes. And so will you. You are strong." His eyes were a mire of hidden emotion, powerfully expressive and unnervingly deep. "There will come a proper time to honor your friend."

These simple, honest words nearly broke her. Glain accepted them with a polite nod, wishing she could trust her voice enough to thank this near stranger properly for his kindness. Somehow he had known what she most needed to hear, and whether he knew it or not, he had helped her.

EIGHTEEN

er hands were shaking so hard she could barely pull on the door latch, and yet Glain's thoughts were clear and focused. As she knocked and opened the door to Alwen's suite, Emrys appeared at the top of the staircase and rushed to follow her inside.

"What has happened?"

Alwen was startled by the abrupt interruption, but Glain managed to block the doorway long enough for the Sovereign to sit straight on the divan and make her best presentation. She looked stronger than Glain expected, strong enough that Emrys might not notice her sunken eyes and sallow skin.

Not that she need worry. Emrys was so agitated, he was unable to restrain himself long enough for Glain to speak, and blurted out his concerns. "There should be double the guard at your door, Sovereign."

"I will first hear what Glain has to say," Alwen said, subtly reminding Emrys of his place. He deferred, but it appeared to pain him to do so.

"Ynyr is dead." Glain had to swallow hard to find enough spit to speak. Tears burned her eyes, and a sob tightened the back of her throat. "We found his body in one of the second-floor guest quarters. He succumbed to the darkling."

"He's been missing since yesterday." Alwen looked sickened. "How long ago did this happen?"

"The trail of the Cythraul that attacked him was too faded to follow," Glain said, consciously measuring her breathing to keep her emotions at bay. "I would have to guess it happened sometime last night. There are no sentries stationed on the second floor. Except for Ilan, who was attending to Pedr, the entire annex would have been empty at night."

"I have ordered a search of the temple," Emrys interrupted. "My men are gathering in the courtyard as we speak."

"If it was still in the Fane, someone would have caught wind of it by now. No," Alwen sighed. "The Cythraul is not a random predator. It comes for the soul it has been sent to take, and then it leaves. It is no longer here."

"We should search anyway," Emrys interrupted. "If it is in the temple or on the grounds, my men will find it."

"And how shall they defend themselves if they do?" Glain was beginning to find Emrys boorish. It was almost as if the weight of command had made him more uneasy rather than more capable. "The Cythraul may not be seeking another kill, but it will fight to defend itself. This I know all too well. Of course your men should make a cursory search, but not alone, and not before we have accounted for the rest of the Stewardry."

Glain turned to Alwen. "I have already ordered the membership assembled in the great hall. It won't be long before they are ready and awaiting your review. Once we are satisfied they are safe, I suggest we then assign the acolytes and the prefects to accompany the Captain's search parties while they secure the Fane, room by room."

Emrys bristled. "And what of the grounds?"

"I don't believe a search of the grounds will be any more helpful," Alwen said, "but we will leave nothing overlooked. We will see first to the membership, Emrys, and then do as Glain suggests."

Emrys acknowledged Alwen's orders with a slight bow, but he was clearly uncomfortable with the decision. As you wish.

"Good," Alwen said. "And if you haven't already, I suggest you welcome Finn MacDonagh back into your ranks. You may find yourself in need of his experience."

"Of course, Sovereign," Emrys said, almost as though he were speaking through clenched teeth. "If that is all, I will see to my duty."

Alwen offered him her most gracious smile and waited until he left the room before reaching out to Glain. "Give me your hand, child."

Glain helped Alwen to her feet and was happy to find she was steady. "Whatever it was Cerrigwen did for you seems to be working."

"Yes, for a time," Alwen said. "Find my robe, and then go get your own. The more composed we appear, the less panicked everyone else will be."

"As you wish," Glain agreed, but she loathed that black robe. "Are you sure you can manage on your own?"

"Yes," Alwen insisted. "I'll be ready by the time you get back. On your way, dismiss the guard outside Nerys's room so that he can rejoin the garrison, and bring Nerys with you. She is still one of us."

Glain's reluctance had almost nothing to do with her distrust of Nerys. Of course, Alwen was right—Nerys should be brought to the assembly. She also should be told about Ynyr, and Glain knew that she should be the one to do so.

"I am so very sorry to hear about Ynyr," Alwen said. "This will be a difficult loss for so many, especially you. I know how much you relied on his friendship."

Glain nodded to avoid having to speak.

"We will find out how this happened and who is responsible," Alwen continued. "And I promise you, this time there will be no mercy."

Glain decided it was past time to voice the suspicion that had been niggling at her thoughts since she'd seen the cloaked figures in the orchard. "I have begun to believe the source of all of this has been in our midst all along."

"So have I," Alwen said. "Go on now. And hurry."

* * *

Glain was annoyed to find Ariane waiting outside Alwen's door. "What are you doing here?"

"What is happening?" Ariane whispered, clearly concerned. "No one seems to know anything."

"You will all know what you need to know soon enough." Glain gestured toward the stairs. "You should be waiting in the meeting hall with the others."

Ariane lingered, uncertain. "How can I help?"

Glain relented, partly to be kind and partly to be rid of her. "Other than Ilan, who has permission to stay with the wounded soldier, everyone is to report to the general assembly. Everyone— do you understand?"

Ariane nodded, eyes wide and worried. All of her recently acquired airs and attitudes seemed to have abandoned her.

"Good. Check the second-floor spell rooms to be sure no one is left behind, and then join the others," Glain instructed. "I will be down as soon as Alwen is ready."

Ariane seemed happy to have something useful to do, and Glain was relieved to have her busy somewhere else. The last thing she needed was Ariane's incessant prying. It was all Glain could do to keep her mind on her duty. Rather than live with the dread any longer, she decided to speak to Nerys first.

Nerys had the quarters opposite Cerrigwen's rooms, halfway down the hall. The sentry standing watch was all too eager to go, having got wind of the trouble at hand. Glain knocked and held her breath until Nerys answered.

"Come."

Glain's eyes began to burn before she had fully opened the door. Already she regretted having taken on this task. Though she and Nerys had never been friends, they had known each other all their lives. Glain was about to heap unimaginable sorrow upon her, and this she would not have wished on anyone.

Nerys was dressed in a simple velvet gown the color of the first autumn leaves and sitting primly on a three-legged stool next to the small hearth, with her hands folded in her lap. Her room was so tidy it was nearly sterile. Aside from a small table beneath the only window, upon which sat the customary implements of a ritual altar, there wasn't a single personal belonging in sight.

Glain hesitated just inside the door, uncertain how to begin. "A general assembly has been called. The entire membership is meeting in the great hall. Alwen sent me to bring you."

Nerys stood. "I don't suppose I will be allowed to wear my robe."

"Please," Glain said. "Stay seated a moment. There is something I need to say."

Nerys lowered herself back to the stool, her expression unreadable. In that awful, tenuous moment Glain saw Nerys in a different light. What before she had perceived as condescension Glain now considered might be nothing more than a naturally distant affect. Nerys was cool and aloof, but that did not necessarily mean she was also disdainful. Besides, Ynyr had loved her.

Glain was suddenly struck with a wounding thought. She had never once wondered *how* Ynyr loved Nerys. They had always been close, like siblings. Had it been more than that? It shaved off another piece of her heart to think it had never crossed her mind to ask.

"I was wondering," Glain said, as surprised by the words that came out of her mouth as she was by the train of thought that had spawned them. Clearly her subconscious was as eager to avoid the real conversation as her heart. "Someone seems to be practicing rituals in the orchard. I have seen them returning to the Fane late at night. Have you any idea who they are or what they are doing?"

"No," Nerys answered flatly, no affect at all. "But I imagine if you were to investigate the orchard you would likely discover what. Ynyr might know who. Perhaps you should ask him."

Glain felt sick. "Nerys, I have difficult news."

She faltered on "news" and thought she might not recover enough to continue. But it had to be said, this awful unbearable thing, and she had to say it. "Ynyr is dead. We found his body in a second-floor guest room this afternoon. He was overcome by a Cythraul attack sometime during the night. Nothing could be done for him. We found him too late."

Glain didn't dare pause until she ran out of breath, for fear she might not get it all out. "I am so sorry," she whispered.

It was so brief a disruption in Nerys's expression that Glain almost missed it, even though she never took her eyes away. Like a cloud passing over the moon, a momentary shadow drifted across her face and then disappeared. Had Glain not seen it, she might have wondered if Nerys had even heard what she said.

"I know he was important to you," Glain said, hoping to honor the loss Nerys must be feeling. "You were very important to him."

Nerys acknowledged the sentiment with a slight nod and then stood up. "Alwen is waiting, isn't that so?"

"Yes, she is," Glain said. "We should go."

Glain searched for something else to say, only to realize how useless it was to try. There were no words big enough to contain what she felt, no sentimental platitudes or customary consolations that would ease the pain. Not for either of them. "And wear your robe. You are still one of us."

* * *

Glain was beginning to think she had developed a physical aversion to the black camlet robe. She could not have it on her person without suffering a most irritating itch. It was all she could do to be still while she called the roll.

She had lost sight of Nerys when the formality had begun, but found her now, standing on the dais with Alwen. This was difficult for Glain to accept, but it had been Alwen's express desire. When Alwen had taken them both aside before entering the hall, Glain was completely unprepared for the directive she had issued. She had protested, but Alwen had pointedly reminded her that there was no one left in the Fane with the skill to carry out her request. Hard as it was, Glain had accepted. The circumstances called for drastic measures.

Glain turned her irritation to Ariane, who had made herself altogether unavoidable. She was stationed front and center at the head of the assembly, as well an acolyte should be, but there was something triumphant in Ariane's posture that made Glain uncomfortable. And where were Euday and Verica?

Without Ynyr, three score and five should be the final tally, with Ilan counted by proxy and Alwen excluded. From the raised dais at the front of the room, she called the apprentices. Once each of them had responded, Glain next read the names of the newly appointed docents. She called the first four names, and all four answered. And then she called Euday.

When there was no immediate reply, she said his name again, louder. The muffled din of a dozen whispered conversations suddenly silenced. And still there was no response. Glain looked to Alwen.

Alwen indicated that Glain should continue, but her concern was evident in the brief exchange of veiled glances. This odd development altered everything. Alwen's plan to reinforce the Fane relied upon the remaining acolytes and the two new prefects, and none of them dared trust Ariane on her own.

Glain circled Euday's name and next read Verica's aloud. As she feared, again there was no answer. Where could they be? To be consistent, Glain called for Verica a second time and then circled her name. She continued with Ariane, Nerys, and finally she came to Ynyr.

It shredded her soul to line through his name, but it was her duty to correct the official record. Glain presented the membership register to Alwen as the Sovereign came forward to address the assembly.

"Three absent," Glain confirmed the record in keeping with the formalities. "Two for whom we apparently cannot account."

"Stand with Nerys," Alwen whispered.

Glain complied, feeling unnerved. These next dozen hours could easily be even more difficult to endure than the last day had been. Now two more of their friends were missing, and Glain found herself in the unlikely position of taking on Nerys as an ally. *How Ynyr would love this*, she thought.

Alwen raised her arms in signal to the guardsmen who were stationed at the entry to close the heavy doors. Emrys and Finn were waiting at the back of the room with a retainer of ten somber-looking soldiers in chain mail and all armed with sword and halberd.

"Captain of the guard," Alwen called out.

Emrys came forward, marching straight through the middle of the crowd. If any of their membership had not fully grasped the seriousness of the situation, they surely did now. Emrys presented himself to Alwen with a clipped bow and then turned to face the audience.

"Murder has been committed in our temple," Alwen pronounced, squelching a flurry of murmurs with a wave of one hand. Her voice rang out with more strength and clarity than Glain was expecting. "The honored and noble acolyte Ynyr is dead."

Alwen let the pronouncement hang in the silence so that the weight of it should be felt. "Twice now the security of Fane Gramarye has been violated. Twice now the Cythraul have entered this castle. Once in a failed attack on the king not even a week ago, and the second, which resulted in Ynyr's demise, just this past night."

Again a flurry of gasps and exclamations erupted, and again Alwen cut it off with a gesture. This was the first that the membership had heard of the attack on Hywel, and taken together with Ynyr's death, it was far more frightening.

"Not even the Hellion horde ever breached the doors of the Fane," Alwen said. Her tone had grown forceful. "Yet, somehow, the Cythraul have found their way in. They have stalked our halls and preyed upon us almost entirely unhindered."

She spoke louder. "There are only two ways the soul-stealers could have entered our midst. Either the veil was weakened to let them through, or the Cythraul were conjured from within it by a summoning spell. Someone in this room provided the means for evil to roam these halls. By the end of this night I will know how, and I will know who."

Silence dropped over the room like a shroud. Glain readied herself for what was coming and tried to ignore the compulsion to dig her nails into her arms to attack the infernal itching. The more serious the situation, the more uncomfortable the robe seemed to be. She felt inside her pocket to reassure herself that the parchment Alwen had given her was still safely tucked inside. Even with the spell and Alwen's confidence in her ability, Glain was unsure.

"There are two Stewards missing," Alwen announced. "If anyone here has knowledge of the whereabouts of the prefects Euday and Verica, speak now."

The assembly stood as if spell-locked. If any one of them breathed, there was not the slightest sign of it. None of them responded. Glain's worry had split between concern that Ynyr's fate had befallen Euday and Verica, and the tiny wriggling worm of suspicion that they were somehow involved.

"As we speak, the soldiers of the Cad Nawdd are searching the grounds and the castle, room by room, stone by stone." Alwen gestured toward the two women at her side. "And while they do their work, Glain and Nerys will inspect the integrity of the veil and do whatever must be done to ensure that our defenses are strong."

She signaled to Glain that she and Nerys should leave, and then continued to address the rest of the assembly. "The rest of you will remain here and submit to my interrogation. If there is evil among us, it will not be for long."

NINETEEN

Hywel paced endlessly, back and forth around one end of the campfire. Odwain and the two lieutenants the king most trusted provided an attentive, albeit reluctant audience for his venting. Odwain was glad for the seats they'd fashioned from two good-sized timber sections recovered from the brush, which had been set like benches on either side of the fire. Odwain sat on one, and the lieutenants on the other.

"Clydog is a fool to think he can hold Cwm Brith, even with a dark wizard backing his game."

It was dusk on the last night they would spend in the White Woods before leaving the relative shelter of the forest for the merchants' byway that circumnavigated the forest. Most of the men were already sleeping, but Hywel was restless and consumed with thoughts of his brother. So much so that Odwain was a bit concerned that Hywel had forgotten that their first duty was to intercept Thorvald's caravan and warn them.

Odwain had come to admire the king, his grace and his prowess, and even his confidence. He could not help but wonder, though, how much of Hywel's bravado resulted from the esteem others conferred upon him and how much he had garnered through his own deeds. Odwain thought of Rhys's father, Bledig Rhi, the barbarian chieftain from whom Odwain had learned that self-assuredness was hard won and respect was earned. Hywel and Bledig were alike in a number of ways, and yet so very different.

"Cwm Brith sits with its back against a pair of rocky hillocks at the head of a small vale. A handful of men can defend the compound a month or more against a siege, if they are vigilant and the house well-provisioned." Hywel spoke his thoughts aloud as he paced. "My father built that lodge to be a stronghold as much as a refuge. A direct attack will fail, no matter how many men storm the walls."

"Then how will you take it?" Odwain wasn't entirely sure that Hywel was inviting discussion, but decided to risk it. Odwain wanted to know how the king of the prophecy plotted his strategies and calculated risks against the gains and losses. Was he reckless, as Emrys and some others believed, or was he wise? "Your brother must have support and resources, or he'd never have dared to challenge you in the first place."

Hywel was almost eager to answer. "The obvious line of attack is through the vale, from the south or the east, but that forces us into the open. I plan to come from the west. There is a section of forest that nearly abuts the compound, small, but thick enough to mask our movements. The woods give way to a clearing about twenty yards wide that separates the trees from the wall. After dark, two men with the proper experience could approach without catching the sentry's notice, steal over the wall and overpower the watch, and then open the gates."

A daring plan and against the odds, but it could succeed— with the right men. Odwain was intrigued. "Wouldn't Clydog anticipate such a move?"

"Likely he would. He'll have his best men on the wall." Hywel paused momentarily to engage Odwain directly, a sly grin widening his mouth. "But we will have the advantage of surprise, and then it's a matter of who has the superior skill. Clydog has yet to outdo me at anything, and that, I would wager, rubs him raw."

"Were you never friends, you and Clydog?" Odwain wondered. The complexities of brotherhood still weighed heavily in his thoughts.

"Not in the least." Hywel's tone suggested that he regretted this truth. "There are nearly seven years between us. By the time Clydog was old enough to squire, I had spent more years in my father's company and, admittedly, in his favor than Clydog had yet been alive. At fourteen, he was fostered at the court of our cousin in Gwynedd, and I've seen little of him since."

"Resentments breed rivalries," Odwain observed. "And now that your father is dead, there is no chance for Clydog to win his admiration. He must hate you for it."

These insights seemed to impress Hywel, who paused again, this time to regard Odwain a little more thoughtfully. "Yes, well, he might have won *my* admiration, and his rightful share of our father's holdings, had he bothered to come for the burial rites and hear the bequests for himself."

"So," Odwain said, "now you must show him the error of his ways and bring him to heel."

Hywel snorted, half amused by the remark. "If such a thing can still be managed, though I have little hope of it. More than likely I'll be obliged to gut my greedy brother and stake his entrails on the ramparts at Dinefwyr as a warning to any other of my kin who might be thinking to challenge me."

"Dinefwyr?" Odwain did not know this place.

One of Hywel's lieutenants obliged: "The seat of Seisyllwg."

"And court of the new realm, Deheubarth," Hywel proclaimed. "Or so it will be known, once Clydog is brought down and all of the provinces are mine."

Hywel stopped to peer sideways at Odwain, beneath a glowering brow and shaggy locks, and then past him at his lieutenants, as if to ask what they thought. One of the lieutenants coughed in a bad attempt to hide a chuckle, and Odwain grew wary.

"I think I am glad you are with us after all, young MacDonagh." Hywel sat on the end of the log facing Odwain, alongside his lieutenants. "Perhaps you can make sense of your mistress for me."

"Alwen?" Odwain was hesitant to speak. This line of questioning could take him dangerously close to betrayal. He owed his fealty to Alwen, even Cerrigwen, before Hywel. "What can I tell you that you haven't already discovered for yourself?"

"Only one thing," Hywel said, quite seriously. "Perhaps the most important thing of all. You've known her most of your life, spent nearly every day of it in her service. If anyone can speak on this it is you, so I will ask. How much do you trust her?"

Odwain was not surprised by the question itself—it was common knowledge that Hywel and Alwen had a contentious relationship—but he was skeptical that anything he had to say on the issue would have value to Hywel. Whatever might be the true motive in asking, Odwain knew enough to be careful in answering.

He could say many things about Alwen—he could say that she was self-righteous and demanding and that she expected as much from those around her as she did from herself. He could also say that she was the closest thing to a mother he could remember, that she had never shown him anything but kindness, and that she was more devoted to her cause and her beliefs than any person he'd ever met. All of that would be true. But none of it really answered the question that Hywel had asked him.

"Madoc entrusted her with the Stewardry and the prophecy," Odwain countered. "I should think that would be warrant enough for anyone."

Hywel's eyes narrowed, and his gaze grew more intense. "I asked how much *you* trust her."

Odwain generally preferred the simple and direct. The mental maneuvering and political ploys favored by kings and courtesans annoyed him. He thought it far more practical to just get straight to the point rather than waste time and effort trying to trick someone into saying what you want them to say. "I trust her more than anything or anyone else I know in this world. I may not always understand the reasons for what she says or does, nor do I always agree when I do, but she has never failed me."

"So you would claim your loyalty is earned then," Hywel queried. "Not just a burden of your oath?"

Hywel was deliberately leading the conversation, and Odwain was done with it.

"I follow no one blindly, not even her. Oath or no oath," he said, looking directly at Hywel. "Prophecy or no prophecy."

Hywel's left eyebrow arched. "You'd make a very poor diplomat, MacDonagh."

Odwain saluted the observation with a shrug and a slight jut of his chin. "Is that good, or bad?"

"I haven't decided, but I will let you know when I do," Hywel said, almost smiling. "I have one more question, if you'll indulge me."

"Alright," Odwain stipulated, "so long as you come straight to the point this time."

"So be it." Hywel gestured beyond the fire ring toward where Cerrigwen lay sleeping, never breaking the steady, pointed gaze he had trained on Odwain. "If it comes to choosing between her and me, which will it be?"

This was not the question Odwain was expecting, but it was far more interesting. Pedr came to his mind, and what his brother had said about his own dilemma in the face of a difficult choice. Odwain also remembered the advice Pedr had given him.

"Well?" Hywel prodded. "Take care how you answer, MacDonagh. I want the truth."

"So be it," Odwain said, squaring himself to Hywel. He would show respect, but without compromise. Once he had believed that duty and loyalty were the same, but Odwain knew better now, and duty had already cost him far more than he'd ever meant to give. "I'm afraid that is a truth I cannot know unless I come face to face with it, Brenin."

"But suppose you did," Hywel insisted. "Tell me honestly. What would you do?"

"I have faith that such a choice shall never be mine to make." Odwain met Hywel's gaze dead on, wondering how this relentless, exacting man would take the naked honesty he demanded. "And so should you."

Hywel held steady, whatever thought or feeling he had well masked beneath a façade of neutrality. But his eyes belied his calculating nature, and Odwain watched them shift from spark to shine as Hywel examined and assessed and adjudged what he had heard, until he came to a determination.

"Tomorrow, we leave the forest for the merchant's road." Hywel stood abruptly, as did his two lieutenants. "But tonight, we shall see how well you can fend for yourself in the White Woods."

Before Odwain had fully made sense of what Hywel was saying, his lieutenants had drawn their swords and flanked him.

"Take a torch and whatever weapons you want. I suggest a good knife be among them," Hywel instructed. "Otherwise, you will go as you are."

Odwain stood slowly, so as not to show defiance or resistance, but neither was he about to submit. He widened his stance and brought his right hand to rest on the grip of his sword.

"Stand easy," Hywel said. "They mean only to make sure you cooperate, should you be of a mind to refuse me. You *will* walk out of this camp, under your own power or theirs."

Odwain would not stand easy. If anything he grew even more wary. It was clear enough to him that he was being put to a test, but he wanted to know why. "What do you expect this to prove?"

Hywel completely ignored his question. "A thousand paces north, straight into the woods, and then true west a thousand more before turning back. My men here will follow far enough to keep you honest. Find your way back here before dawn, or we leave you behind."

* * *

Odwain understood the utter wickedness of the White Woods. He had not been with Rhys and the others when Alwen confronted the devilkin and struck them down, but he had been with Eirlys while their curse consumed her. He had laid her out in the meadow like a corpse on the funeral pyre and waited for the faerie folk to take her away from him. Odwain had survived that horror, and he would survive this.

The first thousand paces he could feel Hywel's lieutenants shadowing his steps, but once he turned west, he knew he was alone. He also knew that the trail he had made on his way in was no longer there. The woods had woven a maze around him; he had heard it whispering in his wake.

The forest was so dark on a moonless night that the torch cast its light only a foot or two beyond arm's length, barely enough to keep him from falling on his face. His legs ached already from the strain and tension of so carefully watching his step.

It didn't occur to him to cheat on his paces until he had already gone more than half way. As he counted six hundred, some shrieking night bird flew out of the brush and startled him enough to make him consider turning back, but honor held him to the rules of the game. Only four hundred paces more.

His last step brought him to the edge of a small spring, which, were it not for the torchlight reflected on the water, he would never have seen until he stumbled right into it. A single footfall farther and his boots would be wet, and maybe the rest of him too.

Neither had he noticed the chill until he stopped walking. Winter was beginning to give way to warmer weather, but the night air still bit. These woods could be the death of a man in far too many ways.

Odwain held out the torch and turned full circle to get a sense of his surroundings. He was fairly certain he had his bearings straight, but his intuition was as skittered as his nerves. Once he was sure it was safe to move, he would move quickly.

As he turned, the light arced with him, chasing back the shadows and whatever might be hidden within them. Each time he moved, a rustle erupted just beyond the reach of his torch. His skin tingled. Something lurked in the brush not six feet from him.

Odwain drew his knife and widened his stance to better balance himself. He stilled his movements and slowed his breathing to bring himself as close to dead calm as he could. Sound and smell were more useful to him now than his sight.

Several moments passed before he heard the rustle again. It came from behind and seemed to be moving south, away from him. Odwain turned toward the sound slowly so as not to provoke anything else that might be hunkered within striking distance.

His ears began to sort the ambient sounds of the forest itself from the transient disruptions made by the creatures dwelling within it. The gurgling spring and the cold night air brushing through the evergreen boughs settled into the background. In the foreground he heard the soft scamper of rodents and other nocturnal beasties, punctuated by the occasional snap and crunch of something slightly more formidable moving about.

Odwain sensed nothing particularly threatening, or even remarkable for that matter—except for the odor. At first it was barely distinguishable from the aromas of forest duff and pine trees adrift in the wind, but he felt an uncomfortable twinge every time his nose caught a curl of it. He knew well the scent of fresh kill.

A stronger whiff reached him, and his senses recoiled. This was not the inviting tang of warm blood and raw meat ripe for skinning. Odwain smelled the reek of human flesh, carried past him as the breeze traveled from northeast to southwest.

He started into the trees, instinctively following the scent toward its source. It was closer than he'd expected. Not even a furlong farther, he broke through the trees and found himself standing knee-high in wild grass and scrub alongside a narrow but well-trod horse path.

This was not the trade road Hywel was headed toward, but even in the near-dark Odwain was certain this path would eventually intersect it. The stench of death was strong here.

He stood on the path and held up the torch so that the light would catch on both sides. A snort and the familiar sound of hooves shifting in the brush drew his attention. On the other side of the trail, a stout Frisian mare waited. The mare was saddled, and standing over something heaped on the ground.

Odwain's gut chucked over in dread, but he crossed the trail anyway. The horse whinnied and tossed her head, but she didn't shy away when he came near. He took the torch in his left hand and reached out to her with his right.

"Easy now, girl. Let's just have a look."

He took the reins and eased her back, lowering his torch to see what lay beneath her. Cloak cloth, plain brown woolen that was soaked through with blood, and good boots. He recognized the make of the boot. Every soldier of the Cad Nawdd was issued a pair.

The body had landed face down in the brush. Odwain let go of the reins and staked his torch in the ground, so he could roll the man over. He readied himself for what he imagined the worst scenario might be, but he was nowhere near prepared for what he found.

"Thorvald," Odwain whispered, heartsick and a little terrified. The warrior's eyes were wide open, staring stark-wide, and his face was a bloodless white, but it was the gaping, sinewy hole where his chest had been that turned Odwain's veins to ice. "How could this be?"

But he already knew. Odwain had seen firsthand the carnage the Hellion rampage had wreaked upon Fane Gramarye. He had witnessed the slaughter of his men—his friends—and been powerless to stop it. Those few who had survived were scarred in body and mind. It still ached where the fangs of their flesh-eating beasts had torn pieces out of his right side.

Odwain pulled fast to his feet, quickly calculating the most likely circumstances and their probable outcomes. When he left, Thorvald had had three men under his command and Cerrigwen's daughter in his charge. On his return he would also have brought with him his brother and Branwen, third Guardian of the Realms. Where one soldier had fallen, so surely had others. And if Thorvald was dead, were the sorceresses as well?

Of all the horrible outcomes that Odwain could envision, this was the worst, though it was not necessarily a fate foregone. There could be survivors. Choosing hope over doubt, he began a quick search through the grass and underbrush near the trees for signs of life.

Working by torchlight was tedious and slow, and required that he come much too close to the bodies in order to see whom he'd found. By the time he had discovered two more piles of remains, he realized the odds of coming upon a survivor were small. If there were any to find, he would need daylight, and help. It was then that he remembered the reason he was in the woods in the first place. He had to reach to Hywel's camp by dawn, and he had only a vague idea where it was.

Odwain borrowed the Frisian mare and headed back into the forest on little more than memory. He was reasonably certain that his natural sense of direction had kept his bearings straight, but the torch was spent. That left only his faith in his instincts.

TWENTY

By the time Alwen had dismissed the assembly and the search of the Fane had begun, the sun was already setting. It took more than an hour just to walk a quarter of the perimeter in the dark, another two to follow the stone walls to the midway mark. Even with a half-dozen torches, there were recesses in the walls or overgrowth where the shadows were so thick nothing short of the noon sun on a summer's day could penetrate. It was these patches that unnerved them all the most, but so far they had found nothing unusual.

Emrys had sent six of his best men with Glain and Nerys, men known for their courage and skill. They had all fought the Hellion and survived, which gave Glain confidence that they could confront anything. And there was no telling what they might find themselves facing this night.

The compound and its lands had been ravaged by the Hellion onslaught, but so had the Cad Nawdd. More than half the regiment had perished, most of them trying to keep the horde from overrunning the main gates, and the rest in the open between the gates and the castle.

"These are sacred grounds," Nerys said, so softly she might well have been speaking to herself. "There should be a monument to the sacrifices made here."

It was a generous and reverent thought, and Glain made note of it. Though the bodies had been burned, the earth held the blood of brave men who had died so horribly in defense of the Stewardry. Their suffering haunted these places, but evil was not hiding here.

"Perhaps when all this madness is passed," Glain agreed. "Perhaps then we shall honor all who are lost to us, in the proper way."

It was too dark to see if Nerys was moved by what she had said, but Glain imagined she appreciated the intent. If Nerys were feeling half the sorrow Glain felt, she knew more misery than she deserved.

"The rear gate next," she instructed. "And then the orchard."

Aside from the orchard, where the White Woods had over-grown weak spots in the wall, it was the rear gate that was the most vulnerable to ingress. Though a sentry was posted day and night, it opened into the forest. If wickedness were to find its way to the Fane, it was very likely to first seek its way through here.

The sentry greeted them and then stood aside so that the officers in their escort could inspect the integrity of the stiles. Nerys took a torch from one of the guards and used the light to get a sense of the surroundings and look for anything out of the ordinary near the wall.

"It is eerie, so near the woods," Glain commented, scratching absently at her arms. "But if the Cythraul were here, their scent has been washed away by the wind."

"I sense nothing at all," said Nerys, still scouring the hedgerows and wild brush. She straightened abruptly and spun around. "*Nothing.*"

A moment passed before Glain realized what Nerys was saying. They both should have been able to feel the subtle harmonic vibrations that emanated from the enchanted mist that veiled Fane Gramarye. Glain had noticed the sensation repeatedly as they had circled the compound along the retaining wall, but not here. This was the evidence for which they were hunting.

"We will need to know how far the breach stretches," Glain said, retracing their approach along the wall. A few dozen steps back she found where the seam had been opened. "I can feel the veil begin to thin here."

She posted one of the soldiers where she was sure the veil was still strong and then began to walk ahead, past the gate, toward the orchard. Nerys was close on her heels, with two of the guardsman right behind. Glain counted nearly a thousand paces before she noticed the warm hum of the veil's magic return.

"Here," she said, pointing to the spot where the nothingness ended. "Mark this place so that we can find it again."

"Before we attempt to reweave the veil spell, we should find the source of the disruption and destroy it," Nerys suggested. "Else our efforts may fail."

Glain agreed. There was little doubt that the persons she had seen emerge from the orchard two nights before had been working magic against them. Anger made her skin crawl beneath the itch of the camlet robe. "I believe we shall find what we seek in the apple grove."

The orchard, with its twisted, spindly-limbed trees was in some ways more eerie than the White Woods, especially at night. The remnants of old magic and the echoes of past blessings lingered at ritual sites like this. There were two sacred places on the grounds of the Fane. The most powerful was an ancient oak tree that stood a few hundred yards farther, on the other side of the faerie meadow. This orchard was the second.

Though densely grown, the apple grove was small and familiar. Within it was a single stone altar, a common place for seasonal blessings and worship that rested at the base of the First One, the original tree that had been the founding source of the orchard. Even in the dark, any Steward could easily find his or her way to it.

"Do you see that?" Nerys stopped her with a hand to her arm. "There, huddled by the tree."

They were still too far off to make out much beyond shadows, but Glain could see a dark bulky form that looked to her like a sack of potatoes leaned against the trunk. She waved the two guardsmen forward and beckoned for a torch.

Light in hand, Glain led the way, edging closer to the ritual tree and the suspicious object beneath it. Even from a distance it was clear the altar had recently been used. Glain could feel the resonance of spell work.

"I smell a blood offering and burnt tallow," Nerys said, her tone tense with anger and dismay. "The magic is fresh."

Nerys started ahead as if she meant to confront the altar, and the sack of potatoes at the base of the tree wriggled as if it hoped to retreat but had nowhere to go. Glain grabbed hold of Nerys by the folds of her cloak to keep her back while the two guardsmen rushed forward.

"Who is it?" Glain demanded, gesturing for the guardsmen to intercede. "Who is there?"

When the only response was a violent wriggle, one of the soldiers gave the shadowy bundle a good poke with the pointed finial of his halberd. The muffled cry that burst forth suddenly brought the sack of potatoes to life, and Glain recognized the shape of a human form wrapped in cloak and hood. A torch shoved close revealed a familiar face in the throes of torment. Euday was bound tight, and muzzled by a hideous magic Glain knew but had never seen. His mouth was sewn shut with enchanted twine, and the harder he tried to pull against the seam, the tighter the stitches cinched and tore at his flesh. It was a vicious hex and very effective.

Her first thought was to free him, but that impulse was quashed quickly by the recent lessons so hard learned. Glain had more than enough reason to be suspicious. And she had no way to know how or why Euday had come to be in the grove, though she would need to find out.

"I say we banish the muzzling but leave him bound," Nerys suggested, "just to be safe."

It was a good idea. Glain stepped closer and bent forward to look into Euday's eyes. He turned away but not before she saw the guilty terror, and in that instant Glain knew beyond any doubt that she had been betrayed. Fury overcame her in a flash of red heat.

"Yes, Euday," she whispered, shaking with rage. "You should fear me."

Glain stepped back and spoke aloud. "I will dispel the hex so that you can speak, and then you will tell me what you know. But be warned, old friend. The first lie that leaves your lips will set them ablaze, and I will gladly watch you burn."

Tears spilled onto Euday's cheeks and glistened in the torch-light, but Glain was unmoved. She reached out with the fingertips of her right hand pursed together in a pincer-like fashion and made a plucking motion as she spoke the command to undo the hex. "*Dadwnud.*"

Euday let out a whimper and wet himself. The stench gave him away, and still Glain felt no pity. She could have chosen a less painful way to release him from the stitching twine, but part of her wanted his suffering. Dark magic would come so easily, if she let it. But it was not vengeance she was after—not yet.

Glain turned her attention to the altar and the herbs, animal bones, and tallow drippings that were evidence of a powerful conjure. "What is this, Euday?"

"It holds the veil open, but only for a few days at a time," he confessed through sobs and bloody spittle. "The spell needs tending, like a fire."

Nerys stooped and swiped the altar clean with the back of her hand, muttering a blessing under her breath.

"Is that what you were doing here?" Glain asked him. "Tending your spell?"

He struggled against the binds, trying to sit up, and failed. "We meet here every third night."

"Who," she demanded. "Who meets here?"

"Verica and Ynyr and I," Euday blubbered. "It takes the three of us to work the spell. But then Ynyr went missing, and when we couldn't find him, Verica and I agreed to meet tonight as we had planned. We thought he would be here."

"Ynyr?" Glain could not believe what she was hearing. "What are you saying?"

"It was him all along. He had Machreth's instructions. Ynyr called the Cythraul against Hywel," Euday pleaded. "We only did as we were told."

"Ynyr is dead," Nerys interceded, her tone flat and unfeeling.

"What?" Euday was horrified. "*Ynyr* is dead?"

"Victim to his own spell it would seem, sometime last night." Nerys moved closer to Euday, as if to menace him further.

"Th—the Cythraul?" Euday sputtered. "That cannot be."

"Oh, but it is." Nerys bent close and snatched a fistful of Euday's hair, yanking his head back so that he had no choice but to look at her. "Surely he did not intend to set the wraiths upon himself, so who, Euday? Who did Ynyr mean to kill?

"Ah—I—," Euday faltered, "I cannot say."

Nerys yanked harder. "Cannot, or will not?"

Still Euday resisted. He set his jaw and summoned defiance. "I *will* not."

Nerys bent close. "Then I will rip out your tongue and feed it to the vermin while you watch."

Her quiet menace had a devastating effect. Realizing at last that Nerys had no mercy for him, Euday's resistance collapsed. He shuddered as desperation took hold.

"The Cythraul were meant for Alwen," Euday blurted. "Ynyr hoped to avenge Machreth's defeat."

"And gain favor with his new lord," Nerys surmised. She glanced at Glain to gauge her reaction, or perhaps for instruction. But Glain was so staggered by what she was hearing that all she could do was shake her head in disbelief.

Nerys let go of Euday's hair and crouched in front of him, seizing him again by the collar of his robe. "Where is Verica?"

Euday shook his head violently. "She never came."

"You fool." Nerys shoved him away as she stood. "Just how do you suppose you ended up trussed and muzzled?"

"Wait." Glain's head was spinning. "Nerys, how can you believe any of this? Ynyr had nothing to do with this. He couldn't have."

Nerys was angry, but also pained. "I wasn't sure until that scroll was found in my room. Ynyr is the only person who could have put it there."

"What?" Glain fell to her knees. She wanted to retch.

"I've always known that he was more sympathetic to the reformers than he ever let show, but I never worried about his loyalties, not really. After the insurrection, though, he became more and more secretive, and when I pressed him, he was so offended, I felt guilty for asking. Then one night, just a few weeks ago, I caught him sneaking into the Fane very late. He was clearly up to something he didn't want known, and I never asked him to explain. I didn't want to know the answer. Things were never the same after that."

"How is this happening?" Glain could barely speak.

Nerys let out a disheartened huff. "Perhaps I should have come to you, but would you have heard anything said against him, especially from me? And what was there to tell?"

Glain gaped at Nerys, gutted.

"When the scroll was discovered," Nerys went on, "I knew it had to be him. The betrayal broke my heart. Ynyr could defend me earnestly without risk to himself, knowing full well that I would be found guilty no matter what he said. You would never believe me innocent, and he counted on that."

Glain was stunned beyond comprehension. She had been stupid and naïve, and here Nerys was speaking to her with all the respect and understanding that she herself had never been shown. It was unbearable.

Nerys frowned and stepped closer, her head tilted to one side as though she were intrigued. "Your robe," she wondered, "how is it shimmering?"

"What do you mean?" Glain looked down at herself and scratched at her arms again, wondering what it was that Nerys was seeing.

Nerys gasped and stepped back, drawing her wand from her sash. With a flourish aimed straight at Glain, she shouted. "*Ymddatod!*"

Glain was horrified, confused. Before she could make sense of what was happening, the black camlet robe dissolved into a wriggling swath of tiny, shiny-eyed spiders. Thousands upon thousands of the hideous creatures crawled over her in their frenzied escape. They fled like fleas from a drowning dog, into the underbrush, where they disappeared into nothingness.

"Great Gods!" she shrieked.

"Are you all right?" Nerys was shaken, but still in control of her faculties. She reached out a hand to help Glain up. "How did you come by that robe?"

Glain had already realized how the black camlet robe had used her. "It was left behind in Machreth's wardrobe."

There was nothing unnatural about that. The proctor's mantle belonged to the office, not to the holder. No one had ever considered that it might have been bewitched.

"His eyes in the Fane," Nerys said.

Glain nodded, sickened by the realization of how she had been duped again and by the lingering sensation of spiders crawling on her arms. "Every time I have worn that robe, he has been there with me."

Nerys acknowledged this truth with a grim nod. "The things he must have seen. Alwen will need to know."

Glain panicked, ransacking her recollections of the last weeks and days, trying to remembered what all she might have accidentally allowed Machreth to witness.

"Cerrigwen's confession," she recalled, which horrified her all the more. "And Hywel's plan to raid Cwm Brith. Oh great *Gods*, Nerys."

"It won't help us to worry about that now." Nerys glanced past Glain to Euday. "What do we do with him?"

Anger swelled in her chest, crowding the hurt and betrayal until she thought she would burst. "The guards will take him to Alwen while we finish here."

"And Verica?"

"In due time," Glain answered, pulling the parchment Alwen had given her from the pouch tied at her waist. "First we reweave the veil spell."

Glain dismissed the two soldiers with a nod and waited as they dragged Euday away. The two guardsmen who had been posted to mark the gap in the veil held their places. The last two took position to watch over her and Nerys while they worked.

It was a complicated conjuration that was meant to be called by a high sorcerer, a mage far more seasoned than either Glain or Nerys. It had been decided that together Glain and Nerys would be as powerful as Alwen alone, at least for the needs of this spell.

To work this magic, they needed oak bark scored with the magical symbols for strength, protection, and endurance; a tincture Alwen had provided from Madoc's private stores; and a blood offering. The incantation itself was in the old language, but Alwen had explained its meaning so that the younger sorceresses could speak the words with intent.

From the velvet bag she carried, Nerys pulled a measure of silk and a tallow wick end. She knelt on the ground to spread the silk over the flat, rectangular altar stone and set the candle upon it. Then Nerys placed bark shards on the cloth in the pattern the parchment prescribed.

While Glain spoke the blessing words, Nerys spilled three drops of the tincture on each of the shards. The wick end sparked to life and both women sighed with relief. They had got it right so far.

Glain knelt in front of the altar, facing Nerys. Using the bone-handled dagger she carried, Glain opened the skin of her outstretched palm with a cut deep enough for the blood to flow freely, and then repeated the ritual wounding for Nerys when she offered her hand. Together they blooded each of the inscribed oak shards, repeating three times the incantation they had memorized.

In so doing, they invoked the power of the four realms—spiritual, celestial, natural, and physical—and caused the elemental magics to converge in answer to the commands within the incantation. Glain begin to feel the familiar shimmering vibration of the veil as it grew stronger. She envisioned the threads of light, energy, and intent intertwining, weaving a patch over the tear in the misty shield that protected the Stewardry from the outside world.

By the end of the third refrain, the spell had done all it could. Nerys offered healing words and bound both their palms. Glain felt gratitude and admiration she had no way to adequately express.

"Thank you," she said, knowing it was not enough.

Nerys nodded, which implied acknowledgment and nothing more. Glain had no expectations, but she hoped it was a beginning. She left Nerys to clear the altar and went to inspect the veil. As she approached the wall near the weakened place, Glain easily sensed the restoration.

"Thank the Ancients," she whispered, so filled with gratitude she could barely contain it.

But the relief was short-lived and the night air cold. A violent shudder overcame her, and one of the guardsmen was quick to offer his cloak. The warm wool quelled the shiver, but a deeper chill remained. Disgust and sadness and self-loathing returned, and Glain forced herself to summon what was left of her resolve. This was but one tiny victory in a heaping mire of deadly betrayals. She could not deny the dark foreboding that the worst was yet to come.

TWENTY-ONE

Thorne observed Rhys from his perch on a nearby stump. He was impressed with how comfortable Rhys had become with the White Woods. This was their third night on the hunt, and though they had yet to encounter the Cythraul or any other real danger, Rhys had learned to handle the unexpected with calm and presence of mind. This was encouraging, but still well short of the training of a true mage hunter.

"Tomorrow we will reach Banraven," Thorne said. "You must be ready for anything."

Rhys glanced sidelong at Thorne, continuing to polish the blade of his boot knife with a swatch of doeskin. "You think that is where the Cythraul have gone?"

"That is where the trail leads," Thorne said, reluctant to mention the dark and deadly presence he had sensed in the dungeon.

"Back to their master." Rhys slid the knife back into the hidden sheath in his boot. "To Machreth."

Thorne nodded. "As I said."

"Be ready for anything," Rhys grinned. He wadded up the doeskin and shoved it into his saddle sack and then settled himself near the fire. "I am."

Thorne was amused by the lad's bravado, but it worried him. Rhys was sharp-witted and skilled, but occasionally he showed the overconfidence that so often afflicted the young. In fact, Thorne suspected that Rhys suffered from more than one of the usual follies of youth.

"Tell me about the girl." Thorne intended the directive to sound inconsequential, a natural turn of the conversation. He had been casually manipulating the topics all evening, under the guise of whiling away the time. It had worked well enough so far that Thorne decided to dig deeper.

Maelgwn stretched himself out between Rhys and the fire, eyes facing the forest to keep watch, but making sure his belly was within easy reach. Instead of answering straight away, Rhys rewarded the greedy warghound with a good long scratch. He was not as adept at hiding personal things as he liked to think, though Rhys did finally meet Thorne's gaze in a halfway convincing attempt. "What girl?"

"The doe-eyed one, your mother's second." Thorne humored him, though they both knew which girl. "What is she to you?"

Rhys looked away again, this time busying himself with tending the fire. "You mean Glain."

Thorne stayed quiet, giving Rhys time to decide what to say, if anything at all. The awkward meetings and forced restraint during that one night in the Fane had made it painfully obvious to him that there was some sort of relationship between the two. It only mattered to Thorne's purposes if Rhys were obligated or had intentions toward the girl, and this he preferred to know sooner rather than later. The Brotherhood required absolute devotion to the cause, and a man at conflict with his loyalties was unlikely to succeed. However, as a rule, Thorne was averse to prying too much into private matters. Any man worth knowing held certain things sacred in his heart, and he respected that.

"I suppose you're asking if I care for her." Rhys was reluctant, but not so much that he ended the conversation. "It's a fair question."

Thorne was amused but kept a sober expression. "Have you an answer?"

Rhys used a half-withered oak leaf to wipe the soot from his hands. "I have feelings for her, but not the ones I ought to."

This was a far more interesting answer than Thorne had expected. "Do you love her?"

"Not in the way I should." Rhys let out a weighted sigh. "Not in the way she needs."

"But it is love, nonetheless, isn't it?" Thorne counseled. "How are you so sure it is not what she needs from you? Have you asked her?"

"No, which is more my point, actually," Rhys said, pulling absently at the moss on the stones they'd used to ring their campfire. "That is a conversation I honestly don't want to have. As fond as I am of her . . ."

"As much as you lust for her," Thorne interjected wryly.

Rhys let half a grin slip. "In *whatever* ways I may admire her, my affection for Glain does not run as deep as hers for me. And even if she were to claim herself satisfied with that, I would not."

"Ah," said Thorne, a little sadly. Men of deep passions were destined to know suffering. "So you are a seeker of soul-met love."

Rhys gave a rueful shrug. "Whatever it is I am seeking, it has to be more than this."

"Seekers of soul-met love pine for something which is almost impossible to find," Thorne warned, noticing Maelgwn's ears, which were alert and pointing toward the woods on the far side of their little clearing. "Such a journey is long and lonely, and often ends in despair."

"So you think me foolish."

"No," Thorne countered. "I like that you know your own heart so well. I only mean to point out that there is a reason that most men, and most women for that matter, will make do with whatever measure of love comes their way. The alternative might well be a life without any kind of love at all."

"A risk I seem to be determined to take." Rhys grinned.

Thorne gave in to a chuckle, watching Maelgwn again. His head was up now. Something in the woods had the warghound's attention. "A true adventurer, you are."

"And what about you?" Rhys's tone was more direct. "Have you a wife or a woman waiting for you somewhere?"

Thorne almost winced. It wasn't as though he hadn't anticipated this question, but it never got any easier to hear. "We are alike, you and I," he said, "Determined to take the risk."

"Good." Rhys grinned at him. "I was starting to wonder if the Brotherhood required a vow of chastity or some such nonsense."

"There was a time, long ago, when the virtues included chastity," Thorne explained, "but that was quickly abandoned. The men of the Ruagaire are devout men, but they are men nonetheless. The life is lonely, and a woman is welcome comfort from time to time."

"The Ruagaire don't marry, then?"

"It isn't forbidden, but most hunters forego a family of their own." Thorne wanted to answer his young friend honestly, but the conversation put him in mind of things he didn't like to think about. "It is difficult to keep a wife and children when your calling claims your soul."

"So, are you still searching for love," Rhys wondered, "or have you given up on it altogether?"

"Eh," Thorne scoffed, trying to keep the melancholy from settling over him. "A true seeker never gives up. But he might learn that finding what he's been looking for isn't the end of the journey."

"You sound like my father just now," Rhys said. "He is fond of saying that loving my mother is the easy part—it's what comes along because of it that's hard. But there's nothing he wouldn't do for her."

Thorne nodded. "And that's what you want for yourself, that same depth of devotion."

"Yes. Though I don't think I've found it yet."

"Trust me," Thorne counseled. "You'll know when you do."

Maelgwn let out a low, deep-throated growl and gathered his hind legs under his haunches. Thorne kept his eyes on the trees beyond the clearing and slowly reached down with his left hand to retrieve his blade from the scabbard laid out on the ground beside him. "We have a visitor," he murmured.

Rhys pulled to a crouch beside the fire, meaning to look as though he were casually tending it, and pulled his boot knife. "There are two."

Thorne was impressed, and annoyed to have been bested. He hadn't picked up the second set of footsteps. "Where?"

"They were together, near the tree line across the clearing," Rhys whispered. "But now I don't know."

Thorne could sense someone, or something, stalking the perimeter of the clearing. Whoever was out there was circling them. Suddenly, a shadowy, hooded figure stepped out of the trees opposite them, and Rhys rose to confront it. In the same instant, Maelgwn sprang to his feet and spun on his tail, snarling at something behind Thorne. Before Thorne could fully react, a ropey bundle flew over his head, and Maelgwn let out a muffled yelp. He had been muzzled by mage tether.

A strong hand gripped Thorne's left shoulder, hard, and steel slid cold and sharp against the base of his throat. "You're slipping, Edwall."

"Am I, Steptoe?" Thorne tensed, waiting for the realization to set in. He had managed to reverse and tuck his sword under his left arm so that it was at just the right angle for a quick gut-tearing upthrust, starting at the groin.

The shadowy figure stepped toward the fire and pushed back his hood. Eckhardt held out his empty hands to show Rhys his weapons were still sheathed, all the while grinning at his brother. "Well played, Thorne."

Gavin pulled back his blade and the threatening grip on Thorne's shoulder relaxed into a friendly roughing. "I owe your mutt an apology."

Thorne laughed. "I dare you to take off that tether."

Gavin stepped around to join the group, and then gawked at Maelgwn in utter amazement. "How is *that* even possible?"

Rhys had already unwound the tether from Maelgwn's muzzle and was scratching him between the ears.

"Maelgwn likes him. Rhys, son of Bledig Rhi," Thorne announced, "meet my Ruagaire brethren—the brothers Steptoe. Eckhardt there, and Gavin here."

"Remarkable," said Gavin, extending his hand to Rhys in greeting, and then to Thorne. "Other than you, Martin was the only man that beast ever let near him."

"We've been looking for you." Eckhardt flashed a warning glare at his brother and then gave Thorne an apologetic look over a warm handclasp. "We have sad news."

"I've heard. Master Eldrith informed me just before he tried to have me taken into custody."

"Eldrith?" Gavin looked at Eckhardt and then again at Thorne. "So you've been to Banraven. When, exactly?"

"Nearly a week now." Thorne cocked a suspicious eyebrow in Gavin's direction. "Tell me what you know."

Eckhardt let out a soft whistle, and two chestnut geldings walked out of the woods. He pulled the bags and bedrolls from both horses and tossed them to the ground near the fire. "Settle in, my friend. There's much to tell."

"What about him?" Gavin gestured at Rhys. He remained standing, but Eckhardt sat cross-legged on his bedroll next to Thorne.

"I trust him." Thorne threw the rest of the wood they had gathered onto the fire. "You can speak freely."

"He is not one of us, Thorne." Gavin was more guarded than his brother. That was usual, but his terseness was not. "The canons of the Order exist for his protection as well as ours."

Thorne's jaw set tight and he shot a glare at Gavin. He did not like to be questioned, not even by a man he called friend. "I said he is with me. Speak, or don't. It's entirely up to you."

Gavin returned the glare with a look of aggravation and concern. He still stood, as though he were seriously considering not joining the group. The dread that had settled in Thorne's gullet turned cold and hard.

"Then so be it," Eckhardt said, attempting to move past the moment. "There isn't time for this, Gavin. It should be enough that Thorne trusts him, unless you no longer trust Thorne."

Thorne's gaze was still fixed on Gavin, whose resistance wavered at his brother's challenge but did not collapse altogether. This troubled Thorne deeply.

"If we no longer trust each other," he said, "then there is no Brotherhood left to honor."

Still Gavin hesitated a few moments more, before relenting at last. He sat next to his brother, opposite Rhys, wary and watchful of the younger man.

"You say Eldrith tried to have you arrested," Eckhardt began. "We heard the same thing happened to Martin, only he did not escape."

Thorne felt daggers stabbing at his innards now. "If it were not for Algernon, I would have shared Martin's fate."

"It seems Eldrith is no longer in control of Banraven," said Eckhardt. "There have been rumors for weeks of an insurrection, that the Stewardry has fallen."

"It still stands, though no longer under Madoc's leadership," Thorne interjected, tipping his head toward Rhys. "The new Sovereign is his mother."

Eckhardt arched one eyebrow in surprise, though he continued as though he were not the least bit impressed. "Martin returned to Banraven to report what he'd heard, but discovered the bad news had arrived well ahead of him. The dark mage had already stolen the sanctuary right out of Eldrith's hands."

Thorne recalled the burning he'd felt as he shot down the chute into the cesspool, and just how close he'd come to meeting the dark mage. "What would Machreth want with Banraven?"

Even as he said it, Thorne knew. Gavin's eyebrows arched as if to reinforce his worst suspicions. The most devastating of betrayals might already have befallen them all.

"Martin's body did not survive the torture," Eckhardt said gently, "but his secrets did."

Thorne nodded because it was the only way he dared respond. The kind of suffering black magic could bring to a man was beyond imagining, and Thorne felt sick. He was also enraged.

"So, Eldrith sacrificed Trevanion to save himself and would have done the same to me. Is that what you're saying?"

Eckhardt offered up an empathetic shrug. "Sooner or later Machreth will discover that Master Eldrith also holds the secrets to Elder Keep, but in the meantime he searches for the three of us."

"What is Elder Keep?" Rhys had been quietly taking in the discussion until now.

Eckhardt and Gavin both looked to Thorne. What Rhys asked was not unreasonable or even unexpected. But having the answer would force him over a threshold that once crossed could never be uncrossed. This was not Thorne's decision to make.

He turned to face his would-be apprentice. "From this moment forward, I will answer any question you ask. But be clear, Rhys. Do not ask unless you are willing to accept the responsibility that comes with having the knowledge. Do you understand what I am saying?"

Rhys gave a sober nod. "I think so."

"Be certain," Thorne warned. "You may not be sworn to the Ruagaire, but we will hold you accountable as if you were."

"I understand."

Though Thorne believed him sincere and committed, he wondered if Rhys had a firm sense of the singularity of the moment. Were the circumstances any less desperate, were they not already in pursuit of a common quarry, and were his mother not Sovereign of the Stewardry, this conversation would never have taken place.

"Alright then," said Thorne. He looked to Eckhardt and then Gavin. Neither man objected, but neither did they offer encouragement. "Has Alwen told you anything of a sacred well hidden beneath Fane Gramarye?"

"Madoc is entombed in the Well of Tears," Rhys confirmed. "My mother almost drowned in it."

Gavin was concerned. "How far has word of the well spread?"

"Not beyond my mother's small circle of trust," Rhys said. "But obviously, it is known to the three of you."

"It is our duty to know," Thorne explained. "In the beginning, the Stewardry was comprised of five orders, and each of those orders had a Sovereign, like Madoc. As the end of their reign drew near, each Sovereign would make a final pilgrimage to the well at Fane Gramarye to shed the wisdom they had collected into the waters so that it was preserved. And then they would journey to their final resting place, to the tomb at Elder Keep."

Rhys was astonished. "A wizards' crypt?"

"In a manner of speaking," Thorne explained. "While the Well of Tears is a bastion of knowledge, Elder Keep is a bastion of souls. Within its walls is the portal through which a mage's essence returns to the beyond."

"A thin place," Rhys realized.

"The *thinnest* place," Thorne corrected. "Nowhere else are this world and the next so close."

"So what have the Ruagaire to do with Elder Keep?" Rhys was nothing if not focused on the point.

To Thorne's surprise, Gavin interjected. "The Brotherhood first existed to protect the balance of power between the five orders and enforce the rules of governance set forth by the Sovereign's council that oversaw the collective. We were once a peacekeeping force thousands strong. Eventually the sects were destroyed or withdrew, until all that remained of the Stewardry were Fane Gramarye and Elder Keep."

"The Fane survived by virtue of the veil, which to this day remains an effective concealment. And of course, its unrivaled military," Thorne added. "The original Cad Nawdd was formed by members of the Ruagaire, you know."

"The Fane also survived by virtue of a pact," said Eckhardt, "as did Elder Keep. Both exist today because the Ruagaire long ago pledged to keep safe the secrets it was created to protect, and to do so at all costs."

Thorne was unwilling to deny the uglier truths. "Not that the Ruagaire Brotherhood hasn't known its dark days. Survival has required sacrifices, and not all of them were noble. Like the Stewardry, our numbers have dwindled to nearly nothing, and our purpose has been altered by time, but we are more than our reputation implies. We are not just a band of mercenary mage hunters."

Rhys took it all in as though it were as easily digested as quail eggs and warm milk. Either he knew more than he admitted, or he was accustomed to hearing unbelievable stories. "So what do we do now?"

"We continue to Banraven and stop Machreth there, if we can," Thorne said.

"It won't be easy travel," Eckhardt warned. "Machreth's demon soldiers search the woods for you every day, Thorne. I'm surprised you haven't encountered them yet."

"The Hellion," Rhys said, his tone edged with bitterness. "It was them that Machreth unleashed on the Fane. It takes three men to bring one of them down, but it can be done."

Thorne was more convinced than ever that his admiration for Rhys was well placed. His experience would be helpful. "I wasn't sure what I was working so carefully to avoid," he said, "but I have sensed something unusual skulking about."

"Never after dark," Gavin observed. "It's strange, but we've never seen them in the forest after sundown. We have been skirting their patrols for the last two days and traveling at night."

"Have you encountered the Cythraul?" Thorne was hoping to confirm his bearings. "We have been following the scent toward Banraven."

"No," said Eckhardt, "but we came from Elder Keep."

"Does Drydwen know?" Thorne had been trying to avoid speaking of her.

"It was she who sent us to find you," Eckhardt said. The careful tone and half-hidden empathy in his eyes only made Thorne feel worse. "Algernon has been sending word from Banraven to us through a new boy he's taken to tutoring, and then we take the news back to Elder Keep. That's how we learned what had happened to you."

Thorne shook his head in bemused exasperation. "Another of Algernon's woodland waifs."

"He calls this one Gelf," Gavin said. "He's a clever lad, and reliable. Or at least he was. We haven't seen him in nearly a week."

"Who is Drydwen?" Rhys asked.

Gavin answered so that Thorne wouldn't have to. "Drydwen is the prioress at Elder Keep."

Thorne stood abruptly. His mood was turning surly, and he was tired of the talk. "We'll sleep in turns," he said, "just to be safe. Two to rest and two on the guard, in two-hour stretches until dawn. Eckhardt and I will stand the first watch."

TWENTY-TWO

By the time they had finished in the orchard and returned to the Fane, the night was edging toward dawn. The great room was empty, and the castle was quiet. There were guards posted in the vestibule and in the halls, giving Glain all the more reason to worry about what had come of Alwen's interrogations.

She dismissed the remaining men of the escort Emrys had assigned and stood staring at the main staircase. At the moment it seemed an insurmountable obstacle. She hadn't the heart or the strength to climb it.

"She'll be waiting for us," Nerys reminded. "The sooner we tell her, the better it will be for us all."

Glain wanted to believe that was true. "I wonder what she did with Euday."

"I would kill him," Nerys said too easily. "But Alwen will let him live. Come on."

Nerys started up the stairs and Glain followed, dragging one foot after the other. She had never known such exhaustion, not even in the long, morbid days of funeral pyres and nursing the wounded after the Hellion had been defeated. But then Alwen had been stronger, and Glain had still had hope. Then she had still had Rhys and Ynyr and faith in her own judgment.

When they passed the second-floor landing, Glain realized that she needed to take the lead, to protect Alwen's secret. She forced herself to pick up her pace and passed Nerys on the stairs. A soldier was stationed outside the Sovereign's chambers.

Glain grew concerned. "Is everything alright?"

"The Sovereign left orders that she not be disturbed except by you," he said. "I believe she is resting."

"Wait here a moment," Glain said to Nerys.

She rapped twice and then let herself in, closing the door behind her. Alwen was sitting in an overstuffed armchair adjacent to the hearth, staring absently into the flames. Glain approached carefully, not wanting to startle her out of her meditation.

"Sovereign?"

Alwen looked up with woeful eyes and an expression of grim resolve. She was too pale, as though her life were draining from her. "What else did you find?"

"Verica is still missing." Glain was reluctant to say more. She didn't want any of it to be true, and Alwen looked so frail. "Nerys is waiting in the hallway. Shall I bring her in or send her back to her room?"

"We can hardly punish Nerys for poor judgment, now can we," Alwen snapped. "Not when we are so egregiously guilty of it ourselves."

The words stung, but no more than she deserved. "The veil is repaired."

"Well, that is something at least," Alwen said. The anger faded quickly, as though she were too weak to hold onto it. "And for what it is worth, you were not wrong about Ariane. She is insipid and deluded by visions of her own greatness, but not treasonous. Euday, however, is a bitter disappointment."

It did not escape Glain's attention that Alwen had avoided mentioning Ynyr, for which she was profoundly grateful. Then she noticed that Alwen was clenching and unclenching her blighted fingers. "Are you in pain, Sovereign?"

"What?" Alwen looked at Glain as if she hadn't understood what she'd said, and then glanced at her fingers. "It's nothing. I am fine."

Glain was not convinced, but it was clearly not a good time to argue.

"Go," Alwen waved at her. "Bring Nerys. There is nothing left to hide, not any longer. And then pour the aleberry. I'm sure we are all in need of it."

Glain retrieved a tentative and almost intimidated Nerys and then poured a healthy dose of the mulled ale for each of them. It took Alwen's insistence to coax Nerys to sit on the divan and take a cup. Glain chose the soothing warmth of the hearthstone, partly for the comfort of it and partly for the vantage point. She was concerned for Alwen.

The Sovereign listened intently while they recounted the events of the evening, nodding now and then in acknowledgment, but otherwise impassive. If Glain had held any hope that speaking about the events in the woods would ease her agony, there was none left by the time they had finished. Said aloud it all seemed even more devastating.

"It is likely Verica fled the compound through the breach in the veil after Ynyr was killed," Alwen said. "Aside from Euday, no one else was complicit in her wickedness, at least as far as my interrogations have revealed. To be sure, I attempted a spirit-faring and consulted the scrying stone, to no avail."

Nerys was brave enough to ask. "What have you done with him?"

Alwen let out a bitter, scoffing huff. "Sent him to rot in the dungeons, though I admit even that is better than he deserves."

"What did he tell you?" Glain wondered.

"No more than he told you," said Alwen. "Though I searched his mind to be sure we had the truth, as he knows it. My probing yielded only his terror and his motivations, which were of no interest to me."

Glain was mildly encouraged. "At least we now know who our enemies are."

"So we do," Alwen agreed. "Nerys, dear child, I believe it is time we are done with secrets, once and for all."

Glain was struck through with guilty panic. Just what secrets did Alwen mean to reveal? The Sovereign stood with considerable effort and walked to the altar table in the receptory. She returned with the black velvet bag that held the bloodstone amulet and held it out to Nerys.

When Nerys hesitated, Alwen placed the bundle in her lap. "This belongs to you now."

"I don't understand," said Glain, thinking as she spoke that there were far too many things she did not fully grasp.

Alwen returned to the overstuffed armchair. "Among the many intriguing bits of information I learned while studying Madoc's papers was the link between the Guardians of the Realms and their lineage. Those of us originally named to the Stewards' Council are each a descendant of one of the founding bloodlines. I am a daughter of the House of Eniad. Cerrigwen is of the Uir legacy, Branwen of Caelestis, and Tanwen a daughter of Morthwyl."

Glain was even more confused. "How does this concern Nerys?"

"Though we have the amulet, Bledig is returning without Tanwen, and time is running out on us. Barring some other sign of her or her escort, I am afraid I must entertain the possibility that Tanwen is lost to us," Alwen said gravely. "And just as I intend to do my best to encourage Ffion to become her mother's replacement, I intend to name a new representative for Tanwen. As Nerys is the last of the Morthwyl line, the privilege falls to her."

Glain could not stop staring at Nerys. "What are you saying?"

"Nerys is Tanwen's sister," Alwen said, "by the same mother, which entitles Nerys to claim the same legacy. The only person who can succeed a Guardian of the Realms is her child. As Tanwen inherited her right through her mother, so does Nerys."

Glain was not sure how to receive this knowledge or respond to it in an appropriate way. It was good news for the Stewardry, for the prophecy, but Glain wondered if it was good news for Nerys. The fair-skinned Nerys had gone unnaturally pale, and though this was apparently not the first time she had heard this information, she was clearly not anywhere near comfortable with it.

Alwen addressed Nerys. "The amulet is safest around your neck. You can protect it far better than I until Tanwen returns or you take her place."

Glain was tempted to ask aloud why Nerys had Alwen's trust. She presumed that Nerys had submitted to Alwen's psychic probing during the investigation surrounding the discovery of the scroll, but Glain was unwilling to leave anything to presumption, not any-more. Still, the only person she knew for certain was still deserving of her faith was Alwen. "If you trust her, Sovereign, so shall I."

Alwen seemed to understand Glain's inference. "If there was ever deceit in her thoughts or her intentions, I could not find it. And I did try."

Glain was satisfied. Alwen's ability to know another person's heart and mind was the only reliable test of truth left to them now. And Nerys was the only ally left—aside from Ariane, but that thought gave Glain a headache.

Though she was reluctant to bring it up, Glain knew there was no avoiding the last remaining task Alwen had entrusted to her. "If Nerys is willing," she said, "I would welcome her help in the search for Madoc's testament."

"A fine idea." Alwen's expression brightened as she looked to Nerys.

Nerys smiled, though she never actually accepted or refused the invitation. Glain decided to take her lack of objection as agreement. Perhaps the only person in the Fane more betrayed than she was Nerys, and Glain was not about to press her for loyalty that had not yet been earned.

"Before I send you both out so that I can rest," Alwen continued, "I have more news. Some good, some less so. First the good."

She sipped from her cup. "Hywel's men have cleared the rubble from the labyrinth as far as the opening to the cavern. I am hopeful they will be able to open the cavern itself within a few days, and we will be ready when the others return."

Glain glanced at Nerys. "Does she know of the Well of Tears?"

"She does now," Alwen smiled. "There are a great many things she will need to learn in very short order, and I will rely on your help.

"However," she said, sipping again at the aleberry, "I'm afraid I am not so sure of Emrys, not anymore. I sensed something disturbing when I entered his thoughts, though just what it was I could not decide. I have asked Finn to keep a close watch on him, and I suggest both of you deal with him cautiously. If you are uncertain about any man of the Cad Nawdd, take your concerns to Finn, or Pedr when he is able."

Glain did not think she could stand to hear another disheartening word. Her eyes ached to close and her dress was still damp. "Sovereign, I believe we could all use some rest."

"Of course, you're right," Alwen said, obviously far from her best as well. "But let's none of us rest too long—evil doubles its efforts while we sleep."

* * *

Eldrith was a coward. In fact, he had come to the realization nearly too late that his cowardice exceeded his arrogance, which he expected would surprise no one but him. Yes, Eldrith was a coward, and a loathsome one at that. If he weren't, he would have done something, *anything*, to save Martin Trevanion from his horrible fate and warned Thorne Edwall away from Banraven rather than invite him into the demon's lair. If he weren't a coward, Eldrith would have slit his own throat when the page had awakened him earlier with word that the dark mage wished to interrogate him next. Instead, he had dressed and sat at his desk, watching the sunrise while sipping at the insidious tea he had brewed from water hemlock leaves and sweetened with heather honey. This death would be slower, and more painful, but it was a civilized end that required much less of him.

His rectory was a fitting last refuge. Eldrith could die here, happily outfitted in the regalia of his office and surrounded by the extravagances to which he had entitled himself during his tenure. For all he knew, he might well be the last master of this Order. A legacy for which the noblest moment would most likely be the last, or so he now hoped. The best Eldrith could ask was to be remembered for his final sacrifice, not his final failing.

The tea was surprisingly mellow, though he had begun to wonder if he had made it too weak. The cup was more than half empty, and he noticed only a mild tingling in his toes. This was troubling. Too weak and he would linger overlong; too strong and the effects, though quick, would be excruciating.

No, Eldrith thought, *I measured the poison generously*. Likely it was his leisurely sipping that was prolonging the end. He gulped half the remaining contents of his cup and settled himself as comfortably as he could in his chair.

He loved this chair and all that it represented. To his own mind, he had been a fair and well-intentioned leader. Even his most foolhardy decision had been motivated by virtue, though it had been guided by arrogance, as Algernon had rightly called out to him.

The tingle in his feet had spread to his lower legs, rendering them useless. He swallowed the last of the tea while he still could and relaxed against the chair back. Soon the paralysis would spread up his body and seize his breathing, then his heart. Eldrith feared the violent convulsions that would overcome him in the final throes of death, imagining his last moments in pain. *Pray they are brief*, he thought, suddenly aware that while he could not move a single muscle below his waist, he could feel every nerve spasm like fire.

Footsteps echoed in the hall outside the door—too soon. Eldrith panicked. Just a little more time for the hemlock to take him so that Machreth could not tear the secrets from him he knew he was too weak to keep. He could feel the crippling heat creep higher, past his groin, to his gut.

The door flung open and Machreth strode over the threshold. Had Eldrith not been so keenly acquainted with the cold-blooded evil that resided beneath those tawny good looks, he might have mistaken Machreth for a nobleman of warmth and benevolence. He'd outfitted himself well in fine leathers and linen tunics confiscated from belongings left behind by members of the Brotherhood, and he kept himself impeccably groomed. The dark mage was tall and lithe and carried himself with the same arrogant charm that overlords possessed, the kind of charismatic confidence that drew support whether it was deserved or not. But his eyes inspired fear, if one dared to look directly into them.

"I hope I've timed this well," he said, smug and superior. He took the cup from Eldrith's palsied fingers and sniffed at the dregs. "You *can* still speak, yes?"

Eldrith was sure that he could, though not for long. It was becoming difficult to breathe. His lungs felt weighted down, and the pain from his limbs and innards writhing increased with every lumbering beat of his heart. Perhaps Machreth would believe he was too far gone. But how had he known?

"Water hemlock," Machreth said. He set the cup on the desk and bent close to sneer at Eldrith, who could no longer turn his head. "Effective, but slow, and more painful than people expect. Isn't that so, Eldrith?"

It was far worse than he had believed. The spasms were so violent, he thought his bones might break, and the burning was beyond unbearable. Eldrith silently begged the Gods for his heart to stop, but he would not speak to Machreth.

"You see," Machreth drawled, perching on the edge of the desk so that he could engage Eldrith comfortably, "it isn't a difficult death you should fear. Death itself isn't difficult at all, really—rather like expelling a breath. And in many cases, as I imagine you are contemplating this very moment, a welcome relief from a state of, well, frankly, misery."

Eldrith thought he had planned it all so carefully. Machreth was amusing himself, like a cat toying with a spider by plucking its legs out one by one. But it would be over soon. He could feel his life leaving.

Machreth smiled. "You're thinking you have beaten me to the endgame. I can see it in your eyes, that expectation of deliverance all men of faith cling to. It *is* near, Eldrith, your death. I can smell it."

He knew he was weeping, tears blinding him and spittle spilling from his mouth, but he could control none of it, not even his bowels. And yet, his heart was still pulsing and his lungs drawing air in shallow, rattling breaths—upon which the faintest of whimpers escaped. Terror filled Eldrith as Machreth's smile widened.

"You need only tell me what I want to know, and I will let the hemlock run its course. If not, I will hold you in this pendent wretchedness until one of us tires of the game."

Machreth waved one hand left to right, and Eldrith felt his existence suspended, no longer progressing toward death or ebbing away from it. He watched, horrified, as Machreth slowly curled his fingers into a clench. Eldrith's body responded as though it were being crushed. He shrieked.

"I knew you would find your voice."

Machreth spoke as though he were coaxing a mule to stable. He relaxed his hand, and Eldrith's agony eased, ever so slightly. Again he prayed for deliverance.

"I still do not understand your resistance, Eldrith. You hardly seem the sort of man to martyr himself for principle, but perhaps I have underestimated you." Machreth glanced around the rectory. "You are Ruagaire, after all—or at least you were before you contented yourself with the trappings of title and the belly-softening monotony of administration. 'Those who can no longer practice are consigned to preach,' or some such banality."

Machreth clenched his fist again, sending Eldrith to new depths of anguish. He felt his ribs splinter and cried out, but he did not ask for mercy. In this awful, bleak moment he knew triumph and honor. He had lost his way, but not his soul.

"You are stronger than I expected, Eldrith," Machreth said, releasing his grip. "But Trevanion lasted three days and still never spoke. I doubt the same shall be said for you."

"Why?" Eldrith gasped. If nothing else, he would die knowing.

"Ah," Machreth said, cocking one eyebrow in mild surprise. "Are you bargaining with your conscience now? Perhaps you are hoping my intentions are less despicable than you believe them to be."

Machreth pulled a cavalier shrug. "If knowing why I seek Elder Keep will help you see your way to submission, then so be it. All the better for both of us, if it puts an early end to this tediousness."

Breath came in labored pants and his mind was befuddled by pain, but Eldrith wanted to hear. He had convinced himself that knowing mattered, if only to make sense of all that had happened to him these last weeks. It was then that Eldrith realized he did not want to die.

"I must confess," Machreth began. "I had no knowledge of Elder Keep until Madoc began to plan his succession. When he named me his heir he began to reveal his secrets. Little by little as I gained his trust, and then as necessity forced his hand."

Machreth folded his arms loosely over his chest and crossed his legs at his ankles, as if he were having a casual conversation with a friend. "The Stewardry and the Well of Tears are inaccessible to me, at least for now. My only recourse is to keep the Fane from regaining its strength and its leadership until I can find a way to reclaim it or time snuffs it out altogether."

"You see,"—he looked pointedly at Eldrith—"I had thought to unite the mages in a new purpose, to make us powerful again by taking back that which was rightfully ours all along. But I have learned these last weeks, as I have traveled among plain folk, that there is no hope of that. The age of the sorcerer has all but passed. I see that now. But neither would Madoc's way have brought us to any better place. He was wrong to put his faith in the kings of men. They will no sooner share their power with mages than with each other. The prophecy was a lie all along."

He shrugged. "But there is still something to be salvaged in all of this, a legacy to build by other means. The future of magic is through the likes of me, sorcerers who will find their destiny in the world by sitting on their own seats of power. It is simple, really. If I cannot lead mages, then I will lead men. And I will do it from Elder Keep."

Eldrith was almost relieved. Perhaps Machreth did not know the whole truth of Elder Keep, all that it was. Still, if ever he found his way there, he would soon enough discover it.

"But I am weary of this." Machreth pulled straight and refocused his attention on Eldrith. A new determination shone in his eyes and his tone reverberated with intensity. "Where is the portal?"

The little hope Eldrith had held that his secrets would die with him, died first. And then his dignity, faith, and courage withered. Eldrith was left with only a few last shreds of honor to cling to, which gave him the strength to stay silent a few moments more. Even Machreth could not keep him alive forever.

"So be it."

Machreth held forth both hands for Eldrith to see, and then ever so slowly, curled his fingers inward. As his bones splintered and vessels burst, Eldrith knew he would fail. Before his organs imploded he would scream and beg, and in the end he would give Machreth what he wanted, just to end his suffering half a moment sooner.

TWENTY-THREE

Hywel's mood was as grim as the air was foul. His men had recovered the dismembered and gnawed corpses of four brave men, which accounted for the original Cad Nawdd complement and their commander. However, Cerrigwen's daughter Ffion was not among the dead. Nor was the sorceress she and Thorvald had been sent to retrieve.

The Cad Nawdd soldiers had hidden away their signature blue cloaks in order to travel unrecognized. Odwain had taken it upon himself to collect the cloaks and any personal trinkets from each of the men so that something of them could be returned to their families. Hywel had ordered a mass grave be dug and what was left of the bodies buried, though like the rest of his men, he would have preferred the traditional rite. Like it or not, Hywel dared not risk the smoke from the pyres giving their position away.

"There are at least four mounts still missing. And horse tracks leading into the trees on both sides of the road." Odwain tied the bag carrying the possessions he'd gathered to his saddle. His affect was sullen, but his disposition otherwise impassive.

Hywel thought of the demon warriors in blood-red armor and the giant man-eating mounts that Odwain had described. "What are the odds that these Hellion beasts and their creatures are still a threat?"

"We'd have seen them by now if they were still nearby. There are tracks along the road, but they are so over-trodden I can't be sure which are coming and which are going. My guess is that the Hellion gave chase if there were survivors, or returned to their lair. I would expect to find their trail in the woods," Odwain said. "Cerrigwen is anxious. She is asking when you will order a search of the forest."

"We've done all we can here," Hywel decided. It was time he conveyed his confidence. Odwain had earned it. "Take half the men and search the south side of the road. I'll take the rest north."

Odwain swung astride his horse and acknowledged the king's orders with a stiff tip of his chin as he sought to take his leave. "Brenin."

The formal gesture was a more subtle barb than Hywel had come to expect from this particular man, but the point was not lost on him. Though he hadn't said so, Odwain was offended by the previous night's test. A man of quality might even feel betrayed. This had not been his intent, and Hywel felt the need to make amends. "Wait."

Odwain turned his mount around and walked the horse back. "Is there something else?"

Hywel took pains to speak with sincerity. "I've met less than a handful of men who could have bested these woods the way you did."

"You flatter me, Brenin." Odwain bowed his head in a show of humility, but his expression was still flat, and his tone carried a hint of sarcasm.

Apparently the compliment was not enough to ease the tension between them. Hywel was annoyed. He was not in the habit of explaining himself, and there was only so far he would go by way of apology to any man. But he did not like to carry regrets.

"I underestimated you," Hywel offered. "I won't do so again."

The grim lines on Odwain's face softened, just a little, but it was enough for Hywel to consider himself forgiven. Odwain tipped his chin again, this time with more jaunt and less grit, and rode away to begin his search.

Hywel watched to see how his instructions were received. As he expected, his lieutenants complied without incident and split their leadership between the two parties. Cerrigwen rode with Odwain and his group into the woods south of the road, while the rest of the men searched the thickets nearby. Hywel decided to look on his own for the horse tracks Odwain had seen along the northern tree line.

In the frosted leafy mud he found impressions left by two distinct sets of hooves headed into the trees, one leading the other by two full strides. Evidence of life and maybe an attempt at escape, at least. Hywel dismounted, leading his horse so that he could better follow the tracks through the forest duff.

The black gelding had been his favorite since the day the horse was foaled. Hywel had named him Aeron, after one of the old Gods, and had spent countless hours grooming him for battle. He knew his horse as well as he knew any of his men, and trusted him more. Aeron had heart, and he was smart in ways that were not at all horse-like.

Hywel trailed the hoof prints for nearly half a furlong when they suddenly disappeared. The underbrush was thick here, but not so thick that it would so well hide a trail. Either the riders were close, or the White Woods was playing tricks. Hywel drew his sword.

If he were patient, and very still, anything that did not belong to the forest would soon reveal itself. He had long ago learned the sounds of the woods. Some were harmless and some were not, but they were all familiar to him. If something new were about, he would know it.

Hywel alerted to Aeron tugging gently at his bit—a tell sign that the gelding's senses detected something disturbing. Aeron's ears were tilted toward his near side. Whatever had raised the horse's attention was coming from the west but was still too far off for Hywel to hear.

Something much closer interested him more. Hywel had caught the sound twice now, but he had to concentrate to distinguish the soft, rhythmic whisper from the subtle rush of the air moving through the trees. He knew what the sound was and what made it, but not who or why it was still hiding.

"I can hear your breathing." Hywel let loose the reins and stared into a dense thicket of furze bushes a few feet to his right, watching for movement. "I mean no harm to you."

He did not expect a response, not right away. Whoever it was had good reason to be cautious. "We have come from the Stewardry, in search of Thorvald."

"No doubt you've found him by now. Or what's left of him." The mature, deep-throated baritone was steady but forced. "Who sent you?"

"We travel under the banner of Seisyllwg, on the king's business and as a favor to his friend Alwen, the Sovereign of Fane Gramarye. Show yourself." Hywel took a single step toward the thicket, fairly certain the man was injured. "Unless you are unable to do so."

"Stay where you are!"

Hywel took heed and stopped where he was. The man's bark was still strong enough to be threatening. If he were wounded, a true warrior would never let it be known, not until he was certain he was no longer in danger. Hywel did not want to provoke him, but neither did he intend to wait much longer.

"If you want my help, say so and I will gladly give it. Otherwise, I will leave you be. Make your choice, but make it quick. We have sorceresses to find."

Leaves rustled and the furze thicket shook. Hywel stood ready, on the off chance his intuition was wrong, and waited for the wounded man to present himself. He expected the elder and now only son of Aslak, whom Hywel thought he should recognize on sight by the build and strong chin known to mark the men of their clan. And if not, any officer of the Cad Nawdd would have Madoc's peculiar wizard signet sewn on his blue cloak.

But what appeared to him was not a wounded man. It was not a man at all, but rather a very small, very young but noble-looking woman with jet-black hair and milky skin—a princess in plain clothes. She held a long-bladed dagger like she knew how to use it, and there was not even the slightest glint of fear in her dark, defiant eyes.

"Was that a bewitchment," Hywel asked, wary, but intrigued, "or is someone else there with you?"

"Goram needs a physician, though he is too stubborn to admit it." Rather than step back, she took a squared stance between Hywel and the thicket, as though she were the protector. "But before I let you near him, you will tell me who you are."

"*I* will tell *you*?" Hywel's ego was pinched, but he was more amused than annoyed. It was a struggle not to smile at this tiny woman with such a bold nature. "Well, if those are your terms."

"They are."

"I am the king of Seisyllwg." He lowered his sword but did not sheath it. *Let the woman know the limits of her daring*, he thought. "And who, then, are you?"

When she started to answer, the deep-throated baritone cut her off. "Not another word until you are certain he is who he says he is."

Such a look of confoundedness came over her that Hywel felt a little sorry for her. She was young, and worried more for her friend than she was for herself. To be fair, Hywel had a good idea who the woman might be, but he risked as much as she.

"My name is Hywel," he said. "You may know me better as the heir to your prophecy."

As he spoke, Hywel was distracted by a thunderous rumble drawing closer so quickly that there was barely time to take cover, and none at all to outrun it. Aeron screamed and pawed at the dirt, and the young woman's eyes widened in terror. Whatever storm was about to overtake them, it was not falling from the heavens.

"How close are your men?" The man she called Goram lumbered to his feet and rounded the thicket with surprising speed and agility, sword in hand. His cloak was gone and his chain mail and leather armor were in shreds. There were at least three ugly gashes to his torso in dire need of dressing. And yet he made ready to fight. If this were not the son of Aslak, he should have been.

"Not close enough," Hywel admitted, wondering if they were besieged as well.

"Send your horse away. He is no match for what's coming," Goram said, taking position in front of the young woman. "The four-legged beasts that carry them have only one weakness—a soft gut. The heart is just below the gullet. Go low and strike hard there, but mind their toothy grins."

"And the demons themselves?" Hywel slapped Aeron hard on the haunches and watched to be sure the animal had gone a safe distance. "Have they a weakness?"

"None that I have found," Goram said, tossing a wry grimace in Hywel's direction. "Luckily, she has skills that I do not. Draw the beasts off and leave the demons to her."

Hywel flanked the soldier, a rush of tension-fueled blood pounding in his ears. He had barely balanced his weight when the forest in front of them seemed to explode.

A monstrous barrel-chested creature with a bulbous head burst through the trees, gnashing a grotesquely protruding jaw of jagged teeth the length of Hywel's forearm. The creature had staggering height and breadth—it was at least three times the size of Hywel's horse, taller and broader and hairier, and oddly boar-like with its hulking shoulders and thick neck. Its roar rattled his bones.

Atop it sat the demon warrior just as Odwain had described it, clad in gut-red metal that shielded it from head to foot and armed with a two-sided ax. The only part of it to be seen was its eyes, twin beams of fire piercing through a slit in its helmet.

Before Hywel could react, Goram struck first, a finely targeted stab into the mid joint of the beast's left foreleg. Using every last ounce of his strength, Goram forced the blade in until it snapped from the hilt. The animal reared wildly, tossing its head and shrieking in anger and agony, exposing its vulnerable underside.

"Quick," Goram hollered as the force of his blow toppled him into the brush. "Now!"

Hywel ducked under flailing forelegs and darted forward just before the beast's arch reached full crest. It was easy enough to spy the sweet spot, but not so easy to reach it. The beast was too tall. His best chance would come as the animal dropped, but his aim would have to be perfect and the strike full and forceful.

These were the virile, full-hearted moments in which he secretly reveled, when his soul felt afire with the power of holding destiny firmly in his own hands. It was these times when Hywel best knew his greatness, when survival hinged on instinct and cunning and brash decision. Even when the likeliest outcome was a gruesome and untimely death, it was in these moments he felt most alive.

A single, precisely timed lunge gave Hywel leverage to drive a swinging upthrust deep through fur and hide and flesh as the beast dropped back to its feet. He gripped the hilt with both hands, tucked his chin to his chest, and grounded his right knee so that he might withstand the force of the falling weight and stave the beast's breast in far enough that his blade would cleave its heart.

Hywel felt the bulk bow his shoulders as it hit, and the searing burn when his thighs tensed against the crush. He also felt the tear and snap of his blade rending muscle and flesh, and then the subtle rebound of denser tissue just before it imploded. His sword had found its mark.

The beast heaved before collapsing, giving Hywel time to roll out from under just before its massive lower jaw crashed to the ground right where he had been. He scrambled to his feet, alert to the danger that still remained, armed now with only his boot dagger.

"Step aside." The tiny sorceress spoke softly behind him. "Goram needs your help more than I do."

Hywel could not pull his eyes from the giant red fiend standing on the other side of the fallen beast. The demon presented with his battle-axe raised. Hywel yearned to answer the challenge, sword or no sword.

"Please," she insisted. "Move out of my way."

Reason urged him to do as she said, but Hywel actually obliged because he felt compelled by the sound of her voice. He recognized the effects of magic at work on his will, and though he was intrigued by the bizarre effect, he resented it. He was not so stubborn that he would refuse to take the wiser path, but in his own time and of his own volition.

How fortunate for him that the sorceress had not indulged him. The demon had already heaved his axe, sending it tumbling head over handle like a throwing knife, straight at Hywel's head.

As soon as the axe left the fire-eyed demon's hands it charged, bounding up and over the beast's carcass with terrifying ease.

Hywel sidestepped the whirling blade by a hair's breadth and instinctively spun around to engage the red fiend. The sorceress had already put herself in the demon's path, just as the axe head buried itself in the ground at her feet.

She raised her arms, palms facing forward. The demon came to a sudden stop a few feet beyond her reach, as if an invisible wall of stone had sprung up in front of him. He staggered backward a few paces, steadied himself, and let loose a furious howl.

"*Hrejka.*"

The sorceress uttered this one word, in the tongue of the Varangian people. It was a language Hywel recognized but had never learned. As he watched, the demon began to quiver. In agitation or maybe pain, he thought at first, from whatever hex the woman had thrown on him.

The quiver became violent, convulsive, as if something inside were tearing its way out. Suddenly, the demon disintegrated in a final combustive burst. And just as suddenly, the carcass of the giant beast shriveled, twisting in on itself until it was nothing but a steaming pile of innards and gnarled bone.

Hywel was impressed by the young woman and her mighty victory, but he was far more concerned that where there was one red fiend, there were likely to be more. He whistled for Aeron, and by the time he had reached the wounded warrior, the black gelding had returned. Hywel offered Goram his hand. "Can you ride?"

"Yes," Goram said, pulling to his feet with Hywel's help. "But give the horse to her. I will walk."

"You can try, but you will only slow us down." The tiny sorceress was brave and powerful, but also a little imperious. She turned to Hywel. "We'll need more horses and all of your men. The nobleman who led the demons down on us has taken the other woman in our party. We might still be able to find their trail."

"Under what banner did this nobleman march?" Hywel asked, dreading the answer.

Goram hauled himself onto Aeron's saddle, but he was clearly spent. "His flag was emblazoned with a yellow lion rampant on a field of scarlet."

Hywel muttered a foul curse. Clydog had sullied the colors of their house. Hywel had underestimated his brother's hubris. "No need to waste time hunting their trail. I know where they've gone."

"Do you know this man?"

"I do." Hywel took hold of Aeron's reins and leveled a kingly look on the young woman. "However, I still do not know you or your friend here."

"I am Goram, eldest son of Aslak, holder of the oath of the Crwn Cawr Protectorate," the soldier interceded, "and pledged to the service of Branwen, guardian of the Celestial Realm. This is her daughter."

"I am both my mother's legacy and the sole heir to my father's throne."

It seemed the tiny sorceress preferred to speak for herself. Hywel was yet even more impressed. He also appreciated the valuable alliances she represented. "By what name do you wish to be known?"

"Raven," she said, growing impatient. "My name is Raven. Now where is your camp?"

TWENTY-FOUR

Glain waited until Nerys had closed her chamber door, and then took the service stairs that led to the kitchen. Before she could rest, she needed to understand how nearly all of her friends had come to betray her. At the very least, Euday owed her an explanation.

Several apprentices assigned to the scullery were already preparing the morning meal. Glain skirted the kitchen altogether by way of a small passage leading to an alcove wherein was the entrance to the dungeon. The door had been chained for as long as Glain could remember. Now one guard was stationed at the top of the old stone staircase and another at the bottom.

The steps were steep and fractured from age and disuse, and the air dank. Glain questioned the wisdom of her decision as she descended into this place of lost souls, and then she remembered how much she had opened herself to Euday.

His was the first cell of what appeared to be many, stretching down a narrow dirt-floored corridor that disappeared into blackness. The light from two torches mounted in iron sconces at the bottom of the stairway barely reached the bars. Euday cowered in the darkest corner of his cage, as though he hoped the shadows could protect him.

"A fitting home for a traitor," Glain said. Bitterness thickened her tone and tinged her words dark and threatening. "A bereft place, a pitiless void—just like my heart."

Euday did not respond, which only angered her more. Glain took hold of the bars with both hands and rattled the gate, startling him enough that he scuttled even further into his corner.

"I know you hear me, you worm. Just tell me why, Euday, and I will leave you to wallow in your own filth, which is the best favor you will ever have from me again. Why would you forsake the Order? Why would you forsake *me*? Were we *never* friends?"

"How like Madoc you are," he said, as if it were an insult. "You are so convinced that you know best, that yours is the only way."

"And how is Machreth any different?" she argued. "He is every bit as self-righteous as Madoc ever was. But Madoc never chose a path based on his own gain. If he erred, he did so believing he was serving the greater good."

"And how is Machreth any different?" He mocked her with her own words. "His vision also serves a greater good, the good of the Stewardry. What care should we have for the world of men, when they have no care for us? Madoc would have us tie our fates to theirs. Machreth will free us from them."

"So he can subjugate us himself," Glain challenged. "How do you not see that?"

Euday lapsed into stubborn silence, and Glain regretted having come at all. She had been wrong to think having a reason would make the betrayals easier to accept. The hard truth was that none of them had ever truly been her friend—they had curried her favor and used her to further their attempts to aid Machreth. She had been duped, and there was no one to blame for that but herself. Nothing Euday said would make her feel better, and besides, it was Ynyr's explanation she really wanted and would never have.

"I was wrong before," Glain said, her anger abating in favor of mourning. "I do pity you, Euday."

"Save your pity for yourself," he scoffed. "I have made my choice."

"And you shall suffer for it, Euday." Glain sighed, truly sorry for him now. "In ways you haven't even begun to imagine."

Glain felt heavy with sorrow, so heavy her feet could hardly carry her back up the steps. Her entire body was convulsing with tiny rippling shudders, and the tears refused to be banished. Somehow she managed to keep herself upright and composed until she passed the sentry at the top of the dungeon stairs.

She made it as far as a corner of the alcove near the main corridor, just outside the view of the guard, before the emotions overwhelmed her attempts to contain them. Somehow she managed to maintain enough dignity to nod at the two apprentices she passed in the hallway on her way to the main stairs. Why hadn't she thought to go back up the service stairs?

By the time Glain reached the second-floor landing, she was so dizzy she could no longer see where she was going. She shoved open the scriptorium door and slipped inside, beyond grateful to find the room empty. Her instincts carried her as far as the nearest chair, and there she collapsed.

Glain muffled herself with the sleeve of her dress, determined not to let a single sob escape. She would be mortified to be discovered in such weakness, but neither could she continue to pretend to be valiant. It felt as if all the horror and fear and grief of the last few months had joined forces against her—just like her friends. She had no one.

Madoc had been taken, and then Rhys had gone, and now Alwen was in need of all the strength she had left. Glain could not bear it. No one could. It was too much to ask, all that she had been through, and yet the struggle seemed no closer to its end than it had months before. Madoc had spoken so devoutly of faith, especially when there was no more hope. But what had his faith gotten him? Betrayal after betrayal, and in the end an icy tomb, that's what.

Nothing Madoc had intended had come to pass, and if he could not succeed, how could she? Perhaps Madoc had been wrong all along. Perhaps fate meant for them to fail. It no longer mattered, one way or another. Glain no longer cared if Madoc's testament were ever found. She no longer wanted any part of his legacy. She had never been worthy of it anyway. How had he not realized it? Faith was worse than nothing when it was misplaced, and Glain knew this better than anyone.

* * *

Odwain had a difficult time of it, giving Goram and Raven the news from home. Thorvald had been sent to retrieve them long before the Fane had come under attack, long before Madoc had fallen. He avoided the more unpleasant events, especially those that hurt him most to recall, and he did not see the need to expose Cerrigwen to their judgment. Nor did either of them need to bear any more sorrow than they were already carrying.

Hywel waited for Odwain to finish giving his account and then gathered Cerrigwen and his lieutenants around them. Goram's wounds had been stitched and dressed, and he seemed to have had a restful night, but Hywel still made a point of accommodating his comfort. Hywel's less than subtle efforts to encourage the young sorceress to busy herself elsewhere, however, went unheeded. Raven insisted that she remain at her friend's side.

Odwain found the stalemate between Hywel and Raven amusing. He had observed now on several occasions that Hywel had a particular admiration for mages, one that held his ego and arrogance in check. Though he never actually deferred to them, he did respect them. And this particular mage seemed to have impressed Hywel more than most. And so it was that the young sorceress was permitted to stay.

"You say my brother has command of these Hellion soldiers?" Hywel was having difficulty digesting this. "They answer to him?"

"Blindly," Goram explained. His voice was strained from the pain, but he was no longer in danger of dying. "So much so that I am surprised we encountered that last one. Soon as the little prince got hold of what he had come for, the slaughter ended and the entire contingent left with him."

"Ffion," Cerrigwen said. She had been quiet these three days past, but an emotional tumult roiled just below the surface, threatening to test her restraint. She was fragile. "He came for her."

"Yes," Hywel said. "But he will not allow her to come to harm. She is too valuable to him. Ffion is the means to his end."

Odwain was only now beginning to piece together the underpinnings of the situation. "He intends to supplant you with her?"

"Not directly." Hywel took a moment to think his logic through. "My first guess is that he plans to use her to manipulate me into some sort of concession. But if Machreth is his benefactor, Clydog will owe him something in return. It could be that 'something' is Ffion."

Cerrigwen stiffened.

Hywel took pity and redirected the conversation, asking her about Goram's condition. "Can you make him ready to ride by midday?"

"I am ready to ride now," Goram insisted, forcing himself to sit up.

The young sorceress rose up on her knees for leverage and pushed him back flat with both hands placed squarely in the center of his chest. Either Raven was stronger than she looked, or Goram didn't have as much fight in him as he wanted everyone to think.

"Midday is soon enough," she said.

"Well?" Hywel looked to Cerrigwen. "We can't leave him here."

Whatever else he might think of Cerrigwen, Odwain had to admit she was a miraculous healer. She had done her best for Eirlys, when the black curse had curled its way through her veins and sucked her into a dark sleep. He had never believed Cerrigwen was the cause of it, as others had, but he would never truly trust her. Still, if any healing magic could help Goram, it was hers.

"No, nor could he stay even if he wanted to," she said, assessing the wounded man and the situation in her thoughts. "His only choice is to continue to Fane Gramarye. If he is anywhere near able, his first and only duty is to get Raven safely there."

Odwain reinforced her point. "We cannot risk losing another of the Guardians of the Realms."

"He will be ready," Cerrigwen said, pulling loose the healer's bag she kept tied to her belt. "It won't be a pleasant journey, but he will survive it."

Hywel's lieutenant tipped his chin toward Cerrigwen. "But can this sorceress fend off the demon army?"

Odwain wanted to laugh at the sheer naïveté of it. Whatever the younger sorceress had done, it could not compare to the power Cerrigwen could wield, even without the help of her amulet. "She is all the magic we need."

Cerrigwen offered the slightest of nods in Odwain's direction and then set to preparing her concoctions. He then spoke to Goram. "Have you had any word at all from your father? Aslak was dispatched weeks ago to intercept your party with news of the insurrection."

"He met us some miles inland, half a day after we landed on the shores of Mercia." Goram said. "He gave us the route we were to take to the Fane, before heading southeast to join some other warrior in search of the last guardian. The plan was to meet again along this path, before it joins the market road. It seems we got here first, as there has been no sign of him so far."

"It is not safe to wait," Hywel said. "Not without more men, and I can spare you none. Take your sorceress home, Goram, and report to Alwen all that has transpired here. We will press on toward Cwm Brith by way of the route you were to travel. And should we encounter Aslak along the way, I will recount to him what has happened."

Goram accepted this with the stoic suffering Odwain had come to admire in all of the men of the Cad Nawdd. One man's sacrifice was nothing when held against the loss the world would know should they fail to bring the guardians together. At least that was what Odwain told himself in the darkness of his own mind. So much loss and so little time taken for grieving were taking its toll on them all.

Hywel waved the conversation to the side so that Cerrigwen could focus her attention on Goram. "I want this camp struck and cleared before noon. We will follow this path as far as the trade road, to honor my word. But then we take to the woods again until we reach Cwm Brith. Tomorrow night should see us where we need to be."

"Will your plan still work," his lieutenant asked, "now that we've demons against us as well?"

Hywel shrugged. "Once we are inside the walls, all we need to do is find the girl and kill my brother. How hard can that be?"

There was a moment of sober silence while each of them calculated their chances. Odwain couldn't be sure who snorted first, but they all knew the whole idea was just shy of impossible. There was a chuckle, and then Hywel broke out in a whole-hearted guffaw. Soon they were all lost to laughter, but the relief was short. There were beds to bundle and horses to saddle. Come midday, nerves would be tight and tempers short as they rode the final miles to Cwm Brith.

* * *

"They feed on my livestock as if it were grain," the copper-headed youth muttered, staring out the tall windows in the dining hall at the hideous monsters and the disgusting beasts they rode. "I should advise you not to leave this lodge. They will devour you as soon as you set foot in the yard."

Ffion wasn't certain he wanted a response, not that he had seemed to notice her silence thus far. The man-child she had been brought before was tedious, and he liked the sound of his own voice. He frightened her—not because he himself was so intimidating, for he was not, but because of the dark forces he controlled. The creatures under his command had killed wantonly in order to get to her, and she had no doubt they would devour her just as he said.

He turned from the window to examine her again, as if he hadn't already looked her over more than once the last hour. "I wonder. Do you know who I am?"

"No," Ffion said plainly. She preferred to be direct, provided she could do so without revealing too much. "But I know where I am."

"You do?" He was surprised, for a moment. "Ah, well, of course you do. You were born at Cwm Brith."

Now Ffion was surprised. What did this person know of her birth? Perhaps she should know him, but she was sure that she did not. He was younger than she, by several years. Clearly he thought himself the master of this estate, which meant he must be kin to the man who owned it. He seemed to her merely a very brash boy with a great deal of power and very little experience, which was yet further reason to engage him cautiously. *Best to stay quiet*, she decided.

"You would know something of Cadell, then," the man-child continued. "Perhaps you even remember him."

Indeed she did know something of Cadell, enough to be wary wherever he was concerned. It was true that she had been born in his house and lived here with her mother for several years. She remembered the lord of Cwm Brith as a fearsome man, though he had been kind to her on the few occasions she had caught his attention. Anything else she knew came from her mother, which amounted to little more than vague warnings against ever crossing his path, and that he had fathered the king of the great prophecy. This redheaded lordling, however, could not be Hywel.

"He is dead now," the man-child continued. "Did you know?"

"Who are you?" Ffion's frustration erupted. She wriggled against the tie that bound her wrists again, only to regret it more than before. The leather bit even deeper into her skin. "Why have you brought me here?"

His mood was immediately altered by her outburst. The welcoming tone was now cold and harsh, and his expression no longer friendly. "Beware the mage tether. The more you struggle, the tighter it binds. And lest you have some other trick in mind, you should know it also prevents your magic from working."

Ffion panicked, though she was careful not to let it show. He had already taken her wand, and if she could not use her hands, she had no hope of escape. And how could he know what she was?

"I am Clydog," he said, "the youngest son of Cadell. My birthright has gone ignored far too long, first by my father and now by my brother. There are debts to settle, and you are here to ensure they are paid."

"What sort of nonsense is this?" Ffion's befuddlement must have shown, for she made no effort to conceal it. "What value could I possibly be to you or your brother?"

"You needn't trouble yourself with such worries—not just yet." Clydog merely smiled at her as though he thought her aggravation amusing. "Hywel will come, and when he does, you will understand."

"It is my mother who will come, not Hywel," Ffion said. "And when she does, you will wish you had never brought me here."

Clydog blanched ever so slightly, and Ffion was sure she saw his confidence waver. He was quick to recover his airs, but she sensed she had struck a weak spot. He was all too aware of who and what her mother was.

"Perhaps you know something of Cerrigwen," she said, mocking him with his own platitudes. "I assure you, however, that she is *not* dead."

Again he smiled, as if she were ignorant of some larger scheme. "Perhaps not, but I think it unlikely she will be coming for you anytime soon."

Lies, she knew. What he said made no sense. It was nothing but an attempt to unsettle her. Ffion reminded herself that silence was often wiser than words. It would gain her nothing to argue against him.

He frowned, as though he were gathering thoughts that were reluctant to come together. "But of course, you could not know of your mother's treason. You've only just returned to these lands."

Ffion realized he was taunting her, trying to weaken her by undermining the source of her strength. Her mother was no traitor.

"In fact," he mused, sauntering closer to her. "I wonder if you have even heard of the insurrection at Fane Gramarye."

More lies, Ffion told herself, but she refused to show him any reaction. Let him guess what she did or did not know and what she did or did not believe. Let this boy play his silly games.

He shrugged as though he thought the matter insignificant and turned away from her, this time to stare at the fire in the huge stone hearth at the head of his hall. "It would interest you to know, I suppose, that your mother came here, hoping for my father's protection. I offered her my hospitality, but she refused."

Clydog turned to look at her again. "When last she was seen, several days ago now, it was at the end of a mage hunter's leash. By now she is languishing in the dungeons at Fane Gramarye."

Ffion was finding it harder and harder to keep still. She had endured all the slander and insult she could stand, but she knew fighting it would gain her nothing. No wonder to her that Clydog's family had disowned or discounted him. He was a vile little brat full to the brim with a soppy mix of self-importance and entitlement. Still, she worried that even some small part of what he said could be true. No. Her mother would come.

Clydog waved to the soldier standing just outside the dining hall. "I think we've had enough chat for now. I am sorry to say Cwm Brith is no better equipped for a lady's comforts than it ever was, but your room is clean and private. This man will be standing outside your door, to see to your safety and your needs."

To keep her contained, more like, but Ffion gave a curt nod in a false-hearted show of courtesy and followed the soldier up the stairs to the living quarters. She was surprised how well she remembered the way. But then, Cwm Brith had been the first and only real home she had ever known.

TWENTY-FIVE

They had been standing at the edge of the forest for more than an hour, watching for movement. Thorne had been expecting to see the Hellion soldiers that Gavin and Eckhardt had described, coming or going from Banraven. So far, there had not been a single sign of them. No sign of anything else either, which worried him more with each passing moment.

"Banraven looks deserted," Gavin said. "Could be the dark mage and his legion have moved on."

"And left nothing alive," Eckhardt added.

"Could be." Thorne was not so sure. "Or could be a trap's been laid in case any of us were to come looking."

"But I'm not one of you," Rhys said. "Someone has to go. Why not me?"

"Won't Machreth know you?" Thorne asked. It was a good plan, at least in theory, but there were still risks. "It might be smarter to send Eckhardt or Gavin in your clothes. It's the Ruagaire cloak and the ring that give us away."

Rhys snorted and mounted his horse. "Is that what you think?"

Thorne looked askance at the brothers Steptoe. "Are we so obvious?"

"Yes," Rhys said. "I'll signal all's-well from the gate, unless I am unable. In which case," he grinned, "I will expect to be rescued."

Thorne returned the grin, meaning to be encouraging, but he had concerns. "If you pass through without signaling, we'll assume all is *not* well."

Rhys tipped his chin in salute and rode off across the small field that separated the White Woods from the grounds of Banraven. By the time he had reached the bridge over the moat, Thorne was uneasy. He mounted, expecting Gavin and Eckhardt to follow.

"Better to prepare for the worst than to hope for the best," he said, watching Rhys approach the gate.

"The gate is open," Eckhardt said, swinging astride. "Is that Algernon, Thorne? Your eyes are better than mine."

"It could be," he guessed. The man greeting Rhys was the same size and stature as the elder and had the same shuffling step. "Even if it is, there's no telling what's going on inside."

"At least there is someone still alive," said Gavin.

Thorne was glad of that, but he would be gladder to see Rhys give the signal. "What is he doing?"

Rhys had dismounted and had begun to lead his horse through the gate. Thorne cursed aloud and yanked hard on the rein to pull his horse out of the furze hedge he was munching. Gavin and Eckhardt responded instinctively to Thorne's movements, and just as all three men began their charge toward Banraven, Rhys turned to wave. Thorne cursed again and eased back on the reigns.

Gavin laughed. "Had you worried, did he?"

"Yes," he muttered. There was no point in denying it. "That boy is too brash for his own good."

"And you would know," Gavin pointed out. "Two of a kind, you and him, and don't pretend you don't see it."

"I see it," Thorne muttered again. "That's what worries me."

"He was made for this life, Thorne," Gavin said. "And don't pretend you don't see that either."

Thorne reminded himself to offer gratitude for his friends. He felt it, always, but neglected to show it as he should. Martin's death would haunt him all the more because he had not treated their last parting as though there would never be another one. A mistake he would not repeat.

Elder Algernon awaited them all in the courtyard. Two bedraggled boys took the horses to stable, and a third, carrying a bucket and ladle, stepped forward to offer the riders water.

Eckhardt grinned at the boy and took the ladle. "So you've survived after all."

Thorne supposed this was Algernon's messenger, the boy called Gelf. Eckhardt seemed genuinely pleased to see him. Clearly this Gelf had made a lasting impression on the hunter, and Thorne took note. Perhaps Eckhardt had found his own apprentice. At least Thorne hoped so; the survival of the Brotherhood weighed heavily on all three of them.

Rhys was circling the small ingress, as if to get his bearings.

"Banraven is a circular keep," Thorne offered, thinking Rhys might not be familiar with the design. "Through that door is a corridor lined with living quarters and service rooms that goes all the way around, beginning and ending in the same place. There is an interior courtyard, a sort of garden, in the center of it all.

"Curious," Rhys said. "Is it always so quiet?"

Thorne and the Brothers Steptoe turned to Algernon, who had yet to say anything. The old man was more haggard than Thorne had ever seen him. But there was no mage sign, and the keep did feel deserted.

"Is it safe to speak here, Algernon?" Thorne was weighing the wisdom of trusting anyone found in Banraven, even Algernon. "The last time I was here, you nearly led me to my doom."

Algernon bristled. "It was me who got you out of trouble in the end."

Thorne held his tongue, thinking instead that Algernon could have easily warned him away from the keep instead of inviting him in that night. One day he would have the whole story, but for now, he would wait.

"Where *is* Eldrith?" Gavin demanded, his distaste for the master unfiltered by his tone.

"I suppose I should show you the rectory," Algernon said, pointing through the main entrance. He led the way across the foyer and through the central garden, to the doors on the far side of the circle nearest the rectory. He moved much more quickly than Thorne recalled from their last meeting.

Algernon stopped just outside the rectory and cleared his throat. "Eldrith is dead. You'll find his body in there. Haven't had the time or the inclination to clean up after him yet. Take a look so you can see for yourselves what that dark mage is capable of, and then you'd best be on your way. Eldrith didn't have Trevanion's strength, not that any of us thought he did, but what matters to you is that Machreth is already on his way to Elder Keep. Left just more than an hour ago with that bestiary he calls his personal retinue."

Algernon stepped aside and scowled at them all. "Well, go on. Have your look."

One by one, each of the Ruagaire took a turn at the door and offered a blessing for Eldrith's soul. Rhys did not look, though Thorne knew the young man had seen Machreth's handiwork before. It was unpleasant, Eldrith's broken corpse, and Thorne could not begin to imagine what Martin must have suffered. Best that Rhys not look, especially not now. There were more pressing worries.

"What does Machreth want with Elder Keep?" Thorne turned back the way they'd come, eager to leave.

Algernon scampered to keep up with him. "It was difficult to hear everything through the false wall."

"But you heard enough," said Thorne. He'd almost forgotten how skilled Algernon was at eavesdropping, but this was the first he'd ever heard of a false wall in the rectory. He imagined Eldrith had never known.

"Well," Algernon huffed, trying to catch his breath, "it seems he intends to make Elder Keep the seat of his enterprise and use its resources to bolster his strength. He made some lofty comment about ruling the world of men if he couldn't rule the world of mages, or some such foolery."

Thorne slowed his pace so as not to tax Algernon so much he couldn't walk and talk. "Do you think he knows what Elder Keep hides?"

"I suspect that *he* suspects," Algernon admitted, dragging his feet to a stop once they reached the outer courtyard. "No way to tell what all he knows, but Drydwen will need your help."

"Algernon," Thorne asked carefully, "where are the others?"

Algernon sighed. "Of the six elders who were alive when Machreth came here, there are three left, including myself. They are hiding in the sanctum—in prayer, they say. In fear, I say, but I intend to join them as soon as you leave. Aside from the three of us, there are a handful of servants still scrounging about. The three of you are all that remain of the hunters."

Gavin made an unintelligible noise that Thorne took for a cross between anger and anguish. He felt the same. He also had qualms about the details, including how it was that some survived and some did not. Algernon had not told everything he knew, but for now Thorne was far more concerned about Drydwen.

Eckhardt and Rhys retrieved the horses while one of the stable boys threw open the gate. All four mounts had fresh provisions tied to their saddles, and Thorne threw Algernon a nod of thanks as he hauled himself up.

Gavin was already astride, thinking just what Thorne was thinking. "If he has only an hour or so lead, we can still get there ahead of him."

"If we ride hard," Thorne said, spurring his horse to a gallop before his backside had fully settled into the saddle.

* * *

They had made better time than Hywel had expected, even with the hour lost at the crossroads where they'd encountered the Cad Nawdd captain, Aslak, and Alwen's barbarian mate, Bledig, who traveled with one of his tribesmen. Their travels had been unsuccessful; every inquiry in Ausoria had failed to turn up any sign of Tanwen, the guardian of the Physical Realm. She had never arrived in the small village that was to have been her refuge. The need to deliver this dire news, coupled with Thorvald's death, had made Aslak anxious to be on his way, but Odwain had insisted that the Wolf King and his companion join the raiding party.

The request irked Hywel, at first. Had he not owed Odwain a debt of respect, he would have dismissed the request without half a thought. In the end he had agreed, in no small part due to Odwain's accounts of Bledig's daring exploits against the Hellion in the battle for the Fane. Alwen's barbarian was sure to be an asset at Cwm Brith, and possibly another valuable ally in the campaigns ahead. To learn something of this renowned warrior on his own, Hywel invited Bledig to ride beside him for the rest of the day.

"By now Aslak will have caught up to Goram and his charge," Hywel said, attempting to coax a conversation. Bledig was a contemplative sort, not unlike Odwain, though the Wolf King was decidedly less brooding. "I'm surprised you were not as eager to return to Fane Gramarye to deliver your news to Alwen personally."

A sly smile tugged at the corners of Bledig's mouth. "Oh, I'm more than eager, but Odwain seems to think I'll be of use on this raid of yours, and I'd much rather go back with something to brag about."

"I haven't much stomach for failure either. It leaves a sour taste." Hywel understood that Bledig counted his return without the sorceress as a defeat. "Your friend, is he as good a swordsman as you?"

"Domagoj?" Bledig grinned and glanced over his shoulder at his companion, who rode with Odwain, a few horse lengths behind them. "Some might say better, but not to my face."

Some might have dismissed such talk as bluster, but Hywel interpreted it as candor. "He was with you, then, in the battle against the Hellion and their beasts?"

"Saved my life," Bledig said. "More than once."

Hywel was impressed, even a little relieved. "Then we are lucky to have you both with us."

"It takes two men, at least, to bring one of the mounts down," Bledig offered, as though he were testing Hywel's knowledge and experience.

"The Hellion demons are easier to kill, big and slow as they are," Hywel smiled, "though I admit it helps to have a sorceress on your side."

Bledig laughed. "It always helps to have a sorceress on your side."

They passed the rest of the afternoon in comfortable silence, though Hywel grew more and more expectant the closer they came to Cwm Brith. They reached the small woods that abutted the estate long enough before dark for Hywel to send out a scout team to assess their approach and any unexpected resistance.

It seemed that the battle with the Cad Nawdd guard had cost the enemy just as much, as only a handful of Hellion soldiers and their evil beasts stood between them and the main house. With Bledig's experience and Cerrigwen's magic, they stood a fair chance. Hywel was feeling almost as much confidence as he did dread. It would still be an ugly battle.

Hywel watched as Cerrigwen walked toward him. It had taken her nearly an hour to approach him. He'd been told that she suffered from some sort of madness, which he expected would make her restless and unpredictable, but Hywel had noticed her hemming and hawing ever since they'd arrived in the small forest. He was wary, yet also curious, and determined to be kind. This sorceress had not only known his father, she had borne him a child.

"I have been watching you, Hywel," Cerrigwen said. "Clydog will never be half the man you are."

"You would know better than I," Hywel admitted. Her comment felt like flattery, but it seemed sincere. "It is years since I've spent any time in his company."

Cerrigwen drew close enough to speak privately. "Your father made him what he is."

"My father made me what I am," he countered, "but Clydog and I are nothing alike."

Cerrigwen cast a doubting look at him. "You are more alike than you think, but not in the ways by which a man is measured. You are bold, resourceful, and wise because your father ensured that you would be. Cadell doted on you. Clydog is desperate, uncertain, and reckless because Cadell ignored him. Remember that."

Hywel knew there was truth to what she said. Cadell had been a harsh man, and Hywel couldn't help but wonder how his father had made Cerrigwen who she was. "Why do you tell me this?"

"Great men become great in moments of unconquerable crisis, in the face of impossible decisions," she explained. "It is their actions in these moments that determine how they will be remembered."

Hywel was reminded of Glain and her dreams. She had offered him similar counsel. "I will do what must be done."

"I trust that you will," Cerrigwen said plainly. "All that matters to me is my daughter. There is nothing I will not do to save her."

Hywel respected her honesty, and he understood the warning in it. He was also starting to wonder which of them Clydog should fear most—Hywel or Cerrigwen.

* * *

Glain sat bolt upright, confused and shaking. It took several seconds to realize she had awakened in the scriptorium. The dream was still vivid, invasive, making it difficult to focus on her surroundings. And the horrible, heart-rending sadness was worse than before. Sleep had brought her no relief, none at all.

The dream had changed, but not how she had hoped it would. In the new vision, the first stag arose enraged and bested the second, overpowering his brother buck and crushing him beneath his fierce, thrashing hooves. Glain took this to mean that when faced with a final choice, Hywel would make the most ruthless one. Not that he would be wrong to do so, but she feared he still did not fully understand the consequences, or the lost opportunity.

Tears of hopelessness filled her eyes, but Glain forced them back. She noticed the air was warm around her, but her bones were still cold. The fire was fresh. And there was honey cake and tea, long gone cold. An attendant had been in the room while she slept—however long that had been.

Glain ate the cake and sipped the cold tea, knowing it had been hours, if not days, since she'd last eaten. If she had any memory of her last meal, she was unable to recall it. Alwen had cautioned against wasting time, and here she was still in a damp, dirty dress she'd been wearing for the past two days.

Glain dragged herself to her feet and forced them to carry her onward, dreading the inevitable encounters in the hallways and on the stairs. If only she had gone back to her room earlier. At first glance from the doorway, it seemed she had been granted a little luck.

There was but a single soul standing in the second-floor hallway. The wounded soldier, Pedr, appeared to be testing his strength. His back was turned to her. If she were quick, she could cross the hall to the stairs before he noticed. The last thing Glain wanted was to be forced into polite conversation.

And then it occurred to her that although polite conversation was not appealing to her, it might well benefit Pedr. She was the Proctor of the Stewardry, the mistress of the house. It was her duty to see to his comforts, even if doing so undermined hers.

"Well met, Pedr," she called out. "It is good to see you up and about."

He turned and walked toward her, more steady on his feet than most men would have been in a similar state. His arm was supported by a sling, to keep it immobilized so there would be no pulling on the half-healed injury to his shoulder, but Pedr was obviously much improved. He seemed taller and broader than when she'd last seen him. This time his color was healthy, but his expression was still grim. He did, however, seem pleased to see her.

"Did you find the tea and cakes?" Pedr asked.

"Yes," she said, surprised and a little embarrassed. "Thank you."

"The attendant did the work," he deferred. "I merely made a suggestion."

Glain suddenly felt unbearably self-conscious. "I was just on my way to change my dress."

Pedr brushed aside her concern about her appearance. "I don't see how you could have got half the sleep you need, especially in that chair, but some is better than none. You must remember to keep up your strength."

Glain could only nod in response, for fear her voice would fail and embarrass her all the more. Twice now this man she barely knew had offered her the most unexpected and perfectly timed kindness. She couldn't begin to think how she deserved such gestures, but she was grateful.

The slightest smile lifted Pedr's lips as he turned to leave. "I'll leave you to your business then. Ilan has made me promise to walk the length of this hall at least a dozen times, and I'm only halfway through."

She waited for him to be on his way before making a quick escape up the stairs. If she had been in her right mind, Glain might have been flattered. As it was, she was all the more confused and uncertain. She would feel clear-headed and purposeful with a fresh dress and her familiar white robe.

By the time she reached her room, Glain was desperate to feel clean. The sensation of a million spy-eyed spiders still lingered on her skin. She tore off her clothes and looked for water to wash on the dressing table under the window. The pitcher was full and the water cold, but that didn't matter. She sluiced it over herself and began washing. And then she saw it.

Every inch of her froze. From the corner of her eye she caught a glimpse of parchment resting on the ritual altar against the wall to her right. Glain was afraid to look, but she already knew what it was.

Naked and still dripping with wash water, Glain turned to face the altar, disbelieving her own eyes. Carefully placed between a candlestick and the silver bowl she used for divining was the missing scroll. Madoc's wax signet was unmistakable. The seal was still attached, though the parchment had obviously been opened.

Glain felt both elation and angst, which caused a sickening lurch deep in her stomach. How had the scroll come to be here, and when? She tried to remember the last time she had been in this chamber. On the day Ynyr had been found dead, that morning she had slept on her bed. But was that yesterday or the day before? She no longer knew.

A shiver forced her to cover herself, but she dared not take her eyes from the parchment as she dressed. Even as she outfitted herself with her wand sheath and the acolyte's white robe, she stared at it, debating whether she could stand to touch it.

Glain was not happy to have discovered the scroll. She had been honest with herself that very morning when she had hoped it would never be found. She had renounced all that it represented. But how could she deny it now, with the dreaded thing sitting within her reach?

She could destroy it. No one would ever know. The person who had left it for her would never speak up for fear of being found out. Even if someone were to accuse her, all she need do was deny it. Glain would be believed.

With a snap of her fingers and a whisper, the candlestick on her altar was lit. After a sputter of spark and old wax, the flame grew strong and steady. Glain picked up the scroll at one end and held the other end over the flame.

The smell of singeing velum tickled her nostrils, and the smoldering ink dust stung her eyes. When the roll end finally caught fire, she sobbed aloud with relief. It was so simple. The only proof of her secret would be ash in a matter of moments.

With no living relations to attest to the fact, no one ever need know of Madoc's grandniece. The truth of her birth would stay safely hidden, and Glain would never be expected to accept rule of the Stewardry. The Primideach dynasty would end with Madoc's legacy unless she came forward to assert her claim on his throne. This, Glain had promised herself, she would never, ever do.

But she would. How could she not? Glain snatched back the scroll and smothered the burning edge with her sleeve. There was no escaping who she was and what she was born to become, no more than Alwen could make herself into something she was never meant to be.

TWENTY-SIX

Every time he rode toward Elder Keep, Thorne experienced an emotional assault. Anticipation lifted his spirits and strangled them at the same time, suspending him in a state of bliss and misery. In this way, coming here was far worse than leaving, because as soon as he arrived, he was forced to begin counting the hours until he would have to go.

This time Thorne also felt fear for Drydwen's safety, which was a new torment. He always worried, but not so much that he was tempted to abandon his duties. He would, for her. But there was little in this world that could threaten the prioress and survive her retribution, especially with the power of the temple surrounding her. She had never needed his protection, not really, and even now Thorne was not entirely sure there was anything he could do. But at least he would be there, and by all odds, well ahead of Machreth.

Eldrith had known only the one documented route to Elder Keep. Thorne and the Brothers Steptoe had discovered many others in their years patrolling the White Woods, some of them shorter and quicker. No one knew these woods better.

Thorne felt Eckhardt studying him with concern, which annoyed him almost as much as it honored him. He wanted to pretend he was unaffected by his fears, but that was a lie Eckhardt would never believe. "Stop worrying, Brother."

Eckhardt snorted, as if to say Thorne's comment was useless, and then tossed his chin in Gavin's direction. The other Steptoe had finally taken to Rhys and was giving him something akin to a history lesson as they approached. There was little known of the origins of the crypt, and what was known was as much lore as it was fact.

Elder Keep was believed to be the oldest structure in the enchanted forest. Carefully orchestrated deceits had helped it survive the Romans and the fall of the old ways. Time had eventually erased its existence from the memories of those who would destroy or pervert it.

The Ruagaire believed the sanctuary had been built by the Ancients themselves, who had entered the world of men through the portal concealed within it. Elder Keep was the first of the sacred sites and the origin of the five bloodlines that had founded mageborn societies. Thorne was a bit of a skeptic when it came to most of the legends he'd been taught during his training, but he believed everything he'd been told about Elder Keep. He had stood before the portal and felt the convergence of the realms. There was no more powerful place.

To the unknowing eye, the keep appeared to be little more than the ruins of a long abandoned manor house. The moss-covered stone ramparts were nearly indiscernible from the natural backdrop, which helped avoid accidental discovery and discourage the curious. But behind its walls was a small and thriving community of mageborn refugees subject to the prioress and dedicated to the preservation of an ancient shrine.

When they reached the tiny clearing at the face of the keep, it was near dusk. Rhys was concerned. "There is no light. Are you sure there's anyone inside?"

"We're in time," Eckhardt said with a heavy sigh of relief. "No mage sign out here, not yet."

Thorne smiled to himself. No mage sign that anyone else would sense. He could feel Drydwen long before he could see her. She was already waiting behind the doors at the top of the temple steps.

Eckhardt and Gavin reined up and indicated Rhys should do the same.

"Give him a minute," Gavin said.

Thorne had already dismounted and was no longer listening to anything but his own needs. By the time his foot reached the first step, the doors were thrown open and she was there. The flame-haired goddess who haunted his dreams and the only woman he would ever love.

What Thorne felt was rarely aligned with how he behaved. His training compounded his nature, which enabled him to remain tightly controlled at all times. This was the most comfortable state of being for him, and the reason Thorne was so good at what he did. But Drydwen had the power to undo him with a smile.

Thorne stopped dead at the threshold of the steps, partly because his sense of propriety told him to and partly because he needed a moment to steady himself. He was always surprised at how much the sight of her affected him, how desperately he missed her.

"No harm has come to my house, Thorne. Not yet," Drydwen said, bemusement softening her mouth. "You can breathe easy now."

There was no force in all the realms that could have kept him from her. Drydwen was in his arms before he even realized he was reaching for her. She overwhelmed him with her unique essence—the heather-honey scent and the wine-red hues of her hair and her lips, and the soft warmth of her skin. The aching was agony, but the joy was sweet. If a woman's kiss could cure a man's ills, hers was all the healing magic he would ever need.

"Thorne." There was urgency in Gavin's voice. "Your mutt is here."

Drydwen pulled away. "I'll have your horses brought inside and see that the others are well hidden. I will wait for you in the crypt, Thorne. Find me there when you're through."

She managed to make him smile despite his doubts. Thorne looked for Maelgwn. The warghound's hackles were high and his teeth were bared. He remembered the dark mage's scent. Machreth was coming.

"Get the bags before they take the horses, and bring them up here," Thorne called to Rhys.

Attendants appeared as if from nowhere and led the horses to a hidden entrance behind the structure. Drydwen was already gone to the crypt to protect the portal. She would allow no living soul to pass through it, in or out. And he would allow no one to get that far.

Gavin and Eckhardt retrieved the saddle sacks and joined Rhys at the top of the temple steps. The mage hunters armed themselves with sword and knife and septacle and mage tether, and then retreated behind the temple doors. The first room was a foyer, in ruins, and a crumbled back wall that revealed the old courtyard and shrine. This was a ruse to deter anyone from noticing the opening at the right side of the foyer. Through this doorway was a short, narrow corridor and stairs that led into the true temple and the crypt that housed the portal.

"What is your plan?" Rhys asked.

"We'll make our stand here, out of sight," Thorne explained. "Let Machreth think he was the first to arrive. With luck, he'll leave his Hellion escort behind and investigate on his own. When he comes in here, for a moment or two he'll wonder if he's in the wrong place. At first glance all he will see is ruins, and he'll think the place abandoned. That's when we'll strike."

It was their only hope, really, to catch him off guard. If Machreth were to have even a moment to react, he could easily destroy them all. Mage hunters were resistant to the effects of magic, but not immune. And Machreth was the most powerful sorcerer Thorne had ever confronted.

Rhys was ready and willing. "Where do you want me?"

This stopped Thorne dead in his tracks. Rhys was in no way prepared for this. He would be less than useless on the first line of defense, and likely to give them all away. Thorne and the Brothers Steptoe were trained to deflect a mage's keen senses. Rhys, talented though he might be, was not. Thorne's faith in the boy was strong, but so was his need to protect him.

Thorne pointed to the corridor. "I need you to hold the ground between me and Drydwen. That leads to a stairwell. At the bottom you'll see the double doors that open to the crypt. Take your position there. Drydwen will spend her last breath protecting the portal to the fifth realm. If Machreth passes the three of us, he must not get to her."

Rhys accepted his orders and left to prepare his defense, and Thorne began planning contingencies in his head. He was not so arrogant as to think himself capable of controlling every outcome, but he was confident enough to know he was likely to get the best of most of them. It helped to consider every conceivable situation, which was how he prepared himself for battle.

Gavin and Eckhardt had secured themselves behind rubble on either side of the foyer that concealed them from view without obscuring their own line of sight. Thorne took cover behind the collapsed wall that revealed the courtyard.

Thorne looped the chain attached to his septacle around his right wrist and cradled it in his palm. The spell catcher was their only defensive weapon against a sorcerer like Machreth. It was also the only tool they had to diffuse the sorcerer's power long enough to subdue him with mage tether. This could best be done by a combination of distraction, speed, and brute force. Like hobbling a wild boar, but far more dangerous.

At the right moment, Thorne would draw Machreth out. When magic was unleashed against him, he would manipulate the spell catcher and capture the energy in one of the seven chambers. The septacle worked like a shield, except that it absorbed the blow instead of deflecting it. When the opportunity presented, Gavin and Eckhardt would move in to overpower Machreth, and Thorne would bind him.

"I can feel them," Gavin whispered.

Thorne gave a nod to signal he could as well. The mage sign was so strong that it was already uncomfortable. He concentrated on assessing what was approaching. Large mounts with riders, four or maybe five, and a normal-sized horse bearing one person. Machreth's traveling party was small, but fierce. Now to wait and see whether Machreth would come in alone.

The riders gathered in front of the temple and then split up. At least four mounts headed off by pairs in different directions. Scouts. Thorne was not particularly concerned that they would find the other entrance to Elder Keep, though it was possible. For now, he needed to trust in his plan and his friends.

A single set of boot steps on the temple stairs—a good sign. Thorne glanced to his right, at Gavin, and to Eckhardt on his left. Both men were ready.

Machreth paused at the top of the stairs and then pushed the door inward, slowly. Thorne thought it interesting that the dark mage dressed all in black, like the Ruagaire who hunted him. He was cautious too, taking his time to assess the foyer before entering. Only then did Thorne consider that upon seeing the ruins, Machreth might not bother to enter at all.

He nearly panicked for nothing, as in his own good time Machreth did indeed come inside. Thorne assumed the sorcerer to be as well informed and intelligent as he was ambitious and powerful. Plan for the worst and then hope for the best, as Thorne always said. Machreth would anticipate ruses and camouflage.

Timing was everything. And once the fight began, it would be fast and furious and swift to whatever end the fates decided. Thorne tensed, preparing to draw Machreth's attention.

Machreth noticed the opening to his right almost immediately and rather than moving into the room as Thorne had expected, he headed straight toward the passage. Eckhardt had already anticipated the changing strategy and stepped between Machreth and the stairwell, fully armed for engagement.

"Hah!" Machreth shouted as he stopped short, but not in surprise. "I wondered how long you would wait to reveal yourself."

Thorne cursed himself under his breath. Whether the black mage had sensed them or had merely anticipated a defense of some kind, the brethren had overestimated the element of surprise.

"You've come far enough," Eckhardt threatened. "Stay where you are."

Machreth laughed. "Or what, mage hunter? *You* will stop me?"

Thorne tensed, but it was crucial that neither he nor Gavin react too soon. Only Eckhardt was exposed, and it was possible that Machreth did not know their full number or their positions. If they were to have any chance, they would need to wait for Eckhardt to engage the sorcerer, but he was vulnerable in the open on his own.

Machreth barely hesitated. The sorcerer drew his weapon with a sweeping motion that was as fluid and elegant as a fencer's lunge. His assault was swift, sure-minded, and deadly. Eckhardt caught the first wand strike easily enough, capturing the burst of magic in his septacle. But the force of it staggered him, and he was unable to recover fast enough to block the second. Eckhardt's natural immunity saved him from death, but the spell energy seared his side open like the slice of a hot blade.

Thorne and Gavin were already in motion before Eckhardt collapsed. Thorne reached the mage first and grabbed for his hands, hoping to break or snatch the wand before Machreth could use it against them. The other immediate danger was from a cursing gesture, which Thorne hoped to avoid by binding Machreth.

"Gavin!" Thorne had a good grip on Machreth's right wrist, but the sorcerer still had control of the wand. Thorne could hear Machreth muttering something in the old language under his breath. "Mage tether, quickly."

Gavin charged from the opposite side, knocking the sorcerer off balance, but not enough to give Thorne the leverage he needed. Machreth was quick, lithe, and unexpectedly strong. The three of them grappled furiously for several long minutes while Gavin tried to force the slip loop he'd tied in one end of the mage tether onto Machreth's free wrist.

"I've almost got the bind on him!" Gavin cried. "Don't let him loose now."

Machreth howled and thrashed. Thorne threw his elbow into Machreth's chin twice, and then once to his nose, but still could not yank the wand from his grip. Finally, Thorne managed to pry back two fingers, which weakened Machreth's hold just enough for Thorne to knock the weapon loose.

The wand clattered against the broken stone floor. The distraction gave Gavin the opportunity he needed to force the tether over Machreth's left hand and cinch it tight around the wrist. Thorne worked to pull Machreth's right arm back so that Gavin could bind both hands behind him. But the sorcerer had a will of iron and strength to match; he would not be subdued.

An unexpected and painful jolt to the gut caught Thorne by surprise. Machreth's well-placed knee thrust cost Thorne his breath and his balance, long enough for the sorcerer to gain sure footing and a solid stance. Before Thorne could recover and redouble his grasp, Machreth escaped and dove for the floor.

"Thorne!" Gavin shouted, planting his feet and throwing his weight back in an attempt to pull Machreth up short. He still had the loose end of the mage tether in his hands, but not for long. "The wand!"

Thorne reached out blindly, caught a fistful of black wool, and hauled on Machreth's cape with everything he had. He felt resistance, at first, and then the fabric tore. The black mage was free, and before Thorne could overtake him again, Machreth hit the floor and curled, scooping up the wand and tearing the leather cord from Gavin's gasp as he rolled back to his feet.

"The mighty Ruagaire Brethren," Machreth gloated. He stood between the mage hunters and the opening to the stairwell, armed once again with his wand, seething with rage and smug in his apparent triumph. "It is difficult to kill your kind, but I have discovered that it can be done."

Thorne was reminded of Martin Trevanion, his thoughts conjuring visions of the many horrors he imagined his mentor had endured. He felt for the septacle he had chained to his own wrist and sidled slightly to his right, hoping he could shield the wounded Eckhardt who lay motionless on the floor nearby. "If you intend to try, give us your best."

For a few moments, Machreth regarded Thorne with something akin to bemusement. Then his lips began to move as though he were whispering to himself. Thorne's heart began to race and the nape of his neck stung like skin split open by the lash of a dungeon whip. He cupped the septacle in his palm and silently begged whatever Gods might hear him for grace.

The air around them hummed. Thorne could feel the vibration and the quickening heat it created. Machreth raised his hands, his wand directed overhead, and the walls began to shake. It wouldn't take much more for the stone ruins to crumble. Machreth meant to bury them.

Thorne looked to Gavin to see if his friend had the same thought and noticed the angle of his gaze. Following Gavin's line of sight, Thorne saw what Gavin had seen—the mage tether was still cinched around Machreth's wrist. So long as he held his wand, the sorcerer could not remove it. And so long as it remained, Machreth's power would be slightly weakened by the binding hex that was embedded in the tether. This was the best opportunity they would have to take him.

On faith and instinct, Thorne lunged. By the time his thoughts caught up with his impulse, he had already made contact. The charge sent Machreth staggering backward, and then Thorne could have sworn he saw lightning strike just before he felt the floor falling away. He had taken them both over the threshold and tumbling down the steps to the crypt.

Thorne careened into the stairwell wall halfway down and thudded to a stop on his knees, a few steps from the bottom. Machreth had landed in a sprawl on the antechamber floor below and was already on his feet by the time Thorne could haul himself to a stand. But Machreth was no longer concerned with Thorne. He had found the crypt.

A half-dozen thoughts flashed through Thorne's mind in the same instant. The lightning strike had been Machreth's spell energy being dispersed, and the Brothers Steptoe had surely borne the brunt of it. It was likely they were trapped or injured, and in either case unlikely to come to his aid in time. The only thing standing between Machreth and the portal was Drydwen, and the only thing standing between Machreth and Drydwen was Rhys.

Again Thorne reacted on impulse. He sprang from the steps and spun around Machreth, blocking his path to the chamber doors. Machreth smiled and with a swipe of his wand, tossed Thorne like a feather on the wind, slamming him against the solid oak planks hard enough to break the hinges and cave the doors in.

Thorne was winded and his vision blurred. He was vaguely aware of a stabbing pain in his left shoulder and of Machreth stepping past him. He tried, but Thorne could not move. He was unable to keep the sorcerer from entering the chamber.

"Well," he heard Machreth say. "If it isn't Alwen's man-child."

Thorne sickened at Machreth's satisfied tone. As fierce and determined as Rhys might be, he was nothing but a momentary irritation to the black mage. Thorne fought through the haze in his head and forced himself to his knees, only to discover a more formidable Rhys than he had expected, standing between the black mage and Drydwen.

Rhys had drawn his sword and taken an offensive stance, which alarmed Thorne, but not as much as the hungry, covetous look he saw overtaking Machreth's face. The black mage was looking past Rhys, even beyond Drydwen. He had seen the opening to the fifth realm.

The portal resembled an unusually large wall mirror, a solid luminous oval framed in greenish marble tile. Yet the surface was not like glass or metal or ice. It was pearlescent, though not truly opaque. The aperture substance was ethereal and diffusive, like a crystal-dusted mist cloud, but it appeared to have the density of thick liquid. To Thorne's eyes, it was a thing of immeasurable beauty and astonishment. Through this opening, souls passed into an unknown plane. There was a spiritual essence emanating from it that brought him to a state of reverence every time he was near it. Thorne believed the portal was the origin of all the mysteries in the world.

The black mage took a single step forward, and Rhys leveled his sword in warning. It was a futile gesture that terrified Thorne, but one he would have made himself. Machreth hesitated, as though he were considering the risks, and then dismissed Rhys in favor of Drydwen.

Machreth looked at her closely, a slow smile spreading over his face, a look of recognition. "They are searching for you in Ausoria, and all this time you have been here."

Thorne looked to Drydwen. "How does he know you?"

"Tanwen," Rhys muttered. "She is Tanwen."

"My given name is Drydwen," she said almost defiantly. "Tanwen is a name that was bestowed upon me, one that I was not permitted to refuse. A lifetime ago now, and long forgotten."

Thorne was confused and frustrated. He staggered to his feet, trying to figure out what to do. Drydwen was not armed, not even with her wand. She was offering no resistance, but she had placed herself directly in harm's way, and Thorne could not see a way to intervene without making things worse.

"No matter," Machreth said, reaching out with his wand hand.

Rhys responded swiftly, swinging his sword sharp and hard on Machreth's outstretched hand. The blade edge struck the wand, not the flesh, splitting the weapon in two. Thorne was awestruck by his young friend's precision.

Drydwen held out a hand to caution Rhys and intervened before Machreth could react. "I do not possess either the authority or the magic to stop you, Machreth, but even if I did, I would not. The portal will decide your fate. For your own good, I will caution you. No living being has ever crossed into the fifth realm through this portal and reemerged, and there is no way to know what you will find on the other side. This is power you do not understand."

"I have no intention of passing through the convergence," Machreth said. "I intend to command it."

Drydwen's eyes widened in surprise, and then she laughed. "Well, that I simply will not allow. You may leave through the doors to the temple, or you may leave through the portal, but either way, you *will* leave."

Only then did Drydwen draw her wand. Machreth swept Rhys aside with a wave of his hand, throwing the young swordsman hard against the far wall. He then raised his hands and Thorne envisioned a horrible hex battle that was sure to end in Drydwen's death. He lunged for Machreth, but it was Maelgwn who saved her.

From the dark recesses of the stairwell, Maelgwn sprang like a whip snap. He landed in front of Drydwen and spun on Machreth, snarling and gnashing his teeth. Thorne scrambled back, instinctively blocking the stairs. The warghound advanced on the sorcerer, maneuvering him away from Drydwen—and toward the portal.

Whether stopping Maelgwn was beyond Machreth's power or he was simply too startled to respond, the advantage belonged to the warghound. Maelgwn's instinct to protect took hold, and the beast struck. Machreth recoiled and lost his footing. He teetered precariously close to the portal aperture, clawing at the marble framing to keep himself from falling. For a moment it looked as though Machreth would recover, but his momentum carried him into the fall. His fingers slipped, and Machreth was gone.

The convergence swallowed him. Thorne had no other way to perceive what was happening. When Machreth's form passed through the aperture, the portal shimmered like shifting sunlight on water, and then it went black.

"Drydwen." Thorne was stunned. The room felt cold. "What has happened?"

"This is beyond my experience," she said, turning to speak to him. A look of concern displaced her perplexity. "You are unnaturally pale."

Thorne scowled at her. "What are you talking about?"

"Thorne," she said, clearly distressed, "you are bleeding."

He heard what she said, even noted his own surprise, and then all awareness of himself vanished.

TWENTY-SEVEN

Thorne's sensibilities returned some moments later as Rhys was helping him slide to a seat against the stone wall near the stairwell. Drydwen was peeling back the layers of torn clothing from his left shoulder, which was more than a little uncomfortable. And now, he noticed, he could in fact see what had so disturbed Drydwen. The black leather chest plate and the tunic beneath were sopping wet from neck to waist and had turned the color of rusted iron. He *was* bleeding.

"The portal?" He strained to see past Rhys.

"The convergence has rebalanced," Drydwen said. "Now keep still so I can look at this wound."

"Later," Thorne argued, trying to pull his legs underneath him so he could stand. They would not comply. "I need to find Gavin first. And Eckhardt—he was hurt."

"You've lost too much blood, Thorne," Drydwen explained calmly. "You might manage to get to your feet, but you won't be able to hold yourself upright for long."

"I'll go," Rhys said. "Stay where you are."

Thorne was in no condition to argue. "Machreth unleashed some sort of spell in the temple, trying to cave in the walls and bury us. The stairwell might even be blocked at the top."

Rhys had already started up the steps. "Maelgwn came down and went up again. It must be clear."

Thorne had forgotten the warghound. "The Hellion scouts Machreth brought with him will still be nearby."

"Your dog can take care of himself." Drydwen was examining his shoulder. "And if the Hellion soldiers return to the keep, I will deal with them. Your wound needs stitching."

Thorne winced at the thought. The shoulder was painful enough as it was. "But you have better ways for mending such things."

"Even I can only do so much." As she spoke, he felt a numbing tingle in the flesh beneath her touch, and warmth flushed through him, not unlike the effects of an exceptionally fine wine. "This gash is very deep, and the sinew is peeled away from the bone. There *will* be stitching involved, but not until we get you somewhere more suited for it. Can you stand now?"

Thorne was pleased to discover that he could, though not with ease. He needed the wall to steady him, but he was on his feet. "The pain is better."

"A temporary effect," Drydwen warned. "Let me help you up the stairs."

"I can manage." Thorne refused her attempt to take his good arm, on principle, though his common sense warned against it. Hauling himself up each step was more difficult than he had expected.

He waved Drydwen ahead of him. The last thing he wanted was for her to see him struggle. "Go on."

She hesitated long enough to tilt a disapproving glare at him, then shook her head and went ahead of him up the stairs. "Have it your way then."

Gavin's voice and the sound of more than one pair of boot heels echoed in the stairwell, and Thorne was dizzied anew with relief. Rhys met him at the top of the steps to offer his hand. This time, Thorne was eager to accept.

The temple foyer was littered with freshly scorched rubble, but the ceiling had not fallen, and the three good walls were still intact. Eckhardt was on his feet, and with Drydwen's help, propped himself on a stone bench in the garden courtyard beyond the old ruins. Several of her devotees appeared to offer aid. One of them stepped in to care for Eckhardt's ugly side wound so that Drydwen could care for Thorne.

"He needs tending more than me," Thorne told her. Eckhardt was not as badly wounded as he had feared, but it was serious enough.

This time she looked at him with thinly veiled aggravation. "We have many healers here. He'll be well cared for. Unless you'd prefer I see to him rather than you."

Eckhardt grinned at Thorne. "That would suit me just fine."

"I know it would," Thorne joked. "But now that you mention it, I think I'll keep her to myself."

Gavin, however, had no stomach for grins or good humor. He was decidedly grim and was covered with stone dust and pebble. "Is it over?"

Thorne was not sure how to answer. "Drydwen?"

"In all my days as prioress of this keep, only once has anything ever emerged from that portal," she said, "and only then in answer to a summoning."

"What does that mean?" Gavin stood rigid, tense with anticipation. He was spent, and frustrated, as they all were. He also wanted assurances more than he wanted explanations.

Drydwen forgave his biting tone and answered him with more grace than he deserved. "If Machreth somehow survived the journey into the fifth realm, it may be possible for him to return, but only if the portal is opened to him. The only way that will happen is if I bring him back or am unable to prevent someone else from doing so."

"So it's *not* over," said Gavin. His brow furrowed and his eyes narrowed in distrust. "Not truly."

Thorne straightened as best he could to face Gavin's skepticism. "It is over for now."

"That is not good enough," Gavin said. "Not at all."

Thorne nodded. He agreed, but there was no point in belaboring a point for which there was no resolution that would satisfy any of them. "Any sign of Machreth's Hellion soldiers?"

"No, but we should keep watch." Gavin dusted off his leggings. "What about the Cythraul you were hunting?"

Drydwen looked surprised. "Cythraul?"

"My young friend and I were in pursuit," Thorne said. "The wraith scent led us to Banraven and then to Machreth."

She shrugged. "If Machreth summoned the wraiths, they are no longer a threat. They would not survive him."

Gavin perked. "Then you think him dead?"

"No, but I cannot know for sure. If he does exist beyond the portal, in whatever form, his power no longer extends to this realm. He can work no magic here—not without a collaborator."

Rhys had been watching a sparrowhawk sitting on the bud-covered branch of a hazel sapling. Something about the bird seemed to fascinate him. "What exactly is the fifth realm?"

"There are four earthly realms—the celestial, the spiritual, the natural, and the physical. The fifth realm is an unearthly realm. It is the otherworld," Drydwen said. "An existence alongside our own, separate and yet connected. Many people believe it is both the beginning and the end of all things. I do not know the truth of that, but I do know it is the origin of all magic."

"Thin places," Rhys spoke slowly. There was something in his tone that troubled Thorne. "Are they also portals to this fifth realm?"

Drydwen studied him more closely before answering. "Yes, in some ways."

Rhys nodded, but he had taken to staring at Drydwen with what Thorne could only describe as suspicion. He might even have considered it contempt, but that seemed out of character. Still, it was odd. The tension eased when one of Drydwen's devotees brought her a healer's bag and she turned her attention again to Thorne.

"The light out here is good," she said. "Better to stitch that gash now than later."

Thorne sat on the end of the bench where Eckhardt had sprawled, to allow Drydwen to work on his shoulder. He watched Rhys for a few moments more, wondering why the young swordsman was so irritated. "What bothers you so?"

Rhys ignored Thorne and spoke directly to Drydwen. "You know you will have to go back to Fane Gramarye, if for no other reason than to explain."

Drydwen didn't even bother to acknowledge him. Thorne was curious. He had questions of his own, but he had planned to ask them later, in private.

"Men of honor have been sent to find you, put themselves at risk searching for you in a place you have never been." Rhys took a step closer. "Madoc is dead."

Thorne felt her hesitate. There could be only one reason this news would matter to her. Drydwen *was* Tanwen, one of the four sorceresses conscripted to the Stewards' Council pledged to serve the king of the old prophecy.

He did not find this hard to believe. When he had first encountered her in the White Woods all those years ago, she had been on her way to Elder Keep and in need of safe escort. He had known she was running. From what or whom he had never asked, and she had never told. Everyone carried secrets, and it was Thorne's way to let secrets rest—unless and until he needed to know.

Rhys shot Thorne a dagger-eyed glare. "You do know who she is, don't you?"

"Thorne knows very little of my past," Drydwen interjected. "And apparently you know more than you should."

She finished her stitching and wiped her hands with a linen cloth before turning to face Rhys. "Who sits on Madoc's throne now?"

"My mother," Rhys said, taking a more respectful tone. Drydwen was intimidating when she wanted to be. "But only until his heir is found, and then she will take her place among the Guardians of the Realms."

"Yes, but who is your mother, boy?" Drydwen demanded.

Rhys blanched, but he spoke up. "Alwen. My mother is Alwen."

Drydwen nodded as if she recognized the name. "Well then, son of Alwen. Tell your mother this. I have no intention of return-ing to Fane Gramarye, not now or ever. I left that life behind me long ago. I never wanted it. Elder Keep is my calling. It is where I was always meant to be. This is where I belong."

Drydwen hesitated, as though she were niggled by regret. "Tell Alwen that the bloodstone is hidden in one of the second-floor spell rooms. She will understand."

To Thorne's surprise, she then turned on her heel, without a word or a glance in his direction, and left them there in the court-yard. If he had been sure of his legs, he would have followed her, out of concern. Then again, he had questions he was fairly sure she was not ready to answer.

"That was ... unexpected," Eckhardt said to Thorne. "Did you know?"

"No." One of the devotees offered him a sling for his left arm, and another brought water to Eckhardt. "But then, I never asked."

"How could you be with her all these years and never have asked about her past?" Gavin wondered.

Eckhardt let out a wry chuckle. "Because then she might have asked the same of him."

Gavin's eyes widened as his good sense finally caught up with him. "Well, none of us wants that, now do we."

Eckhardt slapped Thorne's good shoulder. "Your apprentice here has a lot to learn. You might want to start by teaching him how to avoid offending the prioress of Elder Keep."

Thorne wondered how Rhys would react to Eckhardt's presumption. The offer of apprenticeship had not yet been extended, not formally. It seemed Rhys was more distracted by other concerns.

"I didn't mean to upset her," said Rhys.

Gavin snorted. "Yes, you did. But you have your reasons."

Rhys conceded the point with a terse shrug. "She has abandoned a duty only she can fulfill. There are consequences to her decision. It begs a challenge."

"It is her choice to make," Thorne counseled. He felt compelled to defend Drydwen, although he thought he understood why Rhys had taken issue. "And it is not for you to judge her."

"I am not judging her," Rhys argued. "I am holding her accountable."

Gavin made an effort to end the discussion with a lesson on faith. "I expect Drydwen holds herself accountable. And if there is a tithe to pay, the fates will extract whatever is due, one way or another. That is the way of things in this world."

"There is no less honor in the service she has chosen than the service she has forsaken," Eckhardt added. "In the end, what does it matter what she chooses, so long as it benefits the greater good?"

"There is also the issue of free will," Gavin pointed out. "We are all of us free to choose our own calling, or at least we should be."

Rhys seemed to take a new attitude, one of contemplation rather than accusation, but he was clearly still troubled. The more Thorne observed him, the more he realized that Rhys was at odds with himself, not with Drydwen. He was struggling with his own decision, and Thorne decided the time had come to settle it.

"Even you," he said. "Even you are free to choose your own calling, Rhys, son of Alwen. You are right. There are consequences to every decision. Lives turn on them, which is why they should never be made lightly. But it's time you made yours."

Rhys looked at him with trepidation. "I don't know what you mean."

"I think you do," Thorne said, "but let me make it plain, so there will be no misunderstanding. I have need of an apprentice, and I have decided it should be you. There will be sacrifices, demands I am not free to share until you declare your intent. The initiation will be difficult, and the life, as you've begun to see for yourself, is even more so. But the opportunity is yours, if you wish to take it."

"I would like nothing more," Rhys answered earnestly. "But—I..."

Thorne was through waiting for Rhys to slay his inner demons and come round on his own. "But you don't feel free to choose your own life, is that it?"

"I *am* free to choose," he protested.

"Ah," Thorne said, "so you are afraid of the consequences. Are they really so dire? Will kingdoms fall because you fail to lead them? Will people starve without you to feed them?"

"No," Rhys said, half apologetically, "but my father has no other heir, and I have already sworn an oath to the Crwn Cawr."

Thorne dismissed his concerns with a shrug. "So your father will choose another successor, and the Crwn Cawr will release you from your pledge. What else worries you?"

Rhys stalled, as though he were at a loss for what to say. Thorne did not believe he had any other real burdens. What stopped Rhys from claiming the destiny he wanted was his fear of disappointing his loved ones. As far as Thorne could tell, this was a manufactured fear—one that Rhys had conjured up in his own imagination, but it was real enough to him. It was also an honorable concern, but it was baseless.

"If there is nothing else to keep you from doing so, make your stand. Make it now," Thorne demanded. "Is the Ruagaire Brotherhood your calling or not?"

Rhys was not as quick to answer as Thorne would have liked, but he respected a deliberate man. Thorne would not, however, reward the hesitation with patient silence, at least not for long. And apparently neither would the Brothers Steptoe.

"Declare yourself and be done with it," Gavin goaded.

"It is a rare offer," Eckhardt added. "And you can be sure it won't come again. Not from any of us, and we are all that's left."

Thorne wrapped a bit of encouragement around his expectations, but this was the last he would say on it. "You are suited for this life. There is no doubt about that. But your whole heart must yearn for it. Either it does or it doesn't, and I need to know which. Speak now or never, Rhys."

Rhys took a deep breath, and let it out slowly. He looked as though he were about to confess to a crime. "It does. I declare myself for the Brotherhood."

"So be it." Thorne was pleased, despite the young swordsman's reservations. It was not an easy decision, nor was it without a price. "You were right about one thing, Rhys. Someone will have to explain all of this to your mother."

Rhys sighed and gestured at the sparrowhawk. The bird was still quietly perched in the tree. "I think she already knows."

TWENTY-EIGHT

The slow-burning rage Hywel had been cultivating since he'd headed for Cwm Brith had collided with the sense of foreboding he'd felt since they'd arrived. He would do what must be done. He had no choice. But Hywel was not ignorant of the cost, and more and more he regretted the decision Clydog had forced him to make. Glain's disturbing dream still haunted him.

Killing his brother was the one sure way to end the threat Clydog represented, but it would also tragically weaken his father's line. There would be other costs as well, costs that Hywel was trying to ignore: the loss of the brother bond that would never be realized and the unrivaled power their united legacy might someday produce. If only he had been given a chance to reason with Clydog, things might have been different.

It was too late for reason now. In the thick stillness of the moonless night, Hywel's advance contingent was stealing toward the nearest corner of the outer wall. He'd ordered the first strike to be carried out by three soldiers who knew the compound as well as he—his two favored lieutenants and oldest companions—and a highly skilled bowman who had served in his father's army for many years. Once they had scaled the wall and subdued the night watch, the team would open the gates for the rest of their small force. And so they waited at the tree line, armed and mounted and determined to succeed. Or to die trying.

"Keep close to Cerrigwen," Hywel advised Odwain. Aeron had begun an anxious hoof dance and was pulling against the reins. "She might be vulnerable to Clydog's human soldiers while she confronts the inhuman ones."

Odwain nodded, his eyes trained on the ramparts. "The first guard is down. Can you see the other?"

The second man over the wall had quickly and silently strong-armed one of the two guards walking the parapet. Hywel watched as the third of his advance raiders, the bowman, scaled the wall and positioned himself behind the southwest corner buttress.

"There, on the right." Hywel pointed at the soldier rounding the southeast corner. Almost before he had finished his sentence, the bowman took aim and downed the second guard, signaling to Hywel with a furtive wave. It was now safe for the rest of the raiders to begin a careful advance across the twenty-odd-yard clearing between the trees and the compound.

Hywel had divided his remaining warriors into two factions so that they could flank the gate on both sides for their approach and then mount a split attack once they were inside. Five of his most fierce and experienced men accompanied Odwain and Cerrigwen, while Bledig and the remaining three rode with him.

The contingent drew single file into the wall shadow, each half taking position on either side of the gate. In a matter of minutes they would have entry to the compound, and if all went well, the advantage of surprise. Hywel felt the familiar niggle of agitation that erupted just before battle. He was eager for it.

Almost before they were fully positioned, Hywel heard the scrape of the massive wooden gate bolt being dragged cautiously through its metal bracings. His heart thudded against the confinement of his chest, and rage surged anew. Hywel alerted the others and tensed, prepared to spur Aeron into a charge.

One of his lieutenants pushed one of the heavy, hinged gate doors open a few inches and squeezed through. "Nearly four dozen soldiers, asleep in the barn and stable," he whispered.

Hywel was surprised. "How many of the Hellion marauders?"

The lieutenant held up five fingers. "A half dozen at most, scattered throughout the grounds."

Hywel nodded, feeling more confident. He backed Aeron away to give him room and signaled to the others. "Throw the gates."

A few moments later, both halves of the massive barricade began a slow outward swing, and Hywel let loose his riders. Two men from each of the two small companies made straight for the large outbuildings, bolting the stable and barn doors from the outside by jamming muck rakes and pitchforks and whatever else they could find through the curved iron handles. Odwain and another man lagged to close and bolt the gates to keep anyone or anything from escaping their attack. The rest of Hywel's command rode hard toward the scattering of monstrous creatures, banking both right and left in an effort to corral them inside a loose circle. Cerrigwen, astride her silver mare, waited just inside the walls.

One of the blood-red Hellion soldiers, the one Hywel took to be the leader, hefted a pole mace the size of a birch tree above his giant horn-helmed head and let loose a furious roar. The battle cry was a sound every warrior knew, be it man or animal or demon beast. His minions rallied to mount, but big and strong as they were, the warriors themselves were slow on their feet. It was their sure-hooved gargantuan mounts that were the real danger. Already they snarled and snapped their daggered jaws, straining against their harnessing as they waited to be released.

Hywel hoped Cerrigwen would be quick with whatever magic she intended to wield. He had instructed his riders to keep moving, circling and darting to avoid engaging the enemy as long as possible. It would take two soldiers to bring down just one of these demons, and if they lost even one man, it would be one more than they could spare. Hywel eyed the giant Hellion general heaving himself atop his behemoth and hauled Aeron out of his gallop and into a skittering prance a few dozen paces away.

By the time the four soldiers who had cut away to secure Clydog's army returned to the regiment, Hywel was beginning to doubt his entire plan. As he turned to look for Cerrigwen, a great bellow resounded from the opposite side of the yard, followed by the clang and scrape of sword metal against armor. Bledig, the barbarian warlord, had engaged one of the Hellion riders, and the battle had begun.

"Stand down!" Hywel shouted at his men, wheeling Aeron back on his haunches.

Somehow Bledig and another soldier brought down one of the beastly mounts and immediately doubled up against its rider. A lucky victory in a foolish fight, and Hywel did not expect the others to fare so well should they follow Bledig's lead.

Hywel turned Aeron full circle, seeking Cerrigwen. He needed her now, before the Hellion cut down every last man. But she was not where he expected her to be.

"Balor's balls!" Hywel cursed. Two more of his men had engaged another of the Hellion warriors. He wheeled Aeron a half turn to his left. Where *was* that bloody sorceress?

He saw her then, already dismounted and approaching the fight. Odwain was walking right behind her, leading both her silver mare and his chestnut Frisian. Hywel jabbed Aeron's ribs with his boot heels and turned the stallion's nose toward Cerrigwen. He could do little more now than keep himself between her and the danger while she worked her spell.

But it was over before he reached her. Just like the tiny sorceress in the woods, Cerrigwen raised her arms as she walked, palms facing forward. He could not hear the words she called out, but it appeared as if the demons did. They and their mounts turned all at once, as though she had called them to her. But the Hellion did not charge.

Cerrigwen shouted out again, words Hywel again could not make out. The demon warriors began to writhe, struggling against themselves as if they were trapped in place and fighting to break free of unseen bonds. And then they began to howl in agony and fury.

Hywel pulled up, unsure his approach was wise. As he watched, the Hellion soldiers began to quiver, just as he had seen before, their mounts along with them. The shuddering turned to violent spasms, and then again, as he had witnessed in the woods, the demon legion disintegrated in a fiery burst, leaving nothing behind but piles of burnt bone, seared gut, and melted armor.

Cerrigwen drew down her arms, took a deep breath, and turned to look up at him. "It is done," she said.

"Half done," he said as he dismounted, pointing toward the lodge. "Clydog will be waiting for us with his personal guard."

Hywel took account of his men and their whereabouts. Bledig had already gathered most of the raiders to contain the captured men in the outbuildings, and three others were already on their way to guard the rear of the main house. Two more were waiting for him, just outside the front door.

"How many men will he have with him?" she asked.

Hywel was already walking away. "Not enough to worry me."

Before he'd taken two full strides, Cerrigwen brushed past him. Hywel reached out and grabbed her arm as she passed. Cerrigwen spun on him, wild-eyed and fury fueled. Hywel was a little worried that he had the same look.

"Wait," he demanded. "We'll go in together. Where is Odwain?"

"Not far behind you." She glared over his shoulder and then glared straight at him. "Do you want Clydog dead or alive?"

"Alive," Hywel said, "for now."

She sighed and scowled, as if she were disappointed. "Why?"

Hywel was hard pressed to explain. He had arrived at Cwm Brith fully prepared to wring the life out of Clydog with his bare hands, just for thinking to oppose him. But now that he was here, standing on the grounds as master of Cwm Brith once and for all, Hywel could afford to feel pity. "Whatever he has done, he is still my brother."

Cerrigwen's expression softened only a little. "Then keep yourself between him and me. The last time the little prince and I met, I cursed his foolish soul. Should he or anyone on his order dare cross my path, that person will come to an unpleasant end."

Hywel was surprised but impressed. "Perhaps Clydog will be more easily persuaded to see reason with you along."

Cerrigwen cocked an eyebrow and very nearly smiled. "If my first impression of him is any indication of his nature, I believe he will agree to anything to save his own skin."

Odwain caught up to them. "The men are in position behind the lodge."

"Then let's go," Hywel said. "But leave Clydog to me."

"As you wish, Hywel," said Cerrigwen, "but if he harms my daughter, not even you can save him."

"Agreed." He would not deny her retribution, not that he could even if he wished. Besides, if Clydog were so stupid as to irk the sorceress, then he deserved whatever he got.

The door to the lodge stood wide open to the small foyer, which led directly to the grand hall. This was the only room on the main floor, aside from the kitchens. Hywel had last seen his father alive here, entertaining his cronies over the spoils of the hunt—buck shank and boar hocks with warm ale and tall talk. Good times had been had here, far better times than these.

And then Hywel saw Clydog, standing behind a young woman seated in Cadell's chair at the head of the enormous rectangular oak table in the center of the room. All lanky limbs and copper-colored curls, just as Hywel remembered him, only taller now and bearded. The situation would have been laughable had not so much been at stake.

Clydog was flanked by four guardsmen, and as Hywel drew full into the room, he realized that Clydog held the woman with his right hand on her shoulder and the other resting the edge of a long-bladed dagger at the base of her throat. "Have you met our sister, Hywel?"

"I haven't yet had the pleasure." Hywel stepped to the near end of the table. The young woman looked a great deal like Clydog, who favored their father. They shared red curls and fair skin, and there was something similar in the shape of their mouths. "But this is hardly the time for a proper introduction."

Clydog's gaze shifted and his expression sobered beyond grim as he saw Cerrigwen enter the room. Hywel noticed that Clydog was careful to keep himself squarely behind Ffion. It was clear how much he feared Cerrigwen.

Ffion smiled at her mother. Her hands were clasped together and resting on top of the table, but her wrists were bound. Mage tether, Hywel assumed. Clydog had left little to chance.

Cerrigwen stood next to Hywel, on his left. "Let my daughter go, and I will let you live."

"Send the vile witch away," Clydog shouted at Hywel, his grasp on Ffion cinching tighter as he grew more distressed. "Get her out of here. I will speak to you and you alone."

Hywel was struck by how young Clydog seemed. Inexperience and desperation often led to rash acts, and Clydog had obviously stepped well beyond the bounds of his abilities. This could end in only one of two ways.

"You are in no position to bargain with me, brother," Hywel said. "Your army is mine now, as is this lodge, and you have nothing else that I want. I suggest you make whatever deal you can with the sorceress and hope I am feeling generous enough to leave you your life when this is over."

"Let me leave." Clydog attempted to barter with Hywel anyway. "Once I am safely away, I will let the girl go."

Hywel snorted. "To go where—back to our cousins in Gwynedd, to plot my undoing all over again? You will never be king so long as I live, Clydog, and I promise to live a very long time."

"The prophecy speaks only of a son of Cadell," Clydog countered. He was still clinging to his dead ambition. "It does not call you out by name or by birth. I have as much right to claim our father's legacy as you."

Hywel shook his head, suddenly sad. "The prophecy was never our father's legacy, Clydog. It is my destiny. It has always been mine."

"Machreth pledged *me* his patronage." Clydog said this as if he believed it still mattered.

"To help you defeat me and bring the other kings under your control so that he could rule through you. And you have failed." Hywel was as disappointed as he was outraged. "No son of Cadell could be such a fool. You are less than nothing to Machreth now. You must know this."

Hywel could see in his brother's eyes that he did, but his pride would never let him admit it. In Clydog's mind, he could take no other stand. There was no honorable retreat available to him. If he were to concede now, Clydog would be less than nothing to everyone who mattered.

"I still have our sister here." Clydog wrested Ffion to her feet and sidled to his left, as though he intended to move toward the door. The four men who were meant to protect him backed away, distancing themselves from Clydog. He would have no help from them. "Machreth wants her more than he wants you dead. If I leave here alive, so does she, at least for now. But if I die, she dies first."

"The only way you will leave this lodge alive is under my guard." Hywel edged around the end of the table to the right, blocking his brother's escape on the near side. Cerrigwen waited on the other. "You have another choice, brother."

"What choice?" Clydog was tilting dangerously toward panic. He held Ffion so that she shielded him from her mother and worked at something knotted on his belt, but Hywel couldn't see what it was. "I will kill her if I must, Hywel. Don't pretend her life means nothing to you."

"Of course her life matters to me, as does yours," Hywel said, surprised by his own sincerity. He had begun to understand Clydog for the lost boy he was. Their father had failed him, and that could never be redressed now that Cadell was dead. But perhaps Hywel might make up for some of it. "We are all family here."

"Family?" Clydog squeaked out a wild, unhinged laugh. "We are no better than hungry dogs, you and I, trying to kill each other off to get at the table scraps." He tossed his chin toward Cerrigwen. "*That* witch was just one of many mistresses, and her daughter here is nothing more than spilt seed our father forgot to wipe up when he was done."

"Ffion is more than that, and you know it." Cerrigwen was losing her patience, and her temper. "Cadell let her live because she tied him to the Stewardry as much as Hywel. You will not harm her because she does the same for you."

Hywel could see Cerrigwen tensing from the corner of his eye. She worried him, but so did Clydog. He had something clutched in his right hand, and his blade was pressed too deep into the flesh of Ffion's throat. It had already drawn blood, and she was afraid.

"Stand away Hywel, you and your men," Clydog demanded. "Let me pass."

Hywel had almost forgotten Odwain and the others. They had taken a stand behind Hywel and Cerrigwen, at the doorway. Cerrigwen would strike soon, and Hywel would not be able to stop her. Nor did he think he should. They could not let Clydog leave with Ffion.

"Lay down your blade, Clydog. Let Ffion go, and submit to me." Hywel made one last appeal. "I will spare your life and even offer you terms. We *are* brothers."

"You let none of your enemies live," Clydog snarled. "You are just like Cadell. You'll spare me now only to have me killed later."

"I cannot forgive what you have done, but neither can I forget that you are also a son of Cadell." Hywel took great care with his words and his tone. He could not stop thinking about how Glain had interpreted her dream of the two stags, and he wanted Clydog to believe him. "If you will submit to me now, I will make you my vassal. I swear it. You will have your life and the land and title you deserve."

"Why should I trust you?" Clydog challenged, still convinced that he had a chance to escape.

Hywel stared him down. "You have no other choice, but death."

Cerrigwen stepped toward Clydog, her hands held out and open, as if in conciliation. "I will free you from the curse and Hywel will let you leave, just as you asked. Take Ffion with you as guarantee, if you must, and free her once you feel safe."

What was Cerrigwen doing? Hywel glared at her, angered. She had no right to speak for him, and he had no intention of letting Clydog leave, with or without Ffion. And then Hywel realized neither did she. She meant to draw his attention long enough for Hywel to pull Ffion away.

"Only loosen your grip on that blade a little," she said, inching closer still. Her tone was calm but stern. "You're hurting her."

"All right then." Clydog backed into the corner, still shielding himself from Cerrigwen with Ffion's body. But he did ease up so that the blade was no longer cutting into her skin. "Undo your blood curse, sorceress, and tell Hywel to stand aside."

Cerrigwen waved Hywel off, and he backed toward the entry just enough to give Clydog reason to believe he would comply. Then Cerrigwen drew in her hands, closed her eyes, and began a quiet chant in a whisper too low for Hywel to hear. The thought struck him that he had no way to know whether she were actually removing one hex or calling another. The same thought must have occurred to Clydog, because he panicked.

In a sudden frenzy, Clydog booted Ffion to the floor and hurled whatever he had been holding in his right hand at Cerrigwen. It was dark and loosely formed, like a clump of damp soot. The clump struck Cerrigwen in the face and exploded in a cloud of black silt, momentarily stunning her. Clydog leapt over Ffion and charged Hywel as if he intended to barrel over him to get to the door, now clutching the knife in his stronger right hand.

Hywel reacted on instinct and a little anger, standing with his left shoulder forward so that he could take the blow and still throw his strong arm. He was taller and heavier than his younger brother, who turned out to be smart enough not to make a direct charge. Instead, Clydog attempted to make a glancing pass on the right side, but Hywel stiff-armed him across the chest and threw him off his feet. The block laid Clydog flat out on his back, winded.

"That was too easy." Hywel bent over, twisted the knife from his brother's grip, and drew his sword. "Get on your feet, you cowering whelp. Stand up to me like the man you should be."

Odwain had already pushed past them to help Ffion, but she threw him off, scrambling to her feet shrieking. Cerrigwen was still on the ground where she'd fallen.

"Odwain!" Hywel took hold of Clydog's tunic and yanked him up, tempted to throw a punch for good measure. "Is Cerrigwen all right?"

When there was no immediate response but Ffion's weepy mumbling, Hywel turned on Clydog. "What did you do?"

Clydog was staring past him, to where the others were crowded around Cerrigwen. "I—I don't know. Machreth said it would stop her."

Hywel had shown all the benevolence he had in him. He shoved Clydog back against the wall, pinning him across the throat with his left forearm and raising the knife he had taken to place the tip between his brother's eyes. "Is there no end to your stupidity? Why would you use any weapon without first knowing what it was or what it would do?"

He dragged Clydog across the floor to where Cerrigwen lay. He was so exasperated, he was no longer sure why he hadn't already killed his brother. Ffion was on her knees, with her mother's head in her lap, and Odwain stood helplessly by. Cerrigwen was not moving.

Ffion looked up at him, her face filled with shocked rage and streaked with tears and blood. "He's *killed* her."

Hywel felt sick. Not only had Clydog killed a Guardian of the Realms, he had used Machreth's black magic to do it. Alwen would rightly demand vengeance—and worse, Clydog had now earned an extra measure of Ffion's hatred. How could Hywel justify sparing him now? If it weren't for Glain's damnable dream, he wouldn't even be contemplating it. Because of her, Hywel now felt compelled by the fates to find a compassionate resolution for them all. Unfortunately, he hadn't one.

Just then Bledig and the rest of the men barged through the front door, coming to see what had happened. They were quick to take Clydog's four remaining men into custody and then stood by with the others. Hywel shoved Clydog at Odwain and bent to offer Ffion his hand. To his surprise, she accepted his gesture and allowed him to help her up.

Hywel was uncertain how to proceed. He did not know this sorceress, this sister to whom he now found himself inescapably indebted. Worse, he had neither reason nor right to expect her allegiance, or even her benevolence. He wondered if Ffion knew that her mother's death had changed her fate and what that meant. Hywel knew, and it worried him.

Ffion faced him, unexpectedly stoic and composed. "Have my mother's remains prepared. We will return her body to the Stewardry, where she belongs."

"Of course." Hywel waved at the men gathered in the doorway, but as two of them moved to comply, he reconsidered. "Perhaps you'd like to take a moment alone with her, first."

"No." The anguish he had seen before was no longer evident, but there was anger in her voice. "The sooner we leave this place, the better."

Ffion turned and moved toward Clydog, which made Hywel nervous. He followed but did not block her path. She was entitled to face down the man who had taken her mother's life, even to take his fate into her own hands.

"What would you have me do with him?" he asked, half dreading her answer. It would be difficult to deny her blood, if that were what she wanted. In the end, keeping her favor was far more important than protecting his brother. Glain's dream be damned, he decided. Hywel had done all he was willing to do for Clydog.

Ffion stared long and hard at Clydog, but whatever she was thinking or feeling was well hidden. Too well hidden for Clydog's liking—Hywel could see his brother's lower lip tremble.

At long last, she dragged her heavy-lidded glare from Clydog's face and turned it on Hywel. "You have already promised him his life."

"If he conceded," Hywel reminded her, "which he did not. He was never going to leave this room alive otherwise."

Ffion nodded slowly and sidled her gaze back to Clydog. "Nevertheless, that was what you wanted, is it not?"

Hywel was almost as surprised by his own answer as he was the question. "Yes."

"Then so be it," she said flatly, looking up at Hywel again. "I will leave his fate to you, on one condition."

Hywel nodded and waited for her to continue.

"My mother's one wish for me was that my father would acknowledge my existence." Ffion was firm and self-possessed, as though she had always known of her sire, which Hywel was fairly certain she had not. "She sacrificed everything to claim my birthright for me and to protect me against those who wanted to use me to gain it for themselves or to kill me to keep me from having it. Which of these are you, Hywel?"

"Neither," he said earnestly, feeling surprisingly humbled. It was a truthful answer, but he did not expect her to believe it. "Neither."

She arched one eyebrow, obviously skeptical. "Then I imagine a king who is willing to forgive a brother he hardly knows for plotting against him would also be willing to acknowledge a sister he never knew—especially if she also bears one of the keys to his destiny."

So she did know. Hywel felt a new admiration for Ffion. "I imagine he would, especially a sister who so well understands the value of her alliances."

She almost smiled. "We are of a kind, I suppose."

"No," Hywel said. "We are kin."

TWENTY-NINE

Glain had led Nerys by the nose for two days, continuing a
search for something that had already been found. It was
unconscionable, she knew, but Glain was not yet ready
to reveal herself. Still, she could not continue to say nothing for
much longer. Alwen was worsening.

Nerys now knew how ill Alwen had become, and between the
two of them they had managed to keep rumors from rising. The
membership was nervous enough without worrying that their
leader was weak. Though hers was still the final ruling, Alwen
had essentially been forced to abdicate the throne, leaving Glain
to attend to all that she could.

During the time that the duties of Sovereign had been
secretly hers, Glain had managed fairly well, considering how
ill equipped she was. However, Emrys had become difficult
these past few days, challenging Finn's authority at every turn.
Alwen had refused to speak to him since the interrogations the
night Euday was captured and Verica disappeared, and Emrys
was taking his demotion hard. Several times in the last two

days he had sought Glain out, begging for Alwen's audience. The more she tried to dissuade him, the more distraught he became.

"She will not see you," Glain insisted, standing her ground firmly in the foyer, though more and more curious to know what was plaguing him. "I think it would be best if you could just make peace with yourself for now."

Emrys looked at her with defeat in his eyes. He was disheveled and looked as though he had aged a decade overnight. "There can be no peace for me, not until Alwen hears me out."

"I am so sorry, Emrys," she said, honestly, "but there is nothing I can do."

"I think there is," Emrys snapped, turning suddenly hostile. "I think there is plenty you can do."

Glain was confused and unnerved. She was beginning to think he'd gone a little insane. "I am afraid I don't know what you mean, Emrys."

"I gave you back your scroll," he said in a harsh whisper. "I made sure it came to you. You owe me something for that."

"What?" Glain was stunned. Emrys made no sense. "*You* put the scroll in my room?"

"What you do with it is your business," he rasped, trying to keep his voice low. "That scroll is your burden to bear, but how I came to have it is mine. You must let me speak to Alwen."

Before Glain could gather words to respond, Finn charged through the door with Aslak on his heel.

"Gods grace us all!" she exclaimed. Glain felt as though she had been delivered from the jaws of a hungry serpent. "You've returned at last, and not a moment too soon."

As she spoke, Glain realized that Finn was ashen and Aslak, harried and unkempt. "What is it?"

"We've come straight from the saddle," he said. "I must see Alwen, right away."

It was only then that she saw the wounded soldier standing behind Aslak and the small woman beside him. They were all of them road weary, but there were others who should be with them and were not. The news Aslak brought could not be good, and whatever confessions were burning within Emrys would need to come out. It was useless to hide anything anymore. The time had come to let the fates have their way.

"Come with me," she decided, indicating to Emrys that he should come too. "But you should know: Alwen is not well."

She led the group to the third floor and stood, uneasy, before the doors to the Sovereign's chambers. The sentry saluted his returning captain. Aslak's homecoming was a glad thing for them all—even Emrys, Glain imagined.

"Wait here," she said, hoping to give Alwen a little time to prepare. "I will announce you."

Glain pushed in on one side of the double doors and closed it quickly behind her. To her astonishment, Alwen was already robed and waiting in the Sovereign's throne. Nerys stood nearby, ready and waiting to intercede should Alwen need her help.

"How did you know?" Glain asked.

"A little bird showed me," Alwen said with a smile, attempting a light-hearted reference to her spirit-faring abilities. "I went out on a limb this morning and then floated away on a breeze."

Glain was bemused, but also concerned. It was unlike Alwen to be so whimsical. "Are you alright, Sovereign?"

"Less and less every day," Alwen said, still smiling. "But I won't need to be for much longer."

This was the closest Alwen had come to admitting how frail she was becoming. Glain was so guilt-ridden, she could hardly speak. "There is something I should say before the others come in."

"Go on," Alwen said, expectant but calm.

"The last scroll," Glain admitted at last, "Madoc's testament. It has been found."

Alwen's left eyebrow arched. It was all the reaction she let show. "Where?"

"In my room, two days ago." Glain avoided looking at either Nerys or Alwen. "I have just learned that it was Emrys who put it there for me to find."

"Emrys?" Alwen was aghast.

"That is all I know," Glain said, finally reaching behind her to pull the scroll from her sash, where she'd tucked it for safekeeping. She held it out to Alwen. "I think you have already guessed what it says."

"I will hear you say it aloud, Glain." Alwen was stern, but not angry. She accepted the scroll and cradled it in her lap. "For your sake, as much as mine."

Glain swallowed her fears and regrets and summoned her pride. "I am Glain, daughter of Alric and Brigid, granddaughter of Saoirse, grandniece of Madoc, and the last mageborn descendant of the Primideach bloodline."

She took a deep breath and let the rest out. "I am the one true heir to the Stewardry at Fane Gramarye."

Nerys let out a small sigh, which was a far more restrained reaction than Glain expected. She waited dutifully for the reproach to come, for Alwen's disappointment and frustration. But Alwen seemed only relieved.

"At last," she said. "We'll speak more on this later, but now go let Aslak in before he loses his patience and breaks through the door."

Glain did as she was asked and waited for Aslak and the others to gather in the receptory, before joining Nerys at Alwen's side. Alwen stood to greet Aslak and even embraced him. Glain had not seen her express such affection since Bledig had left.

"It's the aleberry," Nerys whispered. "I believe she's taken too much."

Glain wanted to giggle. It was a silly thought, but it could well be true. She decided to be watchful, just in case, while she listened to Aslak's horrible account.

Aslak and Bledig had joined forces weeks before and failed to find any trace of Tanwen. On their way to rejoin Thorvald's caravan on the road home, they'd met Hywel's cadre, who were waiting with word that Ffion had been abducted and that Thorvald had been killed attempting to save her from the Hellion raiders. Goram, Aslak's eldest son, had been badly wounded. It was decided that Bledig would lend his sword to Hywel's campaign, and Aslak would see Goram and the sorceress in his care safely home.

"This sorceress"—Alwen indicated the small woman with a tip of her chin—"she is your charge, Goram?"

"Yes," Goram said, stepping forward. His face was bruised and battered, and there was an obvious gore wound to his side that had to be causing him pain. It was clearly a struggle to stay upright, but he did. His lanky limbs made him look even taller than his brother, and his coloring was not as fair. But just like Thorvald, Goram had Aslak's strong jaw, broad brow, and remarkable strength. "I bring you Raven, daughter of Branwen of Pwll."

Alwen leaned forward as though she were trying to get a closer look. "Come forward then and be recognized as a child of the guild."

"I come to claim my mother's legacy," Raven announced.

"Then your mother has passed on," Alwen acknowledged. "How did she meet her end?"

"She became ill late in the last harvest season. There was nothing to be done but to watch her fade away." Raven paused to take in a full breath, as if to bolster her courage in order to continue. "She did not linger long."

"You are very brave to have journeyed so far to take on such a burden." Alwen took a moment to regard the young sorceress more carefully. "Your devotion honors her memory. As do your looks, child. But for your youth, you could pass as her twin."

Raven almost smiled. "Her bloodline runs strong in my veins."

"Which is why you are here," Alwen said. "Tell me, Raven. Do you know who I am?"

"Alwen, High Sorceress and guardian of the Spiritual Realm and leader of the Circle of Sages." Raven recited the titles as though she had worked hard to memorize them.

"Yes," said Alwen, fingering the amulet at her throat. "For the time being, I am also Sovereign of the Stewardry at Fane Gramarye. It is that title that requires me to be certain that you are who you say you are. Show me your proof, Raven, daughter of Branwen."

"The pendant burns in your presence." Raven pulled a silver chain over her head, and with it, her mother's talisman. She held the necklace out to Alwen. "I bear the moonstone, the Key to the Celestial Realm."

Alwen took the pendant into her hands and turned it backside-up to examine the casing, just as she had the bloodstone amulet Nerys now wore. Hidden in the engraved embellishments was the wizard signet, etched into the silver by Madoc himself. This mark testified that the amulet and its owner were true.

"The power of the amulets grows stronger in each other's company." Alwen glanced at Nerys, as though her words were meant for them both. "The heat is called the quickening. The key will reveal itself in this way only to its true owner."

If Nerys were sharing the experience, she hid it well. Glain watched from the corner of her eye, feeling her old suspicions rise, until Nerys made a subtle move to reposition the pendant.

Alwen returned the moonstone to Raven. "Never again let this leave your person. Not unless I and I alone command you to do so."

Raven rehung the pendant around her neck. "Am I now a sorceress of the Stewardry?"

"As your mother entrusted you with her secrets, I presume she also entrusted you with her knowledge," Alwen said. "You are trained, are you not?"

"I know the traditional arts of your guild. My father's people are known as the Norse. They have their own magic, which was also taught to me."

Alwen was pleased. "What of your inborn gifts? Are you an oracle like your mother?"

Raven clasped her hands in front of her. "I can read the moon and the stars, and capture their light in the scrying stone, but my foresight is not always clear."

"You need time and practice, but you are indeed a sorceress of the Stewardry." Alwen signaled Nerys to bring the guard from the hall. "You may take your leave now. I hope you will feel welcome among us. The sentry will show you to your mother's rooms and find a healer to make Goram more comfortable."

Alwen waited for the sentry to escort the newcomers out and then straightened herself again as she faced those still remaining in the room. She had the scroll in her hands, and Glain felt her knees weaken. "There is just one more piece of business I shall conduct as Sovereign."

Glain started to object, but Alwen waved her off.

"I hold here Madoc's last testament." Alwen raised the scroll for all to see. "There will come a time to officiate this properly, but I am too tired and too ill to fuss over protocol now. I enlist all of you as my witnesses. If any of you object, leave now."

Glain could not believe what she was hearing. She half expected someone to walk out or argue. Alwen waited a full minute, and then continued.

"This testament names Glain as Madoc's heir. I doubt this surprises any of you, but it was important that we have this proof of his intent. As of this moment, I relinquish my standing as Madoc's proxy in favor of her birthright, and thereby proclaim Glain the true and rightful Sovereign of Fane Gramarye. From now forward I assume my own rightful place, as leader of the Stewards' Council. The time to join the guardians and the power of the keys to the realms is coming, and I must prepare."

Aslak was the only one among them brave enough to voice what they all were thinking. "Are you strong enough, Alwen?"

"Oh, I know it looks doubtful," she agreed, "but I have reason to believe that the joining ritual itself shall be my salvation. You'll just have to trust me, old friend."

Aslak smiled at her with genuine fondness. "And I suppose I'll just have to trust that you know where to find another guardian or two."

Alwen laughed. "As it happens, Aslak, we are overrun with guardians. Fortunately, Nerys is of Tanwen's bloodline, and I have no doubt that Ffion will be returned to us safe and sound. With Raven and me, the circle will be complete. And just this morning it was reported that Hywel's soldiers have finally opened the cave that contains the Well of Tears."

"And so the prophecy will be fulfilled after all," Aslak said.

"So it would seem." Alwen pulled herself out of her throne and turned to Glain. "This is yours now."

Emrys shoved past Finn, who had been doing his best to keep Emrys contained. "Sovereign, a moment's grace, I beg you."

Aslak stepped between them. "Stand back, Emrys. You should not even be here."

"It was she who let me in." Emrys gestured wildly at Glain. "I ask only to be heard."

Finn, who had not said a single word, spoke directly to Alwen. "We'll deal with Emrys, in our own way."

"No," Alwen said, staring quizzically at Emrys. "If it is my judgment he wants, let it be so. If Glain will allow it, of course."

Glain thought the entire scene bizarre, but no more bizarre than Emrys having been in possession of the scroll in the first place. "There are questions that only he can answer, and if he wishes to unburden himself, I think we should hear him out."

Aslak stepped aside and Emrys stumbled forward, falling to his knees at Alwen's feet. "I have failed you."

"You have failed yourself, Emrys, and thereby us all, though we are still waiting to know how and why. Say what you have come to say, Emrys, so that we can be done here," Alwen said.

And so it was that Emrys gave a sordid account of his fall from grace and how he had come to be Verica's consort. To everyone else it was clear how easily he'd been duped, but Emrys told a tale of true love for which he had sacrificed everything, including his honor. He had denied the signs of artifice and never allowed himself to question her. But on the night he'd sent his men to search the grounds, Verica had come to him, offering the scroll in return for his help. She had said that she'd turned Ynyr's spell against him so that she might claim his victories as her own when Machreth returned one day to establish the new order; and that now she wanted his help to put Euday out of her way as well. It was then that Emrys had realized what she was and how low he had fallen. In a fit of rage and self-loathing, he had killed Verica and stuffed her body beneath the floorboards in the abandoned dormitory in order to hide his own treason. Trusting that Euday would be discovered, Emrys had left him where Verica had abandoned him bound and blindfolded in the orchard. Finally, he had delivered the scroll to Glain's room as an act of atonement, but it had not delivered him from his guilt.

When Emrys had finished, none among them seemed to know how to respond. Finn was stiff with fury, and Aslak looked sickened. Nerys was so staid that her feelings were a mystery, and Glain simply felt sad.

"Well?" Alwen looked to Glain. "Shall I answer, or shall you?"

"It is your forgiveness he came for," Glain decided. "Perhaps this should be your last act as Sovereign."

"Very well." Alwen retook her seat on the throne and looked long and hard on Emrys. It was a pitiful sight, this once honorable man reduced to a sniveling wretch.

"Finn," she said at last. "I shall leave his final fate to you and Aslak. Military justice has jurisdiction in this case, but whatever else you may decide, he cannot remain here. Glain need not suffer yet another traitor in her temple."

She turned then to Emrys, who had been forced to his feet by Aslak's less than kind hand on the neck of his tunic. "For my part, Emrys, I give you forgiveness, just as I would any poor fool who lost his way and tried to find the way back—but it is Madoc you have truly betrayed, and there can be no forgiveness for that."

Emrys seemed comforted. The confession had given him the peace he was seeking, but Glain was not so sure she was glad for him. Her own spite reminded her that she had much yet to learn about grace in leadership. Alwen was far kinder than she would have been.

"Now," Alwen said with finality, pulling once again to her feet and turning to Glain. "This is your throne at last."

THIRTY

Glain found Bledig no less intimidating now than before he'd left to retrieve the last sorceress. There was a brusque warmth to the big, swarthy barbarian, but his gruff sense of humor often caught her off guard. In this way, Bledig reminded her of Rhys. Father and son also looked very much alike: the same dark hair and twinkling green eyes, which caused her to miss Rhys all the more. But Bledig had never seemed to take to her, and Glain could never quite tell what he was thinking. His devotion to Alwen, however, was unmistakable.

By the time Bledig and the others had arrived that morning, Alwen had become so weakened, she could barely stand. The blight on her hand had spread the length of her arm and was edging toward her heart. Ffion, as capable as she was, and even with the moss agate talisman she had accepted in honor of her mother, did not have any healing magic that seemed to do any good. Bledig had been at her side now for hours.

"I have asked Finn and Odwain to oversee the last of the excavation," Glain explained. "They are doing what they can to make it safe for us to reach the well. Nerys is preparing Ffion and Raven for the rite. It's nearly moonrise, but we will be ready."

Alwen was pleased, but she also seemed sad. "And tomorrow you will be on your own."

Glain had decided not to think about tomorrow, but she gave Alwen what she hoped was a reassuring smile. "Hywel would leave now, if he could. Some of his Gwynedd kinsmen are threatening another uprising. The king of Seisyllwg has been gone too long from his court, he says. The sooner he is seen at Dinefwyr with his brother and his Stewards the better."

Hywel's day is dawning, Alwen said, taking a careful tone. "You should know that Machreth has eluded us yet again, though he is no longer an immediate threat. Rhys intends to take residence with the mage hunters at Castell Banraven, but I think this does not surprise you."

"No," Glain admitted. It saddened her, but it did not surprise her.

Alwen offered her a sympathetic nod. "You have a new ally in Drydwen, the prioress of a temple called Elder Keep. I suggest you make plans to visit her very soon."

"What is Elder Keep?" This was not the question Glain most wanted to ask, but it was the most appropriate at the moment.

"As I said, make plans to visit the prioress. She will tell you what you need to know." Alwen was tiring too quickly. "I have left you my instructions and notes, along with Madoc's writings, on his desk."

Glain noticed the worry etched into Bledig's brow. "Enough talk for now," she said. "Let me pour you some aleberry."

He followed her to the hearth. "She may not be strong enough to survive the rite."

Glain shared his concern, but she also knew what was at stake. "The prophecy cannot come to pass until she joins the Circle of Sages and leads them to Dinefwyr. The fates turn on this moment, Bledig. It is a risk Alwen is willing to take."

"What if I am not?" Bledig muttered. "I could put an end to this now."

"But you won't," Glain said gently. Her heart hurt for him. Bledig had already sacrificed his daughter to the prophecy, and now the fates might well take Alwen from him. "And neither will I. We will trust her to know what she is doing, just as we always have."

Bledig clearly resented this truth, but he did not deny it. "Then there is nothing left to be done but wait."

Glain gave Alwen the cup and began aimlessly pacing the Sovereign's chambers. These were her rooms now, though the idea was as strange and awkward to her as the indigo velvet robe with the gold brocade that she was wearing. At least it did not itch.

Soon Aslak and Finn arrived with Goram and Odwain, ready to help Bledig escort the sorceresses to the hidden cavern in the labyrinth beneath the Fane. Pedr had charge of the castle defenses while the ritual was being performed, a decision Glain had come to quite easily. Her circle of trust had dwindled to only a few, but she had begun to build again on the strength and character of this one man.

Nerys was waiting with Raven and Ffion in the hall. Hywel and his lieutenants led the way, with Glain close behind. Out of respect and care for Alwen, the procession was slow and cautious. Even for the hardiest among them, the narrow tunnel was still difficult to walk. The labyrinth had been rendered largely impassable except for the single passageway Hywel had ordered his men to clear.

The cavern that contained the Well of Tears was almost too cold to withstand. Tallow-oil lamps had been staked at even intervals around the cistern, tingeing the frosty white cave an eerie, fluttery yellow. Misty vapor hung in the air above the rocky dirt floor, and the walls were coated with thick layers of ice. The well waters were still a black crystal solid, as frozen and unyielding as the day Madoc had been trapped within their depths.

Robed in the indigo velvet mantle in which she had first arrived at the Fane, Alwen made a brave attempt to carry herself with ease and dignity, but the effort was difficult, and it showed. The first time she stumbled on the uneven cavern floor, Glain was sure Bledig was going to leap to the Sovereign's aid, but he managed to stop himself short. Glain admired his restraint and shared in his agony. Though they would both respect her need to appear commanding, the struggle was painful to watch.

The second stumble brought Alwen to her knees. Bledig came forward and offered her his arm. The gesture was both noble and loving, and it brought tears to Glain's eyes. Alwen allowed him to help her to her feet and escort her as far as the well. Once they reached the edge of the pool, Alwen seemed to find new strength. She stood tall on her own, and Bledig stepped back into the shadows.

Alwen searched the marble sill surrounding the well and then knelt. She gestured to the others. "Look for the symbol that represents your realm, and take your place."

As they moved to obey, she nodded with satisfaction. "This is just as it should be, just as my vision revealed to me." She waited until each of the others had claimed a position in the circle and then removed the lapis amulet from around her neck and placed it upon the altar symbol carved in the marble before her. Alwen nodded to Ffion, Nerys, and Raven, indicating that they should do the same.

One by one the keys to the realms were laid upon their corresponding inscription—the moonstone and the stars, the bloodstone and the flame, the moss agate and the tree, the lapis and the rippling waves. Instantly, the jewel at the center of each pendant began to glimmer with an inner light that radiated a soft, warm glow. Each pendant emitted its own brilliant, colorful blaze. It was mesmerizing.

With her arms raised wide toward the sky, Alwen called upon the Ancients, invoking their power and their presence. The cavern floor shuddered.

"Where one arc ends another begins," she pronounced. "Let this circle be forever forged."

The glow from each jewel swelled, surging stronger and brighter, until the colors converged in a blinding flash of white. And just as quickly as it had begun, the joining ritual was complete. But there was more magic to be done.

Alwen looked to Glain and beckoned her closer. Glain stood beside Alwen and watched as she drew a bone-handled dagger from the velvet pouch at her waist. Alwen drew the blade across the palm of each hand in a single, sure swipe and waited for the blood to run. Alwen then placed her hands, palms down, upon the glossy black crust that capped the Well of Tears.

Madoc. Glain heard the beckoning whisper in her mind.

Again the chamber floor trembled. Glain watched, transfixed, as the solid surface of the well wavered. Madoc's visage appeared beside Alwen's reflection, and Glain gasped aloud. The vision held for a moment and then faded.

The earth beneath them pitched and rolled, and a thick, snowy mist formed above the tarn. Frigid air turned humid, and with a hiss the frozen crust dissolved. The waters turned a limpid, fluid blue. And then they began to roil.

Glain's heart stopped and her breath stalled in her throat. Something seemed to float to the top and settle just below the surface. Alwen reached into the well with both hands, and when she withdrew them, she was holding the staff that had been lost with Madoc when the well had swallowed him.

"Your hand," Glain whispered, noticing the lightening skin on the fingers of Alwen's afflicted hand.

"Yes," Alwen said. "I can feel the darkness leaving me."

Then Alwen stood and handed over Madoc's staff. Next, she removed his signet ring and held it out to Glain. "These belong to you."

Glain was elated and grief-stricken all at once. Her legs went numb, and every inch of her erupted with gooseflesh. As she took the staff and ring into her hands, Glain finally felt that Madoc was gone. The difference between knowing it and feeling it was immeasurably vast, like a chasm separating the place you need to be from the place you are. Though there was no comfort in the feeling, there was resolution. She was Sovereign now.

Alwen reached for her amulet. "Nerys, Ffion, and Raven— once you reclaim the pendant before you and place it back around your neck, it become yours to honor, to protect, and to wield. The amulets are separate, but they are also one. You will come to understand this, but so long as the circle remains unbroken, the amulets bind us together. Never, ever let it leave your person."

Alwen rehung her pendant, waited while the other sorceresses followed her lead, and then reached for Glain's hand. "Now for you, dear child. You must drink the waters."

Still clutching the staff, Glain knelt beside Alwen. Panic crept up from within. "What will happen when I do?"

"I felt nothing at all," Alwen said. "But whatever blessing I might have received was tarnished when the well was fouled. I have no idea what will happen to you."

Glain had been sure before, but now she was uncertain. The waters had the power to change her in ways she had only imagined. The dream-speak—the language of the subconscious through which the generations of Sovereigns before her would bestow their wisdom—was an awesome and terrifying privilege.

"Madoc would say this is a test of faith," Alwen said. "Faith in what is for you to decide."

Glain set the staff aside. This had been her dilemma all along. In what did she believe? The more she had tried to answer this question for herself, the more confused she had become.

Perhaps the trouble lay in the attempt to define her faith, as if it were a finite thing. Perhaps faith was not a fixed point on a moral compass or a precise measurement on a scale of intent. Perhaps it was an eye toward what could be as much as what was. In this moment, all she really needed was the courage to take a risk on the unknown.

Glain cupped her hands together, gathered well water into the bowl of her palms, and brought the ice-cold liquid to her lips. She sipped at it cautiously, not knowing what to expect. The water tasted of nothing. The water tasted of everything. All at once she decided that this test, if it were a test, was to find her faith in herself. With a whispered prayer for grace and luck, Glain swallowed the rest in a single, daring gulp.

* * *

"You are stronger than you know."

Glain awoke uncertain. The room was dark and quiet except for the warm glow and soft crackle of alder wood burning in the hearth. She was alone on the divan in her own rooms. But she was sure she had heard a voice.

She spied Alwen's aleberry pot, resting in the coals. Alwen had left it behind as a remembrance and given her the recipe along with a gift of parting wisdom. Glain smiled as she recalled Alwen's "wisdom": one draught, medicinal; two draughts, sedative; and three, a very bad idea.

The quiet reminded her how empty the Fane was now. Hywel had taken with him Alwen and the Circle of Sages, and with them had gone Bledig and Finn and Goram. Bledig would not be parted from Alwen. And though Glain had officially disbanded the Crwn Cawr Protectorate, in recognition of a duty fulfilled, Finn and

Goram had insisted on continuing to serve the Guardians of the Realms.

Though their numbers had dwindled further, the Fane was still a functioning refuge. Glain intended to continue the traditions of the Stewardry as long as there were still Stewards in residence. Machreth had been right about one thing—their way of life was dying.

In the meantime, Aslak had happily retaken command of the Cad Nawdd militia, pledged Glain his support, and made Pedr and Odwain his first officers. Pedr was glad to be able to stay as long as he liked in one place, and Odwain would never leave the Fane for long, not as long as he could still find some essence of Eirlys in the faerie meadow.

But whose voice had awakened her? Glain poured herself a cupful of aleberry and returned to the divan to contemplate the fire. She remembered a dream, a familiar dream. A regal stag, preening atop a hill, master of all he surveyed. This time the vision had ended where it had begun. Glain took this as a sign that Hywel's course was well set, at least for now. The whispering voice, however, had not been a part of her dream.

It had come from somewhere else in her subconscious. Glain laughed aloud as the realization came to her. The whisper was a message from the beyond. This was the first stirrings of the dream-speak. It was Madoc's voice she had heard.

Glain heard a gentle rapping on the outer door. "Come."

Pedr entered, carrying a meal tray. "You slept through the supper."

"Thank you," she said, setting her skirts to rights and hoping her hair wasn't wildly out of place. "Someone should have come for me."

"I'm sure at least one of your attendants meant to, but I discouraged it." Pedr was not the least bit apologetic. "You never take enough rest."

Glain couldn't help but smile. "So you've come out of your way just to bring a tray any one of a dozen novices could have managed with less than half the effort?"

"Not exactly," he admitted, setting the tray within her reach. "Aslak asked that I let you know that his inquiry has been concluded. Emrys has been banished."

Glain acknowledged the judgment with a sorrowful nod. She had expected this. "I suppose he is still pressing for me to make some decision about Euday."

"He didn't mention it just now," Pedr said, "but yes, he is. And he is concerned about your plans to visit Elder Keep."

Glain gave a dismissive wave. "I need to understand what has become of Machreth and what danger he still poses to us. I also need to understand who the prioress is and what it is she has sacrificed so much to protect, and that means I must see Elder Keep for myself."

"His concerns are well-founded," Pedr insisted. "Your safety is uncertain outside the Fane."

Glain understood the risks, but this was a journey she knew she was meant to undertake. After the Well of Tears had been freed of its hex, she had begun to experience powerful dreaming visions of a temple she knew could only be Elder Keep. The temple itself seemed to beckon her. Even Alwen had instructed that she go. In the last several days the compulsion had become more insistent and filled with such foreboding that she dared wait no longer.

"Tell Aslak to take whatever precautions he thinks are wise," she ordered. "But we will make the pilgrimage as planned. I want no more discussion on this matter, Pedr."

"As you wish." Pedr let one sensitive matter drop, but only in favor of another. "And what about Euday? Shall I tell Aslak you're still not ready to decide?"

"What if I *can't* decide," she mused, more to herself than to Pedr. Glain had been avoiding the issue for days. She did not want the first act of her Sovereignty to be an order of execution. "What if I don't *want* to decide?"

"Wouldn't that, in and of itself, be a decision?" Pedr asked. "Deciding not to decide?"

An odd truth, she thought, *but truth nonetheless*. "I don't like your point, Pedr, but I can't disagree with it."

Pedr fussed with the fire as if he felt the need to make himself useful. "Seems to me, either way Euday is left in the dungeon. No better, no worse."

"Neither better nor worse is not good enough," Glain said. "I have kept him alive this long only to interrogate him. There are still so many unanswered questions. But the membership deserves satisfaction, and Euday has earned his sentence. The decision is made; it is now just a matter of carrying it out."

She sighed, frustrated with her own reluctance. "If a leader hasn't the courage to carry out the laws she has sworn to uphold, what good is she?"

Pedr frowned and folded his arms over his chest, peering at her as though he were surprised she hadn't figured out the answer for herself. "A thoughtful, well-considered ruler who does not rush to action is not necessarily lacking courage."

Glain felt silly, but reassured. "How is it you always know just what to say and just when to say it?"

Pedr prepared to take his leave. He was ever careful not to overstay. "Sometimes it's easier for others to see us more clearly than we see ourselves. You'll do what must be done." Pedr paused as he passed through the door. "You are stronger than you know."

* * *

Lexicon of the Stewardry

Castell Banraven *("Raven's Peak")*
The home of the Ruagaire Brotherhood.

Cad Nawdd *("Army of Protectors")*
The castle guard at Fane Gramarye.

Crwn Cawr *("Circle of Champions")*
The protectorate created to accompany the Guardians of the Realms into hiding.

Circle of Sages
Also known as the Stewards' Council, a circle of knowledge and power forged by the joining of the four Guardians of the Realms.

Coedwig Gwyn *(The White Woods)*
The magical forest near the ancient Welsh village of Pwll that shelters Fane Gramarye.

Cymru
The lands known today as the Kingdom of Wales.

Cwm Brith *("Gray Hollow")*

A fortified hunting lodge built by King Cadell of Seisyllwg.

Dream-Speak

The language of the dreamer, the timeless tongue with which the Ancients pass their wisdom to the Sovereign in the shroud of a dream. The power can only be gained by drinking the waters of the Well of Tears.

Elder Keep

Also known as the "wizard's crypt" or "bastion of souls," the Keep contains a portal to the Otherworld through which the Sovereigns pass at the end of their earthly days.

Fane Gramarye

The magic temple and last stronghold of the Stewards, hidden in the enchanted forest of Coedwig Gwyn near the village of Pwll, located in the province of Ystrad Tywi in the land of Cymru.

Guardians of the Realms

Each born only once a generation, the four Guardians of the Realms are descended of a magical bloodline that carries a unique affinity to one of the elemental dominions. The four realms and their lineages are the Spiritual Realm from the House of Eniad, the Celestial Realm from the House of Caelestis, the Physical Realm from the House of Morthwyl, and the Natural Realm from the House of Uir.

Hywel Dda *("Hywel the Good")*

First son of Cadell of Seisyllwg, heralded as the only ruler to unite all of Cymru under one hand and credited with the codification of the first written, binding law of the land.

Keys to the Realms

Four talismans that channel and amplify the elemental forces of the universe:

- Lapis Lazuli—key to the Spiritual Realm
- Moss Agate—key to the Natural Realm
- Moonstone—key to the Celestial Realm
- Bloodstone—key to the Physical Realm

Mystical Realms

The four earthly dominions: Spiritual, Celestial, Natural, and Physical; their elemental forces: water, air, earth, and fire; and their corresponding magical arts: empathy, augury, metamorphosis, and regeneration.

Norvik

A tiny fishing village located on the Frisian islets near the Danish borderlands, south of the River Eider; homeland of Aslak, great captain of the Cad Nawdd and leader of the Crwn Cawr.

Obotrites

Nomadic Slavic tribes, also known as the Wend.

Ruagaire Brotherhood

A centuries-old peacekeeping force originally commissioned to enforce the laws of the mageborn societies. The Ruagaire are defenders of the old ways and mercenary hunters of rogue magic. They are born with a natural resistance to magic and live by a strict code governed by four virtues: veracity, loyalty, righteousness, and forbearance.

Stewardry

A sorcerer's guild devoted to the stewardship and teaching of the old ways.

Well of Tears

The enchanted pool whose waters hold the ancient secrets of the Stewards. By drinking of the sacred waters, the knowledge and experience of all who have come before is passed from one generation to the next.

Hierarchy of the Stewardry

The Principals of the Ninth Order

Madoc — Grand Sorcerer and Sovereign

Machreth — High Sorcerer turned black mage, once Madoc's chosen successor

Alwen — High Sorceress, Mystic, and guardian of the Spiritual Realm

Branwen — High Sorceress, Oracle, and guardian of the Celestial Realm

Cerrigwen — High Sorceress, Healer, and deposed guardian of the Natural Realm

Tanwen — High Sorceress, Alchemist, and guardian of the Physical Realm

Glain — Acolyte, Oracle, Proctor pro tem of the Ninth Order, blood heir of Madoc

The Levels of Mastery

Sovereign — Supreme Leader and Grand Sorcerer or Sorceress

Proctor — Second to the Sovereign, High Sorcerer, Heir Apparent

Docent — High Sorcerer or Sorceress

Acolyte — Accomplished mage, attendants to the docents

Prefect — Second rank

Apprentice — First rank

Novice — The beginner's class

The Legacies

The Mageborn Dynasties (The Ancients)

Primideach	— Prime or First
Caelestis	— Celestial
Eniad	— Spiritual
Morthwyl	— Metamorphic
Uir	— Regenerative

House Aslaksson

Aslak	— Chieftain of Norvik and famed captain of the guard
Goram	— First son of Aslak
Thorvald	— Second son of Aslak

House of Dinefwyr

Cadell ap Rhodri	— King of Seisyllwg
Hywel	— First son of Cadell
Clydog	— Second son of Cadell

Clan MacDonagh

Fergus, the elder

Finn	— Brother of Fergus
Pedr	— First son of Finn
Odwain	— Second son of Finn

Tribe of the Wolf King

Bledig Rhi	— The chieftain
Alwen	— His life mate
Eirlys	— Daughter of Bledig and Alwen
Rhys	— Son of Bledig and Alwen
Domagoj	— Blood brother of Bledig

Acknowledgments

uthors owe eternal debts of gratitude to so many wonderful, supportive people—friends and family, who buoy us with words of encouragement (and the occasional meal or libation) to keep us from steeping too long in self-doubt, and fellow writers and colleagues, who tirelessly lend their hard-earned expertise so that we produce the best work we are capable of creating. I thank you all, but there are a couple of folks whose contributions to this book deserve special note.

That this series ever came into being at all is due in no small part to the kind and well-studied Lynn Lewis, a historical writer pursuing her own dreams of publication. Lynn studied history and art at the University of London, and recently completed a novel based on the life and career of Hans Holbein, court painter to King Henry VIII, entitled *Dance of Death*. Lynn's generous sharing of her knowledge of the history, folklore, and culture of the Cornish and Welsh peoples provided me with the factual fodder I needed for my grand fantasies. Lynn, I cannot thank you enough, and hope one day to find a way to return the favor.

The other people I can never thank enough are my editors—Alex Car, who brought me into the fold at 47North and made all of this possible; Jennifer McCord, who taught me the publishing industry from the inside out; and Betsy Mitchell, who knows just how to help me shape my amorphous creative pulp into something infinitely more artful and meaningful than I ever envisioned. Betsy, you are the Empress of Editorial Awesomeness, and I bow to your greatness.

And finally, to the ladies who guide my professional journey and keep me on course, I offer my most heartfelt thanks—my agents, Jennifer Schober (who started me off on this incredible ride) and Nalini Akolekar (who picked up the reins and continues to spur me on).

HISTORICAL NOTE

irst, let me just state straight out that this book should *not* be considered a work of historical fiction. It might loosely pass for historical fantasy, but it is in fact more myth than anything else. Although the Dream Stewards series is indeed set in a real-world historical context, the novels themselves are in no way intended as an academic interpretation of the political machinations of tenth-century Wales (Cymru). I am, at best, an armchair historian with a penchant for mythology and folklore—particularly Cornish and Welsh.

This is not to say that there is no actual history in this fantasy series. The world of the Dream Stewards is built in and around the life of a real king, Hywel Dda (Hywel the Good), whose significance is not widely recognized. This is largely due to the exceedingly few primary sources or official records from which to reconstruct the social landscape of this period. Even if it had been my intent to shed light on the military strategies and political maneuverings of the time, it would be extraordinarily difficult to do so. The historical documentation of the post-Roman era in the lands of the Britons (essentially Cymru and Kernow, which are known today as Wales and Cornwall) is scant. There is more unknown than known, and the surviving accounts are constantly being reinterpreted.

The ninth century was a transformational era for the Britons (as the original peoples of this region were known). Following a particularly tumultuous half-century in which the northern kingdoms of Powys and Gwynedd fought to maintain their independence against both the conquering forces of Mercia and Wessex, which were under Danish occupation, a new era begins to emerge. By mid-century, Hywel's paternal grandfather, Rhodri Mawr (Rhodri the Great) had established himself as the first High King of the Britons, having now claimed both Gwynedd and Powys under his reign. Rhodri's far-reaching control established a foundation for relative stability between the smaller principalities and created a defensive alliance that all but repelled the Mercian threat and contained the Viking incursions in the east. Both Mercia and Northumbria continued to struggle against the Norse, whereas the kingdoms of the Britons were relatively unscathed. It bears noting that what is now known as southern Wales was never overrun by either Norse or Saxon raiders, due in large part to Rhodri's success in defending his borders. However, Rhodri's stronghold would be divided by his death.

In keeping with Welsh law, Rhodri's holdings were divided between his three sons. His eldest, Anarawd, retained the traditional lands of the Merfynion dynasty and became the new ruler of the vast and powerful northern kingdom Gwynedd. Cadell was given lordship of the southern kingdom in Ceredigion, and Merfyn inherited Powys. This positioned the sons of Rhodri to maintain control through collaboration. However, having also inherited the cunning and ruthless ambition of their father, the elder sons were not content. In particular, Cadell campaigned for dominance, immediately killing his brother Merfyn to gain control of Powys. And by the time of Hywel's birth circa 880 AD, the relationship between his father and uncle was likely as contentious as it was cooperative.

Although the surviving sons of Rhodri were united in their vision of an independent nation of Britons, they were fierce rivals in the bid for who would control that nation. The record reflects few battles of note after Cadell's death circa 905, but it is to be assumed that the struggle for power between Gwynedd and Seisyllwg was ongoing. The known history indicates that Hywel continued his father's conquests. And though there is no evidence of a true rivalry between Hywel and his younger brother Clydog, given the family legacy I have assumed such for the purposes of storytelling. There is, in fact, evidence of cooperation between the sons of Cadell, as the two appear to have ruled jointly until Clydog's somewhat mysterious death in 920 AD. It is at this point that Hywel emerges as the most powerful king of the day.

Hywel ap Cadell, who is both a foundational and a pivotal character in *The Well of Tears* and *The Keys to the Realms*, is arguably the most significant of all the Welsh kings. Hywel continued to gain control of lands and titles through inheritance, marriage, and brute force until 920 AD, when he also claimed Gwynedd and established the kingdom of Deheubarth. He continued his reign over this new nation until his death in 950 AD. Deheubarth did not long survive Hywel, and the individual territories eventually wrested back their independence.

However, Hywel did have a lasting legacy. Though it should be assumed that he accomplished his political feats with his fair share of ruthlessness and brutality, he apparently also had a sophisticated and far-reaching vision for himself and his peoples. Hywel understood the necessity of alliances in creating a state invulnerable to outside influence and invasion, and established a policy of conciliation with England that offered him the ability to maintain stability and a formidable line of defense. But perhaps his most laudable accomplishment was the codification of a body of laws that addressed issues of local governance, property rights, and social conduct, which remained in effect for many generations following his death.

The reign of Hywel Dda ap Cadell came to be known as the "age of peace," which brought a heretofore-unknown era of unity and stability to a region that had existed for generations in an unending state of upheaval. The stuff, as they say, of legend.

Hywel's is a story that begs to be told, and given the mystery surrounding his life, I began to envision the convergence of unknown forces that might give rise to such a remarkable reign. The lack of empirical evidence only made the place and period more appealing to me. So many holes in the reality to patch with fantasy—and yet still pay homage to the history that is known to be fact. In researching the world of the Dream Stewards, I spent more than ten years compiling and poring through the most reputable and generally recognized materials I could find (you will find a partial bibliography at the end of this book). Using the historical record and the natural world as a backdrop, I fabricated a magical realm adjacent to the mortal one and wove the threads together.

The Dream Stewards series is set during the formative years of Hywel's reign and focuses on his rise to power. To the best of my ability, I have honored the rich cultural and political legacies of Cornwall and Wales, lands for which I have a personal affinity and familial connection. But being an author of fantasy, I have also imbued the known history and lore with a culture and mythology of my own making. Although the magic system and society I have created may resemble any number of ancient agrarian-based religions (including Druidism), it is not a reflection or extension of any one in particular. Instead it is an amalgamation of philosophies, doctrines, beliefs, and practices that are common to all—resulting in a unique and original concept.

Suffice it to say, if you were looking for a story rife with bloody battle scenes depicting marauding Viking hordes overrunning the Britons, or an examination of the Druidic mysticism of the Celts (which did not actually exist in Cornwall or Wales), you did not find it in these pages. However, I am hopeful that the story you did find carried you away on a fantastical adventure that was both exciting and meaningful.

My true intent with *The Well of Tears* and *The Keys to the Realms* (and any future installments of the Dream Stewards series) is merely to pay tribute to an unsung hero by exploring how the mysterious and magical realms that exist alongside what we know to be real might have played a part in his real-life story. I hope you are enjoying the journey as much as I am.

Awen á bendithion...

About the Author

Photograph © Brian Huntoon, 2000

Roberta Trahan is a former journalist and marketing professional who always wanted to write a book - and so she did. Her first novel, The Well of Tears, was published in 2012.

The Dream Stewards series was inspired by generations of Roberta's family history originating in Cornwall and Wales, as well as the culture and mythology of her ancestral home.

A Pacific Northwest native, Roberta currently lives with her family near Seattle, Washington.

BIBLIOGRAPHY

(a partial list of resources and suggested reading)

Alfred the Great: Asser's Life of King Alfred & Other Contemporary Sources. Transl. by Simon Keynes. (Penguin Classics edition, 2003).

Berresford Ellis, Peter. *The Druids*. (Grand Rapids, MI: Eerdmans, 1995).

Charles-Edwards, T. M. *Wales & the Britons, 350–1064 (History of Wales)*. (New York: Oxford University Press, 2013).

Crawford, Christina. *Daughters of the Inquisition: Medieval Madness: Origins and Aftermaths*, 1st ed. (Tensed, ID: Seven Springs Press, 2004).

Herm, Gerhard. *The Celts*, 1st ed. (New York: St. Martin's Press, 1977).

Lloyd, J. E. *A History of Wales from the Earliest Times to the Edwardian Conquest*, vol. 1. *Wales—History to 1536*. (New York: Longmans, Green & Co., 1911).

Reston, James, Jr. *The Last Apocalypse: Europe at the Year 1000 A.D.* (New York: Anchor, 1998).

Roesdahl, Else. *The Vikings*, 2nd ed. (New York: Penguin, 1998).